THE HEIRLOOM PEARLS

Kate Nixon

THE HEIRLOOM PEARLS

ISBN Number: 978-1482643367
First Edition 2013

For Randy and my girls

"Though the mills of God grind slowly,
 Yet they grind exceeding small;
 Though with patience he stands waiting,
 With exactness grinds he all."

Henry Wadsworth Longfellow

Una voce poco fa
qui nel cor mi risuonò;
il mio cor ferito è già,
e Lindor fu che il piagò.
Sì, Lindoro mio sarà;
lo giurai, la vincerò,

Act I, Scene II, *Il Barbiere di Siviglia* (The Barber of Seville)
by Gioacchino Rossini

Part 1

Chapter 1

Louisville, Kentucky, March 6, 1859

"Help me. End this."

The old man's sputtered words broke through the low tones of wood on wood as the rockers scraped the bare floor and thirty-seven-year-old Isabel waited. His weak voice drew her from the soft prayers to the Blessed Virgin.

Isabel raised the wick in the oil lamp and watched the light halo the headboard and cast his wan face and wispy gray hair half in shadow. When she leaned over him, his hand came out of the dark and gripped her sleeve with surprising force.

"Now," he said with more effort.

Isabel bit back her tears and shook her head.

"I would do it for you," he gasped and squeezed tighter.

Isabel glanced at his hand and did not doubt his words. She remembered how her attention had remained riveted to his gloved fist when he pulled the reins taut while his new horse Spartacus bolted under them. His knuckles threatened to rupture the seams of his riding glove. A few minutes later Spartacus fell, and they tumbled onto the dirt track.

Once her father took in the horse flailing with its broken leg, he brought out his pistol. Speaking words of comfort, he knelt and stilled the horse. The tears in his eyes had startled her more than the sound of the gun.

She nodded at the memory, but her father misunderstood and shut his eyes.

"God bless you," he whispered as his hand brushed her skirts before falling back into the shadows.

Guilt attacked her, and her heart and soul battled for control. Did she love her father more than she feared hell? In quick secession, she debated whether to end his pain or ensure her eternal damnation. She went with her heart instead of her soul and decided on mercy.

Isabel swallowed against the sharp-edged rock in her throat and gripped the unused pillow by her father's head. When she had almost reached his face, the sound of his death rattle stopped her.

"Thanks be to God," she whispered and let the pillow drop. Then she made the sign of the cross and collapsed into the rocking chair. Her guilt redoubled and immediately crowded out her relief as it also distanced her grief.

"Poppa, intercede for me," Isabel prayed.

Death erased all the pain from his face. With a trembling hand, she closed his eyes and pulled the sheet over him.

Isabel rocked and recited the familiar and comforting prayers as she worked her fingers along the smooth, glass rosary beads. The blessings of forgiveness and inner peace washed over her. She placed her trust in God's forgiveness.

She remained unaware of the passage of time until the clock in Saint Jerome's tower struck three. Roused by the deep tones of the bells, she rose from her chair and became once again the mistress of the house and the elder sister.

It did not take Isabel long to prioritize what she needed to do. She would wake Helen and tell her their father had passed. Then she would send the gardener for the priest and undertaker. In the meantime she would write notes to her five brothers, so the gardener could deliver them tomorrow after breakfast. That way she and Helen would have finalized the funeral plans long before any of the family called at the house.

When her hand turned the doorknob, she also realized that she was at last free. With her head held erect, she glided down the hall. Her life was now her own. No one, she vowed, not even her older brother James, would ever interfere again.

~~~

After she finalized the funeral plans with the priest the next morning, Isabel returned to her room with the maid to inspect her mourning dresses. Three were in no need of repair or updating, and she asked the maid to take them downstairs for pressing. She put the other four aside for the dressmaker and had just opened the jewelry box to select the jet and silver mourning jewelry for receiving her afternoon callers when the maid returned.

She gave a short curtsy, glanced down, and mumbled, "Mr. James, he's downstairs in the parlor. He says to tell you he'll wait for you." The maid fidgeted with her crucifix.

Isabel, tired and still haunted by her father's last request, fought back her impatience. "What else, Susan?" she asked.

"He seems right angry."

"Does he now?"

The maid bobbed her head.

Fury swept Isabel's fatigue aside. How like her eldest brother to ignore her request to call after lunch and intrude before she was receiving callers. Well, she thought, he can just stay there until she was ready to come downstairs.

"Did he ask to see Miss Helen?"

When Susan answered no, Isabel dismissed her. "It will be fine. No need to wake my sister. You can tell him I will be there directly. Also, please set out the good tea service and some of Cook's gingersnaps. Then come back to help me dress."

~~~

Twenty minutes later, Isabel, laced into her best black dress, strode into the parlor. She considered the tall stocky man. His red hair was a few shades darker than hers, except for the encroaching gray streaks. He stood by the blazing fireplace. In addition to the black crepe band on his arm, he wore a scowl above his trimmed beard. His face had the same stony expression he had always used to bully her from the time they were children.

Her resolve sparked. She was no longer that child, seven years his junior. Ignoring his coldness, she sat in her favorite wing chair and poured tea. He took his cup but remained on his feet.

"James, sit down. It makes my neck hurt to look up at you."

He glared but refused to sit. Isabel lowered her head and took a small sip of tea. She would not be drawn into his game. Out of the corner of her eye, she saw him return his cup to the tray with a bit too much force. The bone china cup rattled in the saucer.

"Izzy," he began.

She had always hated how he taunted her with that name. She could not help herself and glowered at him. He smirked and drew a creased piece of paper from his pocket.

"What sort of message is this?" James unfolded the note in slow deliberate motions. "Father passed away peacefully early this morning at twelve after one. Since Helen and I will be occupied with the funeral details in the morning, please call this afternoon after one," he read with ice in his voice.

When he lifted his eyes, she registered the intense chill in them.

"I assume," he said in the same tone, "you sent identical notes to all the family?"

She met his look and did not waver. "Yes, verbatim."

"Why didn't you notify us last night?"

"You were not needed. Helen and I handled everything."

"It's more likely you did everything yourself."

She refused to let his words bait her and instead offered the plate of cookies. His scowl deepened. He was so angry his mustache quivered.

"But why should you have planned the funeral? There are seven of us."

"Be reasonable, James. It would take days for all of us to agree. Helen and I know what Father wanted. He told us."

She fixed him with her own determined look. "After all, we were the ones he saw every day. We were the ones who cared for him until the end."

"You're too high-handed, Izzy, always have been. Why do you have to have things your way?"

"This is Father's way, not mine."

Her sense of triumph increased as his complexion grew more florid by the moment.

"So be it, out of respect for him. I'll not be the one to turn his funeral into a circus."

James stalked toward the door. When he reached it, he turned and glared. "Remember, a falcon, tow'ring in her pride of place."

Isabel shivered and whispered the rest of the quote from *Macbeth*.

"Was by a mousing owl hawk'd at and kill'd."

Chapter 2

Louisville, March 9, 1859

David Smith mixed with the rabble on the gangway and shoved his way to the wharf. With luck, the noise from the engines and the stevedores yelling at the slaves hauling bales might mask any alarm his victim or the captain could raise.

Once free of the mob, he smoothed his black suit coat and tilted his bowler hat a little more to the left. His first steps were rapid until he reminded himself to ease away from the waterfront. David set his pace to right above a stroll.

Don't draw attention he thought as he looked for an escape route through the cluster of dirty brick warehouses. He calmed when an opening in the crowd appeared. Reassured, he merged with the other men who also wore black suits and carried walking sticks.

When he reached the shopping district, he noticed the women parading by in their fashionable hoop skirts. The cheerful feathers on their bonnets caught the sunlight and stirred in the cool spring breeze. He tipped his hat to the most attractive ones and was rewarded with smiles.

But his heart was not in a bit of flirtation. Instead, he fought down his inner turmoil. "Damn it," he voiced after he replayed how the extra jack had slipped from his sleeve. His luck had finally run out. He was done gambling on the riverboat circuit. No amount of practice in front of a mirror could make up for his slowing fingers. He faced the truth. At thirty-five, he had lost his ability to shuffle and stack the deck.

Mindful of the mud, he moved deeper into the city. Behind him the sounds from the riverfront faded. At the most he had thirty minutes to find a place to hole up while the captain summoned the police. He figured he had to hide an additional hour until the riverboat resumed its journey upstream.

Next on his agenda was a change in his appearance. The easiest and cheapest was a visit to a barber and have his goatee removed and his blond hair trimmed, so he could move on to a new plan that involved a fresh mark and resulted in some money.

Guided by a tolling church bell and a tall spire, David walked five streets away from the river and then paused. In front of him, a red brick cathedral and its grounds sprawled over a whole city block. At least one hundred carriages lined the wide avenue. A long ribbon of somberly dressed people went up the cathedral's grand steps and through the carved wooden doors.

This had to be a funeral he thought. Today was not Sunday or one of those Holy Days of Obligation he remembered from catechism class. With luck, the captain and his boat would be far upriver before the church emptied.

David looked at his shoes. A few swipes with his white linen handkerchief took care of the dust. With quick fluid motions, he refolded the cloth and returned it to his pants pocket before he straightened his cravat and cuffs. When he was as presentable as possible, he joined the mourners in line to pass through the open doors.

Almost the last to enter, he waited his turn. An usher indicated a seat on the end of the back pew and handed him a funeral Mass card. A quick read told him the deceased was a seventy-five-year-old widower named James McIntire. The old man left behind five sons and two daughters and a gaggle of grandchildren. The card listed orphanages, hospitals, and other benevolent societies the family supported.

So, David noted, the recently departed was a man of some social status. There had to be over five hundred mourners crowding the church. Rows of young children sat in the front center pews. All were dressed alike in dark blue uniforms. He would have bet his last gold coin on the chance the nuns in charge of the children were attending in hopes of more money and less unmotivated by grief.

The low murmurs ceased. The first words of the funeral Mass, *requiem aeternam*, came from the nave. David watched the priest lead the casket carried by six men. The pall bearers were close in age and appeared related. All were about the same height and had various shades of red hair. Two women, one slender and thin, the other, shorter and stouter, followed the casket down the aisle toward the apse and the sunlit rose window. Their veils, black and long enough to reach their gloved hands holding bibles and rosary beads, hid their faces.

David's thumb brushed the raised letters on the engraved card. His intuition told him there was something here for him. It took him a few minutes to see it. The daughters had to be spinsters since they retained their maiden names. Good, he had a way with old maids. He could probably find an angle to play.

He flipped the card and saw the invitation for mourners to gather at the family home after the interment. His luck had definitely turned. He could feel it. The reception offered another good place to hide. While he was there, he could also root out more background on the sisters.

David leaned back and waited for the Mass to end. Louisville receptions were probably the same as the ones his mother had dragged him to in Cincinnati. People might claim they went to pay their respects, but he knew they also went to gossip.

~~~

David stepped into the McIntire foyer and noticed two women seated on a wicker sofa and dressed in full mourning regalia. They had escaped his attention at the funeral Mass. The elder one, with a dowager's hump and ear trumpet, reminded him of the long-widowed society mavens who lurked at any important event. The younger one had to be her hanger-on companion. Their eyes were not on each other but rested on the people walking before them. No one stopped to speak. Only a few nodded. He too went by them and stood before a nearby painting where he could watch and eavesdrop for a few minutes.

"What will Isabel and Helen do now that their dear father has passed on?" asked the older, wrinkled woman.

Her hands, in mourning gloves, stroked a remembrance brooch at her neck.

The second woman, at least twenty years her junior, replied, "For sure not marry. They're on the shelf. Both are well over thirty if they're a day. And since they're as rich as Croesus, they won't have to marry." She emphasized the words with a flutter of her black-trimmed fan.

"Such dutiful daughters. I'm sure no one expected their father to outlive his wife by so many years. Those girls certainly gave him the best part of their lives."

"What else would you expect from their convent education?"

The older woman nodded her agreement. "I heard old McIntire signed over all his assets to them."

"To Isabel. My George told me it was her idea. Poor Helen doesn't have the sense God gave a goose. I remember her from my daughter's cotillion. She was flighty then, and she hasn't changed a bit."

"What a pity there are so many younger heiresses available this season," the older woman said with a tone David recognized as false. "Even with their father's wealth, Isabel and Helen aren't attractive anymore."

"Isabel's certainly too old." The younger woman's fan fluttered again. "Helen might have a chance if her waist were tinier. But with her short stature, every extra pound shows. It's such a shame."

"My dear, it happened to most of us by that age."

~~~

David took it as a good omen that he had been right about the McIntire sisters being spinsters. It was even better their social crowd had labeled them much too old to be in the marriage sweepstakes. His luck just kept building.

It was time to cross into the formal double parlor where polite nods paid his way through the crowd. Murmured "my sympathies" carried him past the first line of lesser relatives. He recognized them from their black armbands. Their lower status left them to mingle around the huge Boston ferns placed along the walls.

At the far end of the room sat the only two women in the crowd without hats or veils. There could be no doubt that these two pale-faced women were the bereaved sisters. They were close in age and wore their red hair styled the same, gathered into chignons. According to the gossips in the foyer, the slender one was Isabel, and the other Helen. Side by side, they received condolences from the visitors.

David worked his way through the small groups of people and joined the ill-formed line passing before the sisters. There were about ten people before him when a tall stocky man with auburn hair turning gray blocked his path.

"Sir, how can I help you?" The man's unmistakable Southern draw did not mask the hard authoritative edge of the question.

David stepped from the line and offered his hand. "Mr. McIntire," David guessed because of the man's hair color. "D. J. Smith, of Pittsburgh. My deepest sympathies on your father's passing."

"Do not mumble. Speak up," McIntire said as he returned the handshake.

In a louder voice, David repeated his words.

"And you knew him how?"

"Not personally, you understand, only by his reputation as a benefactor. I hope I'm not intruding, but when I heard about your loss, I wanted to pay my respects."

"Thank you for your kind words," the older man said. "I'm James, the eldest son."

"James."

The soft feminine tone turned David in the direction of the new voice.

"Will you introduce me to your friend?"

David fought back a smile at the hint of coquetry in the word introduce.

"Mr. Smith, may I present my sister, Miss Helen?"

David gave her his most charming smile and a slight bow.

"Will you escort me back to my chair, sir?" she asked.

He nodded to James and gave Helen his arm. Behind him, David heard James say, "Good firm handshake."

A soft, little laugh came from Helen, "James has always talked to himself. Since his hearing has diminished, his volume has increased."

David patted her gloved fingers and smoothly lied, "I understand, my oldest brother does the same. It's one way we know what he's thinking."

They reached Isabel who was pulling her hands from the hold of an elderly woman.

Helen leaned toward her sister and interrupted in a stage whisper. "Isabel, this is Mr. Smith. He told James he has heard about Father's charitable works all the way up in Pittsburgh."

With a flutter of her fan and eyelashes, Helen turned her attention back to David. "Am I correct, sir?"

"Yes, Miss Helen speaks the truth, Miss McIntire. Your father's generosity is certainly well known. May I offer my sympathies on your loss?"

"Thank you for calling today, Mr. Smith," Isabel said. Her tones almost matched her sister's in pitch yet lacked the flirtatiousness. "Please have some refreshment."

David gave a sight bow before asking, "Miss McIntire, may I fetch something for you?"

Isabel met his gaze no longer than necessary before she declined his offer. He noticed her eyes seemed to be hazel one moment and blue another. When she looked to the next caller, David knew he had been dismissed. So he bid Helen goodbye.

Three down, four heirs to go. He surveyed the parlor. In the nearest corner were two men in their twenties with black armbands and hair shades between those of the brother and the two sisters he had just left. The only difference between them was one wore his hair in curls while the other's hairline had begun to recede. David remembered seeing both on his side of the casket during the procession.

Now their heated discussion and occasional glances over at the sisters held his attention. They had to be some relation to the McIntire clan. David sauntered closer and pretended to look at the family curio collection.

"Coverture is what it's called," the balding man said.

"How can it benefit us?" the other asked.

"First, we have to find some dumb fool to marry Isabel. As soon as she marries, the husband controls her property. Then we use him to get back what she made Father sign over to her."

"Wouldn't it be easier to work with her and not bring in some outsider?"

"Hell no. Tell me the last time Isabel cooperated with us. She wouldn't even allow us any say on the old man's funeral."

David eased away. This was certainly turning out to be his lucky day. The younger McIntire brothers were unhappy and greedy. And coverture, what could he do with it?

He decided to make one last circuit of the room before he headed toward the door. When he passed some well-dressed men congregated near a spittoon, the words 'the younger James', 'overextended', and 'doesn't control a large enough share' caught his attention. He slowed to hear more.

"Won't be long before we can foreclose on James and his distillery." The oldest man accented his words with a small smirk.

"I urge caution. The war can change everything," a thin, nervous man said.

"Only if Lincoln gets elected," a third spoke in a harsh tone.

"There won't be any war. North, south, it does not matter. We're all business men," the first man said.

~~~

David strolled back toward the business district and kept an eye out for the police. The few officers he passed did not seem interested in him. The riverboat was probably long gone. He assumed he was safe.

Good, he was clear to move on to his next venture. He would need rooms for the next few days while he explored other weaknesses within the McIntire family. He was intrigued by what he had discovered so far. Their finances shaky, the brothers splintered, Helen a flirt, and Isabel had no suitors. The family was a straight flush if the last card, coverture, was the right one.

Even if the cards broke the right way, he would still need some way to finagle himself into the family's social circle and woo Isabel. But he would risk a few of those precious gold eagles he always kept back to stake himself. His mind played out several schemes. By the time he walked into the lobby of the Galt House, he had decided upon the simplest.

~~~

On Monday morning, it took about thirty minutes searching in the vicinity of the courthouse to find the saloon he needed and the right man. Inside the sixth place, the dim, sour-smelling room was the same as the others, but among the four customers, one was sitting under a dingy window. He was in his mid-twenties, eating instead of drinking, reading a book instead of engaging in the political argument over state's rights taking place at the bar. His dark hair was a little too long on his collar, his suit a little too worn. Stained and bulging saddlebags rested next to him on the bench.

David sat on the bench opposite the young man and waited for him to look up. When he did, David asked, "Are you a lawyer?"

He then laid two silver half-dollars near a greasy spot on the table.

"Not yet, I take the bar exam next week. Why, do you need one?"

"Just some help with a legal term."

David watched and waited. The young man moved his gaze to the coins and then back to David.

"I'll be glad to help if I can," he said.

David slid one coin halfway across the table but kept his index finger on it.

"This is for the information. The second one is for your silence."

"Fine by me, what's the word?"

"Coverture," David said. He slid the coin the rest of the way and removed his finger.

The young man's face brightened at the word. "Interesting concept. Let me review Blackstone for the salient points of law."

He pulled a worn volume from the nearer saddlebag and read. The expression on his face changed. A frown came and went as he scanned

11

a few more entries. At the last passage, he gave a decisive nod.

He looked up and said, "Sir, coverture has a long established history. In sum, a widow or an unmarried woman eighteen years or older has the legal right to buy and sell whatever she owns. However, once she marries, the law considers said woman and her husband to be one person. Therefore, the husband subsequently gains control of said assets as long as they are married."

"You are telling me the husband may buy and sell anything his wife owns?"

"Yes, unless otherwise specified before the marriage."

The young man gave the passage one more glance before shutting the book with care.

"Usually the woman's parents require this protection before giving permission for the couple to marry."

"What do they want to protect?"

"Property, household items, or slaves."

The young man's words were what David wanted to hear.

"Good, good."

The second coin joined the first.

~~~

David moved on to the next part of his plan. He walked into the front office of the McIntire Distillery and was surprised when the sour mash smell was so strong inside that it made his stomach rebel. He presented his card to the young male clerk and would have bet the youngster was some lesser nephew because of his red hair and frayed sleeves which rode a little too high on his wrists.

David insisted upon a meeting with Mr. McIntire. The young man, who gave his name as Hugh, offered a feeble resistance at first, but David cowed him. Calling card in hand, the clerk surrendered and walked down the hall to the right.

While David waited, he moved to the front window and gazed out at the riverfront. Smoke unfurling from the riverboats reminded him what rode on this meeting. If James McIntire bought his pitch, David would be set for life. If the meeting went south, he knew he might have to slink back home and ask his family to take him in.

Fifteen years ago he had ridden out of Brecon on a horse stolen from his father, and he never wanted to see his tiny part of Ohio again. Sweat broke out on his forehead, and he just had time to mop it away before the young clerk returned.

A few minutes later, David entered a room ruled by a partner desk piled with stacks of papers. James sat at the desk and swore under his breath as he worked his way down a ledger sheet. Yearly account books behind glass doors emphasized the long history of the firm.

David cleared his throat to get James' attention. The older man put his finger on a line near the end of the page. Then he glanced at the calling card by the ink well before he gave his visitor a once over.

"Smith, is it? Do I know you?" James frowned.

Undeterred, David leaned across the desk and offered his hand. "Slightly, sir, from your father's funeral."

Though James' frown deepened, David did not wait for an invitation. He placed his hat and walking stick on the chair next to the one he claimed for himself.

"But let me promise you upfront that you'll not regret our meeting today."

"Get to the point, man."

"I propose a partnership. I can guarantee one thing. When we act together, we'll eradicate all your financial problems. With my help, you can dissuade the bank from foreclosing."

"Sir, you're woefully misinformed."

David ignored the words and their icy tone. Instead he kept his attention on James' face. There was a hint of curiosity in the man's eyes, but there was also a sense of wariness.

"I'm a very busy man," James continued, "and I certainly don't have time to listen to foolishness. Please leave."

He returned his focus to the ledger.

"It's in your best interest to hear me out."

David remained seated. He still had a few cards to play, and short of young Hugh muscling him out of the building, he had nothing to lose by staying.

"Do you know about coverture?"

James looked up and shook his head.

"It refers to a married woman's legal status. Once your sister Isabel is married, she no longer controls her own property. Her legal rights vanish the minute the marriage license is signed."

David punctuated the point by snapping his fingers, and James blinked.

"How do you know so much about my family?"

David turned the question aside with a dismissive wave.

"You need Isabel married to a man like me. I can woo her and be your partner at the same time. Think of it as similar to Hannibal's pincer strategy at Cannae. You, with your distillery on one side, and me, with coverture rights to Isabel's holdings on the other, against your bankers. We can win. I bet you'll agree too, once you think about it."

David picked up his gloves and walking stick. "I'll give you two days to decide. You can reach me at the Galt House."

"What's in it for you?"

"Cash. I need to build my nest egg for a few years."

James rubbed his nose for a few moments and then gave his answer. "Your deadline's meaningless. We McIntires never rush to judgment. It has stood us in good stead for many generations."

"I bet your father and grandfather didn't have to contend with younger brothers looking for their own husband for Isabel. They want to control who she marries."

David stood and after gathering his things, strode for the door. This is it, he thought, bluff the man.

When he reached the hall, he turned, "Remember, two days. Don't bother young Hugh. I'll see myself out."

Outside the closed door, David paused and knew he had won when James' words came through the transom.

"Isabel married to him and me with her property? By God, it'd serve her right."

After a sour laugh, James continued, "I just might see what old Herndon has to say about this coverture business."

~~

The next evening, while David dined with James and his family, he poured on the charm to James' wife Elizabeth. He found women past a certain age so easy. The old chestnuts about being a child bride and having a youthful step worked wonders. Even though Elizabeth was stout, plain, and had even more gray in her hair than James, she pinked up like an unmarried girl.

Afterwards the two men retired to the walnut-paneled library and negotiated the details of their partnership over cigars and sipping whiskey. By eleven o'clock, they had almost concluded their plans.

"To review," James said, "I'll arrange for you to meet and court Isabel. You'll have a year from now to marry her."

"Agreed, and within six months of the marriage, I'll begin selling her assets to you. Everything will be in your hands within three years."

"Yes, you'll also be the new vice-president at the distillery."

"For an annual salary of one thousand, five hundred dollars."

David raised his glass in a mock toast.

"Good God, man, the sum is too extravagant."

David put down his glass and waited until James stopped his bluster about the high cost of doing business.

"Not when you consider I need to set myself up as a gentleman of a suitable class for your sister."

"One thousand," James countered.

"Split the difference with me, and consider what this investment means to you."

"Agreed."

James' hand was unsteady when he put the number down in his notebook.

"But if you fail to marry, you'll resign your position and leave town."

"You have my word, sir."

Chapter 3

Louisville, March 30, 1859

Isabel sensed a smile play behind her veil as she gloried in her secret and walked out of the parish hall with her hand resting lightly on James' arm. They had just concluded their first monthly meeting as the newest board members of the Catholic Charities for Louisville.

James, as first-born son, inherited his seat. She, though, had earned hers by accompanying her father to his different boards during his last years. Those meetings served as an education. She had sat, quiet and demur, and absorbed every bit of information. She was confident the men did not realize they had shown her how money bought power. Enlightened, she had made demands on her father.

One was when the time came, she, along with James, would also serve on this board. And true to what she had learned, the extra gift of money her father had promised to the parish upon his death sealed the agreement with Father O'Connell.

The cathedral's clock struck a quarter past two as a few board members lingered on the steps. They offered their sympathies to her and James, and soon several walked down to the busy avenue. Yet James seemed to find excuses to stay. She could not think of what was his reason to stand around and visit. It was not like him. He never cared for the social niceties.

Isabel nodded to old Mrs. Chinn and tried pulling a bit on James' arm. This delay had gone on long enough. It was time to return home and remove the heavy mourning cloak and veil. She rejoiced that only six more months remained before she could fold her black clothes once again into the cedar chests. Her mother's jet jewelry did help relieve the somber dark of her ensemble, and she would be in a lighter veil by summer and could catch more of a breeze. Men had a much easier experience with deep mourning. All James had to do was put an armband on his usual dark suit.

At last he gave into her prompts, and they moved down the steps and onto the street.

"Wasn't that man coming toward us at father's reception?" James asked after they walked a few minutes.

She could not see the man clearly through her veil and said, "James. I need more explanation than that. So many men came to honor him."

"The one from Pittsburgh, you remember. He told us about Father's reputation spreading so far to the east. His name was easy to remember. Smith? Yes, that's right, David Smith."

A few minutes later, the man named Smith shook hands with James and turned to her. He gave her a warm smile and raised his bowler hat.

~~~

"I hope today finds you well, Miss McIntire."

The smile made Isabel remember his kind offer to bring her some refreshment, and she sensed a blush grow under his scrutiny before the man turned his attention back to James. She was now thankful for the full heavy veil.

Isabel used the black lace to hide her examination of Mr. Smith. He was only a few inches taller than she, and she liked the way his smile reached all the way to his green eyes when he laughed at one of James' inane jokes. His most charming feature, she decided, was the way his blond hair curled, just a bit, right above his collar. She did not mind that the men talked for a few minutes about the races at the new Woodlawn Course.

When James asked him to accompany them on their walk, Mr. Smith agreed and somehow maneuvered himself so that he took her arm. The sidewalk was too narrow for all three to walk abreast, and James dropped back. For the next few minutes, her new acquaintance again offered his condolences, hoped her faith would help her through her time of trouble, and with another tip of his hat said good-bye.

~~~

Once they were back in her parlor, she felt her brother's eyes on her while she removed her hat and veil and rearranged a few loose hairpins in her chignon.

"I think," he said, "the meeting and walk were good for you. Some color has returned to your face."

"Nonsense, it is the veil's doing. You men have no idea how hot these things are," she answered and sat in the chair opposite his.

"I have something to discuss with you," he said and leaned closer. "You've always been a pretty good judge of character. It's about Smith, the man we just met."

Isabel tried to fight down the blush she knew was growing on her cheeks.

"For your club?"

"No, for the distillery. I thought he might be a good addition to the sales department."

Isabel could not believe that he was actually asking her opinion. "Where are you expanding our market?"

"East, I'd like for us to crowd out some small distilleries between here and Lexington."

"I have been in favor of that move for years. And as far as Mr. Smith goes, I agree. I do believe he has never met a stranger."

Isabel found herself giving slight nods of acknowledgement to others as she searched the congregation for Mr. Smith's blond curls. When she found him seated two rows in front, her heart danced at a higher tempo until she reined it in and regained her senses. But his presence distracted her attention from the homily again.

However, she was not the only one who noticed the coincidence. Helen was all atwitter on the carriage ride home. "Mr. Smith is always so gracious when he stops to say hello to us."

"Take care, Helen, better not make too much of it. He talks more to James and Elizabeth."

"So true. But have you noticed how some of the mothers make sure he speaks to them and their marriageable daughters? No? Well, Isabel, the race is on."

"What do you mean?"

Helen giggled, "The race to the altar."

～～

The next Sunday morning, Isabel sniffed as Helen stood beside her at their front door while waiting for the gardener to bring the carriage around.

"Are you wearing scent?" she asked.

"Just a bit."

Isabel was about to chide her sister on how women their age should act, but let the moment go. If Mr. Smith found Helen ridiculous, so be it. If he fell for such an obvious ploy, he deserved his fate. Isabel vowed she would not demean herself.

Unease settled over her as she had a glimpse of her future, growing old in her elegant, lifeless house with no one for company, if Helen won Mr. Smith's affections. But Isabel would not stoop to the same level as her sister. If she chose to enter what Helen called the race to the altar, she would remain a lady.

~~~

On Easter Sunday David Smith came to the family celebration at James and Elizabeth's house. When Isabel saw his place card next to hers, she offered her sister-in-law a silent thank you. This was her opportunity to show Mr. Smith how a true lady conducted herself.

His table manners were a bit disappointing though. They were not quite up to her standards. He used the cheese knife for buttering his roll and looked at the finger bowl as if he had never seen one before. But his conversation was witty. She enjoyed his comments about the outrageous hats he had seen at church during the early Mass.

"Mr. Smith," Helen spoke across the table in her silly, girlish way, "you just wait until you see the ladies' hats at the spring races. Last year I wore a bright pink one, crowned with a cloud of butterflies."

"I'm sure it was one of the best ones there, Miss Helen," David smiled. "And Miss McIntire, what did your hat look like?"

When he turned his attention on her, she had difficulty putting her thoughts in order. Finally she was able to speak.

"I did not attend the races last year."

David's smile dimmed a little. "Maybe this year?"

James answered before she could. "What a grand idea, Mr. Smith, why don't you join the family. We've had a box for years."

~~~

After lunch, Isabel's heart filled with joy when she realized her high standards had carried the day. While the children formed small packs and scoured the lawn for the hidden Easter eggs, Mr. Smith asked her to walk in the gardens. As they stopped to admire the early spring blossoms of daffodils, he told her about his life of moving from one business opportunity to another up and down the Ohio.

"I'm what you might call a rolling stone," David confided with a slight shrug. "As soon as I'd conquered one challenge, I'd move on to another. But lately, I've been thinking it may be time to settle in one place."

He gave her a meaningful look and led her to a seat under the loggia, carpeted overhead with ivy.

"Do you enjoy living in Louisville?"

When she answered yes, he asked about her favorite pastimes.

"I enjoy the opera. I have had season tickets ever since I was a girl."

"Opera is something I also enjoy. I try to attend whenever I'm in Pittsburgh or St. Louis."

Her heart thrilled with his answer, and she asked, "Have you ever been to the Louisville Opera?"

"Unfortunately, I've never had the opportunity to attend. But maybe this next season," he said, and his lingering gaze transmitted shivers through her. "What performances have you enjoyed?"

For a few minutes she was too befuddled to answer. "Almost all of them," she at last managed.

"Tell me your favorite part of your favorite opera."

"It would have to be Rosina's aria."

She took a deep breath and shared with him something she had never said aloud to anyone else. "When she sings '*Si, si, la vincero,*' I admire her spirit."

David nodded and asked her about other operas. She lost all track of time as she shared the glories she had seen on the stage.

When their walk finished, he gave her a small bow and brushed her hand with a kiss. He nodded to Helen pretending to appreciate the rose bed. "Please excuse me, I must thank Mrs. James before I leave."

Isabel watched him speak to her sister-in-law and turn around to tip his hat to her before he departed. Helen glared at her while Elizabeth smiled.

~~~

In May the family celebrated at the Falls of the Ohio to mark the end of the school year. David again joined the family. He seemed to enjoy organizing the baseball game for the younger children. After he lost several rounds of horseshoes to her brothers Patrick and Stephen, he stopped by the picnic area for some iced root beer.

"Ladies," he nodded to Isabel, Elizabeth, and her other sisters-in-law.

"Mr. Smith," Elizabeth spoke first. "You certainly have a way with children. Do you come from a large family?"

Isabel noticed his eyes flicker and harden momentarily before he answered, "Yes, Mrs. McIntire."

After he removed a bottle from the washtub filled with ice, he returned to the horseshoe game.

Disappointed, Isabel watched him go. Why had she not thought of a comment clever enough to keep the conversation going? She knew her sister would have.

~~~

A few mornings later, Isabel was alarmed when Elizabeth called before nine.

"Is something wrong?" Isabel asked after they were seated in the parlor.

"No, and I hope, after you hear my reason for coming today, you will let me return on my usual Thursday afternoons."

"Whatever do you mean?" Isabel noticed Elizabeth seemed a little nervous. Her sister-in-law kept smoothing her skirts.

"Please do not think I am a busybody, but while we were at breakfast this morning, James mentioned something about Mr. Smith."

Isabel could not stop the blush growing on her face. With a kind smile, Elizabeth reached over and touched her arm.

"The family has noticed how much attention he gives you…"

"What are you trying to say?" Isabel interrupted.

"James told me such good news this morning. It seems Mr. Smith is quite taken with you."

Isabel knew her blush deepened. She fought for control of her heart and thoughts. A nod was the best she could do.

"I shall invite him to our house for my birthday next month and again for yours in July, but only if you agree. Believe me, you cannot wait until your mourning period is over to reciprocate his attentions. The man will not be unattached long."

Isabel laughed, "You want to be my matchmaker?"

"Who else would be better? I can arrange it so you always sit next to him at dinner, and only if you say so, James could pass on encouragement to your Mr. Smith."

Isabel could not help herself and giggled. "But he is not my Mr.

Smith."

"Not yet," Elizabeth returned a giggle of her own.

, – – –

The evening of Elizabeth's birthday, Isabel found herself partnered with David against their hosts at whist. Although David claimed he did not know much about the game, the two of them won most of the hands before they broke for a cold buffet.

"May I escort my Lady Luck to dinner?"

The expression coming from his eyes melted her heart.

Isabel let a smile dance across her face. As she walked arm and arm with him to the sideboard, she said, "I seem to have the most unusual luck when you are my partner. Are you sure you are not familiar with this game?"

"Cards have never been part of my recreation," he said. "Don't you think my skills are improving?"

"With practice, they will probably become even better."

"We'll see, but," David gave her a soul-reaching look, "What's more important is we'll get to be partners again at your birthday celebration next month."

Isabel's heart skipped a beat and soared. Her dreams were coming true. She, not Helen, would win David. Against her will, the balcony scene of Rosina swearing she would prevail flickered through her mind and embarrassed her. When had she become a character in an opera? Did she not have more depth than Rosina displayed as she pursued her man? It took Isabel a few minutes to reassure herself. She certainly had worth and dimension. There were her charity work and patronage of the arts. And respect. She did have society's respect.

~~~

David paced his expert seduction with military precision. He held longer conversations after each Mass. Another strategy was casually joining her on the street when she moved from shop to shop. He escorted her home and carried her bundles. After a little more time, he placed his hand over hers when it rested on his arm. Without fail, he attended the weekly family dinners at James' house.

~~~

In July, with five months of the wooing year already spent, David rejoined his prospective brother-in-law in the library. With the windows open to capture any breeze possible on the humid late afternoon, the two men smoked cigars and planned the next stage.

James laughed, "I happened to overhear Brian and Patrick yesterday. Their topic was their coverture scheme. It seems my youngest brothers have yet again failed to act quickly enough."

"So they've finally found someone?"

"Can you believe it? They've at last managed to recruit their own candidate, a ne'er-do-well gentleman farmer from Bardstown. Long on pedigree, chronically short on funds."

James leaned forward. "They plan the introduction soon. It's imperative you claim her before he makes his move."

"It's also important to not overplay our hand. If I press too soon, it will appear in poor taste. She is still in mourning. You don't want her bolting."

"Good God, man, she's not a young simpering girl, and you don't want her acting like one when this other man shows up. You've got to have her hooked before he gets here."

"All right." David stubbed his cigar in the ashtray beside him. "The parish ice cream social's next week. I'll ask her to accompany me, without Helen. Can you hint to your wife about Isabel moving into half-mourning a month early so she can wear something with a bit more color. It's damn hard to play the love-struck suitor when your adored one is all in black."

"I'll see what I can do," James answered with a wry smile.

"Good, we'll make a much better picture when I take her hand and help her from the carriage. All the old gossips will stretch their necks to look at us and comment on her clothes and what a handsome couple we are. If Louisville's like every other place I've lived in, word will soon get around. Everyone will know she's spoken for."

~~~

Their arrival at the church social exceeded David's plans. He heard a few women set to buzzing when Isabel, in a purple silk dress striped with lavender and silver, stepped from the carriage. Clusters of women whispered and watched them walk arm in arm toward the main tent. The glowering reactions from the two youngest McIntire brothers near the stand of magnolias almost made him burst out in laughter. If those fools only knew what they had set in motion with their strategy of coverture, he thought.

David was satisfied. Soon he would exchange Isabel's assets for cash. In three years, he could return to Pittsburgh a rich man. He had been saved from Brecon, after all.

Isabel set her wedding for February eleventh. David had insisted they marry before Lent even though the full year of mourning was not over. So only the family attended.

She had to surrender some of the extravagant plans she had made long ago with her school friends. But a few of her long-held plans came true. One was the Loughlin lace veil her mother claimed had come over with her grandmother. Thus had begun the tradition that every bride, including any women marrying into the family, would wear the antique lace.

The dressmaker had complained matching the veil to the exact shade of ivory satin would take a great deal of extra work. But on her wedding day, Isabel saw the effort was worth it. The gown's fitted bodice accented her slimness. Her mother's lace fell from her auburn hair, framed her face, and ended at the hem of her full skirt. She was so happy she had chosen not to wear a hoop when she saw how the graceful skirt brushed the carpet.

The last item she put on was the heirloom multi-strand pearl choker, also from the Loughlins. But, unlike the lace, no woman in the family had worn the necklace since her mother's passing so many years ago.

~~~

At the nave of the church, Isabel met James and kissed him on the cheek.

"Thank you, you brought David into my life. I never thought I would ever marry."

His smile vanished, and he looked almost haunted.

In alarm, she asked, "Are you ill? You look like you've seen a ghost."

He shook his head, but his knees wobbled. His hand grabbed the doorframe for support.

"Do you need to sit down?"

"No, not at all."

He took out his handkerchief and wiped at his face. "It's only….I mean I never realized before how much you remind me of Mother."

"I am so sorry she is not here," Isabel said as they started down the aisle. "I am certain she and Poppa would have approved of David. Surely you agree?"

James did not answer her. Instead he grew paler and had to dab his handkerchief to his forehead again.

~~~

Isabel found married life exhilarating. She and David moved into the master bedroom, where she enjoyed physical love for the first time. Now she understood the sly smiles her sisters-in-law made when they had referred to their marital duties. Her social calendar also blossomed. Soon the newlyweds were booked for the opera, theater, and fancy balls.

However, two worries nagged and clouded her happiness. One was her sister. Helen did not accept Elizabeth's offer to move in with her and James and stayed instead in her childhood home. Invited to many of the same social functions as the newlyweds, Helen accompanied them. But it seemed to Isabel that each dinner and party diminished her sister's spirit.

When several hostesses hinted that it was becoming more difficult to partner Helen at dinner and cards, Isabel tried to bolster her sister's spirits with shopping for imported fabrics and visits to dressmakers.

Then came the dinner party at the Whites'. The guest of honor, a Mr. L.T. Rodes, mentioned he was a cousin of the First Lady.

"Why Mr. Rodes," Helen interrupted the man's harangue about how unfairly the press treated dear Cousin Mary. "Is there any truth about Mrs. Lincoln selling the manure from the White House stables for ten cents a wagonload?"

The room froze into a dead silence. Isabel heard some women murmur and saw them bring out their fans. Helen smiled and did not glance her way. Mr. Rodes sputtered. Isabel looked to David for help, but he gave up his effort to stifle his laughter and covered his choked laugh with a cough.

"By Jupiter, she put him in his place, didn't she," the man on her right said in a stage whisper. "Well played, Miss Helen."

His voice boomed across the table, and he raised his wine glass in a salute. "Most interesting gathering I've been to in months. Thank you for turning the talk from the war." He winked and drained his drink.

Mrs. White finally gained control of her dinner party. She rose and announced the ladies would now retire to the parlor. "Gentlemen, please join us after your brandy and cigars."

The pitying side-looks the other women gave Isabel in the parlor told her Helen's social life was over.

After they arrived home, Isabel followed Helen to her room.

"Helen, how could you bring up politics? You know Momma always said no lady mentions politics or religion at a dinner party."

"He was such a hideous man. I watched him talk and talk. It was a disgusting spectacle. He never cleared his mouth before he spoke. No one else had any opportunity to say a word."

"You mean no one else paid any attention to you."

Helen made a little moue. "I wish to retire, Isabel. Surely your husband awaits you?"

~~~

Isabel's second disappointment was children. During the first three years of marriage, she had conceived and delivered five early babies. They all died within hours of leaving her body.

After the fifth child, Doctor Reynolds laid down the law. "My dear," he said as he patted her hand. "I've known you ever since you were born. No one else knows you as well as I. So, I must insist you practice abstinence. I've discussed the matter with David, and he agrees."

"So you, David, and God are denying me children?"

"I don't know about God's part, but I do know this. Another pregnancy could kill you. Today, I barely stopped the hemorrhage. Next time, I might not be able to. But you are a fortunate woman. Not all husbands place their wives' needs above theirs."

Part of Isabel's core shattered. Dreams of her children at play in the yard and opening birthday presents died. She felt resentment claim her soul. Why were her brothers blessed with so many children and she none?

Chapter 4

Louisville, April 13, 1863

Prioress Justina felt her sixty years. The spring rains brought out the aches. Each throb in her knees recalled how many times she had knelt at prayer in the cathedral's damp and cold. On days like this, she wondered if her prayers had ever done any good.

Within the past hour, a new twinge started at the base of her neck. She knew it came from the hours she had spent bent over the account book. Although the convent's donations had increased after the war economy brought money to Louisville, the war had also brought more soldiers. As a result, these men fathered more children and food prices rose. The orphanage's monthly balances predicted she would need more funds for the needy children under her care.

The account book, still open before her, did not offer much hope. The easy items, such as extra candles and new textbooks, were already gone. Also the ledger showed the income from their bakery had disappeared with the advent of the war. These days flour was too expensive to go into the sisters' fancy breads.

A glance outside her window reminded her of the sacrifices their order had made since the war began last year. The sun dried the rain off the rows of sprouting corn. Not only had the sisters turned their rose gardens into vegetable patches, they had also halved their own food portions.

This year most of the nuns gave up their noon meal, so there would be more food for the children. She was concerned about some of the older nuns who also fasted. They were growing too thin to fight off illnesses. After she had mentioned this in the chapter meeting, she overheard some of the younger sisters' whispers that at her age, she would also be in danger this winter if she kept winnowing away.

These worries and others haunted her preparations for the annual tour next month. She knew the floors would be waxed, the woodwork polished, and the windows cleared of flyspecks and dirt. Sister Valeria had volunteered to make sure the children were clean and orderly. The board would see the war had not cost St. Jerome's its dignity.

The prioress tapped her pencil against the ledger and considered how she could shake loose more coins from the wealthy parishioners. God willing, maybe this year, Mrs. Smith would attend the annual tour. Her two-year absence from the tour meant the children had gone without her customary gifts. The food and clothing came in handy, but the young ones especially missed the toys. Of course, Justina thanked God every year when Mr. McIntire fulfilled his father's bequests, but he did not understand the children the same way his sister did. He always arrived empty-handed.

With some effort, Justina made it out of her chair when the bell announced mid-morning prayers. Her long strand of wooden prayer beads clicked and signaled that she was stepping as fast as she could toward the chapel.

~~~

Justina looked up from her account book in the lull after the mantle clock chimed eleven. Footsteps came closer to her office. She recognized their pattern and replaced her pen in the holder. She answered "Come in" to the knock on the door.

"Good morning, Sister, God be with you," Father O'Connell said.

"Good morning, Father, may God also be with you," Justina said and eased her way up.

"Be seated, Sister."

The stout man walked with a slight limp to the chair by her desk.

Age was overtaking him as well Justina thought and waited for him to lean back.

"You seem happy," she said.

His round face broke into a wider smile. "I could tell you it's because God has blessed us with such a fine spring day," the priest spoke.

"But there is some other reason?"

"Yes, I've been at Mrs. Smith's."

His smile was infectious. The prioress found herself smiling in return.

"She's attending the board meeting?"

"Let's just say, Sister, a little bird told me a secret."

"And are you going to share it with me?"

Father O'Connell leaned closer and stage-whispered, "It'd be in our best interests to have our most attractive children where they can readily be seen. This year Mr. Smith will also be joining us." He ended his secret with a wink and a nod.

"From our lips to God's ear, may they see a child to adopt. Will they be wanting a girl or a boy?"

"Can't say either way."

"Does Mrs. Smith prefer an infant or a toddler?"

He shrugged. "My best advice to you is to have your chosen children where the Smiths will notice them."

"Yes Father, thank you, this is good news."

The priest soon left to call upon the elderly sisters in the infirmary, and the nun closed her account book. She took out a piece of paper from her desk drawer and thought about which children might most appeal to Mrs. Smith.

Justina thought six-month-old William and Catherine the best choices from the infant room. Cheerful, they followed the sisters with their eyes when the nuns moved about the room. No teething yet meant they did not have any red splotches on their faces. William had a wondrous wreath of brown curls no visitor or caretaker could ever resist touching. Catherine's morning-glory-blue eyes latched on to anyone who met her gaze. The prioress made a note to dress them in the newest, unstained uniforms and place them with some toys in the first crib.

The two four-year-olds were easy, Etta and Colin. Sister Justina thought the little girl had several factors in her favor. There was the child's red hair the color of poppies along with her green eyes and angelic voice. If the Smiths could hear Etta sing during the tour, they might consider her. But the sisters would have to keep the girl from indulging in one of her infamous temper tantrums.

Colin was just as fetching with his dark wavy hair and warm hazel eyes, and his disposition was so much better. A few months ago, she and the sisters had discovered his talents lay in drawing. Justina added Colin and Etta to her list and plotted how she could present them. She noted dress last, put in schoolroom, away from older students, by their names.

Lastly, she included Nancy and Edward from the elementary class. The girl's face was delicate yet strong, and her honey-colored curls and bright amber eyes gave her a serene air. Edward was strong and the tallest eight-year-old. His dark brown hair fell neatly along its natural part. His gray eyes hinted at his ever present ability to find humor all around him.

She wrote Edward was to assist the men with their hats and Nancy to offer the ladies some cool water and sugar cookies.

She sat back, pleased with her plans.

"Father O'Connell should be quite happy with these children. Enough variety to make the choice seem real, and few enough to make the choosing easier."

~~

On the eve of the tour, Sister Justina called Sisters Valeria and Anna to review their plans for the last time. Their goal was to conclude the meeting before sunset so there would be no need to light the lamps.

Justina led with her report. "Mary Michael reports all the rooms, including windows and ceilings are in fine condition. Each room will have a few fresh flowers."

At the word, flowers, the three of them looked out the windows opened to the gardens sprouting green.

"The good news is the spring blossoms are at their colorful peak. We've saved our few lilacs for the mustier rooms. Redbud branches are to go into the airier rooms."

"I made my rounds this afternoon to check on all six children," Valeria said next. "William and Catherine still have no sign of teeth so they're not fussy and their complexions remain clear. Their crib and clothes are ready. In case the Smiths decide not to go all the way into the room, they'll still see the babies in the front crib."

On her list, Justina noted this task done.

Valeria continued, "Etta has practiced a song an hour every day for two weeks. I have decided she's to sit on a stool and sing to her doll."

"Not the one missing an eye and an arm?" Anna frowned.

"It's her favorite," Justina reminded her subordinate and shifted to relieve the pain in her right hip. "She won't part from it without a scene. You recall the last temper tantrum when I tried to remove the food stains from her doll?"

"Yes, she wouldn't allow anyone else to pick it up after she flung it down on the floor and stomped on it."

Anna pointed her finger heavenwards. "The child's temper must be curbed."

"You were so patient with her, Justina," Valeria said.

The prioress appreciated the turn in the conversation and nodded her approval to Valeria.

"I just offered it up. Etta needs love and compassion, not punishment. I'm sure God gave her such a special voice for a reason. Our task is to help her find its purpose.

Anna shook her head. "Although she's blessed with a special gift, her willfulness won't do her any favors."

"She'll need that spirit to survive. Out there." Valeria countered and pointed to the window.

"The child also needs to know the wisdom of obedience and how to conform," Anna warned. "And conform she must if she's to make her way in the world. No one will take on a disobedient apprentice."

Justina knew they would never be in agreement over Etta and ruled, "So we'll renew our efforts to tame her willfulness. As for tomorrow, we shall let her have the doll. We don't want her to have a fit of temper, do we? And the other children?"

"Colin found some animals, bears and foxes, in a book," Anna continued. Valeria turned in her chair, so she did not have to look across the table at Anna.

Justina sighed. Sometimes, the adults were worse than the children she thought, but she nodded for Anna to finish her report.

"Colin's been working on his animals with Mary Clemens every afternoon. His drawing has improved. Nancy and Edward have practiced their tasks. He can carry a hat to the cloakroom without bending the brim. She can now serve the water and cookies from a tray without any mistakes. They're prepared for tomorrow."

"Thank you for the good reports." Justina folded her hands over her written list. "I've inspected the kitchen, dormitories, chapel, and schoolrooms. All the gifts the current board members have given us are in use. In sum, we present the image of a grateful community. We've used our gifts wisely. Yet, at the same time we're still in need. Can you think of anything I've forgotten?"

When the two said no, Justina closed the meeting. "We will join the others for evening prayer. Let us all pray God moves the board to evermore generosity and leads the Smiths to adopt."

Chapter 5

Louisville, May 25, 1863

Isabel stood by the convent's entrance and tried not to show her impatience. Though the bells of St. Jerome's had just signaled one o'clock, none of the other six board members seemed to mind the wait for Father O'Connell. Certainly not David, who, she saw, made the best of the delay.

Her husband appraised the two other wives who wore spring frocks the colors of her prized dark pink roses. The women held David's attention with their beguiling laughter and graceful gloved hands fixing a curl or straightening an earring.

Isabel knew she, with her dark clothes, stood in sharp contrast, without even a nosegay to add a bit of color to her ensemble. Her height, accentuated by her slimness, made her resemble a crane dressed all in black. The women, whom she decided were much too old to flirt with her husband, looked like jeweled hummingbirds.

But, she told herself, it was important to remember her real purpose of the tour today. She wanted a family, and the orphans were her only hope. With God's help, together, she and Father O'Connell would persuade David. She had already prayed for success. Now she replayed the vincero aria in her head for courage.

At last the priest opened the doors. He greeted each board member before he led the group to the reception room. An older boy, introduced as Edward, took the men's hats. His companion, a girl called Nancy, offered cookies to Isabel and the two women. More impatient with each passing moment, Isabel declined.

Father O'Connell must have noticed. After he once more thanked them for their service, he bustled them out into a window-lined hallway. Sunrays reflected off the polished poplar wood paneling and warmed the passage.

When the priest turned the corner to go down another hallway,

Isabel paused. Before her were two niches. The first one held the candle-lit statuary of St. Jerome. Mary with the infant Jesus occupied the other. After she made her silent prayer asking them to intercede for her today, she moved on.

~~~

Their next stop was the infants' room. Isabel saw Sister Justina by a crib with two beautiful babies. One had a set of curls. The other had the brightest blue eyes that fell on her and held. Isabel heard the nun say, "Our older girls assist." It was a speech she had listened to before. Instead she broke from the board members at the open double doors and approached the crib.

Sister Justina moved aside and said, "Here we have William and Catherine, both about six-months-old."

"Hello William, hello Catherine," Isabel said. "What lovely babies you are."

They looked up at her. William raised his arms, and Isabel said to Sister Justina, "Is it all right?"

"Of course, William loves to cuddle."

He snuggled up against her breast, and Isabel thought how complete she was with him in her arms. Her contentment broke when David touched her elbow.

Isabel turned so he could see the baby in her arms. "He is so precious," she said. "Look at these curls and his big smile."

"Yes, yes, but you must come along Isabel, remember what the doctor said."

Isabel heard the old man's advice again. 'Your nerves are fragile. Do not become overwrought.' She ever so slowly put the baby back in his crib. Her arms suddenly seemed so weightless and empty.

"Mrs. Smith, do you wish to continue?" Justina asked, "You look quite pale."

"Yes, the toddler room is next?"

"Same schedule as always, then we move on to the schoolroom."

Isabel fell in step between her husband and the prioress and walked down the hall to the toddler's dormitory. There, the children played with a few dolls and blocks, but no child seemed as engaging as William. She considered how she could leave the tour and return to him while the prioress led the way to the schoolroom.

"Most of the children," Justina said, "in here are six to ten. They should be in their geography lesson. However, we do have two special younger children, Etta and Colin, with the older students today. They have both shown early talent so we're giving them extra lessons. You will hear Etta sing. I believe you will all be quite taken with her natural gift."

"And the boy?" Isabel asked.

Justina smiled, "His drawing talent is quite remarkable for one so young."

Father O'Connell brought them to the open door. The schoolroom took up the entire second floor of the girls' wing. Thirty students sat two to a bench in a room graced with windows on three sides. A young nun stood in front of a six-foot map of the United States. After she pointed to the states one by one, the students in unison recited the state's name and capitol.

After listening to the children correctly name a few geography facts, the priest walked toward the north window.

"This is Colin," he said.

The boy was so engrossed with drawing the picture of his bear he did not even look up.

From her side of the group, Isabel noticed a red-headed little girl seated on a stool and rocking a doll. Sunlight flooded the music area of the room. The beams of light caught the girl's braids and showed that unruly wisps had escaped from their confinement.

Isabel moved closer. The scene reminded her of the golden moments in the theater when she had seen the curtain begin its ascent. Now, just as in the theater, the audience conversation lowered, and the voices from the far side of the room receded. A soft Gregorian chant fell over her and held her captive.

The little girl closed her song and raised her face to look over the visitors. Leaving her stool, she walked toward Isabel and held out her doll.

"You've got red hair like Polly and me. What's your name?"

"My name is Mrs. Smith."

Isabel knelt down to the little girl's level. "What is your name?"

"My Christian name is Bridgette. But Sister Justina calls me Etta. Cause she can't get Bridgette out in time."

"In time for what?"

"To stop me when I'm in trouble."

"Are you often in trouble?" Isabel laughed.

"Sometimes. But Sister Justina says I'm getting better. She tells I have to try harder because God is busy."

"Busy with what?"

"With the war and helping others. I can't take up all his time. I have to be real good."

"I am confident you are very good."

Isabel touched the girl's shoulder and rose.

~~~

Elated, Isabel stepped into the carriage outside St. Jerome's. Father O'Connell must have shared her hint about adoption with the sisters. She could not remember such adorable children on the previous tours.

Her spirits stayed high all evening during the usual weekly meal with her brother James and his family. Especially when James shared with Elizabeth how much he enjoyed the little girl's song. For once, Isabel did not ache with being childless when her brother's seven children in their matched robes came in to bid the adults good night.

Instead, Isabel imagined a family chosen from the orphans, clad in her favorite Royal Stuart tartan, with the same nightly ritual at her house.

~~~

"David, did you find those children adorable?" she asked on their short buggy ride home.

"Certainly, my dear."

"I think we need to adopt them. We have so much to offer."

"You don't want all of them, do you?" He had taken on a teasing tone.

Isabel ignored David's attempt to trivialize. "Not the two older ones. I heard Mr. Percy and Mrs. Chinn discuss how they would find positions for them. But the other four would be perfect for us."

"Four's too many at one time."

"They are so special." Tears filled her eyes. "I knew as soon as I held William, he was meant to be mine."

"You're not strong enough to supervise four young children. It'd take more staff, at least one more maid. I don't think you realize how much care and time children need."

"I do know my arms suddenly felt empty when I put him back in his crib."

Isabel returned to the wondrous moment she saw William and the other child side by side.

"The little girl Catherine looked sweet. I wished I had had the chance to hold her."

"Maybe older children will be easier."

"You mean the two children in the school room? The little red-headed girl? She would certainly look like one of the family. We could give her voice lessons. Or would you prefer a boy?"

"This is a weighty decision. My advice is to pray for guidance. In the morning you'll have a clearer head."

He patted her hand and closed the subject.

In her dreams, Isabel pictured the four orphans with opened Christmas presents, play time in the side yard with a large collie, and kisses for her and David every night complete with the lingering scent of soap from their baths. Bedtime stories of Mother Goose and fairy tales followed by sweet kisses and hugs wove through her dreams.

She awoke determined to adopt them all, the quicker the better. Two boys and two girls would be a nice family. Somehow she would have to convince David they needed to adopt them every one of them.

Chapter 6

Louisville, May 26, 1863

David's dreams plagued him. Scenes from his childhood featured his younger sisters and brothers. Memories of their vivid diaper smells and snotty noses disrupted his sleep and stayed with him through the night. He did not wake up in a good mood. He lay in his bed and listened to the sounds of the well-ordered house come awake. Not one discordant note resonated in the morning routine of muffled voices that rose from downstairs and of doors opened and closed with restraint.

However, David faced the cold truth during his morning shave. From his take on Isabel's expressions yesterday, he realized they would have to adopt at least one child. He had seen how his wife's eyes softened when she held the infant and lingered on him after she returned him to his crib.

He would not accept four children and their interruptions to his home life he decided on the way down to breakfast. The family outings with the pack of McIntire nieces and nephews running amuck had long ago dissuaded him from having a large family. Money figured into the decision as well. He did not like the idea of the extra expense which went along with children. More importantly, he had paid the price for the life he now had. Wooing and bedding Isabel had been work. He deserved peace and quiet.

By the time he reached the dining room, he had determined how he was going to play the morning scene. He would agree to one child now, preferably the red-headed girl, since girls were easier than boys, or so his mother always said. He would add the promise of another one child or two in a few years.

Anything to keep Isabel distracted, so he could capitalize on the rumors of the new massive coalfields throughout the state. Investments in them would certainly increase his secret financial holdings. By God, he loved the stock market. He found this gambling even headier than cards. His holdings now included transportation stocks in railroads and canals. If the market held, in a few years he would turn out to be a rather wealthy man in his own right. Then he could leave this flea-bitten town and go to a real city, New York or Philadelphia, someplace where he could snare another heiress with his good looks and charm. And polish, he added to his list of attributes. He had to thank Isabel for the thin veneer of class he now wore. She had been a excellent teacher. David, buoyed by his decisions and plans, sat down to a hearty breakfast of eggs and grits.

"Good morning, my dear," he said and lowered his newspaper when Isabel joined him.

His first thought was his wife was not in her usual black. Instead she wore a dark green silk day dress, trimmed about the collar and wrists with lace. Second, he noticed she looked more rested than he remembered in a long time. The determined jut to her chin broadcasted that the Isabel he had married was back.

"Good morning, David. I am glad you are still at home this morning," she returned his greeting with a smile. "Would you like more coffee?" she asked and rang the bell to summon the maid.

"No, I do need to be off to the club soon. How did you rest?"

"Very well, thank you. I followed your advice. Last night I prayed for guidance and awoke this morning with God's answer in my soul." Isabel's face lit with happiness. "He has chosen us to adopt those four children since we can give them so much."

David knew better than argue with God. So he put his plan into action.

"Why don't we invite Father O'Connell to lunch at the Galt House and discuss your wishes with him?"

"Wonderful idea, David, I shall send a note to the priest house and ask him to join us at twelve thirty."

"Fine, I must be off now. I'll meet you here about noon."

~~~

David's first stop after heading out the door was the priest house. It had taken him a walk of only two blocks to come up with the gist of the conversation he wanted to have. By the time he had reached his destination, he had rehearsed his lines and had them down pat. The housekeeper, a diminutive woman dressed in faded black and whose age he could not even begin to guess, answered his knock.

"Father's in the study. I'll tell him you're here," she said and cleaned the flour from her thick fingers.

"I can see you're busy this morning, Edith. Making your angel biscuits for Father's dinner tonight?"

"Bless your heart, no, sir. Just his bread. I was ready to turn the dough into the pans to rise when you knocked."

"I'll just take myself down the hall to his study." David inclined his head in that direction. "I wouldn't want to be the blame for his bread failing to rise properly. My mother was always quite particular about her bread making too."

"Thank you, sir, it would certainly be a great help."

A minute later, Father O'Connell called out a cheerful "Come in" after David's knock.

David noticed the man had his usual smile on his face. The priest rose from his seat behind the large walnut desk and shook hands. Through the narrow ceiling-to-floor bare windows framing the desk, the priest's prized rose beds showed great promise for the summer.

"Sorry to interrupt your morning work, Father."

"Not at all, Mr. Smith, I'm here to be of assistance to my flock. I hope everything is fine with you and Mrs. Smith."

"We're in good health. But it's Mrs. Smith I've come to see you about."

"Sit down, and tell me how I can help you."

Father O'Connell indicated a rail back chair. David inwardly groaned and sat on the chair's edge. He remembered sitting in the hard seat during previous visits and wondered yet again if the priest used the chair to discourage long talks.

David leaned forward in a futile attempt to find a comfortable angle. "Those unfortunate orphans yesterday touched my wife's tender heart. She prayed last night for guidance."

He spoke the next words in an undertone. "This morning she told me God has advised her to adopt four of the children we saw yesterday."

"God be praised. Which four would that be?" Father O'Connell matched David's volume and clasped his hands in front of him where they rode on top of his round stomach.

"The two infants in the first crib and the red-headed girl and the boy who draws."

"The first would be Catherine and William in the crib. The older ones are Bridgette and Colin. This is glorious news."

"But she can't take on all four children at the same time. The doctor would never allow it. You see, she's not strong enough."

"I'm not quite sure I understand. Surely, your wife won't be the only one in your household to mind the children."

"No, of course not." David straightened. "We have ample help and will even hire on another girl. It's Mrs. Smith's mind and spirit I'm talking about. She'll want to supervise every detail of their lives. My concern is that she's not yet recovered from her losses. I fear she'll suffer a relapse."

"Ahh, what do you suggest?"

Father O'Connell sat back further into his chair and rocked with his hands on the chair arms.

"One child, two at the most. I know she was particularly taken with the small baby William and the little girl Bridgette."

The priest considered and rocked at a slower pace. "I can see the wisdom in your thinking. There's a reason nature spaces children about a year apart."

"She will send you an invitation to join us for lunch today at the Galt House. I'd appreciate it if you would persuade her to begin with one child. Maybe later we would add another in a year or two. The little girl would be the best one to start with. Girls are more compliant, aren't they?"

"Yes, generally so." The rocker stopped, and the priest leaned forward again and fixed David with his intensity. "But there was a girl infant yesterday in the same crib. It's been my experience most women prefer an infant over a toddler."

"I agree if they're young and healthy women. Unfortunately, Mrs. Smith is neither. Two infants would be too much for her."

Father O'Connell rose from his chair to indicate the meeting had come to a close. "I'll also pray for guidance on this matter."

After giving David a pat on his shoulder, he promised to see him for their luncheon. David thanked him for his time and shut the door.

His next stop was to see the younger Walter Herndon, who had taken over his father's law practice a few years before. After he was shown into the attorney's small private office furnished with a desk and only two chairs, David sat down on another uncomfortable visitor chair.

Walter, a man whose mutton chop sideburns were his only distinguishing trait, remained seated and shuffled the papers he was working on into the center desk drawer.

"How may I help you today, my friend?" he asked from behind a desk that now held only a small stack of blank paper and an ink set.

David recapped how he and Isabel were interested in the adoption of one child, possibly two from St. Jerome's.

"How difficult and time-consuming is adoption, Walter?"

"Fairly simple. Don't worry. We use a standard form. Our office has overseen the process for other families. The first step is acquiring Father O'Connell's approval. I assume he agrees."

"Informally. Do you need written confirmation?"

"No, I always check because he has to give permission. No sense preparing documents if he'll not put his John Hancock on them."

"What happens then?"

"You will sign the papers." Walter began a list. "I'll get us on the docket. On the appointed day, I'll take the documents to the circuit court where the judge will approve the adoptions and order them entered into the pleas record."

"Then the child is legally ours?"

"There's one last step. We have to post a notice in the newspaper to indicate your intention to adopt the child." This task also went on the list.

"Why?" David did not like the idea of all this family business printed in the paper.

"We have to give fair notice to any relatives."

The pen went back to the ink set.

"What happens if someone shows up in court to say the child isn't an orphan, or worse. What if someone comes to the house and says he won't make any trouble if I pay him to go away?"

"I'll not lie to you. It's possible. But what the Sisters of St. Jerome do is to record a new name, given and surname, for each child abandoned at their home. Is the child you're interested in an abandoned child?"

"Yes, that's what the nuns told us yesterday."

"Good, no problem then." Walter picked up his pen and added another entry to his list. "About six months after our first court date, you'll have to return and take an oath. You'll swear you intend to legally adopt this child. I also suggest you prepare a new will."

"Why?"

"Both you and Mrs. Smith should have an updated one to protect your new heir. You should also consider whom you would want to act as a trustee for your estate. This should be a person you would trust to oversee your child's rearing if either of you should die while the child is a minor."

"I suppose James would be the best."

"I couldn't agree more."

David read the upside down words James and trustee on the paper.

"Remember," Walter said, "your heir will inherit your and Mrs. Smith's considerable assets. You'll want someone responsible to look out for the child's best interest."

"I had no idea it was this complicated."

"It's not for most people. But the McIntire family assets do continue down to the grandchildren and beyond, in perpetuity." Walter put the pen down and paused for questions.

The words in perpetuity gave David the sinking feeling that somehow James and Isabel had tricked him. He just barely mastered his anger before he asked, "What do you mean?"

"It's quite a story. My father told me the late Mr. McIntire wished to protect his wealth for posterity since during his long life he had witnessed the three generation cycle of wealth too many times. You've probably seen it yourself. One generation builds the foundation of wealth. The second generation capitalizes on it. But by the third generation, maybe because life has been so easy, the descendents waste not only the profits, but also the capital. Old Man McIntire was quite adamant. He wanted some guarantee his wealth would be protected from irresponsible children or grandchildren. Did you know he was the third generation in the business?"

David shook his head. The sinking feeling found new depths. He remembered from his Latin that perpetuity had to do with forever. He did not like where this conversation seemed to be headed.

"No?" Walter continued. "McIntire was proud he had maintained the family wealth and didn't want it at risk after his death. So my father set up a trust for him about seven years before he died."

David experienced *déjà vu*. His luck had changed, and the cards had turned against him. What had the old man done? Walter's voice called him back.

"Though my father advised Mr. McIntire it was impossible to manage from the grave, so to speak, he devised an irrevocable trust fund. It turns out a certain percentage of the interest is available to the family each year, but the capital can never erode." David willed himself to hold his rising anger in check, so he could find the loophole for that damnable word irrevocable. One had to exist. He only had to find the right angle.

But the image the self-satisfied lawyer presented did not help.

"Let me get this straight," David tried to keep his tone conversational. "Not all of the family wealth is available to the McIntire's heirs?"

46

"Correct."

"How much?"

"Privileged information for blood relatives only. Mr. McIntire was down tight rabid about who was privy to the trust's details."

The lawyer's last statement almost cost David his calm demeanor. Only by calling upon the ability he had learned years ago when he sat at the gaming tables did he succeed in masking his emotions. His strong will power neutralized his voice.

"So any children we adopt would not have the same information as their cousins?"

"Interesting point in law." Walter made another note on his list. "I'll have to research it."

"What else can you tell me about this trust?"

Walter paused and seemed to weigh his words. "I'm barred from sharing specific financial details. What I can tell you is this, the majority of the late Mr. McIntire's estate is bound up tight, and no one can manipulate those assets. Mrs. Smith, along with her brothers and sister, learned after their father's death that each is entitled to one seventh of the annual payout of interest. When you married Mrs. Smith, you assumed the right to control those funds as well as her ownership in the distillery and some assets her father signed over to her."

Alert for any defect the lawyer might reveal, he said, "Go on."

"If the market continues to hold, any grandchild of the late Mr. McIntire should have a comfortable lifestyle. Not as "high on the hog" as their parents because of the sheer number of offspring the parents could potentially produce, you understand. In sum, any children you and Mrs. Smith adopt will certainly have some inheritance."

"The interest from the perpetual trust."

"Yes, fortunately for your children, the elder Mr. McIntire did not differentiate between his natural grandchildren and any adopted ones." The lawyer gave a rueful smile. "I can tell you this has been a lesson for me on unintended consequences. You see, my father never anticipated either daughter would marry, let alone have children."

David sensed panic erode his calm façade. "And what happens if, God forbid, my wife dies before me?"

"The same result applies to her brothers' estates. The interest passes to their children. If they are minors, their trustees control the funds."

It took him a few moments to absorb the last bit of information. "So I can not expect anything from the McIntire family trust."

"Only what Mrs. Smith has left from her inheritance as one of the seven children and from her arrangement with her father. As long as Mrs. Smith is alive, you'll, of course, benefit from the trust. Last time Mrs. Smith asked me to go over her accounts, I saw a good part of those funds went for household maintenance, correct?"

David's throat dried and closed. "When?" he squeaked.

"A few months after your marriage. Has your financial picture changed much since then?"

David managed a weak shake of his head.

"Good, I like to keep things status quo," Walter nodded. "But remember, upon her death, those funds would cease to come to you."

~~

Somehow David closed the conversation and left Herndon's office. He needed a place to sit and beat his anger back, fast. No good would come of losing his temper.

His club, the Athenaeum, was one block north. He had enough time to sink into his favorite Chesterfield chair, steady his nerves with a small whiskey, and think before lunch at the Galt House.

A few minutes later, amid swirling clouds of smoke from the other members, he took his seat and ordered a whiskey. His hands rested on the worn arms of the burnt umber leather chair while he waited for the white-coat attendant to return with his drink.

As soon as the first glass arrived, David ordered a second. This one he sipped. After he emptied his glass and put it on the table next to him, he faced his situation. The undeclared amount of wealth, untapped and out of his reach, let alone control, infuriated him. He knew part of his anger rose from his wounded pride. He did not like being bested by a dead man.

How had he fallen from being the creator of his own con game to a bit player with so few moves left to him? But maybe he could make this work to his advantage. The first possibility, wooing Helen if Isabel died, made him shudder.

David pushed himself out of the deep chair and headed home. His determination grew with every step toward home. He was not ready to concede. But keeping Isabel happy and busy was more paramount than ever. He did not want her to grow suspicious about the siphoned off assets. Damn it, he had fulfilled his part of the contract with James. Isabel's shares in the distillery were now under her brother's control as were the other properties specified in their contract. David also wanted to continue living off of her. There was no way he wanted to touch his own steadily growing reserves. Those funds were his, for his own use.

Fortunately, Isabel's failed pregnancies had provided cover for his arrangement with James. She was not curious about her finances. But the situation could always change. Therefore, he had to keep her busy.

Resigned, David accepted his fate. He would have to agree to more than one child. With luck, Father O'Connell might convince Isabel to limit their family to only a toddler and baby.

~~~

At the Galt House, David shook hands with the priest and watched Father O'Connell thank Isabel for the invitation and the opportunity to try the new French chef's dishes.

"Mrs. Fleming told me the other day," the priest said, "about the delicious pheasant and thick chicken soup. But the pickled beets weren't to her liking. She claimed her family recipe was better."

"The pheasant is on the menu again today with green peas," Isabel read from her menu.

"Excellent."

The three had the best table in the dining room. Through the large plate glass windows, David looked out at the Ohio, and as course followed course, he watched the small craft maneuver around the riverboats. One by one the boats moved from his line of vision, and still the word adoption had not come up. When the chess pie arrived with refills of coffee, David concluded he would have to steer the conversation since the old priest must have forgotten the purpose of the meal.

But after Isabel took one bite of her pie and shoved it aside, she told the priest she wanted to adopt four of the orphans she had seen on yesterday's tour.

"Mrs. Smith, I'm so thankful you found the children agreeable yesterday. Any one of those four or the others we have in our care is worthy of adoption."

"Father, when I looked at those children's faces yesterday, my soul quickened."

David sat silent and watched tears come to her eyes.

"I wanted to gather them in my arms and never let go. That has never happened to me before in all the years I have toured the Home. Somehow, I know those four children will be perfect for us."

The priest took his time in answering. First, he used his napkin to wipe a bit of pie crust from his mouth. Then he refolded it and replaced it on his lap.

"My dear, we pray all of our children find homes. However, I have to tell you we've never allowed so many at one time to go into the same home. Our past experience tells us it's better for the child, as well as the family, to begin with one or two children, unless they are siblings."

All conversation stopped until the waiter left after refilling the cups and the priest stirred two teaspoons of sugar into his coffee.

"The little ones," Father O'Connell continued, "we're discussing are not related in any way. Just unfortunates some desperate souls chose to leave at our gate instead of abandoning them."

"I can see the wisdom of your policy," David interjected. "Can't you, Isabel?"

"Yes," she agreed with him though he noticed how disappointment flickered on her face.

"I suppose we could certainly go back to Saint Jerome's again in a year or two and adopt the others," he said, and her eyes lit up.

"I'm certain you'll be happier with the decision to start with one or two children now," the priest said and added another teaspoon of sugar. "Something else to consider is that even in nature rarely do we increase the size of our family by more than one at a time."

"How soon before we can bring them into our home?" Isabel asked.

"Since you and your family have been on the board for so long, we can dispense with most of the procedures we usually follow. Isn't Walter Herndon your attorney?"

The priest looked at him, and David nodded yes.

"We've worked with him before. I recommend you consult him." He turned to Isabel and said, "It won't be long before you can have little William and Etta in your arms again."

"I can hardly wait. Maybe we could bring them to our home for visits before all the legal work is completed?"

"Well, it's highly irregular. Let me discuss the matter with Sister Justina. Now, do you have any more questions?"

"No, thank you. You have been helpful. I appreciate your wisdom," Isabel said to the priest.

Next she turned her attention to David. "We can prepare their rooms right away and hire a new girl to help mind them."

The priest drained his cup and let his glance linger on Isabel's almost pristine slice of pie.

"Something else, Father?" David asked.

"No, no," he leaned back and patted his stomach. "I must go. Mr. and Mrs. Smith, I thank you for the luncheon and more importantly your willingness to adopt these precious little ones."

Father O'Connell rose from his chair. "My blessings on the both of you," he said and left.

"Come my dear, I'll take you back home before I go visit with Mr. Herndon. I have an hour before my next appointment. We're agreed on the two children, correct?"

There was a glow to Isabel's face when he came around to help her rise from her chair. His confidence was restored. Soon, he thought, she'll be so busy she won't have time to think about money matters.

"It is true, David, we shall have children at last. I have so much to do."

"I'm sure you will get it all done." Taking her arm, he guided her out of the hotel dining room. "What are our plans for the evening? I've a late appointment at my club today."

"Our calendar is clear tonight. The theatre is tomorrow and a debutante coming-out ball for Colonel and Mrs. Quisenberry's daughter on Saturday."

"Good, good. Sounds good," David answered with his mind already returned to scheming how he could maneuver some of the McIntire trust money into his control.

Part 2

Chapter 7

Falls of the Ohio, June 2, 1866

David brought his new roan horse to a stop at the edge of the park grounds and did a rough head count. Almost fifty people had gathered for the annual family picnic along the fossil beds. By God, he hated these McIntire outings.

"Not one of those pampered gentry would last a day on a farm. No one in his right mind leaves his comfortable house and comes out here to sit on dirt," he growled and headed to a large shady maple to tie his horse. Growing up in the country had robbed him of any romantic ideas about fresh air.

"Damn, the mosquitoes'll carry us off before noon." Bowler hat in hand, he swatted the pests and approached James and Stephen. David saw Stephen was also using his hat to chase the insects away and crowed to himself that at the rate the younger McIntire was losing hair, he'd be completely bald within two years.

"Ready to find some good fossils today?" Stephen taunted.

David winced from the jab beneath his brother-in-law's words. Last year, Stephen had found a nearly intact trilobite before a spring thunderstorm called a halt to the contest and picnic. According to the family rules, he was the winner and entitled to be the fossil judge this year.

"Luckier than ever," David said.

The foundation of his boast was not a lucky feeling. Instead he had hired some college students to go out and collect a few specimens in March, when the annual cycle of freeze and thaw forced a new crop of fossils to the surface. Four prime ones lay in his vest pockets right now. One thing he knew was there was always an angle to play.

"Good thing the rain's stopped." James scanned the sky and headed toward the other adults. David and Stephen fell in beside him.

"I know," James said, "the children have their hearts set on going in the water. Are your Willie and Etta excited about today?"

David looked at his other brother-in-law and wondered anew why a man with such important business to think about would pay attention to the idle thoughts of children. The world was full of far more weighty events and consequences.

"The picnic is all they have talked about," he lied. It had been at least three days since he had even seen the children. They were Isabel's business, not his.

Soon, the men reached the area where the servants had set the food hampers and folded blankets under some shady oak trees. The two youngest McIntire brothers, Patrick and Brian, were already in attendance and served the women food from the hampers. The small group sat on the riverbank but was far enough away to avoid accidental splashes once the children were given permission to run into the water.

David had to admit his younger sisters-in-law did look comely in their new pastel walking dresses. The latest style was daring as it allowed women to display their ankles. Isabel also wore one of the new style dresses today in heliotrope. Helen, of course, was in her usual black silks. She continued to wither and wrinkle while Isabel seemed to reverse her aging and now appeared much younger than her sister. He remembered that the first time he had seen them, they had looked much the same age.

Shouts from the old buffalo trace diverted his attention. Mr. Collins, the family's tutor, and Miss Arnold, the Smith's nanny, had the children organized in races. The hard-packed earth made an excellent racecourse clear of the spring mud. The three-legged races looked to be popular with the older children. The younger ones balanced eggs in spoons and rushed to cross the finish line first.

Etta was noticeable not only for her bright hair, but also for the way she gained ground. She might even win if she maintained the pace. Willie struggled to catch up to her. When the egg dropped from the spoon, he caught it. At once his pleased look changed since the egg broke apart in his hand.

David heard Patrick laugh, "Guess Cook didn't hard boil them first. More fun that way, don't you think?"

James joined in. "But look at the little man. Not even a tear."

David had a surge of ridiculous pride followed by amazement before disgust took over. Was this what his life had become? Another man's favorable statement about his son made him proud?

Willie stood still and wiped one hand and then the other on his shirtfront. The egg smear grew larger, and his hands moved faster. David looked around for Nanny Arnold. The egg race had ended, and she was herding the children to the finish line of the other race.

A glance back at his son showed the boy had sat on the ground and dug in the dirt. Bits of leaves and soil stuck to his shirt, his face, his fingers, and his legs. He looked a proper mess.

A memory from David's childhood tumbled forward. The kitchen garden, not for the plants but for its small bugs and worms. He was six years old and all by himself in his favorite place. He could almost feel the heady rush of freedom again along with the whispering presence of the captured insects that danced on his fingers and up his bare arms. An internal echo sounded his mother's hollers from the kitchen door and her stomping feet. He stood stock still and relived the whole episode.

When he had seen her clenched fists, he knew he was in for it. The tears rushed down his face, and heart-stopping terror pounded in his chest.

"David Anthony Smith, don't you know any better than to run off and roll around in dirt the minute my back is turned? You're about the most senseless and worthless child I ever knew."

"Ma, I didn't mean to do nothing wrong. I was after some bugs." He bent over and tried to clean himself off.

Her left hand hauled him upright, and her right hand shook his frame.

"Go get yourself a switch, and it'd better be thick enough this time."

~~~

David jerked back to the present. Fueled by his long ago impotency in dealing with his mother's anger, he strode toward Willie.

"Come on son, let's get you cleaned up a little. There'll be hell to pay if you sit down to eat and look like a chimney-sweeper." David took Willie's hand and drew him up. "I think we need to go to the river."

He noticed Willie's pleased reaction and added, "Not to play. We've got to get you looking like the little gentleman you are before the ladies see you, right?"

"Right Poppa."

They found a small clearing at the riverbank, away from the

shallow wading area. Fifteen feet down, a man dressed like a tradesman fished in the rain-swollen water. The two men nodded. David took out his crisp clean handkerchief and bent down to moisten it. During the next several minutes, he managed to clean the smudges off Willie's face. He no sooner turned back to soak the cloth when he heard the splash.

He looked behind him. Willie was gone. Down the riverbank, he saw the fisherman take off his hat and rush toward the water.

"Where is he?" David called.

"About three feet to your left," the stranger shouted before he plunged into the current.

David flung himself into the river. When he came back to the surface, he saw Willie. It took forever to close the distance to the boy. David's first grasp failed. Willie looked back at him, his face barely submerged underwater, white-eyed in panic, and mouth open. David lunged again. He caught hold and brought Willie out of the river. Reunited they clung to each other. The fisherman joined them, and they waded back to the riverbank where David saw Isabel and most of the family had massed.

"He's fine, just fine," David shouted. "Willie, look around and wave to your mother."

Isabel had Willie in her arms before both of his feet were out of the water. Isabel and her family hurried back up the path.

David put out his hand to the fisherman. "You have my gratitude, Mr. ?"

"Mueller, Roman Mueller. Glad I could help," he said over the handshake. "Your boy's real lucky. Tricky undercurrent out there today. Besides, that river don't give up its dead."

David shivered and not from any breeze. "The name is David Smith. Come see me Monday evening at the Galt House. I'd like to buy you a drink."

"Sure, Mr. Smith."

Mueller took a few steps away before he turned and said, "There's something else."

"What?"

"Ever hear of near-drownings?"

"No, why?"

"Funny thing about them. It's almost like the river can't let go once it gets ahold. Best keep an eye on the youngin' for awhile."

"What do you mean?"

"Keep him sitting up straight. He's got to cough up the water he swallowed."

David thanked the man again and walked back to rejoin his family, and a long dormant feeling reawakened in him. The emotion was so raw he struggled to take in breath. The vestiges lurked far in the past. He was nine and stood in the barn with his father. Before them wobbled the newborn foal promised ahead of time as his birthday present, his first horse, Ajax.

The unconditional love David had for his horse back then had today transferred and intensified the moment his hands drew Willie from the water. The weight of his epiphany staggered him.

"My God, this is fatherhood."

Chapter 8

"Practice, practice, it is most important you practice your breathing, Miss Etta." Monsieur Chastain leaned forward and repeated, "Practice, practice" again.

Seven-year-old Etta thought the white-whiskered man reminded her of a big crow dancing on a branch. She did not like his shrill voice and black clothes.

The tone her teacher used was similar to the one Mr. Collins used when the boys refused to settle down and his ears got all red. Monsieur had run out of patience.

"I don't want to practice. I want to sing songs," Etta answered.

At the same time, she kicked over the music stand and folded her arms over her chest. The vocal arrangements scattered about her feet.

"You are a fortunate little girl. None of my other students have such an elegant music room."

She followed his glance at the uncurtained doors where the morning sunlight crept toward the piano. When his eyes moved to the fireplace on the opposite wall, she saw her mother seated below the large mirror. Her mother looked upset also. Her cheeks were red, and her fingers gripped the arms of the chair.

Etta decided the lesson was over. She stomped towards the door of the music room and gave no answer to her mother's command to stop and say she was sorry to her teacher. But inside she remembered a part of a score her mother had sung with her last week. It was in Italian. The only words which made any sense were *la vincero*. These were the ones she sang, sotto voce, on her way to her room.

~~

From the second story window seat overlooking the street, she brushed back the curls her temper tantrum had loosened and watched the hated Frenchman leave the house. Her disappointment grew when she realized he was not angry. The man turned left at the end of the front walk. The hope he would quit and never ever return wilted. Instead he strolled up their street and tipped his hat to Mrs. Merriman and her silly children.

Her focus turned to the sounds from downstairs. They were not from her mother. Nanny Arnold and her brother Willie had returned from their morning walk.

Lunch and supper in the nursery came and went with no mention of her bad manners. Etta did not understand. Never before had one of her bad deeds gone unnoticed for so long.

At seven o'clock, she and her brother followed their usual routine and joined their mother and aunt in the small upstairs sitting room. The cheerful rose and spring green floral wallpaper did not calm her nerves. She knew there had to be a punishment for her bad manners with the voice teacher. What was unknown was what kind her mother had planned and when it was going to take place.

Her mother and aunt sat across from each other at the round marble top table and planned the upcoming Thanksgiving dinner. She heard them talk about menus and where to seat all her aunt and uncles. A side-glance to her mother and aunt told her she and Willie were being ignored as they played on the Turkish carpet runners by the low-burning fireplace.

Willie had set up an army camp with his toy soldiers and horses. With only a few pieces of artillery left to put in place, the two armies were almost ready for their cavalry charge. Etta scooted closer with her doll and looked back at her mother and aunt. They were still occupied.

"It'll be our first Thanksgiving here since Father died," her mother said.

"We should have the family over before Midnight Mass also this year."

"Wonderful, the children are old enough now to stay up and participate."

Etta felt restless. The pressure of waiting for her mother's scolds reached the breaking point. She snatched her brother's tin horse and cart away from him. He gave up without a fight. Etta knew he would, even though he was almost as big as she was. He squalled and ran to their mother.

"Momma, Etta took my toys," Willie sobbed.

Etta watched both women look up when he flung himself into his mother's skirts. Their gaze moved to her. She sat in the middle of the army camp with the seized toys in her hands. She scattered the neat lines of soldiers with her feet and stared at her mother.

"Bridgette Clarissa Smith, stop at once. You'll say you're sorry and give your brother back his toys immediately," Momma said.

"Such an ungrateful little girl you are," Aunt Helen said. "You have so many playthings yourself. Why do you need your brother's?"

Etta clutched her booty and said one word, "No."

Momma rang the silver bell on the table. No one spoke until Susan arrived. Her mother said, "Miss Etta is ready to retire. Please summon Nanny Arnold to put her to bed."

Her mother's calm response made Etta angrier. She flung the horse. It landed close to her aunt's slippered feet. Willie, in the midst of his sobs, must have kept track of what she was about because he ducked behind his mother. Etta was quite pleased with the result.

When Willie cried louder, Momma picked him up and commanded, "Etta, sit in the chair until Nanny gets here. It's a good thing your father isn't here to see how you've behaved tonight. He'll be disappointed when I tell him. Your punishment will be no dessert for three days. You'll also get up early tomorrow and go to first Mass with me and confess."

Aunt Helen rushed over and grabbed Etta by the arm. Etta was surprised her aunt was so strong. With one arm, the old woman forced Etta into a chair and leaned in close. Etta shrank back from her aunt's oniony breath and anger.

"You'd better be careful, girl," Aunt Helen said in a low voice. "St. Jerome's will always take you back if we decide you're too much trouble."

Etta shuddered. Her aunt, always dressed in severe black, reminded her of a bat swooping down to attack. Etta could not remember the first time she had heard her aunt's threats. What she did know was they were never spoken to Willie. Etta was not quite sure who the we meant or exactly how much trouble was too much, and she never asked.

Flashbacks haunted her, the dreary orphanage, the nightmares of getting lost in the maze of the large buildings, and the fear she would never be a good girl.

"You come from a bad seed," Aunt Helen hissed. In a louder voice, she said, "Young lady, if you were mine, you'd not be able to sit down for a week."

Etta saw Nanny enter the parlor and nod to her mother before approaching her. "Come Miss," Nanny said and stuck out her hand, "it's bedtime for you."

Etta rose from the chair and took Nanny's outreached hand. For a second, she considered she might drop the cart she still held and crush it underfoot on her way out of the room. But Nanny Arnold had horrid ways of revenge. Etta still had a sore patch on her head. Three days ago she had pushed Willie down into a mud puddle, and when Nanny undid the braids and brushed the snarls from her hair, Etta had winched at each yank and pull.

"Thank you, Nanny," Momma spoke. "Be sure and have Miss Etta ready for Mass at six thirty tomorrow morning. She'll be joining Miss Helen and me."

The nanny gave a small curtsey and guided Etta from the room.

Etta's conscience accepted her punishment of early bed, no dessert, and first Mass as righting her earlier wrong to Monsieur Chastain. She had paid for her bad behavior.

~~~

The following Saturday Etta entered the music room at her usual time. The practice sheets were absent from the music stand. The voice teacher sat in a chair close to Momma in front of the unlit fireplace. Etta noticed he had on country clothes. He had also stuffed his brown trouser legs into his boots. He looked like her father and uncles did when they all went to the Falls for their family picnics.

"Good morning, Miss Etta," he spoke and gave her a real smile from behind his dark moustache. Etta noticed he looked happy, especially in his brown eyes. The squint was gone.

"Good morning, Monsieur Chastain," Etta replied and performed the expected curtsey.

"Today there will be no voice lesson, no practice, practice. Exactly what you asked for last week, yes?

She nodded in victory and thought for a minute that she had won. But then why was he here?

"We are off on an excursion, a little trip to the country. Your mother will be joining us."

"Come Etta. Fetch your coat and hat from Nanny," Momma said. Dressed in a deep purple silk day dress with a paisley shawl, she rose from her chair. She also had on boots.

The voice teacher followed them out the door. The family waited under the front portico until the carriage drew near. Monsieur swung open the door and helped Momma to her seat before he turned to her. "Miss Etta, I am certain you have questions, but I shall answer them when we arrive. Until we reach our destination, your mother and I will discuss music and the opera season. You will listen, yes?" She agreed. Her curiosity overrode her willfulness.

Careful not to disturb her mother's skirts, Etta took her seat. Monsieur entered last and sat opposite. He tapped his walking stick on the ceiling, and the carriage started out the circular drive onto the broad avenue. Too soon the sound of the horse's hooves changed from the dignified clip-clop she liked to a dull sound. When she pulled the curtain back, she saw they were on a country dirt road. Etta did not see anything of interest and let the curtain drop. Bored, she settled back into the seat.

The adults still discussed the Louisville Opera season. She heard about the great operas of New York and London. Etta tried to ignore their conversation. However, the longer the trip lasted, the less bored she grew. She was surprised about how much she enjoyed their talk, especially when Monsieur explaining a tricky aria from Wagner's *Rheingold*.

When the driver halted the carriage, Etta pulled the curtain again and saw a small red brick house surrounded by fields of grass and white fences everywhere. She moved her head farther out the window, and a flash of horses caught her attention. Horses of every size and color surrounded her. Their elegance made her breath catch.

"We have arrived at Colonel Quisenberry's," the Frenchman spoke over her shoulder. "Mr. Mahan has agreed to show us around. Ah, here he is now."

Etta noticed at once that Mr. Mahan was a man dressed in rough work clothes and dirty boots, but polite. He opened the door, raised his hat, and said, "Welcome Mrs. Smith. I understand you want to see the colts first." He helped Momma step down.

"Yes, thank you." Momma raised her silk parasol and waited until Etta climbed out.

"This must be Etta," the overseer said and smiled at her. "Do you like horses, little one?"

Etta, shy before this tall, friendly man, only nodded.

"Good, you're going to see some real pretty ones today. We'll start over here." He pointed to the left.

"Miss Etta," her teacher said when they stopped at the fence, "This is your music lesson for the day, horses." About twenty colts frolicked before them. "First I want you to look at how these animals gallop."

Mr. Mahan then spoke, "They're out here away from their mommas for a little exercise. We want to see what they can do."

Etta watched the colts dash about in the field. They were similar in size. The only differences were in their coloring and markings. She thought her teacher had gone mad and lost his senses. But being outside and taking a coach ride without her whiney little brother was much better than practicing her scales and breathing.

"Tell me what you see when you look at them run," Monsieur Chastain said.

"They're playing with each other."

"Yes, they are like children. Now look carefully at the way they run. What are their differences?"

Confused, Etta looked at him and at the horses again. She turned back to him and said, "They all run the same."

"Is it true, Mr. Mahan? Do they all run the same?" the teacher asked.

"No sir, not at all. Out there we've got about three potential great horses."

"Which ones, Mr. Mahan?" Etta asked and looked back at the colts.

"See that black colt with the white forelocks? She's the strongest runner so far. There's also the bay drinking from the trough and the dappled one with a white star above her nose."

Etta watched the three circle the fence but could not see what the trainer talked about.

"Let us move on to the yearlings next," her teacher indicated to Mr. Mahan. "Miss Etta, you noticed all the colts had the ability to run, yes? But what you did not see was their natural talent. Only someone trained can spot it in animals so young. Remember only three out of those twenty have the chance to succeed."

Etta took another look back at the colts and still saw only young horses run and sprint.

"Here are the yearlings," Mr. Mahan pointed out. "I followed your instructions, Mrs. Smith. The yearlings with real promise are here in this small corral."

"Miss Etta," Monsieur said, "This is your second lesson. Watch these two horses carefully. They are the ones with natural talent and the ability to learn. They have a good chance of becoming winners." He turned and indicated with his walking stick, "The rest of the yearlings over there in the other field will never be famous."

The three adults stood off to the side. Etta walked around the corral and peered through the openings at the horses. They seemed to enjoy circling the enclosure. The larger one took off on a fast gallop until he reached where she stood. When he stopped, he tossed his mane and snorted.

"This is Endeavor out of Perilous Trek and Lightening," the overseer said. "Isn't he something else? He likes a carrot and his nose stroked after he races." He put his hand in his pocket and stretched out his other hand towards the horse's nose. Only after Endeavor saw the carrot the trainer had pulled out did he allow the man to pet him.

Momma asked, "Out of these horses Mr. Mahan, how many will be winners next year at the races for two-year-olds?" Etta somehow had the idea this question was about her.

"Only one, ma'am."

Etta looked from the horseman to her mother and next to her teacher and asked why.

Monsieur was the one to answer. "Only one of them matches his natural talent and ability to learn with the desire to win. The other will never be a winner. *Note bene*, your third lesson is winners have the desire to win. Without it, no amount of talent or ability to learn will make you famous or a winner."

Etta moved back to the corral and looked over the horses. Monsieur had lied to her. The lessons today were not about horses. They were about her. She knew she had talent. All the sisters at St. Jerome's had told her God had given her the gift of music and urged her to use her voice in His work.

However, no one had ever explained she was special because she had talent others lacked. She turned back to look at her mother and teacher. The warmth her pride brought faded. She realized they wanted her to accept that talent was not enough.

"Fine," she muttered so no one else could overhear, "but I'm not a horse. And I don't want to practice, practice, practice."

She said the last sentence in the same way Monsieur did.

Etta saw the adults thank Mr. Mahan. They waited for her to remember her manners.

"Thank you Mr. Mahan for showing me your horses," she dutifully said before climbing back into the coach.

The driver had no sooner snapped the reins when Monsieur returned his attention to Momma and began the discussion about opera again. This time he had small books he called playbills.

Etta considered taking a catnap when the words "Have you ever seen such fancy silk princess ball gowns" made her change her mind.

"What princess ball gowns?" she asked.

"The gowns the first ladies of the opera wear," Monsieur answered.

"When they attend the opera?" Etta was interested in dressing up like a princess.

"No, when they perform the lead. Would you like to see some pictures?"

She took the offered playbills. Her teacher was right. On the covers the princesses wore long flowing gowns trimmed in bows. Sequins and beads covered the dresses. The layers of lace-trimmed skirts swirled about the princesses' feet. The bodices had matching sequins and lace.

But the decorations did not stop there. These women wore shiny necklaces and gold bracelets. What Etta liked best were the hairpieces. Each of the women wore her hair on top of her head and was crowned with either a tiara she knew had to hold diamonds or jeweled combs and feathers. Without any difficulty at all, she pictured herself with those beautiful items. She wanted to decorate her hair just like the first ladies of the operas did.

"You will notice, Miss Etta," Monsieur Chastain said, "only the princesses wear these fantastic creations. The other women wear much simpler clothes. The princesses are like the horse Endeavor we met today. They have the natural talent, the ability to learn, and most importantly the desire to win. Do you have the desire to win?"

Glimpses of twirling light-filled dresses, the delicious swish of the underskirts, and best of all the sparkling tiaras played through her head.

"Yes, I have the desire to win," Etta mouthed her teacher's phrase.

"Good, next week we'll renew our breathing lessons."

"When do you give me a princess gown?"

The teacher looked surprised. Etta failed to understand why. She was sure he had promised dresses.

"When Monsieur says," her mother said, "you have mastered your breath control, I'll order one."

"What do I have to do for more dresses?"

"You'll have another gown when you've mastered Italian vowels and a third when Monsieur says you've mastered volume and perfect diction."

"May I have one now? I know how to read music."

"Touché," Momma laughed, "what color would you like?"

"A light blue one with sparkles and bows. I don't like dark blue."

The next Saturday, Etta paraded before her mother in the music room until Monsieur Chastain arrived. Each rustle and crinkle of the robin egg blue satin dress proved how special and beautiful and powerful she was. She had earned this dress. No one in her family had her natural talent or determination.

The music teacher's words stopped her performance.

"Miss Etta, what a lovely gown you have. It's quite becoming."

"Thank you, Monsieur," she said with a small curtsy. "How soon do you think I can master breath control?"

Chapter 9

Louisville, March 19, 1867

"The blue princess gown," eight-year-old Etta demanded and glowered up at Susan.

Etta's mind was set. Until she got her way, she would stay in her flannel robe and slippers, even if it meant a standoff in the nursery. Etta stood with her arms crossed. Susan leaned down with her hands on her hips and mouth in a straight line. Out of the corner of her eye, Etta saw Willie scoot back from the edge of his bed to the wall.

"Miss Etta, your mother said you must wear this brown dress to school. Now hurry or you'll be late."

"I won't, I won't wear that ugly brown dress, and I won't go to school."

"You like school. You get to play with all your cousins. Mary Margaret is your best friend."

"You mean we get to sit on hard benches in Uncle James' smelly attic and listen to Mr. Collins go on and on."

Susan leaned even closer to her. "You don't want your mother to come in here, do you?"

"I don't care."

"Don't give me that look. You'll care when I tell your mother."

Susan straightened up. "I'm going to get Willie ready. In five minutes you had better be dressed, young lady, so I can do your braids."

In the time it took the maid to see to Willie, Etta hatched a plan, her most brilliant one yet. Stage one was to dress in the brown dress and wait. When Susan turned back to her and asked which color ribbon for her hair, Etta smiled and chose blue.

Once Susan finished her braids, Etta went off to wage the battle of the morning with the real enemy, her mother.

In the breakfast room Etta was surprised to find her mother was not alone. Aunt Helen was also there, but her aunt's appearance at the table did not alter Etta's plan. She sat down between the two women and fired the opening shot.

"It's not fair, Momma. The only time I get to wear my princess gown is for music lessons and the opera."

"You need to save your gown for good," Momma said over a letter she was reading.

"You won't let me wear it to church."

"It is not a church dress."

"It's getting tight," Etta persisted. "I've been so careful with it. It's almost new. It's not fair."

"What do you think is fair?" asked her mother after she put the letter down.

"I want to wear it to school."

Momma looked at her. Etta saw her mother's frown lose its downward tilt. The expression meant to stop talking and wait for the answer.

"Hmm, you make a good argument. At the rate you are growing, you will be out of it in a few months."

Etta sat still, barely breathing. She may have won.

"Those gowns do cost a small fortune. It does seem a waste to wear them so seldom."

Momma took a sip from her teacup while Etta silently urged her mother to announce her decision.

At last she spoke, "I shall let you to wear your princess gown one day a week to school. Which day would you prefer?"

"Wednesday, we go to school more on Wednesdays than any other day."

"Wednesdays it is. Now finish your breakfast, so you will not be late."

"So tomorrow I can wear my princess gown to school?"

"Yes."

"And you'll tell Susan I can wear it?"

"Yes, Etta, as we agreed."

~~~

An hour later, Etta and Willie joined eight of their cousins and Mr. Collins in the attic schoolroom. She never understood why one of the pretty rooms downstairs could not be used instead. The attic was dark and smelly from the gaslights. The chalk dust made her sneeze. It was worse in the winter when the coal stove added more dust and another layer of odor. The only things she liked in the room were the few glass cases that held fossils, stuffed birds, and animal tracks set in plaster of Paris. What she hated most about the room was she could see only bits of sky and tree branches through the high narrow windows.

"I get to wear my princess gown tomorrow," Etta told her three girl cousins, Mary Margaret, Rosanna, and Mairead after the teacher turned to write on the blackboard.

"No, you're not," Mary Margaret answered.

"Yes, I am. You just wait and see. Tomorrow, I will be a princess."

"Miss Etta, pay attention. Stand and recite your poetry lesson."

Etta smirked at her cousin and whispered, "Yes I am, I have won the battle."

Then she hummed her favorite lyric *la vincero* before she recited "Paul Revere's Ride" from memory.

~~~

The next morning Etta was gracious in her victory. There was not one hassle over getting out of bed, not one tear flowed down her cheek. By the time Susan finished with Willie, Etta had made her bed, picked up her part of the room, dressed and waited for the maid to button up her dress and arrange her hair.

The calm continued. Etta was not thrown off by her aunt's unusual appearance at breakfast. She remembered to use her napkin and even asked to be excused before she pushed in her chair and left her mother and aunt at the table. The grown-ups' conversation reached her the same time she closed the dining room door.

"Maybe I should order a few more princess dresses, Helen."

"It was a peaceful morning. Such a pleasant way to start the day," her aunt answered. "I might make it a habit to join you more often for breakfast on Wednesdays and not just on my charity mornings."

~~~

Later in the afternoon, Isabel received a note from her sister-in-law Elizabeth. It seemed the school day had not gone smoothly. Could Isabel come at two, before Mr. Collins dismissed the children?

~~~

The grandfather clock chimed two when she entered Elizabeth's well-appointed parlor. On the tea table were four place settings with the good china and silver.

"Who else will be joining us?"

"The other girls' mothers."

This meant her sisters-in-law, Leah, mother of Mairead, and Shannon, whose daughters Mary Margaret and Rosanna were close to Etta in age.

Isabel sat down, and while she unbuttoned her gloves, the doorbell rang. Soon the last two guests walked in. They, like her, were dressed in their best hats and most stylishly flowing day dresses. Leah in a tasteful peacock blue that accentuated her creamy skin and delicate features. Shannon, however, wore an unfortunate apple green that did nothing for her complexion or expanding girth. They all perched like tropical birds in their chairs.

Elizabeth served tea and recounted what had happened during the morning. "It seems Etta's princess dress has started a revolt among my other nieces. Thirty minutes after school began, the other girls stormed into my sitting room. They said it wasn't fair Etta got to dress up and they didn't. They also declared they wouldn't go back to school until they also have princess gowns. They were so serious with their lips stuck out and their arms crossed. I barely managed not to laugh."

Elizabeth smiled, but Leah and Shannon did not. Isabel stirred her tea, and a flash of her bright yellow dress in the matching pier mirrors caught her attention. In that instant, she realized the girls upstairs in the schoolroom were much like their finely-dressed mothers downstairs.

"I told them they had to return to class," Elizabeth continued, "and reminded them that they were not speak to me again in such a manner and they had to apologize to Mr. Collins for the disturbance in his classroom. They agreed, and I said I'd think about their grievance, but I was making no promises."

Shannon reached for another finger sandwich, her third Isabel noted.

"Mary Margaret," Shannon said, "asked if she could wear a special dress today, but I thought it was more of her foolishness."

"So they went back to class without any trouble?" Leah asked.

"They did. I followed them up the stairs. When I reached the schoolroom door, I saw six little boys and one splendidly dressed little girl working on their sums."

"Anything else happen?" Leah asked over her teacup.

"Yes, at lunch Mr. Collins told me the girls refused to talk with Etta. She pretended their shunning didn't bother her, but she seized any opportunity to flounce and twirl. When she sat, her skirt needed a great deal of smoothing. He predicted that by dismissal time, the tension between the girls will be at the flaring point."

Isabel spoke for the first time. "I had no idea it would cause this type of problem. I suppose I can rescind my promise she may wear her favorite dress on Wednesdays."

She noted Leah and Shannon sent each other a look which said they did not believe her.

"But I would rather not. It means so much to her."

The two women exchanged a nod.

"I might have a solution," Elizabeth said. "Let's remake some confirmation dresses for the girls by next Wednesday. Leah, do you still have Tara's?"

"Yes, I suppose your idea might work," Leah said.

"It'll probably fit Mairead. Mary Margaret and Rosanna may have the ones I put back for any possible granddaughters," Elizabeth said. "I think they can be put to better use now. Maybe these dresses will return peace to the schoolroom."

Isabel appreciated Elizabeth's suggestion and effort to stop the sniping, both in the classroom and here in her parlor.

"I agree," Shannon answered first.

Leah nodded and nibbled on her sandwich.

"Etta was a perfect angel today when she was getting ready for school. I am sure," Isabel said and rested her eyes on Leah and Shannon, "you will find it the same for your daughters."

Elizabeth headed off Leah's answer with a question of her own. "How to you feel about offering deportment lessons on Wednesdays since the girls'll be dressed up?"

"Just for the girls?" Shannon asked.

"Maybe we could include the boys, especially my Ian," Elizabeth said.

"What a wonderful idea," Isabel laughed. "Willie may not want to wear fancy clothes, but at least he can learn some manners."

"Ryan could certainly benefit from learning the right way to behave in public," Shannon said and accepted her third cup of tea and another sandwich.

"Who would lead these classes?" Leah asked.

"I'll speak with Nanny Arnold. She could take care of the girls," Isabel offered. "Maybe Mr. Collins can teach the boys?"

Chapter 10

Louisville, May 18, 1870

David rewarded eleven-year-old Etta with a cheap bracelet and ring set in green glass, and her tiny sobs quieted. He watched the bracelet slip over her slender wrist. She moved it so the glass shimmered in the light from his lamp.

"Remember," he told her and rose from her bed, "Momma doesn't have any jewelry this fine. Only Poppa's big girl gets presents like this."

After he saw her nod, he left and closed the door to her bedroom. Quick steps took him back to his room where he poured himself a celebratory drink. His plan had worked almost perfectly. There was a minor problem when she turned reluctant, but after a few quick drinks from his flask, she became quite compliant, maybe even forward.

Through his drunken haze he pictured himself as a suave, distinguished gentleman awakening a nubile young woman. Over his final drink of the night, he replayed how last week he had decided to make Etta his plaything. Isabel and Helen were at cards and discussed the children as usual. Most evenings he ignored their conversation. However, that night the word maturing caught his interest.

"You are so correct, Helen. Etta is maturing so quickly. I think it is time she had her own suite of rooms now. She does need her privacy," Isabel said.

"It is more important to keep in mind she and Willie are not related. I hope you have talked to her about being a lady and what is proper for our class of people?"

"Not yet, she is still too young and innocent."

"Nonsense, her sort of class indulges in improper behavior at a much earlier age."

"Helen, how can you say such a thing?" David heard the anger in Isabel's voice and in the way she slapped her cards down on the wooden card table.

"You know I'm right. Remember the lecture at the college last month?"

"I disagreed with everything that distasteful man spouted."

"The visiting professor had the scientific research to prove his theories. Education and clothes will not really change a person. You have to face the fact, breeding will out."

"He cannot be correct. Otherwise, all our good works have no benefits."

David heard Helen snort and move to the other side of the room. The tension hung between them until Willie and Etta came in and Helen left. He watched. Isabel treated them as innocents. He however, for the first time, saw a young girl, not a child. Her flaming hair and alert eyes enticed him as well as the swell of her budding breasts. Her goodnight kiss convinced him she was seducing him. After all, they were not blood. She was an orphan who should be grateful for everything he had given her.

Now, a week later it was time to savor his victory. He raised his glass in a toast.

"She's mine."

Chapter 11

Falls of the Ohio, June 3, 1871

Etta waited impatiently as she felt the carriage wheels roll over the rough ground of the buffalo trace by the river. She hoped she would soon see her cousin Connor.

In the pocket of her pink gingham dress was the family's graduation gift to him, a gold watch chain. Her fingers touched the wrapping, and she could not wait to have a few special moments to give him his present. It had taken only two requests before her mother agreed she could. It must be because she was so grown up for her twelve years.

When the carriage turned, she saw him. Before the wheels came to a complete stop on the packed earth, she had the door opened. Her mother's words "Etta, remember you are a lady" had no effect. Ignoring Willie's plea to wait for him, she jumped out and dashed toward Connor with one hand in her pocket to keep the package safe.

When she joined him at the end of the lane, he stood in the middle of a bunch of her McIntire boy cousins.

"Look fellas, at this scrollwork." Connor held the most elegant pencil she had ever seen.

"It's real eighteen carat gold. Run your fingers along the stem. It's made from genuine ivory, off an elephant."

"African or Asian?" asked her cousin Sean.

She gave Sean her best withering look. Just like him, always the smart aleck and now he tried to make fun of Connor on his day.

"Come on Etta, be nice," Connor said and offered his pencil to her for inspection.

He must really like her. She did not even have to ask. She thrilled to how the ivory warmed to her touch and the gleam of real gold shone much richer than her brass pretties.

But Connor took back his pencil too soon and started to walk away.

Disappointed, she shoved her hands into her pockets and found the package.

"Wait, Connor. I helped Momma choose your graduation gift. I hope you like it," she said and held out the small package.

Her heart danced at his smile and thank you and then slowed when he turned to go. As she watched him head toward the adults, she planned their next encounter, when she would ask if she could keep the pencil safe for him when he went fossil hunting in the river.

Etta saw him collect other gifts along with hugs and handshakes from the aunts and uncles. After he talked his mother out of a few cookies and put his opened packages in the picnic basket, Etta did not see the pencil go in.

Connor picked up a burlap bag. When he called for the cousins to go with him to the river, she joined the group and worked her way forward to walk beside him.

"I'll hold all the stuff you've got in your pockets so it won't get wet when you go into the water."

"Don't you want to join us?"

"Not today, Momma says I'm too old to play in the water unless I watch the younger ones. I'll just hold on to your valuables."

He stopped and stared at her. "What do you want in return?"

"A pretty rock for my collection, nothing else."

She twisted and swirled her skirt.

"You've got to be real careful with my new pencil. I wasn't supposed to bring it today, but just I had to show the guys."

"It's the prettiest pencil I've ever seen." She gave him her best smile.

"Boys don't have pretty pencils. We have handsome pencils. Keep it safe for me, promise."

~~~

Etta watched as Connor and the cousins waded toward the shallows where the best fossils rested on the riverbed. He looked back a few times to check on her, and she would wave and smile. Then Connor stopped. The loose fossils had grabbed his attention.

At this point, Etta rejoined the rest of the family in the main picnic area and sat at a far table. From her vantage point, she saw Connor put most of the specimens the young cousins offered into his burlap bag. When the younger children tired of collecting, they came back to the riverbank. Connor with his older brother Jamie stood in the middle of the fossil field and sorted out their best finds.

Several times Etta pulled the pencil from her pocket. The sunlight showed the fine lines in the ivory and the pencil glowed with magic. With this pencil, she realized she could be a writer of spellbinding stories and forget about voice lessons. Everyone knew authors did not have to practice, practice, practice.

When she looked up to check on him, her two cousins had reached the riverbank. Connor hefted the burlap bag on his shoulder with little effort. He did not seem to mind the water seeping from the bag and down his front and arm. When he looked up at her, Etta waved and headed to the woods. She had another plan.

~~

"Etta, where are you?" Connor called.

She looked under a tree branch and saw him at the tree line.

"Over here Connor. Come see what I've found." From the noise he made, she knew he was closer.

"Come see the buttercups." She just had time to kneel in the middle of the flowers and pose before he found her.

"Sit down beside me," she said and patted the ground.

Her arm stretched just so, and the fabric on her bodice tightened. His eyes moved to her bosom. His mouth opened and closed a few times before he sat down and thrust a pink-streaked quartz toward her.

"For you, for your rock collection."

"Thank you so much, Connor. I will put it under my pillow. My dreams will be of you."

He blushed and said, "Would you like to see what I found?"

She moved even closer. She let her knee touch his and stay there. Then she leaned forward and said, "What did you find?"

He had to clear his throat before he could answer. "A trilobite, very rare. See, it's intact." His blush deepened. Not broken, I mean."

Etta did not move her gaze from his face to the rock. "Uh-huh."

He blushed more and said, "We better get back now."

He stood up and put the fossil back in his pocket.

"Come on."

"Help me, please."

Connor bent down and took her outreached hands. When he pulled, she lost her balance and fell against his chest. She made sure her breasts pressed into him.

He said nothing, only dropped her hands and walked away. A few steps, later he turned and faced her.

"Thank you for keeping my pencil." He stayed put and stretched his hand, palm up, toward her.

"Your pencil is the most beautiful one in the whole world."

He waited, hand still out. "Could I have it, please? I would be so grateful."

"It's mine, for graduation. I can't give away my gift."

"I'll trade you for it."

"Nothing doing, give it back," he opened and closed his hand in front of her.

"I'll give you kisses for it. Special kisses," Etta ignored his hand and narrowed the space between them.

"Here." he reached into his pocket and brought out the trilobite. "Take my new fossil instead."

"Silly, I don't want a fossil." She moved even closer and in a lower voice said, "Do you want to touch my hidden magic flower?"

Etta could not tell if his face grew redder from embarrassment or anger.

"Give me back my pencil right now, or I'll, I'll tell my parents what you said."

"I was just teasing you. Here's your stupid pencil."

Etta got the pencil out of her pocket and threw it at him. He grabbed for her. His hand caught on her arm and held onto her sleeve. It ripped. She twisted out of his fingers and ran away, in tears.

~~~

Etta watched the scene unfold when she got to the edge of the woods. The adults turned, alerted by her bawling. Next their heads raised beyond her to see Connor running behind her.

She knew from the shocked expression on his face that she had done something wrong when she mentioned her price for the pencil. She had better come up with a story soon since he might outrun her and get to the adults first.

When her mother met her, she pointed to her torn sleeve and back at Connor before she flung herself into her mother's arms.

"Connor, Connor, he…"

"I didn't do anything. I didn't hurt her. She wouldn't," he said.

She waited to see if he would continue with "give me back my pencil."

But he did not, probably because he would sound like a baby. At that moment, she knew he would not say anything either about her offer to trade for the pencil.

She had won.

~~~

Etta sat beside Momma on the parlor sofa and waited for the questions to begin.

"Tell Momma what happened. Was Connor mean to you?"

Etta, more experienced with being in trouble, knew better than blurt out answers like her stupid cousin tried to do.

"He asked me to take care of the stuff he had in his pocket. He had a new pencil."

"Yes." Momma touched her hand.

"He didn't want it to get wet when he went into the river for fossils." Her mother's expression was still calm. "So I put it in my pocket. I was very careful, Momma."

"I am sure you were."

"Then I decided to pick you and Aunt Helen some flowers. And I went into the woods." A sob interrupted her words, and she teared up. "But I got lost and got real scared."

Her mother pulled a handkerchief from her pocket and handed it over. "What happened with Connor?" Her mother's little frown told her it was time to finish the story.

"I was so happy, Momma, when I heard him because I knew he'd rescue me. I called so he could find me. When I saw him, I ran and gave him a big hug. But I dropped the pencil. He got angry at me. He pushed me away and tore my dress. I got scared all over again. And I ran and ran and ran."

Etta threw herself into her mother's lap and cried real tears. She knew she had to be convincing because today she had done something very wrong.

"My poor child, of course you were frightened. I want you to promise me you will never again go into the woods by yourself. It is not safe."

"I promise," Etta said after she raised her head, "I'll be more careful." She made her lower lip tremble and renewed her tears. "I'm so sorry, Momma, I lost all your pretty buttercups and violets."

Isabel hugged her. "The important thing is you're unharmed. Tomorrow, we shall go into the garden and you can pick some flowers."

"Thank you, Momma."

"Now go upstairs and dry your face and rest. You are excused from dinner tonight."

Etta left the parlor and started up the stairs. The sound of a door opening made her stop and linger in the shadows of the landing. It was her father. He came out of his office and moved toward the parlor. After he joined her mother, she tiptoed back down the stairs and eavesdropped on her parents.

"Tell me what happened. If anything improper happened with Connor, by God, he'll," she heard him say.

"Nonsense, David," Isabel said and told him Etta's version of events.

"You're quite sure she told you the truth?"

"Why would she lie? She is an innocent child."

"You probably didn't ask the right questions, Isabel. You don't understand males."

"I grew up with five brothers, remember? Now, I am going to see about Etta's supper tray. It has been a trying day. I suggest we all turn in early."

"Are you going to talk to James and Elizabeth about this?"

"Why? It was a childish misunderstanding and nothing more. Things will return to normal sooner if the adults make no fuss."

~~~

Two days later, Isabel had an early and uninvited visitor. At nine o'clock, Elizabeth swept into the dining room on the heels of the maid. Her sister-in-law had not even waited for Susan to bring back word they would receive her. Isabel could not believe the bad manners.

"Please serve Mrs. McIntire a cup of tea and some toast," Isabel spoke to the maid with a hint of well-placed frost.

"Thank you, Susan, I would enjoy a cup of tea," Elizabeth said and pulled her fingers from her gloves.

Elizabeth made small talk about Brian, the only bachelor brother left, and his new young woman, until the maid reentered.

"Thank you, Susan," Elizabeth said, "And please thank Cook also."

Isabel and Helen sat and waited. After a small sip of tea, Elizabeth began. "I've come this morning, so we can discuss what happened at the picnic. We have to consider what is best for both children and help them through their distress."

"Whatever do you mean? There is no one troubled in this house," Isabel replied and reached for her cup.

"I'm so glad Etta's no longer upset. However, Connor is still bothered."

Isabel sighed and put down her cup. "It was one of those childish arguments children sometimes have, in particular high spirited ones like Etta. It is better we adults do not interfere. They will work it out. Connor misunderstood, nothing else."

"You aren't concerned about what Etta said?"

Isabel noticed Helen, beside her, stirred in her chair. "What do you mean?" Isabel said.

"She wanted him to trade his graduation pencil for a few special kisses, and, and," For a moment, she broke eye contact with Isabel.

"Yes?" Helen said.

Elizabeth straightened her shoulders, let out her breath, and leaned forward to whisper. "She asked him if he wanted to touch her in a magic place."

Helen gasped. "I think it is time you left," Isabel said and stood.

Elizabeth stayed seated and said nothing. Isabel did not even try to control her anger.

"I will not have such improper words spoken in my home and around my children. Why do you bring this filth to my family? I do not know how you were reared, but in the McIntire household, we never talked about these sinful matters. Have you forgotten? Etta is only a child."

Elizabeth let the words linger before she also stood up and met Isabel's glare. "You must understand why I am here. A girl her age is much too young to trade kisses for possessions she covets." She slid her fingers back into her gloves. "I want to help in any way I can."

"You can help by taking your impure words and ideas out of this house. My family and I will not attend any family gathering unless you apologize this instant. You are an old busybody. Leave."

Isabel held to her threat. The family did not attend Elizabeth's birthday party in June. When Elizabeth sent a gift and card to Isabel in July for her birthday, they were returned, unopened.

Chapter 12

Louisville, April 18, 1873

"Railroads and coal," David said over the most recent east coast newspaper his club had to offer.

His broker, Dylan Hogan, sat in next to him as David relaxed in his favorite dark leather chair.

"I should buy more," David continued. "Hold them until they almost peak and then push a quick sale."

He had long dreamed of being richer than the McIntire family, especially the old man he had never met. After all these years, his pride rankled over how James Sr. had outsmarted him from the grave and drove him to take greater risks.

Hogan, a serious man of forty-five with a perpetual crease of worry on his forehead, snapped his paper closed. "There're whispers. This could be the start of a recession. Time to get out, David."

"The Exchange's made up of a bunch of stupid sheep, not a backbone among them. The market crash in Vienna last week is an opportunity, especially since the big money men turned tail and ran."

His words caused the crease in Dylan's forehead to deepen even more. "You're ahead, aren't you?"

"I'm not a sheep. There's plenty of play left in the market. You'll see I'm correct."

His confidence had never been higher.

~~~

On May 23rd David again met with Hogan, this time in the broker's office. They made small talk about wives and children for a few minutes before his host made his case.

"I have to tell you the economic outlook has become more uncertain. You have too many of your assets in railroads and coalfields. Since you refuse to cash out, it'd be better to spread your investments out into more diverse categories," Dylan said and smoothed his few stray hairs over his receding hairline.

David knew this gesture was his friend's tell. "Dylan, you bleat like an old woman. You know the saying about faint heart."

"Listen to me. You have too little in liquid assets. Keep in mind the other old saying about all your eggs in one basket."

"You'd never have survived as a gambler on the riverboat circuit with those weak and unsteady nerves. This country's going to grow westward. Always has, always will. What's even better is railroads and coal are mutually beneficial."

David, tired of Hogan's dire warnings, brought out his silver case filled with imported cigars and offered one to his friend.

The man took it and nodded his thanks.

"Some of the bigger brokers," Dylan paused to reach into his drawer for his cigar clippers, "say the market's a house of cards and it's about ready to collapse."

The cap of the cigar fell into the ashtray.

"Of course, that's what they say."

David noticed his tone indicated his impatience and softened his next words. "It's called bluffing. They want people to panic and sell short. Then you know what's going to happen? The movers and shakers will come in and buy the stocks and make a killing."

David snipped and lit his cigar.

"You're wrong. I've played poker. I know betting on the come when I see it," Hogan replied.

"This is a sure thing. Soon I'll be one of those big money men. Think they'll ask me to buy a seat on the exchange then?"

David gave his friend a smile but did not get one in return.

"You can't win. Cut your losses now."

"The big deal's this close." David held his thumb and forefinger about an inch apart before he puffed and let smoke spiral toward the ceiling. "I'm just a few months away from having enough."

"Enough for what? What's driving you?"

"Enough to look down my nose at James McIntire and all his brothers."

"Your brothers-in-law? That's why you take such risks? Come to your senses, man. You're making a sucker play. They've got at least four generations of wealth behind them. You're not going to catch up to them in only one lifetime."

"Watch me," David said, and leaning back, drew on his cigar again.

On September 18th, David read in the newspapers that throughout the country, all the big city banks and brokerage houses closed. The papers claimed the bankruptcy of a bigwig named Jay Cooke had started the financial crisis. For David, the good news was his railroads were not involved. His strategy was to buy stock in as many of the railroads as he could.

When the New York Stock Exchange did not open on September 20th, he was annoyed, not concerned. How could he trade with the exchange closed? The newspaper phrase "Panic of 73" did not alarm him. He would not allow rich old bastards in the know rob him of opportunities to build up his wealth.

On September 25th, five days after the exchange halted all trading, Hogan insisted upon another meeting. This time David agreed. His confidence had slipped each day the exchange had remained closed. So when the broker walked into his study at half past seven, David feared Hogan's news.

While David kept his whiskey glass full, his guest outlined the bleak economic picture. The alcohol did not steady David's nerves. He shoved his glass aside and stared at Hogan while the man's words chipped away his last bit of denial.

"David, you must accept the truth. Your assets have dwindled down to almost nothing. Your railroad and coal stock are worth about a fifth of what they were this summer. No one knows when the exchange's going to reopen. Furthermore, no one knows what'll happen when it does. Listen to me, man. The wild ride's over."

David sensed his world was about to fall apart. "I'm down to nothing. You're saying I'm busted?"

"Close to it. Some of your real estate ventures may rebound in a few years. But your immediate plans should be to unload what you can when the market reopens."

David tried to find firmer footing. "All gamblers have a run of bad luck. That's when you double down."

"No, this isn't a game of cards or a game of chance. The economy's ruined."

The future David had envisioned evaporated, and his broker's next words, meant to reassure him, did not.

"But I hear the McIntire fortune's in better shape. James started pulling out of the market a year ago. Smart man. Wish I had too. But your family will weather this. Much better than others will."

~~~

David locked the door of his study after Hogan left and pulled out his ledger book. How could close to ninety per cent of his wealth have turned to dust when before him was a record of spectacular wins marred by only a few losses? If his friend's judgment was correct, he was ruined. He owed more in gambling debts than he was worth. What he had built up over the past few years, one purchase at a time, was gone.

~~~

The stock market reopened after ten days and went to new lows. David followed Hogan's advice and sold everything. After he returned home, he stayed in his study and drank. This routine meant no one called, and he had no reason to come out. The deepening business depression led to many blank evenings on their social calendar.

When he did wander through the rest of the house, he found no comfort. The children's arguments and Helen's persistent snipes at Isabel over the break with the family drove him back into his exile.

The only relief in his solitude came from his visits to Etta. But even these times offered little comfort.

In the deep winter, the power he had over her shifted.

"Next time," she said in January, "You'd better bring me something special."

"Don't you like these pretties?"

"They're worthless. I want diamonds. You wouldn't want Momma to find out about your visits, would you?"

David knew he had to promise her something.

"For your birthday, I'll give you diamonds for your birthday."

Chapter 13

Louisville, February 1, 1874

Etta followed her mother's instructions and entered the parlor at two o'clock. After a quick glance around, she sighed. Momma had tried to make the occasion festive. But her party had no decorations and only three guests. Aunt Helen, in her best black silks, sat beside her mother, who had changed into her fancy gold taffeta. Willie had kept on his tie after Mass this morning and stood by the fireplace.

Ever since her mother had for some reason parted ways with the family, Etta knew she would not have the same special celebration every other girl cousin had on her fifteenth birthday. It was all her mother's fault there was not a table heaped with presents and many guests at her party.

The family custom was when a girl turned fifteen, she received her first earrings and was given permission to wear her hair up. She remembered her girl cousins' birthday parties. Standing apart and itching to be their age, she had watched the older girls pull their ringlets up, rearrange their hair, and turn into young women. At each party, her own fifteenth birthday had seemed so far away.

Her birthday, however, would be a melancholy affair with just the four of them. Not even Cook's fancy pink iced cake alongside the tea things helped. It was not fair she thought as she fought back tears of frustration.

Her mother spoke first. "In honor of your birthday, I have a very grown-up gift for you. Come sit beside me."

Etta took a seat between her aunt and mother and waited. Momma placed a velvet bag in her hands. Etta opened the bag and slid its contents onto her lap.

"These pearls were your grandmother's. I had them restrung." Momma said.

"You destroyed Momma's choker?" Aunt Helen blurted. "You had no right. Her pearls also belonged to me."

"The silk broke," Momma answered her sister. "So I took the opportunity to have them restrung. I have a strand for you, one for myself, another for Etta on her wedding day, and one for Willie's bride."

"Momma," Willie said, "I'll never marry and leave you."

"We shall see, young man," Momma answered him with a smile. "Etta, the jeweler told me chokers were old-fashioned. No one wears them anymore. The modern style is to string pearls with gold and crystals. He made a strand for you with matching earrings. I hope you will enjoy them. I know your grandmother would have wanted you to wear her pearls."

Etta turned and held her hair up so her mother could clasp the necklace. The cold hate in her aunt's eyes made her shrink back.

"Tomorrow, we'll have your ears pierced," Momma said. "Now let me see. How grown up you look. Happy birthday." She kissed Etta on the cheek and asked, "Will you be the lady of the house today and serve at tea?"

Etta thanked her mother and let her fingers brush the strand. She liked how different the gold and crystals were compared to the pearls, and she went to the mirror. With one hand, she swept her hair on top of her head, and with the other held the earrings up to her lobe. She was surprised, she did look older. The light from the chandelier caught the gold and crystals, and against her skin, the pearls took on a glow.

At that moment, she caught sight of her father, in the door, empty-handed.

~~

Etta could not believe he still did not have the promised gift when he sat on her bed in his nightshirt after everyone else had gone to bed.

"You promised me," Etta shouted at her father. "Today, at my tea, you said you had something special for me."

She narrowed her eyes and glared at the drunken, puffy-faced man. His dressing robe was in a heap beside him. In the light from the oil lamp, she saw her father hold in one hand his flask and in the other a necklace of red and yellow glass beads. The necklace looked cheap compared to her pearls, and it was certainly not what she had demanded from him.

Enraged, Etta grabbed the necklace. "These are not diamonds," she hissed and flung her gift toward the door.

"Shhh." Over his whisper was the sound the necklace made when it hit the door and broke.

"You can't touch me again until I have diamonds," Etta shouted before she saw her aunt by the open bedroom door.

"What's going on in here, David?" Aunt Helen said.

"Etta had a nightmare."

"And this?" Aunt Helen said when she reached down and picked up a few of the pieces from the broken necklace.

Etta thought fast. "Poppa woke me up," she worked herself into tears. "He was kissing me here," she pointed to her mouth. "And touching me where he shouldn't."

"Not for the first time, I imagine. You're not fooling me. I now have the proof I need to get rid of both of you. No self-respecting father gives his daughter such a cheap trinket."

Aunt Helen held up a fragment of the broken string of beads and strode out of the bedroom.

Etta looked at her father. He seemed stunned. Unhindered by alcohol and age, she flew out of the room and tried to reach her mother before her aunt did.

~~~

The few seconds it had taken her to get her legs out from under the bedclothes had cost precious seconds. Her aunt had arrived first and stood over her mother and held her proof. The gaslight glared overhead.

Etta heard Aunt Helen's smug words. "Then she said he had kissed her and touched her in improper places. He's a drunkard, and she's a common cheap harlot."

Her mother did not look up when Etta came into the room. Instead the older woman stared at the necklace. Aunt Helen continued, uninterrupted.

"I heard her demand diamonds, can you imagine a fifteen-year-old saying such a thing? I take back what I said about her being cheap. Isabel," Aunt Helen stopped to take a breath, "they have to leave tonight."

Etta realized she had to gain the upper hand and flung herself onto her mother.

Momma touched her head and said, "Sit up and tell me what's going on."

Etta shook her head and sobbed.

"Why are you asking her?" Aunt Helen demanded. "She's a liar. She and your wastrel husband have been carrying on right under your nose, for quite sometime, I suppose, and you've ignored the signs."

Aunt Helen took another deep breath. Etta stayed still but kept an eye on the two women.

"But the girl deserves it. She's a bad seed. Nothing good is ever going to come from her."

Etta saw her mother glare at her aunt and knew she still had a chance to turn this horrible night around. Think, she had to think fast.

Momma's arms straightened and made her sit up. "Look at me and stop crying. Tell me what happened."

"I woke up and Poppa was there in bed with me," she gave what she hoped was a convincing shudder.

"Lies, it's all lies," Poppa stumbled into the bedroom.

"Momma, he was kissing me on the mouth. And he was putting his hands."

"Don't believe her, Isabel. She seduced me," Poppa interrupted.

"Momma," Willie came to the door. "What's wrong? Why's Susan in the hallway?"

Etta, charged by the certainty the next few minutes determined her future, stuck to her story. "Momma, I've been so afraid. Poppa said he'd beat me if I told you what he did to me. I didn't like it, but he said I had to be his big girl."

"Poppycock," Aunt Helen said.

"This cannot be true," Momma said as she clutched the gold counterpane and sank back into the pillows. Poppa made a low noise.

Etta looked over to see her father collapsed on the floor with his head bent into his hands. From the door, she heard Willie tell Susan to get water and the smelling salts.

"I'm so sorry," Etta continued, "I didn't know what to do. He told me he'd send me back to the orphanage if I didn't do what he wanted. I didn't want to leave you. I love you, Momma."

Etta grasped her mother's hand, and when Momma did not respond, she was terrified. She had to come up with some way out of this.

"Diamonds, Helen," Momma asked, "What did you say about diamonds?"

"His ungrateful whore demanded diamonds."

Momma turned to look at her and asked, "Why would you mention diamonds to your father?"

Etta saw her mother's eyes search her face for answers. The air grew heavy over the next few silent moments. Etta wrestled with one reason and another. Not one was believable. At last the perfect retort came to her.

"You old cow, you're deaf. You can't hear right," she ranted to her aunt.

Poppa's words, however, overrode hers.

"She had a nightmare, about the red queen, from her children's book. I went in to comfort her."

Etta collapsed on the floor. She had lost.

~~~

Isabel's throat closed off. With the same speed tumblers of a bank vault click and allow access, her brain lined up all the disparate clues and put them in order. The times David gave into Etta's temper tantrums, the odd moments she had encountered them alone in rooms, the way the girl moved with a certain knowledge of her body, the incident with Connor, and the harping of Helen that claimed the girl was of bad seed. The most damning were the different accounts of what had happened in Etta's bedroom.

Her heart iced, and she took command of the crisis.

"Get out of this room, David, and be out of my house by first light, or you'll live to regret staying."

Isabel watched him pull himself together and lurch into the hall where Willie and Susan stood. Without another word, David shoved his way between them. Willie's face showed tears and disappointment. The smelling salts in the maid's hand spilled out on the floor.

"Susan, go back to your room. You are not to say anything to Cook about what happened tonight. I shall talk to the staff in the morning." The maid bobbed a quick curtsey and went down the hallway.

Isabel returned her attention to Etta. "You will go to your room without another word. I shall deal with you tomorrow." Etta rose from the floor and left the room.

"Willie, take the key ring from my top desk drawer and lock your sister in her room." He wiped away his tears with the sleeve of his nightshirt and stepped toward the dresser. "When you finish, you will return the keys to me."

Isabel cut him off when he started to speak. "Not now, son."

Only Helen remained. "Go to bed," Isabel told her. "There is nothing more to be done tonight. We shall deal with the situation tomorrow."

~~~

Isabel listened to the household settle. Willie walked down the hall with slow footsteps after he returned the keys. In her room, Helen rocked for at least an hour before she must have gone to bed. Etta cried for several hours until she fell silent. Intermittent noise from David's study reached her. He opened and slammed drawers. His footfall on the steps indicated he came up to his rooms. Then he went down the steps and out the side door. The neighbor's dog next door alerted her he was in the carriage house.

Soon he will be gone, out of my life Isabel thought and was surprised by the numbness in her heart. Next the carriage drove down the drive, and the dog at last quieted.

But her thoughts kept sleep at bay. How had she slept so soundly before this night? Why had she not heard him come and go to Etta's room if she could hear all these noises now? More than anything, how could she have been so unaware of these events in her own household?

The memory of her sister-in-law's last visit and offer of help surfaced. Would Elizabeth shun her? Or would the older woman be gracious enough to accept her apology and come if asked?

Isabel had nothing to lose. Since Susan knew what had happened, it would spill out through the town within two days. The gossip would spread from kitchen to kitchen with each delivery the grocers and milkmen made. The cooks would tell the housemaids who in turn would spice the news up when they passed the tale to their mistresses. She could not even guess what form her shameful story would take when the women shared it with their husbands.

Isabel rose from her bed and moved to the desk under the window. Resolved, she took out a sheet of stationery and wrote a short note to Elizabeth. She reread the few words asking her sister-in-law to call at her earliest convenience. Isabel weighed if she should apologize and go into more detail or add she would explain later. The latter seemed better. She could not find the energy to write about the awful things of the evening. She folded the note, sealed it in an envelope, and addressed it.

The fire had died down, and the drafts from the windows chilled her. Climbing quickly back in bed, Isabel hoped sleep would come once she was warm, but her mind would not let go of what to do about Etta. The solution was not as easy as ordering David out of the house. The girl was just fifteen.

Isabel woke with a start and a sense of loss. It did not take long for her to remember the horrible events of last night. They had really happened, and she was the only one who could deal with them this morning. The mantle clock showed six o'clock. Time to rise and get on with her new life without a husband or a daughter.

After she dressed in a somber gray gown and went downstairs with the letter, she paced in the parlor while she waited for the rest of the house to rise. The loss of Etta loomed before her and would be unbelievably painful. Did she really have to carry through with what she had decided?

~~

"Momma, what happened last night?" Willie asked when he joined her in the parlor.

He wore his school uniform of a white shirt and tie under a blue vest and black pants.

She motioned for him to join her on the sofa. "Remember the deportment classes at Aunt Elizabeth's?"

He nodded. "And you learned to be a gentleman and the girls learned how to be ladies?"

He nodded again and looked puzzled. "Last night," she went on, "we found out Poppa and Etta were not acting as gentlemen and ladies do. So Poppa left, and Etta will have to go away for more lessons."

"She can't have them here?"

"No."

"Poppa has to have lessons too?"

Willie swung his legs, and Isabel placed her hand on his knee to still him.

"Yes, he does," she answered.

"Then he'll come back home?"

"Willie, your father will never return to this house."

"Never? Why?"

"His lessons will take a long time. You are now the man of the family."

He picked at a scab on his thumb until a drop of blood formed. Isabel gave him her handkerchief and waited.

Willie sat up straighter. "You'll have to call me William. Willie is no name for the man of the house."

"You are quite right." She hugged him. "From now on, your aunt and I'll call you William."

"But Etta will come back home after her lessons?"

"We will talk about that later, for now, go see Cook about some breakfast."

Isabel waited until her son was out of the room and rang for Susan. It was time to put her plans in action.

~~~

When the maid arrived, Isabel fixed her with a firm gaze.

"Susan, you must keep in mind your position with our family. You are not to say anything to anyone about what happens in this house."

The maid promised.

"Thank you, now I want you to take this key and unlock Miss Etta's room."

Susan took the key Isabel had looped to a bright green ribbon and put it in her apron pocket.

"If you find Miss Etta is not awake, wake her up. Tell her she has twenty minutes in the bathroom before you will serve breakfast in her room. You will stand outside and escort her back to her room where you will lock the door and come back down for her breakfast, understand?"

Susan nodded, and Isabel continued. "Good, after you return my keys, I want you to summon the staff into the parlor."

~~~

After the maid bobbed her curtsey and left, Isabel walked into David's study. From the doorway she could see nothing of his was in the desk or bookcases. In this emptiness, there was only an envelope on the fireplace mantle.

Isabel crossed the room and debated whether to read it or not. Deciding she did not ever want to know what he had written, she threw the letter onto the nearly spent embers in the fireplace.

Empowered by rage, Isabel continued on her way to the parlor where a few minutes later she notified the staff Mr. Smith had left the house and they were not to gossip about his departure or any other events pertaining to the family. She guessed the word had already spread since no one seemed surprised by her announcement. Such was the way it was with servants. They all talked.

She dismissed all except McConkey, the gardener. "Take this letter to Mrs. James. Give it into her hand only, understand?"

~~~

Isabel found it difficult to keep her composure when Elizabeth arrived within the hour and joined her in the parlor. Her visitor did not stop to take off her hat or gloves before she gathered Isabel into her arms and asked, "Has someone died? Why, you look like you haven't slept."

"I should have listened to you, the time you called, about Etta and Connor," Isabel whispered to Elizabeth and hung on. "Please forgive me."

"I do," Elizabeth tightened her hold. "Now tell how I can help."

"First, let me take your things," Isabel said and stood back.

Elizabeth removed her outer attire and gave them to Isabel, who placed them by the tea things. The two women moved to the sofa before the fireplace.

Isabel said, "You were right, about Etta. Seems she and David have been acting improperly for some time."

"Oh that poor child. How did you find out?"

Isabel shared only the barest facts, but still her eyes brimmed with tears.

"I need your advice. What am I going to do about Etta? She must not remain here."

"How can you send her away? She's the victim."

"She's above the age of consent."

"But was she when it started?"

"It doesn't matter. Think about it. How can I let her stay? I cannot send her to school. You know how fast this will travel through the whole town. The shame will ruin her life. Willie will suffer enough as it is. If she stays, he will also be ruined. But worse of all is I can't trust her around Willie."

Elizabeth's protests stopped.

"More important," Helen, dressed in her customary black, spoke from the parlor door, "you know the child came from an evil union."

Helen continued after she sat down beside Isabel on the sofa and took her sister's hand. "She'll never change. There's no place for her any longer in this house. She's not one of us."

Elizabeth looked from Helen to her and asked where Etta was.

"Locked upstairs in her bedroom until I find someplace for her to go."

"I'll take the child in until you find a suitable place."

"No, she has disgraced our family. Banishment is the only solution."

"Isabel's correct. She can't be around any of our family," Helen said.

"My suggestion," Elizabeth said, "is to call upon Father O'Connell. It might be possible she can return to St. Jerome's until he can find an apprenticeship for her."

"Maybe he can help."

Isabel straightened and tried to take comfort from Elizabeth's suggestion. But she felt a sense of foreboding overcome her.

"This ordeal will be so horrid. The gossip, the looks, the shunning." She dabbed at her eyes with her lace handkerchief.

"Only for awhile," Elizabeth offered, "until something else comes along to seize people's attention. Remember, the family will stand beside you."

~~~

Elizabeth's last words did sooth Isabel. She was not alone in this ordeal. The family would rally around her and offer support and solace. But she still had many things to accomplish today, tasks only she could do. She reached deep down for strength, sang *la vincero* sotto voce several times and grew stronger. She was ready to ask for help.

"Helen?" Her sister looked up from her tatting. "Are you receiving any visitors today?"

Helen answered no, and Isabel again rang the bell for Susan. When the maid stood before her, she issued the orders for the day.

"We are not at home except for Mrs. James, Father O'Connell, or Mr. Herndon," Isabel said. "Also please go up and check on Miss Etta every three hours and escort her to the bathroom as needed. She will have all her meals in her room until further notice. Tell Cook to plan on three for lunch and dinner in the dining room from now on."

She dismissed the maid and thought about the other tasks. "In a few minutes, Helen, will you look over some letters?"

"Of course, but then you must go up and change into one of your latest gowns. It's important we keep up appearances. You can't go around dressed in mourning. The servants will notice and talk."

Isabel agreed and touched her sister's arm on the way to the writing desk. After she wrote to the priest and lawyer, she gave the letters to Helen to critique.

"These are good. No need to go into detail. All they have to know is that you want them to call post haste," Helen said. "I also suggest you ask Susan to draw you a bath. Do not worry, I'll send the letters out within the hour."

Isabel started for the door, stopped and turned back to face her sister. "You will instruct the gardener no one else is to receive them."

"Yes, now go calm yourself."

Chapter 14

Louisville, later the same day

After her bath, Isabel sat by the fireplace in the parlor and gathered her thoughts. Soon the men she had summoned would come. She needed their guidance since they possessed the training and experience denied her, but she had no need of their control. The rest of her life was finally hers to shape. The weight of their pending visits grew, and she tried to read. It was no use. Her inner discipline failed. The words passed by her eyes and out of her mind.

Her attention wandered, to the way the light from the flames of the fireplace caught on her bright gold and green silk skirt and her wedding band. The elegant ring, once a symbol of her status as a married woman led to the memories of her courtship and marriage. David had seemed too good to be true. He was better than any man in her adolescent fantasies which had been fueled by the giggling whisperings she and her classmates at the convent shared after lights out. In the beginning, she thought Helen, being younger and more outgoing, and yes, less headstrong, would be his choice. But she had won him, and for a short time her life was charmed.

The heartache from the miscarriages and the loss of their lovemaking had worn her down. She recognized grief had caused part of her to wither. Her family had let her sink down deeper and deeper into the blackness of her mind. Where she found the strength to free herself from melancholy and adopt Etta and William, she did not know. Not from her sister, but maybe from God.

Shame fell over her. She had brought the only scandal in living memory into the family. Incest. This was not done in the best families. How could she face her brothers and their wives? Not everyone would be as kind and comforting as Elizabeth. And all those people at Mass would be a nightmare. But she would get through this with determination and a brave front. No one, not even David or Etta, was going to ruin her.

The insistent sound of the front door knocker brought her back from her reflections. Father O'Connell's greeting to Susan came from the foyer. Her answer was too low to reach into the parlor. Hurried footsteps signaled his approach.

Isabel looked up at his greeting and noticed he had a puzzled expression on his face.

"Praise God, Mrs. Smith. I'm glad to see there's no black crepe or funeral wreath hung on the door."

"Thank you for coming." She set her closed book aside, rose from her chair, and waited for him to cross the room.

"My thought when I read your note was someone had passed. I even asked young Father Boniface to take over my morning rounds."

"I appreciate how busy you are," she said and gave him her hand. "I was about to have some tea. Would you like to join me?" she asked.

His jaw clinched and a slight tinge of red, probably from anger, she thought, mounted his cheek. After a moment, he seemed to master his irritation. It was not misplaced. She had implied in her note he was urgently needed. Yet, he did owe some consideration to her and the family. The McIntires had certainly given enough to the church through the years. Besides, she wanted to set the tone she was in charge and his role was to counsel but not control.

"Thank you, no," he answered and waited until she sat down again. Then he took the chair next to hers. "Tell me how I can help you." He perched on the chair's edge and folded his hands in his lap.

"I need your advice."

"Of course, Mrs. Smith."

"And I ask for your confidentiality." His nod was a bit too measured. "No one except you must know, ever." This time the nod was brisker. "Last night, we had a disturbance in the household."

Her composure crumbled, and she fought to keep her eyes on him. Damn David and Etta, and Helen too, she thought, damn them all for putting her through this.

"You must realize," Isabel began again, "I find it difficult to speak of this matter."

"Take your time." He leaned back into the chair.

"Around eleven o'clock, Helen heard some shouting noises and traced them to Etta's bedroom. She at first assumed Etta was having another nightmare."

He mumbled something. She could not tell if it was from

impatience or encouragement.

"But when she listened at the door, she heard a man's voice."

Tears started. Isabel blotted them with her handkerchief and willed them to stop.

"David was in her room, and Father, he was," she faltered.

Color flooded the priest's face. Several seconds later, he cleared his throat.

"Let me help you," he said. His eyes did not quite meet hers. Isabel nodded. Maybe she would not have to put what had happened in actual words.

"Was he," he let his eyes flicker in her direction before he looked away again, "was your husband committing improper acts with your daughter?"

She shook her head. "Not last night. Helen thinks she surprised them before..."

"Anything happened," he finished for her.

She nodded again. "Helen has been suspicious for some time but never had any proof. But last night..."

"What happened, Mrs. Smith?"

"They both confessed."

"Ahh."

Isabel read in his eyes he really did not understand how she felt. Her family had been ruined in only a few minutes. He listened to people's problems, but what problems did he himself have? She would have to explain.

"I demanded David leave, and he did." The effort to remain calm had exhausted her. She had to pause. The priest waited for her to continue. Isabel took a deep breath and let it out. "William and Susan overheard everything, but he is too young to fully understand what he heard."

The priest cleared his throat. "And Etta?"

"I asked you to call today in hopes you could find a place for her. She also has to leave."

He chased the surprise from his eyes and said, "Sometimes, Mrs. Smith, when we're overwrought, we make hasty decisions we later regret."

"I will never regret this decision. Can you help or not?"

"Maybe," he stopped. His flush returned. "I have a delicate question to ask. Is she with child?"

His words proved too much. Her composure broke into fractured bits, and she gripped the chair arms as her heart pounded wildly.

"I do not know. I did not even consider, no, you have provided an even more necessary reason for banishment."

"Your daughter..."

Isabel did not wait for him to finish. She stood to indicate the meeting was over. He also rose.

"She is not my daughter any more. I will disown her."

"Maybe in time you'll rescind your decision."

"Never, I am adamant, I never want to see her again."

Isabel rang the bell. "Susan will see you out. Find Etta a place soon, or I shall turn her out in the streets myself."

~~~

The second man Isabel had summoned came while she and Helen were at their afternoon tea with William. When Susan opened the parlor door, Walter Herndon hurried in with his satchel.

"Mrs. Smith, I apologize, I couldn't come any sooner."

"The important thing is you are here now. Come join us."

She looked at Helen who made no move to leave. It was probably better to have her stay rather than eavesdrop in the foyer as she did during the priest's visit. Her son was another matter.

"William, you may take a few sandwiches and go outside and play."

"May I ride my bicycle?"

"As long as you stay on this block. Do not wander off."

He grabbed a handful of sandwiches and ran out the door. Herndon took the vacated seat, and Isabel handed the lawyer a cup of tea.

"Mr. Herndon, I called you here because I need your advice."

"Yes ma'am, I'm at your service."

She willed herself to remain calm and hoped her story would grow easier with the retelling.

"I will not go into great detail. It is too disturbing. What you need to know is Mr. Smith no longer lives here. You will deal with me on all business matters now."

Herndon's eyes widened and his teacup rattled on its saucer. His glance followed hers to his hand. He put the china down on the table.

"I don't understand."

"He left last night after, after it was discovered he and Etta had behaved improperly."

She was past the worst part and took a sip of tea. The lawyer looked even more shocked. His face went white. He frowned. Isabel waited until he sorted out what he wanted to say.

"I'm sorry for your trouble." He looked at Helen and back at her. "Was your daughter molested? Do you want me to work with the police?"

Isabel decided she would have to be plainspoken with this man. "No, please, no police. I wish to consult you on a legal matter."

He opened his satchel and took out paper and pencil.

Isabel continued, "I cannot divorce David. The church will never grant me permission. What I need from you is a legal way to remove my husband from my life."

He put down his pencil and said, "I understand your desire to move quickly. However, as your attorney, I must advise you to not be hasty."

"Do not treat me like a child," she fumed. "What you must understand is I consider myself no longer married. You must find a way to make it legal."

"It is possible you may make a decision you'll regret and…"

Isabel had had enough of his dithering. "Mr. Herndon," she interrupted, "You have represented this family for many years and your father before you. I want this matter handled expeditiously. The question seems to be will you handle my affairs, or do I have to find a more capable firm?"

She stared at him until his Adam's apple bobbed under his closely trimmed dark beard.

"Yes ma'am, I can handle the matter for you." He took up his pencil again. "Where has Mr. Smith gone?"

"I do not know or care."

He made a few notes as he spoke, "Maybe desertion or divorce from bed and board can provide some grounds. The latter means you would regain all rights to your property with the understanding you may never again take any funds from your husband. In essence, you would be saying he has left and never intends to return to the marital home."

He looked at her when he finished. Though she had never heard of this type of divorce, it sounded like the legal remedy she needed. There was a small comfort in knowing she was not the only woman ever to face this situation.

"Thank you, you have summarized my possibilities."

"I'm sure we can rush this through the court. I'll keep you informed." He started to put his paper and pencil away.

"There is more," she waited for him to look at her again. "I need documents to disown Etta and a new will, today."

"I can understand about Mr. Smith, but why disown your daughter?"

Helen answered before Isabel could, "The harlot was a willing partner in this behavior and should be punished."

She flinched at the note of triumph in her sister's voice and said, "Mr. Herndon, she is not my daughter any longer."

"As you wish," he made more notes, "I'll draw up these papers immediately. My understanding is you are in control of your own interests now and you want to keep Mr. Smith and Miss Etta from benefiting from any of the McIntire wealth."

"Exactly."

This conversation with Herndon had been easier than the one with the priest, and she was relieved she would never have to tell these events ever again.

"Will you keep William's guardianship the same, in case something should happen to you before he reaches his majority?"

"Yes, my brother James and his wife." He made a mark beside a line on his paper.

"Would you like for me to make arrangements for Miss Etta to go to the county home?"

"Thank you, no, Father O'Connell is seeing to her arrangements."

He checked his notes. "And I can see there might be one more matter to consider."

"Yes?" What could he have thought of that she had not already seized upon?

"In case Miss Etta is with child?"

For the second time today, she had to face the question, and it was not any easier. She reached inside, deep into her reserves, and steadied herself. She hoped her voice did not betray her turmoil.

"Do not put anything in writing. However, if she is and takes it to St. Jerome's, I shall increase my endowment. Please ensure I never know which child is hers. Can you work with Father O'Connell in this matter?"

When he agreed and finished his notations, she dismissed him.

"I am glad you're handling these family matters for us."

~~~

During the rest of the afternoon, Isabel wrote letters and sent her regrets for events on her social calendar. Maybe a few weeks spent out of the public eye would give time for the scandal to wane.

But she grew impatient with Herndon. How long did it take the man to translate her wishes into those esoteric legal words?

The hour hand of the mantle clock had almost reached six when the knocker on the front door sounded. Susan's steps grew louder when she came from the dining room and into the foyer.

Isabel forced herself to remain at her writing desk and gazed outside the nearby window. Though the garden was ice-covered, she knew her prized roses and cannas by the gazebo would soon be in full bloom. Would they or anything else ever bring her pleasure again? She did not want to feel this angry forever.

"Mr. Herndon, ma'am," Susan announced.

The lawyer entered with two young men, only a few years older than William. They looked nervous and had evidently never been in a house this elegant. They stood rooted in the doorway and gawked at the mirrors and high ceilings. She noticed their fingernails were stained with black ink.

When she offered the three of them a seat, Herndon took his and waved the other two towards the foyer.

"Who are they?"

"My law clerks, Mrs. Smith. If you approve the will I've drawn up, they will witness it. Miss Helen cannot since she is a beneficiary."

"I thought you would be the only person to know the contents of my will?"

"Rest assured, ma'am. When it comes time for you to sign, I'll fold the document so all they'll see is today's date and you writing your name."

Now she remembered the procedure. It had been the same with her father's will. All she had seen was the codicil she had insisted upon.

The lawyer's next words brought her back.

"I believe I have drawn up documents that encompass your wishes. Let's start with the will so the boys can get home to their dinners."

Isabel stacked the few invitations and letters to the side of her desk and held out her hand. He opened his satchel and slid out a single piece of paper. After he spent a few moments to look over the document, he gave it to her. Isabel scanned it for flaws while the lawyer stood next to her. There was one requirement more important than any other, and she wanted to see how he had stated it in legal terms. It did not take her long to discover its peculiar phrasing.

'Having borne no children, I restrict any inheritance to my sister Helen McIntire and children of her body and to my adopted son William. He is the only living person who is not a blood relative who has a right to any part of my estate.'

"Nice touch," Isabel said and pointed to the paragraph.

"I hoped it would meet with your approval."

"Yes, call in your clerks."

After she signed, the witnesses added their signatures. Herndon rolled the ink blotter over all their names and dismissed the two young men.

"I have the other documents with me." He placed two more papers on her desk and returned the signed will to his satchel.

Bridgette, the name the nuns gave her, and Clarissa, the middle name Isabel had chosen so carefully for its Latin meaning of bright and its Italian beauty when sung, seemed to stand out on the paper.

Isabel hesitated and closed her eyes to regain her strength. Replaying last night's scene in her bedroom made her stomach twist. But there was no going back. Etta had to go. William was her main concern now. He had to be protected.

The document stated she, Isabel, disowned her daughter Bridgette Clarissa Smith, aged fifteen years, forever and always, as of today's date, February 2, 1874.

Though her hand trembled when she dipped the pen in the ink, her signature was firm. Silently she returned her pen to the inkstand. Herndon blotted her name and removed the paper from her sight, all without saying a word. She was grateful. Replying to any of his questions would have been difficult.

Isabel read the remaining paper. This one asked the judge to recognize she was no longer living as the wife of Mr. David Smith, whereabouts unknown. He had deserted her, and if he did not appear in court to contest the case, she should be granted a divorce of bed and separation. Her mind puzzled before it rebelled over the matter of a court appearance. How could she appear before a judge, someone she personally knew? A light touch on her hand broke into her revelry.

"Mrs. Smith, I was saying you will not be permitted to marry again unless you have a full divorce, but as the church…"

"I have no plans to marry again, ever. Please explain this line about court and contesting the case."

"May I?" he pointed to a chair.

When she nodded, he brought it over and placed it beside her writing desk. He took a small note from his breast pocket and scanned it before he answered, "You need to post a legal notice in the newspaper stating Mr. Smith no longer resides at this address and you're not responsible for any of his debts."

Her anger spiked, and she lost her battle to remain calm. "So I shall have to wash my dirty linen in public after all."

"Not necessarily in Louisville." He checked his paper again. "There's a peculiar quirk in the divorce law some men find useful."

She saw him smile at this last statement until his eyes met hers. She glared at him, and the smile vanished.

"The law requires they post the notice in a general newspaper. The loophole is they don't have to use their local one."

"So women are divorced without knowing it, without a chance to appear in court and contest the divorce?"

"Yes, men even come from other countries to take advantage of our laws."

"But now I get to use it for my advantage?"

"Quite right. I suggest a small paper in Webster County. The newspaper owner and I have an arrangement. I'll send him a wire and get it in this week's paper after I see the judge tomorrow morning."

"When do I go to court?"

"You won't have to. I can handle everything for you."

His words eased some of her turmoil, and she asked her next question. "And how long until this is over?"

"Inside of a month for the divorce. The will is valid now. I'll file the paper regarding Miss Etta tomorrow and walk it through myself."

"Thank you, I knew you were the right man to settle these messy matters."

~~~

Upstairs, Etta heard footsteps and another noise come down the hallway. She feared what this meant. No fight remained in her. The past day and two long nights of crying and stomping and screaming had exhausted her and reminded her of the rat she and Willie had once watched drown in the rain barrel. Lots of frantic movements and no way out.

When Susan had brought breakfast yesterday, her remarks were few and delivered with a sense of cruel superiority.

"The priest and lawyer were here, Miss Etta. There's been lots of talk in the parlor. The upshot is they're looking for a place to send you, a home for wayward women. Miss Helen says that's what you are, a fallen woman and not fit for polite society."

The words fallen woman brought Etta to tears again, and Susan seemed to soften.

"Don't you worry, Miss. Father O'Connell will do right by you. He's a good man."

Someone unlocked the door. Etta looked up from her tear-sodden pillow and saw Susan shoving a battered, dust-covered trunk through the door.

"Miss Etta, Father's downstairs waiting to take you away. Come on now. You have to pack. He says you can bring one trunk with you and suggests you bring nothing fancy. Good serviceable clothes is what he said."

Susan pulled the trunk over to the clothes press. The lid creaked when she opened the trunk.

"Where am I going?" Etta asked.

The fear over leaving her home made her heart race. She looked around the familiar room with pink floral bouquet patterned wallpaper. She could not picture herself living anywhere else. She would be with people she did not know and without her mother or brother, or any of her own things she loved. How could she live without her family, her books, and favorite dolls from childhood.

"I didn't hear before I shut the door," the maid straightened up and wiped her hands on her apron. "I couldn't hear through the door neither. But it has to be better than staying in this room all day and night with only me to talk to. Hurry up now."

Susan returned to inspect Etta's clothes and folded the largest and plainest ones in the trunk.

"I don't want to leave. Why can't they just leave me here? I'll be good, the best girl in Louisville, I promise. Will you tell them, please?"

"I'm sure you would be, but one thing I've learned in my life is that just because you want something, doesn't mean it will be. There's a good lesson for you to learn, Miss Etta. You have to make do with what the Lord's given you."

"I even wrote Momma a letter. Maybe she will forgive me."

"It's possible she will in time. Leave it on the desk. I'll give it to her."

Susan stopped and looked at her. "But you have to leave today. Anything special you want to take with you? I've left a little room."

"My birthday gifts from Momma."

"You'd better keep your jewelry inside your chemise. Don't be showing those pearls off." Susan pointed her finger, and Etta backed away, frightened by the woman's intensity. "You can't trust a soul, not one single person, understand?"

Etta nodded, and Susan continued, "Child, you're going out into the real world where there's no one to protect you. No one to look out for you. And, remember this, there's always some one who wants to take from you, and only a few who want to give you anything good."

Etta shuddered at this warning. The reality she would not be safe or ever see her brother, mother, or any other family again swept over her. She gasped for air and started shaking her numb hands.

"Put your head down between your knees. Take a deep breath. You've got yourself all worked up. Won't do no good, you know."

"I feel faint," Etta said with her head bent down.

"Don't pass out, girl. You've got to get stronger quick. Now get up and go take out one of those chemises I packed for you. I'll get my needle and thread ready. It's down right plain you need some help with surviving."

Confused, Etta nevertheless did as she was told and handed over one of her undergarments. Susan stood in front of the window.

"Step over here and watch what I'm doing." Susan began by forming up a little pocket in the side seam. "It's easy to hide your valuables from men. They never go anywhere close to your monthly linens. My mother told me she always kept some old washed linens with stains she couldn't get out on top of her monthly supply. My father never touched them even when he was desperate for some drink money. You understand what I'm saying?"

"I think so," Etta said, but somehow she knew she missed the import of Susan's words.

"Let me make it clear. One of these days you're gonna find yourself in need of a hiding place for money or jewelry. One you don't want no man to find. Men get real squeamish about women's monthly bleeding and won't have nothing to do with it at all. You can always use that to your advantage. Now do you understand?"

"Yes, but why are you sewing a pocket?"

"Because no stained cloth is going to stop a woman. So you have to have a hiding place on you. A little pocket or two in your underclothes comes in handy for coins and jewelry. My mother always told me to keep a needle and thread ready in my outside pockets so I could hide my valuables. I prefer my pocket in front, under my left arm. Hurry now, put your pearls in here, so I can stitch it shut."

After Etta changed into the altered chemise and one of her plainest dresses, Susan said, "You can help carry your trunk. Better get used to not being the princess anymore."

"Wait," Etta said and moved toward her desk. There she opened the middle drawer and took out the letter address to her mother.

"I'll put Momma's letter here on top. You'll make sure she sees it?"

"I told you I would. Hurry up."

"Come Polly, we're going to a new place."

Etta took her old doll from St. Jerome's off the bed pillow.

Out in the upstairs hallway, she noticed all the doors were closed. Downstairs Father O'Connell waited in the foyer. All the doors she could see were closed on this floor as well.

"Come child, it's time we leave," the priest said and took the trunk from her.

"I want to see Momma and Willie before I leave."

"You must come away now. Trust me, it's better this way."

With her eyes filling, Etta turned to Susan who tried to hold back her own tears. "I'll miss you, Susan."

"You take care and remember what I told you," the maid hugged her.

Etta returned her embrace and went down the front steps. Then she stepped into a wagon with a driver who did not tip his hat or smile. She had never been snubbed before. Servants and hired people always treated her with respect. However, the snub from the driver became her first hint about how others would treat her since she no longer had the backing of the McIntire name and family.

~~~

Each moment the wagon progressed farther from her home brought Etta closer to tears. How could this really be happening to her? It was not fair. Yet she realized she and her father had to pay the price of their sin. Maybe this strange place she was bound for would be a Purgatory here on earth, and one day, she would overcome her stigma and return to her family. She would show Momma and Aunt Helen. She would fight and win this battle. Her favorite opera line came to her and brought her strength, as always. But this time, she realized, she needed courage more than ever.

A few minutes later Etta felt stronger. Out of the corner of her eye, she saw the priest sat with his hands folded. He seemed to wait for her to speak.

"What is this place like?" she asked.

"I've not seen it. I imagine it's much like St. Jerome's. Do you remember your time there?"

Etta nodded but did not tell him the old convent was the scene of her many childhood nightmares.

"This place has a good reputation," he said. "It was started after the war to take in widows and children of veterans killed fighting for the Union cause. Somehow, it turned into a home and workhouse for women in need of a place to live and work."

"An orphanage for adults?"

"Good, you've caught the essence of the situation. My friend, Mr. Fielding, oversees its operation. He has promised me you'll be well taken care of."

"For how long?"

"Until you're trained and can support yourself as a decent woman."

According to her Aunt Helen, all she knew how to do was sing, pretend, order servants around, and throw temper tantrums until she got her way. A shudder ran over her. The future seemed scary.

"Trained as what?"

"Most of the girls are trained as domestics. But," he stopped and stared at her for a few moments. "You and Mr. Fielding should discuss your options fairly quickly."

"Yes, Father," she said.

Her thoughts focused on how much better it would have been if they had left her at St. Jerome's all those years ago. Instead, she had grown up to think she would be a lady of society and supervise a household, and now, all of a sudden, she seemed destined to be a servant.

Part 3

Chapter 15

Frankfort, February 3, 1874

The open wagon carried Etta and the two nuns who had accompanied her on the train ride from Louisville. When the driver slowed at the foot of a gravel drive, she read the plaque embedded in a fieldstone pillar. Home for Friendless Women.

This had to be the wrong address Etta thought and turned to look at Sisters Mathias and Ignatius. But they did not tell the driver to keep going.

He turned the wagon into the drive, yet she could not tear her eyes from the pillar until she felt a gentle touch on her gloved hand. Etta turned back to see Sister Mary Mathias' sympathetic look. Then the horrible realization hit her. This was where her mother had sent her, a place for homeless women. The name of the place was terrifying.

The two nuns remained as silent as they had on the train ride from Louisville. The only human sound came from the driver urging his horse to continue up the ice-rutted drive.

Sister Mathias broke her silence when the driver stopped at the front door of a three-story gray building.

"Will you please carry the trunk just inside the door and wait for our return?"

"Yes, Sister," the driver answered.

When he climbed down and hefted the trunk onto his shoulder, Etta heard his grumbles. The nuns ignored his complaints and followed him through the front door.

Etta hunched her shoulders against the cold and took in her new home. The words on the engraved limestone lintel above the entrance matched the ones on the pillar. The grounds were bare of benches or fountains, and only a few trees were in sight. Although the light accumulation of snow made it difficult to tell for sure, she did not see any flower gardens surrounding the house.

Tears stung her eyes. She was friendless and looked upward to plead, "Please God, let me go back home. I promise I'll be good, I'll never sin again."

The overcast sky kept out any welcoming sunshine, and she returned her eyes to the building. It was so ugly without arches or flower boxes or painted shutters and so different from her home in Louisville.

On her first step into the lobby, Etta met with a smell which triggered a long buried memory. A dim picture of St. Jerome's seeped back. Not the St. Jerome's of her nightmares. Instead she remembered the rooms where she had slept and lived.

After Etta walked past the nuns, her brain sorted and registered the source of each odor. Kerosene, damp laundry, unwashed bodies, fat from cooking, and dust. Collectively the air smelled old, defeated, hopeless.

Etta knew what was before her. Her panic heightened, and she retreated backward until the two nuns tenderly but firmly took her arms and guided her forward to the admission office. Inside, an elderly man, about her Uncle James' age, sat behind a desk. His shirt might have once been white but had dimmed with age, and his black suit coat was faded.

Her next impression was gray, the same color as the building and the sky. His skin tones indicated he never went outside for sun or fresh air. His hair hung in unbrushed waves to his ears, and his eyebrows spilled out and down over his eyes. Even they were gray and had a tired listless look to them.

"Sisters welcome," he said and stood to greet them. "You've brought Bridgette Smith with you, I see. Please be seated. This won't take long. The girl's trunk? She brought just one, as instructed?"

"Yes, Mr. Fielding, only the one. The driver left it outside your office," Sister Ignatius said.

"Good, Father O'Connell sent me the important information. He requested he be contacted instead of the family. So I'll ask one of you to sign your name as proxy for him on these admission papers." He gave Sister Ignatius a pen. "Right here, and here," he directed.

After she signed and returned the paper and pen to him, he said, "Thank you. You can leave the girl here with me now. Please pass on my regards to my good friend Father O'Connell."

He rose from his chair and walked toward the door. The nuns also stood and turned to face Etta. "Remember all the good teachings the sisters have given you over the years," Sister Ignatius said.

"You will be in our prayers, child," the other nun said.

Through the opened door, Etta watched the last two people she knew walk down the hallway. Before Mr. Fielding shut the door, she saw them near the Home's entrance.

How quickly her life had changed. Yesterday she had awakened in her elegantly furnished pink bedroom. Tonight she would sleep in this ugly place. Everyone else from now on was going to be a stranger. This place was called a home for friendless women for a reason. And she was truly friendless. Her knees weakened, and her chin trembled.

"Steady, girl," Fielding said from behind his desk. "Don't you go getting wobbly on me now. Before I turn you over to Matron Luttrell, I need to inventory your valuables. I'll write down what items you have. Your money will be deposited in the bank, and I'll put any other valuables in the vault in my office. We'll both sign the receipt."

"I don't have any money or valuables, sir."

"Nonsense," he shook his head. "Not with the type of clothes you're wearing. Surely your folks didn't send you here without any funds. Hand over your money and any jewelry. There's no safe place to keep them, once you get upstairs."

"I do have ten dollars from my birthday." She opened her reticule and stacked the coins on the desk.

"Here's your receipt," the warden said after he took the money and put it in an envelope with her name on it. "When you leave, any funds unspent and earnings you have left after expenses for clothing, room, and board will be paid out to you. Understand?"

The words rushed over her. She did not understand and looked at him for help. He must have misinterpreted her silence because he moved on to a new topic.

"Good, ready to meet Matron Luttrell? You will address her as such, and you'll address me as Warden Fielding or sir. Understand? I tell all the new ones the same. Good manners are important, especially since you have to make your own way in the world. Come on."

He got up and headed out the door. "Pick up your trunk. You'll have to carry it to the dormitory."

"Yes sir."

Etta struggled with lifting the trunk since it was too wide to fit within her arm span.

He watched her without any expression on his face and said, "Looks like you'll have to drag it. Any marks you make on the floor, you'll have to come back down and clean up when Matron Luttrell's finished settling you in."

After Etta stopped to rest on the first landing, a woman almost as short and stout as her Aunt Helen found them. But unlike her aunt, this woman wore bright plaids which matched her heightened color. Under her white work cap, graying wispy curls surrounded a face marked with good humor and kind brown eyes. Etta liked her at once. She reminded her of Sister Justina.

"You must be Bridgette Smith. Welcome to our Home."

"Thank you, ma'am."

"I'm Matron Luttrell. I answer to that or Mrs. Luttrell."

"Yes ma'am."

"Fine, let's get you settled in."

The matron turned to Mr. Fielding, "See you at breakfast tomorrow morning, sir."

The warden headed back down the stairs.

"Come along, dear. Let me take your trunk." The matron picked up the truck with grace and ease and started up the stairs. Etta followed.

"I've chosen a nice girl for you to sleep next to," Mrs. Luttrell said over her shoulder. "Just one more flight, and we're there. Let's stop here for a minute."

Mrs. Luttrell put the trunk down, sat on the top step, and patted beside her for Etta to sit.

Etta noticed the traces of old wax and melted snow on the worn wood. She hesitated a bit before she discarded the idea of spreading her handkerchief on the step. Instead, she took a seat as if she regularly sat on dirty stairs.

"My job here," Mrs. Luttrell said, "is to keep the Home running smooth. The best advice I can give you is tell no one about your past. Your future is what counts. It's important you muster all your effort to that goal, understand?"

Etta nodded, and the matron continued with her speech, "I hope you're a fast learner. Don't ask anyone else about her past. Mainly because it's none of your business. There's also the fact people usually lie. The past is gone. You need to remember the future, right?"

Etta indicated she agreed. They stood and climbed to the last story.

At the top of the stairs, the dormitory extended through the whole floor. It looked the same as what she remembered about St. Jerome's. Two lines of cots all covered with the same gray wool blankets. Nothing individual marked any of the linens or wall space above the beds. Even the open crates at the end of each bed looked identical. Sitting on one of the far beds was a young girl about her age.

"Lavinia," Mrs. Luttrell said when they reached the girl, "this is Etta Smith. Etta, this is Lavinia Ballard." After the girls greeted each other, Mrs. Luttrell said, "Lavinia, you can help her settle in." Facing Etta, she asked, "Are you hungry?"

"A little, yes ma'am."

"Both of you come by my sitting room before you head on down to the community room. I saved back some food from lunch. See you in a few minutes." The matron turned and left.

After Mrs. Luttrell was gone, Lavinia asked, "You must be pretty frightened, huh?"

Etta's strength vanished. She did not trust herself to speak.

The other girl seemed to understand and took charge. "Let's get you unpacked. Take your coat off and fold it in the bottom of the crate. After you're finished with your trunk, we'll go and have a cup of tea and some food with Old Lute. Hope she has cookies."

There was something funny in the way Lavinia said the name Old Lute, and Etta almost laughed when she repeated the name. "Old Lute?"

"That's what us girls call Mrs. Jane Luttrell, not to her face, mind you. We've got names for all of 'em. The warden's name is Ghostie. Can you guess why?"

"Because he's all gray?"

"Right, Mrs. Sutter, she's the cook. We call her Salty. And the nurse, we call her Icy because her hands are always so cold."

"What's her real name?"

"Mrs. Hensley. Then there's the gardener. His name is Mr. Caldwell. We call him Sniffles," Lavinia laughed.

"Because it's a rabbit's name?" Etta asked.

"Because he's always picking his nose and swiping the snot on his shirt sleeve."

"Ewww, disgusting."

"Did you bring lots of pretty things? I hope you don't mind me asking, but the clothes you have on are so beautiful." Lavinia stroked the sleeve of Etta's blue wool dress. "Your shoes are well-made too. Are you rich?"

Grateful to have a friend, she almost told the girl everything before the matron's advice echoed inside her head.

"No, I'm not rich. A kind lady whose daughter died gave me all her clothes."

"Are those your only shoes?"

Etta could not remember what Susan had packed for her. "Why?" she asked.

"The first year I was here, this rich girl Beatrice came, and she had the most gorgeous red shoes. She had a real right and a real left shoe, like yours."

Etta looked down at her shoes and saw nothing unusual about them until she looked at Lavinia's. Both of her shoes were shaped the same. A fast picture of their gardener's boots came to her, and she understood. Rich people like she used to be had proper right and left shoes. The poor did not.

"I packed in a hurry. I don't remember. What happened to the rich girl and her shoes?"

"There was this other matron, Mrs. Baxter, only we called her Old Battleaxe. She was real mean. Old Battleaxe decided the heels were too high." Lavinia spread her thumb and forefinger apart about two inches. "So off came the heels. Can you see what happened to the shoes?"

"The toes curled up?"

"Right. Give me your shoes, and I'll show you."

Etta sat down on her new cot and took off her shoes. Lavinia put them on and took some steps, walking on her heel.

"What a funny story," Etta laughed.

"It got better the next month. Old Battleaxe made us switch our shoes every month so they'd wear even. When you have shoes like mine, it doesn't make any difference. But when you had shoes like Beatrice wore, it was so funny," Lavinia laughed.

But Etta did not understand why.

"See, first month right on right and left on left. The next month, she looked like this."

The girl switched the shoes and did an exaggerated strut between the cots.

"She had to wear her shoes like that for a month?" Etta burst out laughing.

"Every other month until she outgrew them. Finally some other woman got them. Old Lute threw them out the first day she was here. You came at a good time."

Etta returned to her unpacking and lingered over placing her clothes in the crate. The thought of the long evening with the other women downstairs and an even longer night in this new room terrified her. Somehow she had to find the strength to survive.

Lavinia did not seem to be in any hurry either. She touched every piece of clothing.

"I've never felt woolens or silks this soft." Her fingers moved on to a blue silk day dress. "Your rich lady's daughter must have been real careful with her clothes. They don't look worn at all. Maybe you could write her a letter to thank her and mention how needy we are here."

Etta folded her last dress, a green which matched the color of her eyes, on top and thought of all the lovely clothes and shoes she had to leave behind. In her mind she saw her mother passing them on to Cook and Susan for their various nieces, the custom ever since she could remember.

"I'm sorry, I don't know who she is. The nuns told me about the lady and her daughter."

"Oh well, it was just an idea. Hungry? Let's go." Lavinia led the way toward the door.

"You'll find most of us are easy to get along with here. But watch out for Mazie Raines. She's a magpie."

"What's a magpie?"

"You never heard that expression, huh? I'll show you."

The girls stopped beside the cot nearest the door, and Lavinia leaned down and began to sort through the clothes and bits of lace and ribbons.

"I mean she steals things, little bright shiny things, just like the bird that takes stuff it can't use or eat. None of us has anything valuable. But if you come up short some day, search through her crate."

Etta thought of the chemise and her pearls, safe and sewn up, and gave Susan a silent thanks for her wisdom.

Lavinia pointed out a few cheap baubles and buttons.

"See what I mean. She's really harmless. Kind of odd and lonely. Every month Old Lute goes through Mazie's things and sorts out what doesn't belong to her and returns them. This green glass button belongs to Sophie. She was looking for it yesterday. I'll take it to her when we finish with the matron. Turn right, the washroom's down this way."

"How many women live here?" Etta asked when they were out in the hall.

"There's about twenty to a floor. Each floor takes turns eating, cooking, and cleaning up. You ought to be glad you came this week. We get to eat first, then for the next two shifts we cook and clean up."

The girls entered the washroom and stopped in front of a long mirror hanging over five washbasins. Her new friend's dark curls contrasted with her own. The girls started to repin their hair.

"What do we do during the day?" Etta asked.

"Ghostie must have run a hospital or something in the war." Lavinia rolled her eyes. "He has everything scheduled. What time we eat, what time we bathe, when we get up, when we have to work, and when we go to school."

"We really have to go to school?"

"It's required. That's what Ghostie says every time one of us asks why we have to go." Lavina posed in an exaggerated pose with her right hand on her chest and the other stretched out in front of her. "Every time someone asks why, Fielding stands like this and says 'Education can never be taken from you, my girls. Therefore you must be educated until you are eighteen.' He is such an old prig."

"What's school like?"

"The usual stuff. About thirty of us crammed into one room, cold in the winter and hot in the spring and fall. We have to do math and reading and geography. Most of the kids don't work. But some of the boys are quite handsome, so it's worth it."

"There are boys in the school?" Etta noticed a blush come over the girl's cheeks. "Any special boy?" Lavinia's complexion deepened.

"I've got my eye on Daniel Miller. You can have any of the others, but Danny's mine."

"So after school we study and relax until it's time for chores?"

Etta turned her head from side to side to check the recaptured curls.

Lavinia moved to look directly at Etta. "Some people call this a workhouse. In a way, we're lucky to be in school four hours a day. The older women have to work hard all day."

"What work do you do?"

Lavinia held out her hands and raised the sleeves on her arms. Her hands were red and chapped. Her cuticles wore specks of dried blood. Burns splotched her lower arms. Some of the injuries were old and scarred. Others looked raw and new.

"Can you guess?"

To Etta, her new friend's hands and arms looked like the weekly washwoman's. "The laundry?"

"Right, every day but Saturday and Sunday, until five o'clock. But I should move up after I train you."

"Up where?"

"The mending room where I'll repair the holes in the bed linen and towels."

Etta looked down at her own hands with not a scar or scab on them. Her arms were also unblemished. She did not want her hands and arms to look like this girl's. There was so much here she did not like or want to experience. Maybe she could run away tonight.

On the way down the stairs, Etta asked, "What time do we go to bed?"

"Nine o'clock. No one can use any lamps or candles after lights out. You're not supposed to be out of bed until the next morning. But on our floor, Minnie's been put in charge, and she can't hear too good, so if you have to go to the necessary, be quiet. She won't know it."

"Has any one ever escaped?"

Lavinia looked astonished and stopped in the middle of the flight of steps to stare at her. Lavinia's answer came in a raised voice.

"You've never lived on the streets, have you?" Etta shook her head. "It's mean out there."

Lavinia now spoke in a lower tone. "You're a lot like Beatrice, and it's just not your shoes and clothes. It's the way you carry yourself and how your hands look. You're clean and you've eaten regular. I'd hazard you've never had to work or wonder where you were going to sleep at night."

Etta could not bear the quiet disgust coming from Lavinia's eyes and looked away.

"Once you leave," the girl said, "you can't come back. Fielding won't let you. He says you have one chance to better yourself. You decide you don't want it, he's got lots of other girls and women ready to come in."

Lavinia stopped and took a breath. "I don't know how you got in here so fast. You're lucky it was before you got dirty and in trouble out there."

She next motioned over her shoulder. "You don't want to be here? Fine. Leave tomorrow. That way some more deserving woman can come and take your place. And you can bet she won't escape."

Etta's temper had started to heat halfway through Lavinia's first sentence. She did not like the way this girl preached to her. Just as quickly though, the cold reality of Lavinia's words sobered her. This was the truth about a world new to her, and she was grateful for the advice.

"Thank you, I didn't understand."

"I hope you stay." The girl's smile made Etta feel welcome as did the next words, "I think we can be good friends."

~~~

"Come in girls," Mrs. Luttrell said after Lavinia knocked.

Etta followed her new friend into a sitting room recently wallpapered with spills of pink and yellow flowers, but with the carpet worn thin. Good but frayed and mismatched furniture took up much of the space. All the furnishings reminded her of the castoffs used in the servant's quarters back home. The pillows were ill-made, and Etta thought they were probably sewing projects for the beginning seamstresses. A sense of gloominess touched her. Was she never going to live among beautiful or elegant furnishings again?

"Have some food, girls." Mrs. Luttrell used her knitting needles to point to a cold luncheon placed on the table nearest the fireplace. "You must be hungry. I have a few cookies also, your favorites, Lavinia, gingersnaps."

"Yes ma'am. Thank you."

Etta sat on the edge of the chair, the way Nanny Arnold had drilled into her. After she smoothed her skirt, she noticed Lavinia slouched back into her chair, a cookie in each hand. Etta eased her posture until she also touched the chair back. No one looked shocked or grim, and she was comfortable. Maybe there was something good to being poor. She knew she was about to find out.

Chapter 16

Louisville, May 28, 1874

"I have good news about Etta," Father O'Connell said before he took his first sip of tea.

Isabel gave him a slight nod and waited for the priest to deliver his monthly report on her banished daughter. He had called every fourth Thursday since February with the latest letter from his friend Fielding. Helen's silks rustled. The sound did not quite mask her sister's subdued snort. Isabel accepted that Helen would always consider Etta a bad seed. But the wilting magnolia blossoms visible through the parlor window reminded Isabel life did not stand still. She herself had changed so much since the scene in her bedroom on her daughter's fifteenth birthday.

During the priest's first two visits, Isabel had risen and, without a word, walked out of the parlor when he mentioned Etta's name. After he left, she found the letter on the silver mail tray in the foyer. Driven by anger over the man's insistence, each month she snatched the envelope and marched back into the parlor where she tossed it, unread, into the fireplace. Helen nodded her approval both times.

But last month, Father O'Connell spoke words about forgiveness and the blessing of peace it brings. The center of her heart thawed a bit. She said she would stay for his visit if he would leave the letter and not mention Etta.

The priest agreed, and true to his word, left the letter in the same place as the others. Isabel's resolve weakened when she touched the envelope. Hurt and anger waged against the increased sense of loss over her daughter. She brought the letter back to her writing desk and stuck it into her missal. Helen harrumphed, and her knitting needles clacked her disapproval.

~~~

The next day, after Helen stepped into the carriage and headed to her altar flower committee meeting, Isabel pulled the envelope from the black leather book. When she unfolded it, the crease distorted the priest's name and address and refused to smooth out after her fingertips stroked it over and over. She stopped her hands when she realized she was stalling.

Angry at her cowardice, she turned the envelope over and opened the flap. Without hesitation, she took out the single sheet of paper inside and read it. Some of the words she read resembled the school reports which had arrived at the end of each grading term. The phrase "still longing to return home" saddened her though "making friends" gave her some comfort. A short paragraph described the search for an appropriate apprenticeship. Her pain eased a little, and she knew she would take Father O'Connell's letter when he called in May.

On a golden spring day, Isabel sat with her sister and Father O'Connell amid fresh lilac blossoms and waited for him to begin.

"My friend reports Etta's doing well in her studies and work." Father O'Connell put his teacup down on the table beside him. "I have another letter from Mr. Fielding." He pulled out the envelope and paused.

Isabel extended her hand. The priest met her eyes and nodded. He rose from his chair and gave her the envelope. She folded and slid it into her skirt pocket.

"Is she with child?" Helen asked.

Father O'Connell shook his head.

"Is she in good health?" Isabel asked.

"Yes, Mrs. Smith, she is. Etta's doing well by all accounts. Seems she has a knack for organization and details. You must have taught her well because she's now an assistant to the head matron. Fielding says the Home has never operated so smoothly." He smiled, and his eyes grew soft.

"And her apprenticeship?"

"He says they've found her one with a boarding house where the state representatives and senators stay when the legislature is in session. Frankfort becomes quite busy then, as you can imagine."

"I hope she is maintaining good morals," Helen said.

"Indeed, they have devotions twice a day."

"Not Mass?" Isabel asked in unison with her sister.

"I asked the same question. Fielding told me he conducts interdenominational services. Etta and the other Catholic women may attend Good Shepherd Church, a few blocks away."

"You do bring good news today," Isabel said, and a small kernel of happiness in her heart expanded.

"It's the best place for her since she can't live here with you."

"Isabel," Helen demanded. "You're not bringing her back here, are you?"

"No, of course not, though I am still concerned about her welfare."

"She was nothing but trouble from the minute she came. You should've known she was too old to change. Take pride in how you have been able to shape William into a decent young man. You never had a chance with the girl."

"Miss McIntire, I disagree with you. Etta's high-spirited, yes, but she's never been an evil child. Your sister gave her an opportunity. Maybe after the girl's matured, you will all be reconciled.

"Etta can never come back into this house. It's mine too. I'll not allow such a godless person to live here."

"Surely you believe in forgiveness and redemption, Miss McIntire?"

"Only after a long penitence, Father, a long one that matches her sins."

"I'm sure she's in all of our prayers," he said.

Suddenly a chill crept over her neck. She reached for the bell to summon Susan and she stood to dismiss the priest.

"Thank you for coming today, Father. I do appreciate your kindness toward Etta."

The priest stayed seated. "There's another matter, concerning Mr. Smith."

Isabel turned back to her visitor and noticed his eyes had lost their warmth. "You know where he is?"

A sick feeling started at the pit of her stomach. She sunk into the nearest chair, and her fingers curled on the chair arms. Why could David not disappear and leave her alone?

"It seems he returned to his family farm, near a small town called Brecon in Ohio," Father O'Connell said.

"How did you find out?" Helen asked.

"From his priest. He wired me this morning with news of Mr. Smith's death."

The word death hung in the air. Guilt attacked Isabel. She had never confessed how she had wished him dead and even prayed for God to intervene and strike him down. No one knew prayers seeking forgiveness followed those thoughts. Had God answered only her first prayers?

"How did he die? An accident?"

"No, Miss McIntire. Mr. Smith hung himself in his brother's barn." The priest paused and looked back at Isabel. She saw anger sweep over his face. "He left a note asking his niece Anna to forgive him. She is only ten years old."

"Ten? You mean he?" Isabel could not say the word out loud.

"The priest's letter provided the details," Father O'Connell said.

Isabel shook her head and said, "The poor child."

The memory of the scene in her bedroom where over four months ago her own daughter had pleaded her innocence tumbled forward. "Maybe what Etta said was true, and I've wronged her."

"Nonsense," Helen objected. "You did the right thing. I imagine Etta and David had been carrying on for years. Both had to leave, for the sake of decency and our family reputation."

The priest intervened. "Mrs. Smith, let me bring her back."

"Father," Isabel faltered, "Is it possible I was too hasty and rushed to judgment? Did I wrong my daughter?"

Helen did not give the priest a chance to answer. "Let's see how she reforms. If she's sincere, we can always bring her back later."

Isabel's eyes lost focus, and the room dimmed. A headache radiated from the back of her head to her temples. "I cannot decide now. If you will both pardon me."

Isabel rose, and so did Father O'Connell.

"Yes, of course," he soothed. "I'll call tomorrow."

Helen asked, "Why did the priest wire you about his death?"

"Mr. Smith wanted to be buried here in Louisville. It was part of his suicide note."

Isabel stopped at the door and turned around. His words swirled in her head. She grew weaker and held onto the door handle. "At our church?" she could barely get her question out.

"Not in hallowed ground since he is took his own life," Father O'Connell said.

Helen interrupted, "Where then?"

"Miss McIntire, he'll be buried in an unmarked pauper's grave at Cave Hill. I'll be present."

He turned to Isabel, "If you wish to attend, I'll accompany you."

"Tomorrow," was all Isabel could manage and hurried from the room.

Chapter 17

Louisville, later the same evening

William hurried into the dining room while he tightened the knot of his tie. Only his aunt was seated at the table. She made a show of checking the watch pinned on her bodice.

"Sorry I'm late, Aunt Helen."

"By two minutes," she said, "What is your excuse?"

"My volcano experiment made a lot of foam," he answered and took his seat. "I had to wash off the bench in the gazebo."

He removed the napkin ring and placed the white starched linen on his lap. "Did you smell the vinegar?" Helen shook her head and gave him a tiny smile. "Where's Momma?"

"She must still be resting," Helen answered and picked up the bell to summon Susan.

When the maid entered with three soup bowls on a tray, his aunt asked, "Has Mrs. Smith been downstairs since she lay down this afternoon?"

"No ma'am."

"Will you go check on her please?"

"Did Momma get sick?"

Helen did not answer him until Susan shut the door. "No, only a little tired," his aunt put her hand on his arm. "I want you to remember you're the man of the house now." He nodded. "Your mother had some news today about your father. Did she tell you?"

"No, I haven't seen her since lunch." He was no longer hungry. His stomach churned.

"I'm sorry, son, to be the one to tell you, but he's dead."

William looked at his aunt and tried to make sense of the news. His father was dead. The only thing he could think of was the rat he and Etta had watched drown in the rain barrel. But he sensed there was more to this word. The realization hit. He would never ever see his father again. Tears came and fell down his face.

"Don't cry, William. You need to be strong, so you can help your mother."

He wiped his cheeks with his shirtsleeve. "Nothing's the same. I want him and Etta back. I want things to be the way they were." He fought back new tears.

The dining room door opened behind William, and Susan rushed in.

"Miss Helen, something's terrible wrong with Mrs. Smith. She won't talk or move."

William looked from the maid to Aunt Helen where he saw fear cross her face. She started for the door. Without turning or stopping, she told him to stay put and asked Susan to send the gardener McConkey for Doctor Reynolds.

He obeyed and listened to the women scatter. Susan went through the kitchen and into the backyard where she screamed for the gardener to get a move on and go fetch the doctor.

In the opposite direction, his aunt's steps sounded a rapid beat on the bare wood floor. She headed up the back steps, something he never remembered her doing before.

William walked to the window to wait for the doctor's buggy to turn into the driveway. The house stilled around him. Outside the birds began their night song and the crickets called to the darkening shadows. He missed Etta more than ever and needed her here with him.

Some minutes later, he saw carriage lights come up the driveway. The emptiness of the house gave him the pricklies, and he could not tolerate the wait any longer. He crept down the hallway and toward the front stairs. He was afraid his aunt would be angry if she discovered he had disobeyed. Halfway down the hall, he found her, but there was no anger on her face, only worry.

"Come in the parlor," she said. "We need to pray for your mother."

"What did the doctor say?"

"He is still upstairs."

William followed. He left the door open and crossed to where his aunt knelt before the crucifix on the wall. He joined her and offered his own silent prayer. They were still at prayer when the doctor entered.

"Let me help you to a chair, Miss McIntire," Dr. Reynolds said. William waited until she settled and took his place beside her. The doctor took off his glasses and put them in his front vest pocket. "Mrs. Smith has been stricken with apoplexy."

William did not know what the word apoplexy meant, but his aunt must have. She mumbled another prayer and crossed herself.

The doctor continued, "Paralysis has set in on her right side. Mrs. Smith is conscious though non-responsive when I touch her right arm or leg. Her prognosis is poor. I'm truly sorry, and although it would be best if she were to go quickly, she may linger for a while."

"She'll never get better?" William asked.

"I have never seen an apoplectic recover in my thirty-two years of practice. With your aunt's good care, she may live out the summer. Pneumonia usually sets in despite the best of care. Do not look for her to live through the winter."

William looked from the doctor to his aunt. Her face had paled, and her hands gripped her rosary and trembled. He was scared. He feared he would lose his mother. "Can I see her now?"

Aunt Helen did not answer, and William repeated his question to the doctor.

"Son, only if you don't upset her or..."

William bolted from the room before the doctor finished his sentence.

~~~

Upstairs, William sat and held his mother's left hand. "We can talk this way, Momma. I'll ask you a question and you trace an x on my hand for no and a circle for yes. It'll be like a game. Do you hurt?"

Isabel drew a slow and unsteady x on his palm.

"Good, are you hungry?"

Another x.

"Are you tired?"

Isabel struggled to move her finger in a circle.

"I'll say goodnight."

William kissed his mother on her forehead and left the room.

At the same moment, Aunt Helen came through the door with her tatting. "Do not worry, son. I shall be with her all night."

"Wake me up if you need anything," he said.

"I will, my boy."

"Remember, I'm the man of the house. I can help."

"See you tomorrow."

She hugged him.

"Are you going to wire Etta and let her know about Momma?"

His aunt broke away. He noticed her mouth went straight. "No, it is better we not contact her."

"But wouldn't you want to know?"

"Quiet, you do not want to wake your momma," she whispered with a more insistent tone. With her free arm, she guided him out into the hall and shut the door. "Your sister cannot come back."

"Maybe she can help make Momma better."

"There is nothing she can do. We are all dead to her."

William shrank back from his aunt. "Etta still loves us, I know it. We're all she's got in the world. I bet if you asked, she'd come back and take all the deportment lessons you want. She'd be a lady again."

"Etta will never be a lady. She will never return to our house."

"And if Momma dies, I'll have no one. I'll be all alone."

"You will always have me."

"But I won't have Momma. I've lost Poppa and Etta. It's not the same. I want a family."

William watched her tighten her jaw and heard her sigh before she said, "These are things we have to learn to offer up. Our sufferings sanctify our souls."

~~~

The next morning William rushed to his mother's room before breakfast and found her much the same. Her mouth still drooped to the right. Susan must have taken over for his aunt. She fed Isabel with a spoon. It looked and smelled like the beef stock Cook always made for him when he was sick. His stomach lurched at the smell and memory of how awful it tasted.

Most of the food ran down her chin. After every spoonful, Susan dabbed up the tiny stream of brown liquid.

"A few more swallows, Mrs. Smith. Doctor said you must eat. Cook made this special for you. We all want you to get strong again."

"Show me how to feed Momma, Susan," William said. "I have to know how to take care of her."

The maid put down the bowl on the table beside the bed. "Come out in the hall with me."

William touched his mother's left hand and joined Susan outside the door.

"The important thing, Mr. William, is to move slow. I learned how when I took care of my granny after her stroke. I was real patient with her. You can't get frustrated cause then they get upset and might have another stroke. So you have to do everything slow, just like you have all the time in the world."

"How long did your granny live after her stroke?"

"About a month, but she was real old. But it's different with your mother. She's a strong woman."

"But the doctor said-"

"Stop, Mr. William. There's another thing I learned when I cared for my granny. Never say nothing about them not getting better. Remember, you want them to be calm. When you go back in, look at your mother's eyes. You'll see how the left one moves and follows you. I noticed it when you walked in. Your mother knew you were here before she saw you. She hears and understands everything."

"She did yesterday too," he said.

"And she can still move her left eye today. So she didn't get no worse, a good sign. Now talk with her while you feed her real easy."

William did not find any comfort in Susan's words. He thought he knew what would make his mother better. Impatient, he tried to slow down and not rush the feeding. When Susan said Momma had eaten enough gruel, he kissed his mother and told her he would be back in time for lunch.

"Where are you off to?" Susan demanded.

"Out to ride my bicycle."

"The fresh air'll probably do you some good. Be careful. Your mother doesn't need no more problems."

"I will, I promise."

"You won't get it in your head to wander off, where you're not supposed to be?"

"Uh uh," he lied and eased his conscience by crossing his fingers behind his back.

Downstairs, he grabbed his cap and some cookies before he left the house and cycled out the driveway.

Some loose gravel at the corner made his tires spin. He lost his balance and fell on the cobblestones. But he got right back on the bicycle and did not stop pumping his legs until he reached the priest house.

~~~

"Good morning, I'd like to see Father O'Connell," he said when the

133

housekeeper opened the door.

Edith looked down at him. He felt her glance take in his muddy shoes and his grass-stained knees and his skinned elbow. Then she gave him a tiny smile.

"He's not here right now. He's out visiting. I'll tell him you called for him."

She started to close the door.

"How long will he be out?"

"I can't say. Do you want to speak to one of the other priests?

William considered before he decided against talking with someone else. He did not know who to trust. In his thirteen years, he had learned grown ups had ways to find out information he thought had been secret. Even though Father O'Connell seemed trustworthy, he had to be careful. Aunt Helen might learn he was at the priest house, and he did not want to answer her questions.

"No ma'am," he answered and tipped his cap. "I'll stop by later."

~~~

Back home William changed his clothes and dashed some water on his face and hands before he headed to see Cook. After he thanked her for the big bowl with hot oats and milk, she asked, "Have fun?" and handed him a wet washcloth for his hands and elbow.

"Uh huh," he said and did a quick wipe with his fingers before he shoveled the first spoonful in his mouth. "How's Momma?"

"The same. A Mrs. McCarthy has arrived and taken charge of everything. Also Father O'Connell's here-."

"He's with Momma?" William interrupted and stood.

"No, he's been to see your mother. The nurse chased him out after a few minutes. She said he was agitating her."

"Where is he now?"

"He's in the parlor with your aunt."

William ran to find the priest.

~~~

"I forbid you," William heard his aunt's voice through the closed door, "to talk to my sister about that harlot anymore."

He opened the door and saw the two adults around the tea table. They looked up at him. His aunt's cheeks were flushed. The frown on the priest's face fled, and the man motioned him forward.

"Come join us."

William looked at his aunt who nodded. Keeping his skinned elbow out of her sight, he took a seat beside the priest.

"Have a cookie," Father O'Connell said, "You must be hungry from all your bicycle riding."

William said yes and took a sugar cookie from the plate.

"Wonderful invention," the priest went on. "Didn't have them in my day. Collecting bugs is what we did for fun. Do boys still do that?"

"Yes sir, I like the praying mantis best."

"Reminds me of the time I found a cocoon," the priest said. "Our science teacher had told us there were bugs inside such things. Have you ever found any cocoons?" William nodded his head and finished his cookie. "I was about your age when I found one. I was real careful with it. I put it in the pocket of my jacket. But by the time I returned home, I'd forgotten all about it. Do you know what happened next?"

The priest's laughter surprised William. "No, was it funny?"

"Not at the time, son. One summer morning I heard my ma start screaming. I found her in the hall closet, jumping up and down. On the floor and all over the walls were hundreds of newly hatched praying mantis."

"Shame on you, Father," Helen interrupted, "Telling the boy such a tale."

"William, I'm telling you this story so you'll be careful. I had to catch all of those little bugs and put them outside. Ma was so mad she sent me to bed without my supper."

The priest laughed again and wiped the tears from his eyes with his handkerchief.

William laughed with him and reached for another cookie, but his aunt gave her head a small shake.

The priest stuffed his handkerchief back into his trousers and said, "To this very day, I still empty my pockets every time I come into the house. Ma made it a hard and fast rule."

Right then William thought of the answer to his problem. "Father, can I bring you any special bugs I find?"

"Stop bothering the man, William," his aunt snapped. "And you mean may not can."

"It's fine, Miss Helen. William, I'd enjoy looking at your bug collection. Stop by any time."

"I'm going out to get started on finding more now."

William snuck another cookie and ran outdoors.

A few minutes later, he looked up from the garden and saw the priest head toward him. His heart pounded. He would get to do something important for his mother and sister. Father O'Connell was almost to him when his aunt came out the side door and started toward them.

"You forgot your umbrella, Father," she said.

"Thank you Miss Helen. William, you come and show me your bugs any time, but remember, no cocoons, Edith won't like it."

~~~

Etta answered the summons to Old Ghostie's office. She hoped it was about her apprenticeship. So far, she had escaped the laundry room because Fielding told her she had a talent for running a large house. Somehow, she had absorbed what to do from watching her mother and aunt. Fielding assigned her the tasks to schedule the work shifts, keep the accounts, and deal with the tradesmen.

When Etta opened the door, she noticed Matron Luttrell was also in the room. Fielding did not look any different than usual. Mrs. Luttrell, though, had a sad expression.

"Come in, my girl," Fielding said and gave Mrs. Luttrell a nod.

"Etta," the matron said. "Father O'Connell has sent you a telegram. We thought you might want to read it here."

"Willie, something's happened to him?" Etta fought down her growing fear.

"I can tell you the news isn't about him," Fielding said and rose from his chair. "I'll leave the two of you alone now."

After he closed the door behind him, Mrs. Luttrell pointed to the two visitor chairs. "Let's take a seat."

Etta took the folded paper from her and opened it. The few words told about her father. It took a few heartbeats for it to sink in and to put the pieces together.

"My father's dead. He killed himself because he treated his niece the same way he did me. She was only ten."

"I am so sorry, Etta."

"I'm not."

Etta realized fresh anger against her father was building like a volcano. She stared out the window behind Fielding's desk and enjoyed the strength the anger gave her.

"I'm so glad he can't hurt any more girls." She appreciated Mrs. Luttrell's silence and touch on her hand. "I was so scared he'd find me here and…" She could not finish.

"You're beyond his reach now. I know you don't believe me, but you'll recover. With God's help, you'll become a strong woman."

"Maybe Momma will let me come back home now?"

"You can hope. My advice, though, is to plan your future here in Frankfort."

~~~

After lunch, William pounded up the backstairs to see his mother and found Mrs. McCarthy on guard outside the door.

"You must be William," the thin woman said with her hands folded before her white apron.

He looked at her and did not like her. Except for her white apron and cap she was dressed all in black, like his aunt. Her face also wore a frown, much like Aunt Helen's.

"Yes, ma'am," he said.

Through the open door, he could see his mother's hand at rest on the bedspread.

"Young man, this is a sick room. You may visit before dinner for no more than ten minutes."

"Yes ma'am."

"Also it's good manners to knock and wait to be told to open the door. You must not enter her room until you are invited. Understand?"

William agreed. "But since I'm here, can I see her now?"

Just as Edith had a few hours before at the priest house, this woman's stern look melted. He smiled at her and knew he had won when her hand ruffled his soft curls.

"For a few minutes. Don't wake her up."

William walked around the nurse to the bed. Momma looked so still he feared she must be dead until he saw her eye quiver. He leaned over and gave her a kiss.

"I'll see you later, Momma, I hope with good news," he whispered so the watchful Mrs. McCarthy, knitting on the other side of the bed, could not hear.

On the way out of the room, he remembered his manners. "Thank you, ma'am. I'll be back before dinner."

She returned his smile.

~~~

Outside in the garden, William tried to find some interesting bugs to show Susan or his aunt. One of them would have to give him permission to visit the priest. Luck was not with him. He had only one green caterpillar so far. The wind stirred and blew dust. Its speed increased until the undersides of the leaves turned up. He knew this sure sign of rain would bring his aunt out to the side porch. She was so afraid of thunder and lightening.

A few minutes later he heard her. "William, stop dawdling. A storm is brewing. Come in right now."

He looped his net to keep the caterpillar from escaping and turned to look at her. A huge clap of thunder rumbled. Lightening zigzagged across the darkening, growing thunderheads. His aunt jumped and edged back toward the door.

"Let go of whatever you have in your net," she called through cupped hands.

He obeyed. After putting his catch on a leaf, he headed to the porch steps.

"Tomorrow will be better for bug hunting," she said and held the screen door open. He walked in and propped his net near the door.

"You're right, I'll go to the park. I must've chased all the goods ones away."

"Tomorrow is going to be better than the park. You will go to the Falls in the morning. Your Uncle James and Aunt Elizabeth will be by early after breakfast."

"I don't want to leave Momma all day."

"She would want you to go. You know you will have such fun with Ian and the rest of your cousins."

William recognized the jut of his aunt's jaw and knew there was no arguing with her. Tomorrow he would just have to catch lots of bugs. Maybe his cousins would help.

"Okay, I'll go," he agreed and with his next words, planted the seed for his plan.

"Maybe I'll find something interesting to show Father O'Connell."

Chapter 18

Louisville, May 30, 1874

William, reluctant and fearful of leaving his mother, climbed into his uncle's buggy for a picnic. He felt guilty about the day at the Falls. His mother was so sick and had only his aunt for company.

But Aunt Helen had seen through his pretend upset stomach at breakfast and told him he was going. He did not have to have fun, but he was spending the day with his cousins.

The finger wagging and the shoulds followed. He should be grateful he was healthy. He should be happy the family, and he knew she did not mean his sister and father, were reunited. He should offer a prayer of thankfulness that God had given them a wonderful day with no hint of rain. William surrendered.

At the Falls, he and cousins Ian and Michael captured a variety of insects which included giant dragonflies and a few ambush bugs. After they reached the one hundred count, they put the jars of bugs under a tree. The rest of the day he swam and ate his favorites his aunts had brought just for him, velvet cake, ambrosia salad, and honey-fried chicken. Aunt Helen had been right. He did enjoy being with his cousins again. Plus he had a bounty of squirming and crawling bugs he could show the priest tomorrow.

~~~

The next morning, his aunt would not let him take even the best ambush bug to Sunday Mass. He had to come up with another way to see the priest. During the service, his attention was on his problem, not the liturgy. When he walked out of the church a few hours later, he stopped and waited until Father O'Connell finished talking with the family in front of him.

At last William had the chance to ask his question, "Will you be eating with us today?"

"Not this week, young man. Miss Helen, I believe the Ladies Sodality has me scheduled at your house sometime in July."

"Yes Father, we have your new assistant today."

William knew better than ask if the priests could trade dates. His aunt was in charge of the Sodality again this year, and no one ever changed what they planned.

The day seemed to drag on. He had to stay in his good clothes until the young priest left in the early afternoon. When he checked on the bugs before supper, about twenty had died. He threw them away and transferred the rest of the ambush bugs into a separate jar. By bedtime, five more in the big jar had died.

His evening prayers asked for his mother's recovery, Etta's return home, peace for his father's soul, and help in keeping some of the most interesting bugs alive overnight.

~~~

William woke up at daybreak and pulled his outdoor clothes from under the bed. A few minutes later, he joined Cook in the kitchen.

"Master William, you're up with the birds alright and look ready for the woods," she said after she turned from the stove.

When he got closer, she bent down and frowned. "Aren't those the clothes you wore to the picnic?"

She straightened and put her hands on her hips. "Why didn't they go down the laundry chute?"

"Cause they're clean enough to wear one more time."

"What's going on?"

"I got to show Father O'Connell my bugs this morning before they all die. Can I have a piece of bread?"

"Your momma wouldn't want you going off without a good breakfast," she shook her head and stuffed some more wood in the stove.

"You wait til I get the fire agoing. You need some food that'll stick to your ribs."

"Please," he moved closer and touched her arm. "I'll eat more when I come back, I promise. Let me go now before the good ones die."

Her look softened. "Deal. I'll have a good breakfast of sausage and eggs, maybe even some angel biscuits ready."

His stomach growled, and he swallowed the saliva in his mouth.

"With some apple butter?"

"I'll open a fresh jar for you. Now take this hunk of bread to tide you over. Make sure you eat it before you touch those filthy bugs. No telling where all they've been and what diseases they're acarryin."

William thanked her and gulped the bread while he ran toward the shed. Within two minutes, he had shaken out the dead insects and headed out with ten good specimens of ambush bugs and three dragonflies. He added his net to his jars and rushed downtown to the priest house where the housekeeper opened the door.

"You again," she said. "It's too early to be visiting. Go home and come back later this morning."

"Please Miss Edith." William tried his most innocent look and took off his cap. For some reason he never understood, women never told him no when they saw his curly hair. "I promised Father O'Connell he could see any new bugs I found, and most of them have died, and more will die if I have to wait." The housekeeper did not shut the door, and her frown weakened. "I promise I won't take a lot of time. I understand Father is busy."

Out came her hand toward his head. She, like most women, ruffled his hair and smiled. "Only five minutes. Go around back and mind what you do. I don't want those bugs loose in my clean house."

William waited on the back porch and shuffled his weight from one foot to the other. He could not stand still. His mission was too important.

The door creaked open, and the priest came out, a big grin on his face.

"All this talk of bugs makes me feel young again. You brought me some unusual bugs, have you son?"

"Yes sir, a few, most of the good ones died. The ambush bugs ate parts of them."

William held up his jar. "This is what I have left."

"Let's sit on the back step here. I promised Edith none would escape and come into the house. She reminds me of my mother. Did I ever tell you the story about the praying mantis cocoon hatching out in my house when I was a boy?"

William fought against his impatience and remembered his manners. "Yes, you said you had to go to bed without your supper."

"Good memory, now let me see what treasures you have."

William handed over the jar.

"Can anyone hear us out here?"

"Only God. Edith's busy in the dining room serving my fellow priests."

Father O'Connell put down the jar and looked at William. "What do you want to talk to me about?"

At last, William thought, someone understands. "My mother," he said.

"William, I'm truly sorry. I'm praying for her. Are you?"

"Yes, but there's another reason I'm here." William considered how he wanted to say his next thought. "Will you tell Aunt Helen what I tell you?"

"I can't answer until I hear what it is."

William studied the man's face before making his decision. After a deep breath, he said, "I don't want Aunt Helen to know I'm here."

The priest did not say anything. William went on.

"I haven't had the chance to ask her yet, but I think Momma really misses Etta and wants her back

"Your mother can speak?"

"With her hands." William explained their system.

"Now Mrs. McCarthy's there, and I can't ask her. Aunt Helen would be angry if she heard me. But if Etta comes back home, I know Momma would get better, and the three of us will all be together again."

Tears came to his eyes, and he wiped them away. "You remember Poppa?" The priest nodded. "I know," William said, "I'm not supposed to talk about him, but I still miss him." He ran his sleeve over his eyes again.

"Here's what I am going to do," Father O'Connell said. "I'll finish my breakfast. You go back home and wait. Understand?" William nodded. "Your house will be the first place I go today."

~~~

It took forty-five minutes for Father O'Connell to arrive. William tried not to show how nervous he was when the priest gave Susan his hat and asked to see Mrs. Smith. William then fell in behind the black-clad man as he led the way upstairs.

In his mother's room, Mrs. McCarthy had left, and his aunt was there with her embroidery and knitting on a table next to her chair. William tugged on the priest's coattail.

Father O'Connell turned around and patted his shoulder. "Trust me, my boy," he said in a low voice. "Good morning ladies. How are you,

Mrs. Smith?"

"She's about the same, Father," Aunt Helen answered for his mother.

The priest pulled up another chair on Isabel's left side. "Miss Helen, I can be here for a little while. May I offer you a respite?"

"Thank you, no. I arrived only a few minutes ago." Aunt Helen put her knitting in her lap. "Since you're here, I'd like to speak with you about the Ladies' Sodality and their altar flowers."

His aunt began a long complaint about how her flowers were at their peak this week, and she was not scheduled to place her floral arrangements on the altar until next month. For some reason, Mrs. Fleming would not trade, and it was probably because her own asters were in full bloom this week.

William grew more anxious. How was Father going to get his aunt out of the room? William moved behind her chair and shrugged when he had the priest's attention.

"Would you be willing, Miss Helen, to take charge of arranging flowers for the entrance hall? I can have a table put by the front steps."

"What size table? I would have to bring the correct linen."

"I know how important this is. Maybe you should go over to the priest house now and ask Edith to help you find a table you like, to ensure you'd have the size you prefer."

"I really should stay here," she said and checked the watch pinned to her bodice. "Mrs. McCarthy is due to return in thirty minutes."

"I'll stay with Mrs. Smith until you or Mrs. McCarthy returns." The priest patted his pockets. "Do you have some paper I may use to write Edith a quick note to explain?"

His aunt showed the priest where his mother kept her paper and pen. After a few minutes, his aunt left with her note. William heard the priest say something about Edith forgiving him. But he did not understand what the man meant.

When William took his aunt's place, he looked at his mother's face. Something had gone from her eyes since he had visited in the morning.

Father O'Connell looked at him and shook his head. "I'm afraid we won't be able to ask your mother any questions, my son. Sit and wait while I anoint her and offer a prayer."

William listened to the Latin words and gave up hope. Momma was going to die, and Etta was lost forever. He tried to keep the tears from coming but could not.

After he said amen, the priest suggested, "Let's go find Mrs. McCarthy, and you can see me out."

~~~

Isabel floated in and out of awareness. Some of the priest's words made sense, others did not. She thought William held her hand and wanted to tell him how much she loved him. She strained to make her finger move but could not.

The woman with the soothing hands bathed the left side of her face. There were soft words and a warm dry towel. She drifted until Helen's voice woke her.

The words "relieve you" crept through her fog. Isabel fought to clear the thoughts jumbled in her head. She had to tell her sister something, something from long ago, a promise they had made after their father died.

Helen touched her cheek, and Isabel tried to open her eyes.

"I remember, we agreed," Helen said.

A single tear fell, and something soft crossed her face and stayed. Memories flashed. William in the crib at St. Jerome's. Etta wreathed in sunlight and singing to her doll. And a song from long ago. Darkness followed.

Chapter 19

Frankfort, June 4, 1874

Etta had almost finished the inventory in the storeroom when Mrs. Luttrell found her. "You have a visitor, a Father O'Connell. He'd like to see you in Mr. Fielding's office." Happiness bubbled through her, and she asked, "Has he come for me, to take me home?"

"I don't know. Hurry on up. I'll take over here."

Etta rushed up the stairs. Maybe her prayers had come true. Maybe Momma had at last reconsidered.

"I'll be good Momma. I promise I'll never do anything wrong again," she whispered and knocked on the closed office door. Before there was an answer from Father O'Connell, she had the door open.

"Am I going home? Has Momma sent you to take me home? Please tell me yes."

"Take a seat, child," Father O'Connell said. She obeyed and sat across the desk from him. The priest looked sad and had a tired expression. "I don't have good news for you."

"Is it Willie, is he dead?"

"Not your brother. The sad news is your mother passed away, suddenly, a few days ago."

"Momma?" She sat and tried to breathe, but her lungs did not work. "Momma? What happened to her? An accident?"

"Your mother had a stroke and lingered only a little. She died peacefully."

"Did she say anything about me? Or ask for me at the end?"

"She couldn't talk at all. I'm so sorry. You should take comfort in knowing your mother is no longer suffering."

Etta shuddered. Inside so little strength remained, but she realized someone had to take care of her brother.

"I've got to get home, Willie needs me." As tears overcame her, she gave into them.

Father O'Connell sat and waited until she blew her nose and looked back at him.

"I need you to listen," he said. "I've watched you from the time you arrived at St. Jerome's, and you've always been determined, sometimes a little too much. Now it's your greatest strength. Use it. God gave you your temperament for a reason."

"What next? What am I to do now?"

"You stay here. Remember, we had planned on you staying until you turned eighteen?"

"But I really thought Momma loved me enough that I could go back. I guess she didn't, did she?"

The priest seemed to weigh his words before he spoke again. "The only advice I can give you is to look forward, not backward. My prayers will ask that you have a blessed future with your new life here in Frankfort."

After he left, Etta returned to the dormitory upstairs. Her heart was so heavy, and her slow steps dragged on the wooden floor. Somehow, she kept moving toward the secret hideaway Lavinia had pointed out a few weeks after her arrival. A recess in the corner under the stairs hid a panel which opened up to the attic.

Her friend's words echoed after she crawled through the opening.

"Sometimes it all gets too much, and you need a place to be by yourself. Sophie and I are the only ones who come in here. We've fixed it up with some old pillows and carpets. It can be yours as well. But don't tell anyone else."

Etta reached the sunlit vent in the gable. To block the light, she hung a faded paisley drape, donated by a rich woman during the board's clothing drive last year. Drained, she curled up on the red velvet pillow Sophie had made from an old dress.

In the quiet space, Etta permitted her grief to visit and engulf her every part. Grief not only from her mother's sudden death. But from all her losses, her father's abuse, her brother lost to her forever. With this latest blow, the dream she would eventually return to her childhood home evaporated and added another layer of pain.

These losses spiraled into her earliest sorrows. Leaving Sister Justina at the orphanage. The unresolved misery of not knowing who her real parents were and why they abandoned her. Life had become too much and was not worth the struggle to continue. She cried until she had no tears left.

Her friends woke her when it was time for supper. She was still curled in a ball. Her eyes felt swollen, and the pillow under her face was soaked.

"We're so sorry Etta." Lavinia knelt and hugged her. "We heard Ghostie telling Old Lute about your mother. Don't worry. We won't tell anyone."

"We knew you were different the first time we saw you. Anyone could see you came from quality," Sophie whispered.

"You don't understand. I've lost everything," Etta answered through her tears.

"It's the shock," Lavinia said. "It takes time to get over."

Etta heard the dinner bell. "Leave me alone, go eat."

Lavinia got up from the floor. "Etta, we'll be back. I'll try to sneak some food out for you. Maybe Lute will look the other way."

"I'll put some bread in my pocket for you," Sophie said.

Etta listened to them leave. The girls moved to the panel and down the steps. Their fading footsteps caused her to feel more abandoned than ever.

~~~

The outside light behind the drape had darkened when Etta heard her friends return. Lavinia had an oil lamp. Sophie carried a tray covered with a napkin. It smelled like ham and potatoes.

"Look what Lute allowed us to bring you." Sophie sat the tray before her and removed the napkin.

Etta felt her stomach rumble in hunger.

"You're the cause of a miracle," Lavinia said and knelt beside her. "I don't remember she ever let food out of the dining room before."

"Matron Luttrell broke a rule, one of her own," Sophie said.

Etta sat up and looked at her two friends. "I'm sorry I was so mean to you before. You're my best friends."

"See, you're not really alone after all. You have us." Sophie poured some coffee from a small pot.

"First things first, Etta," Lavinia said. "You've got to eat even if you're not hungry. That's one of the best lessons you learn when you're on your own." She raised the lamp wick. The shadows retreated.

"You never know when your next meal will come." Sophie said as she looked over the plate. "So eat some of this food. When you're ready, we've got some ideas."

Etta ate about half before Lavinia, at last, let her stop and instructed, "Wrap your bread and put it in your pocket, for later. It'll keep for several days."

Sophie moved the tray to the side and said, "Now let's get started on your future."

"I don't have a future," Etta moaned. "Everything is ruined."

"Nonsense, you have a future," Lavinia answered. "I'm sorry the one you wanted isn't the one you're going to get. But you have to ask yourself, do I take what comes my way or do I make the future I want."

Etta considered her friend's words and felt a slight bit of hope. "Like you want to own a hat shop?"

"Exactly, and Sophie wants to own her own bakery. It won't be easy to get. But we know we have to plan and work toward them. You can too."

Etta was torn between envy and despair. They seemed to have their lives all worked out. Did they really have the right idea? But it was so much easier to sit here and not think or even move.

Lavinia touched her arm, and Etta forced herself to focus on her friend's question. "Have you ever had to work hard for something? Not some chore you had to do and got paid for it. But maybe something almost impossible?"

"Yes," Etta answered and smiled a little. She remembered the princess dresses and her singing lessons.

"Good," Sophie replied. "So you know how to work. That'll make it easier," she said the last to Lavinia who nodded.

"What's this idea you've got?"

"We all vow today we'll help each other," Sophie said.

"Now and even after we leave this place. We'll be sisters for the rest of our lives," Lavinia promised.

Etta wavered. A retreat into grief and a slow death seemed less work than what her friends talked about.

Lavinia's words pulled her back. "Keep your lost dream of returning home. But if you stop and think about it, you'll realize it was never going to happen anyway. When you walked through those big doors downstairs, you had already left your old life behind."

At first, Etta shuddered at the truth in these words but soon decided her friends had offered wisdom. Her future was here, in Frankfort, with them. Louisville was gone forever. Father O'Connell was right. She did have strength and determination. She willed her tears to stop and closed her heart to the past.

Chapter 20

Frankfort, July 2, 1874

Almost a month after the priest's visit, Etta returned to Fielding's office.

"I have some good news for you," he said. "Thomas Caldwell has an opening at his boarding house."

He gave her a small smile. It was the first time she had ever seen him look even a little happy. "He wants to offer you an apprenticeship. Both Matron Luttrell and I gave you a good recommendation."

"So I have to leave here?" Etta was torn. Though she wanted to be free of living at the Home, she did not want to leave her friends.

"You'll work eight hours a day over the summer. In September, you'll go to school in the morning and the boarding house in the afternoon. Mr. Caldwell agrees with me. You must complete your education."

Etta realized the austere side of Mr. Fielding was back. "Evenings you'll spend here."

"Will I be earning money?"

"No, an apprenticeship is for training, not earning. But I'll pay you for five hours a week if you continue to help me an hour an evening with the accounts."

"How long is my apprenticeship?"

"It will run until December of seventy-seven," Fielding tried another smile. "At which time, you'll have an education and some valuable job experience."

He slid the contract across the desk and handed her a pen. Etta took it and signed her next three years away. "I recommend you make the most of this opportunity. Because the state legislature meets here, there'll always be the need for boarding houses and people to run them. Some of the newer legislators have to stay in private residences because all the rooms are already taken. Who knows, one of these day you may have your own boarding house."

~~~

Etta joined the staff at Caldwell's, and after awhile, fear of failing her apprenticeship vanished. For the first time she could remember in her life, she had moments of serenity. Yet she never let her guard down. Something, out of her control, could happen and take her happiness away. So she told herself not to trust anyone, certainly none of the male boarders.

Her anger occasionally led to flare-ups, and she went head to toe with anyone, who, according to her, needed it. More than one time she had lashed out at a butcher for shorting her on an order and taken overfriendly salesmen to task when they cornered young chambermaids in the hallway.

In November, a new boarder arrived. Owen Murphy had hair almost as red as hers and hazel eyes full of good humor. His hands and body frame told her he had not done hard physical work. He did not have the hardscrabble lean look farmers had.

She understood when she found out he worked at McCords' music store. His job was to play sheet music, so customers could decide if they wanted to purchase the songs to play at home. During his free evenings, he would use the piano in the front parlor of the boarding house to practice the new songs. Etta would sometimes sing the lyrics as he mastered the music scores. Occasionally, he would indulge her and play parts of her favorite opera.

It took almost a month before Lavinia and Sophie discovered the source of the new songs she sang during the supper shift at the Home. They pestered her for details about the new stranger.

One evening in early December they surprised her. One evening in early December they dropped by the boarding house to walk her home and surprised Owen and Etta at the piano.

The moment Etta led them out the back door of the boarding house, Sophie grabbed her arm and said, "He's so tall and handsome, I adore full mustaches, don't you, Etta."

"He's good looking," Etta said and noticed her friend's face fell a little. "But we're friends, truly."

"But how can you not be in love with him?" Sophie asked.

"I don't have time for such foolishness," she answered.

"I seem to remember you have time to flirt though," Lavinia reminded her.

"It's fun to watch what a look or word can do."

"Yeah, just so they don't get to the point of dueling like those two salesmen a month ago," Lavinia said, and Etta saw her friend had lost her good humor.

"I know, I've learned from my mistake." She gave Lavinia a playful nudge.

"I hope so. That almost cost you your apprenticeship."

Etta sobered. Losing her chance at Caldwell's was not in her plans of becoming independent. "I learned not to flirt so flamboyantly, didn't I?"

"Is it okay, Etta," Sophie broke in, "If I chase Owen until he catches me?"

"As long as we can all still be friends. I don't want to lose either one of you."

~~~

The path of Sophie's and Owen's courtship advanced and entertained her. Sophie flirted with Owen, and within a few weeks, he was smitten. He changed the lyrics of some of the popular songs to include Sophie's name while Sophie for her part baked special little cakes for him.

By spring Lavinia and Daniel had decided to marry when she finished her apprenticeship at the dress shop. Etta also suspected Owen and Sophie discussed marriage.

But she had no romantic interest in any man though several had expressed interest in her. She did not like the way they made her feel when they talked and let their eyes roam below her neck. It seemed they were more interested in her body than who she was.

The legislators, she knew, were mostly married, and though she was beautiful, she realized she was not worth any scandal.

From the hints the businessmen dropped, they seemed willing to walk out with her. Yet Etta did not even consider a future with any man who traveled so much and had so many opportunities for dalliances.

Etta faced the facts. Frankfort was a small town, and the few out-of-town girls who arrived at the Home carried a whiff of disgrace and shame. Since she was one of those, it was unlikely any respectable family would let her marry one of their sons. She was a social pariah, without a proper pedigree.

Chapter 21

Frankfort, April 16, 1876

To nineteen-year-old Ben Darnell, it seemed everyone's eyes were on him while he strode over the wooden sidewalk. He felt every bit a farm boy, smack dab by the state capital building and surrounded by fancy folk.

Ben almost turned around and headed back to the train station. He was scared, almost as much as the time he was eleven and deep into the woods, alone and without his parents' permission. He tracked the wild cat which had killed his favorite dog. His anger melted into fear the farther he advanced on the cat's trail.

The moral from this memory, he now told himself, was fear can make a man perform better. His tracking and shooting had paid off. At the end of the day, he had satisfaction when one careful shot felled the animal.

This time was different, however. He was older. More important, he did have his parents' permission, but only because his mother had been his strong ally. She had stood up to his father and insisted he give his son enough money to start a farming store and a letter of credit.

Lord knows his old man could afford it. He had spent the years after the war snapping up one farm after another in the tax sales until he was one of the richest farmers in three counties. But no one could tell by how the family dressed or lived. The old skinflint was tight as a tick with his money.

Ben's woolgathering made him bump into a man in front of a store. After he tipped his hat and begged the man's pardon, Ben tried to get his bearings. The tall buildings, three and four stories high, confused him. He wondered why here, in the big city of Frankfort, people walked faster and how they seemed to know where they were going and what they were doing.

At the corner, the Farmers Bank stood with marble columns

supporting an impressive portico. Though the bank intimidated him, Ben forced himself to go up the concrete steps and pass by the columns and into the lobby.

Inside was an elegance he had never imagined. The dark carpet hushed his steps. Employees scurried behind the grated windows and desks in back of the polished railings. The people reminded him of the bees in his father's hives.

Ben stood uncertain. Did he go to one of those barred windows or approach a dark suited man at a desk? He was almost ready to retreat when a young boy, about fifteen-years-old, asked if he could help. Dry-mouthed, Ben took out his letter of credit and showed it to him.

"You'll be wanting Mr. Trimble," the boy said. "He's the loan officer. Right this way, sir."

Sir, no one had ever called him sir before. Ben regained some confidence and followed the boy to a desk, close by the opened vault. He took a seat and waited.

"I understand you want a loan, Mr.?" a short man with a well-trimmed beard and clean spectacles said and took the chair behind the desk.

"Darnell, Mr. Trimble."

"Any relation to a Mr. Reuben Darnell of Fayette County?"

"My father, sir."

"Mr. Darnell, let me say how pleased I am you have chosen Farmers Bank. We'll do right by you."

Within five minutes, Trimble approved the loan application and even directed him to several vacant stores on the lower end of Main Street. He wrote out the names and addresses of the landlords and told him what a fair rental would be.

It took several hours to inspect the stores and close the deal for the one he wanted. His choice was the one nearest to the rail depot. He signed the rent contract, shook hands with the landlord, and put the key in his vest pocket.

Pleased with his business accomplishments so far, he walked more slowly through the two rooms. The front windows were flyspecked, and the amount of dirt and dead bugs in the corners told him it had been vacant longer than the six months the landlord had said. Probably more like eighteen months Ben thought. No problem though. He was not afraid of hard work. He knew how to clean.

Over the next hour, he planned his displays and drew up his supply list while he sat on a rickety chair and rested his feet on another one. Sore and throbbing, his feet let him know he had met with more paved roads and sidewalks today than in his whole life put together.

When his stomach growled, it reminded him he needed to find something to eat. He put his feet down, stood and stretched, and looked around his new store before leaving. He heard the key turn the tumblers in the door with a real sense of pride and gave the knob a twist to ensure the lock had caught.

Ben set off, satchel in hand, away from the railroad tracks, back toward downtown, full of purpose. At the end of the block, the scent of sugar wafted from an open door. He had found a bakery. Inside he chose six cinnamon cookies and coffee. The clerk pointed out a bench shaded by a large maple. He stopped there and wolfed down the crisp cookies so like his mother's.

A church bell pealed out a few notes before it rang the hour of four. Ben pushed himself off the bench. He had to get a move on and find a place to board. He walked along Anne Street in search of Caldwell's Boarding House, top on the list of four the banker had recommended.

Ben found the house halfway down the street. He was glad he had the address since there was no sign on the fence advertising rooms to let. The white clapboard house, three stories high, included a wrap around porch with rocking chairs ringing the house. A dark roof crowned the dormer windows. The paint looked a few years old. After he figured how much paint it would take, he stopped himself from estimating how much time it would take to do it right two years from now. He had to remember he was no longer a farmer.

When he opened the wooden gate, an entrancing voice drew him as gently and surely as a silken net. He had never before heard a voice this angelic and pure. The voice was an instrument and somehow reminded him of something stolen from him, the theft unrecognized until this moment. Enchanted, he had to discover the source.

Ben burst into the parlor and with his satchel, thumped down into the nearest chair. The song and piano music stopped. Tongue-tied, he gazed at the woman who stood behind the man at the piano. Ben stuttered his request. Would the angel before him continue?

"Do we go on, Etta?" the man asked after he cleared his throat.

"Please," Ben requested and registered he was looking into the greenest eyes he had ever seen.

"We'll finish up, Owen," the woman named Etta said and returned to her sheet music.

Too soon they ended their performance. Ben stood and tried to repair his social gaucheness. "You must think I have the manners of a mule. My momma would be just so upset with me. Please accept my apology for barging in here."

"Welcome to Frankfort, Mr.?" the woman said.

"Darnell. I'm new in town. I arrived this morning and need rooms. Do you have any available, Mrs. Caldwell?"

"We have a few. But I'm not the owner. My name is Miss Smith."

"And you're Mr. Caldwell?" Ben asked the piano player.

"No, wrong again," the man smiled and shook hands. "I'm Owen Murphy. I live here and work downtown at McCord's. You'll like this place. It's the best boarding house in town. The food is good and plentiful."

"Mr. Darnell, let me show you our rooms."

"Are you finished with your practice? I can wait if you're not."

"Yes, it's time to get back to work," Etta said to Ben after she touched Owen on the shoulder. "The rooms are this way, Mr. Darnell."

He struggled to answer her questions on the way up the stairs but was still spellbound with fog swirling in his brain.

Etta said, "We offer rooms on a monthly basis. Will you be staying that long?"

"Longer."

"Are you the new Methodist minister?"

She stopped and appraised him in his worn suit.

"No, a store, I mean, I'm looking to set up a store."

"Ah, well, the best available room's on the third floor, number thirty-eight."

He was so lost in her eyes that he had nothing to say.

"Would you like to see it?" she asked.

"Yes," he mumbled before he was able to ask why it was the best.

"The other two are on the second floor where the legislators stay. They'll corner you in the bathroom. They won't let up until they've talked you to death."

"That sounds good, Miss Smith."

He liked the word Miss. It was best news of the day. Until he remembered the piano player in the parlor. His heart sunk. She might already be taken.

They reached the third floor. Ben looked down the hallway and saw four plain wooden chairs lined up along the walls.

"Why the chairs?" he asked.

"Mrs. Caldwell thinks there won't be so many visitors for her boarders if they take the hardback chairs into their room. No drinking and gambling going on is what she says. Here we are."

Etta opened a small room with a single bed. He saw a room with a single bed and without one extra frill.

"You can see," Etta said, "the light is good, and it does capture any breeze going by during the summer months if you leave your door open."

"I don't understand Mrs. Caldwell's concern about visitors. There's not enough space for any carousing," Ben laughed and walked inside.

He paused to look around at the bed under the window and the clothes press along the opposite wall. A small walnut washstand with a basin and pitcher on its marble top stood on the third wall.

"If I had any visitor, he'd have to put his chair in the center of the room."

Etta explained, "Most of our guests socialize elsewhere. Mrs. Caldwell doesn't allow any women visitors up here at all. Female callers sit in the parlor, and Mrs. Caldwell prefers they be your mother or sister."

She gave him a smile so dazzling his heart melted. "Will you be having any female visitors, Mr. Darnell?"

Ben found himself smiling back at her. He noticed for the first time a small dimple on her cheek and felt his face go red. Sweat popped out on his forehead. Was it possible she was not taken with Owen what's his name?

"Only my mother, Miss Smith," he managed to answer.

"Mrs. Caldwell will be happy. She runs what she calls a proper and moral establishment. You'll have breakfast and dinner with a clean room and bed for $3.00 a week, paid by the month in advance. Lunches are extra."

"Sounds reasonable, are there any other rules?"

"Don't be late for a meal. There are rarely any scraps left," she smiled her glorious smile again. "Then you'll either go hungry til the next day or have to eat in one of the taverns down on High Street."

"Any more rules?"

She shook her head, and a curl sprung free. He watched it fall behind her ear and rest on the collar of her white blouse.

"I forgot, just one more rule. If you're out past nine in the evening, you'll find the door locked. Mrs. Caldwell believes nothing good ever happens past nine at night. You're out that late, you sleep somewhere else."

Ben thought he had better put a cot in the back storeroom in case he had to work late. This room did not offer enough space for him to do his accounts. At this moment, though, he did not care if the windows leaked.

"I'll take it."

"You don't want to see the others?"

"No, this one's fine. I trust you, Miss Smith."

~~~

"Owen tells me there's a new handsome boarder at Caldwell's, one with blond hair and blue eyes," Sophie said to Etta as the three friends were on their way to school.

"I heard he's really tall and has broad shoulders," Lavinia joined in.

Etta willed her blush to go away and walked a little faster. "He must mean Mr. Darnell," she answered and gave up the battle with her blush.

Sophie said, "He moved in two weeks ago, and you didn't tell us a thing about him, not a word."

"Ah, now I understand the new hair ribbons you started wearing last week," Lavinia teased. "Come on, tell us all about him, or we will just have to go to his grand opening and see for ourselves."

"You know, we'd certainly look out of place at a farm store," Sophie joined in.

"You have to promise," Etta said, "you especially, Sophie, not to tell anyone."

"We do," both answered in unison.

Etta was bursting to talk about Ben. "He seems so different from the other boarders. I mean, he's not polished like the politicians and businessmen, and he seems honest. You can tell he's worked outside. He's got freckles all over his nose. And his poor hands are covered in scars and calluses. He says he earned them from wrong moves with barbed wire and sharp tools."

Etta saw her friends wink at each other. "What is it?"

"Nothing, nothing at all," Lavinia said.

"Owen says he's working hard to get his store open, and..."

"What else, Sophie?" Etta demanded.

"Ben asks him a lot of questions about you."

"Such as?"

"Are you walking out with anyone, what's your favorite color, are you going to continue working at Caldwell's after graduation?"

Lavinia interrupted, "He sounds interested in you."

"Would you like Owen to speak to him about the graduation party

Old Lute's planning for us?" Sophie offered.

"No, I can't invite him. It wouldn't be proper. But maybe you could hint to Owen I'd like the chance to get to know him better?"

~~~

Etta waited for one long month. Ben was friendly but remained silent about calling on her. It was all she could do to not grab him by the lapels and ask why not.

"Owen," Etta sat down on the piano bench after she and Owen finished their music practice. "What's taking him so long?"

"I think he's shy and deliberate."

"How long is it going to take? I know he's interested because he goes out of his way at dinner to tell me about some funny thing that happened to him. When I'm on the porch after dinner, he comes by and talks. He's even underfoot when we practice on Sundays while Mrs. Caldwell's visiting her sister. You have to talk with him again."

"Why?" Owen crossed his arm.

The smile he gave back infuriated her. "Because I can't take the suspense any longer, that's why."

"All right," he laughed. "I'll mention the saying about a faint heart never won a fair lady."

"You could mention the town concert next Sunday in the park."

"And tell him if he doesn't speak up soon, you'll kill him." He turned and started towards the hall. Etta heard him laugh all the way to his room upstairs.

"Men," Etta said, and stormed out of the boarding house to return to the Home.

~~~

Three days later, Etta had just stacked the afternoon tea things onto a tray to carry them to the kitchen when Owen joined her in the parlor.

"The concert's only four days away," she hissed. "Did you talk with him?" Owen reached for a biscuit on a plate and nodded. "What'd he say?" Etta said.

Instead of an answer, Owen stuffed a biscuit dripping with apple butter into his mouth. With exasperating slowness, he wiped the crumbs from his fingers. She struggled to keep her temper under control.

"He didn't exactly say yes, but he didn't say no either." Owen poured some coffee before continuing. "I told you he's a deliberate man, Etta. He's going to have to work up his courage."

Etta lost the battle with her temper. "Are your ears full of wax? Are you sure you understood him? Did you mumble?"

"Give it one more day. Plan on coming with Sophie and me anyway, and I'll make sure he shows up at the park and finds us. Don't worry. Ben can't be hurried. He's a steady one. Remember, he likes to plan and think."

"Oh, I don't have the patience to wait." Etta stomped her foot.

"Well, Princess Storm Cloud," he warned. "Here comes your prince up the sidewalk."

He took her by the arm and guided her toward the parlor. "You don't want him to see you with fire coming out of your eyes, do you? That's better, smile and look happy, and practice this new score."

Both turned to say hello to Ben when he walked in.

"Etta," Ben asked, "Are you ill? Your color's high."

"No, she's a little taken by the heat," Owen answered. "Make her sit down. I'll go fetch a glass of water. Will you keep her company until I return?"

Owen did not even wait for a reply. He headed toward the kitchen.

"Do you need a fan?" Ben asked. "It's quite close in here this evening, isn't it?"

"I'm a little bothered by the heat. I find it cooler outdoors, don't you?"

"Yes, matter of fact, I…I'm thinking of going to the park on Sunday for the concert. Would you like to go, with me, I mean?"

"Yes, thank you Ben, I would," Etta smiled at him and hoped she did not seem too eager. "The newspaper promised the music would be entertaining."

"I think the company will be even better."

Her heart quickened when his fingers traced a light touch along her wrist.

~~~

"What are you going to wear?" Lavinia asked the following afternoon when Etta stopped in the dress shop.

"I don't have anything new, and I haven't finished my blue dress yet."

"How much more do you have to do?"

"I can't move on to the lace trim until I get the right sleeve in. I've taken it out three times already. One more time, and I'll rip the dress into rags or be daring and wear it sleeveless."

"Sophie and I will come over after work and help you the next few nights. It can't be as bad as all of that," Lavinia laughed. "Etta, no one wears sleeveless dresses."

~~~

Two nights later, the girls finished the dress in Old Lute's room.

"Try it on, Etta," Sophie said. "We want to see how you'll look on Sunday."

Once she saw her reflection, Etta had a flashback to her princess dresses and ran her hands down to smooth the skirt. Cotton instead of silk, lace instead of sequins, this dress was nothing like the elegance she had once worn. But she loved this one more because her friends had helped make it.

"You're so beautiful in this color," Sophie asked, "Isn't it called a peacock blue?"

"It does make your eyes greener," Mrs. Luttrell added.

Lavinia added, "I do like the pink flowers in the background. They're so dainty and feminine. Why don't you bring it by the dress shop tomorrow, so you can see how you look in the three-way mirror?"

~~~

Etta arrived at the dress shop and found Sophie had arrived ahead of her. Each held a package wrapped in brown paper and wore an expression of intrigue. Etta was instantly suspicious.

"What's going on and what's in there?"

"We stayed up a little later last night," Lavinia said.

Sophie chimed in, "And made these for you. Hope you like them."

Etta opened the packages and saw a reticule and a cloth cap made with her dress material. "I've never had such true friends. Thank you."

Tears came to her eyes when she looked from her gifts to her friends. "I'd never have finished the dress without your help. And these."

She held up her gifts. "It must have taken you most of the night to finish them."

"Not so long. Now try everything on, and let us see," Lavinia said.

Etta obeyed and modeled the completed ensemble.

"Mr. Benjamin Darnell isn't going to take his eyes off of you," Sophie whispered as she hugged Etta.

Etta giggled and returned the hug before turning to Lavinia.

"You were my first friend here. Thank you again for this." She pointed to her cap. "And your friendship."

"You're welcome," Lavinia's voice caught. "Promise you'll invite us to your wedding."

"Wedding, don't rush us."

Lavinia answered, "Silly, I meant your wedding. Not necessarily with Ben, but I hope you choose to marry him. He's a nice man and worthy of you."

~~

Sophie and Etta waited on Sunday for their young men to escort them to the park. Each was dressed in her finest. Sophie wore a yellow and white plaid dress which set off her blond hair and fair complexion. Mrs. Luttrell fluttered around and smoothed hair and skirts as she chattered away about how they would be the most beautiful women at the concert.

While the older woman talked, Etta found herself excited about the afternoon with Ben. Somewhere in her inner core, she knew her feelings were deeper for him than for any other man she had known. He possessed a stability and substance which others did not.

She also realized she was scared. Her fears bounced around like a croquet ball. Ben might find he did not love her. Or worse yet, they might fall so deeply in love, he would want to marry her. She would have to learn to trust him, and she did not know if she could. Also she would have to surrender the independence she saw in her future. All those emotional chains would bind her if she married. Her introspection ended when Sophie announced she saw the two young men rounding the corner.

"They're both carrying bouquets. Ohh, this is so exciting. I've never had flowers before, have you?"

Etta had an instant and faint memory of her parents presenting her with pink roses after one of her voice recitals and reminded herself that her previous life was over. She was a new person. As far as her friends in Frankfort knew, she had no past.

Sophie twisted a blond curl about a finger, and the motion caught her attention, and Etta refocused on her friend's question.

"No, what kind of flowers are they?"

"They're not roses. Mine are pink and yours are lavender."

All three looked out the side window of the foyer.

"Those are impatiens girls," Mrs. Luttrell spoke over their shoulders. "Stick one or two in your hair, and I'll put the rest in vases for you. Hurry now, go and sit down. Be sure and act surprised when you see the flowers. Puts me in mind of the time…"

Both girls sat down, and Etta winked at Sophie who smiled back. Etta knew they were going to ignore the older woman's reminiscences, as usual. They never really listened to her when she spoke of her past. Somehow Old Lute never seemed to notice that they never asked any questions.

The men entered the foyer and with slight bows, offered the flowers. Etta noticed her hands trembled when she took the lavender flowers. Mrs. Luttrell helped her place a blossom under her hat. Ben let his finger graze her hand before he set it on his arm. The four left in a swirl of skirts.

Etta was pleased her nervousness vanished by the time the foursome walked a block. Owen teased Ben about his tie. Ben pointed out Owen's haircut should improve in about ten days. Their friendly banter had set her at ease.

The couples sat on benches around the bandstand and listened to marches and popular tunes of the day. Although the customary fare for town brass bands was nothing like the Louisville operas she had attended, Etta enjoyed this music more. She and Ben harmonized so well on a few of the songs that the people close to them applauded.

During the intermission, they visited the ice cream parlor. Etta regretted when the concert ended. Lightening bugs flecked the pink and yellow glorious dusk. Evening songbirds accompanied Ben and her. They agreed it was the most wondrous dusk they had ever seen.

~~~

Everything had gone smoothly with Ben after the band concert. Yet Etta had a lingering feeling something was not right. She tried to explain it to Lavinia and Sophie as they styled each other's hair during their weekly gathering in the attic. But her words did not come close to revealing how off kilter she felt.

Lavinia stopped braiding Sophie's hair and glanced at Etta. "You can't give way yet, that's all there is to it."

"Give way to what?" Etta put hair pins in her lap.

"Peace and accepting what comes.

Etta had no idea what her friend meant. "What are you talking about?" She crossed her arms in frustration and anger.

"You still think life's a battle to be won." Lavinia finished the first braid and tied if off. "Probably because you've had to."

Lavinia put down her comb and touched Etta's hand. "We all have, to survive."

Sophie turned so she could face Etta and said, "But one of these days, you'll realize it's not a sign of weakness to accept what you've been offered. Everything doesn't have to be a fight."

Etta struggled to keep her indignation out of her voice. "For example."

Lavinia eased onto her other hip. "Well, take tonight, for instance, when Mazie offered to help you with the potatoes."

"But she doesn't do them right," Etta retorted and could not believe her friends were talking about potatoes when she needed help understanding what was going on with her and Ben.

Lavinia answered, "She does them well enough, and dinner would have been on time, instead of fifteen minutes late."

"The point is, Etta," Sophie said, "Your stubbornness may cost you one of these days. You don't have to have all the answers all the time. You can let someone else make a few decisions."

"You mean I'm bossy?"

"At times, but it's fine because we love you," Sophie said and gave Etta a hug.

"And," Lavinia put her arms around both of them, "most of the time you're right. I'm asking you to listen to others once in a while."

~~

After the lights were out and the women were one by one falling asleep, snores replaced the night coughs and rustlings of bedclothes. Etta replayed her friends' words and compared them to what the adults from her life in Louisville had told her when she was a child. Sophie and Lavinia were right. Most of the time she did not really listen to what others said. Had she always been so? Who except for Willie really loved her for who she was?"

Well, maybe I'm a little bossy, she thought, but I'm usually right. If anyone disagrees with me, they should stick up for themselves and come back at me. How else am I supposed to know? She turned sideways and pounded the lumpy pillow before she fell asleep.

~~~

Ben's courtship continued, and Etta found her resistance vanished a bit more each day. It was as if some barrier, she did not even know she had built, came down stone by stone. A lightness came over her. Chocolate tasted better. The blue in the sky became more vivid. Music touched her more deeply.

Lavinia and Sophie commented on how her face had softened one evening when Etta sat across from them at dinner.

Sophie said, "The little wrinkle between your eyes is gone." She leaned forward and let her finger trace where it had been.

"Do you feel different?"

"Calmer, every day's a bit more peaceful."

"I've noticed," Lavinia laughed. "There haven't been any temper outbreaks for a few weeks. At first, I thought you were getting sick, but you don't look feverish."

"It's Ben. I think I'm in love with him."

Sophie giggled, "Do you feel all butterflyish inside when he looks at you?"

"Yes," Etta answered. "What a good way to describe it. I don't even have to be with him. All of a sudden it overtakes me."

Both the other girls gave each other a look which made Etta feel left out.

"Yep," Sophie said, "You're in love. So are you going to marry him?"

The word marry terrified Etta. Why could things not stay the way they were now?

Lavinia tapped her on the arm and asked, "Has Old Lute given you the talk? I got it almost a year ago."

"Me, three months ago," Sophie shared.

"No, what talk is this?"

Lavinia sat up straight and assumed a serious expression. "The one where she tells you it's important to remain pure and untouched until your wedding night. How true love is based on respect. If he truly respects you, he won't ask you to do anything improper. Marriage has its carnal side and never refuse your husband his marital rights," Lavinia recited.

"Don't forget about the cow," Sophie said.

"Oh yes," Lavinia drawled, "the cow. Don't snicker when she says if the cow gives the milk away for free, the farmer won't buy it."

"Cow?" Etta asked amid swirling anxiety.

Lavinia said, "She means you don't give yourself to any man until he marries you. It's a game. He has to marry you before you experience marital bliss," Lavinia rolled her eyes at the last phrase.

Sophie tsked Lavinia before saying, "She also said she'd answer any questions we might have about the marriage bed, but, of course, only after we're safely married."

During her friends' conversation, Etta's soul shrank. Lavinia and Sophie were so innocent compared to her. She had such secrets buried in her past. She was soiled goods. How foolish she had been to believe she could start over and go to Ben as if she were untouched.

Her inner storm must have marched itself across her face because Sophie said, "Oh-oh, you've got your little wrinkle back again."

"Etta," Lavinia said, "don't worry about Old Lute's talk. It's something she gives to all the girls. Think of it as a last test before getting out of here."

But Lavinia's comforting words fell short. Etta tried to fight off a growing panic and stood. "I don't feel good. I'm going upstairs." This last statement was a lie. She already pictured herself bolting from the side door of the Home and out into the small park beyond.

When Sophie offered to have Old Lute look in on her, Etta answered more abruptly than she planned. "Don't, I need to rest. My womanlies are coming."

Chapter 22

Frankfort, August 14, 1877

Ben stood with Owen at the bar of Doyle's tavern. He tried to ignore the elbow to elbow jostling from the other men crowded around the two of them.

A big fist thumped next to his untouched beer. Its owner bellowed, "If you're not a drinking, you'd better be a moving."

Ben took in the hand and the heavily muscled forearm, dirty and sweaty. Before he could react, Owen grabbed him by the shoulder and pushed him away from the bar.

"Come on, no sense getting our brains beat out. Head for the back."

After they settled away from the rowdy drinkers, Owen said, "You're as flat as the beer in front of you."

Ben nodded. He knew what his friend meant. A confused fog had enshrouded him ever since the week before when Etta had refused to look him in the eye or even talk to him.

"Worse, you've lost your color," Owen laughed. "You don't even look like a farmer anymore."

"It's no joking matter." Ben tugged at his ear and sighed. "Etta won't talk to me, not like she used to. Hell, she won't even stay in the same room with me any more."

"You're not missing out on much." Owen grimaced. "She's got the worse case of pricklies I've ever seen. What'd you do to her?"

"Nothing. One day everything was right as rain. Then boom. She turned into an iceberg." He picked up his mug and drained it.

"Did you try anything with her, improper, I mean?"

"No, I haven't even kissed her yet. All I've done is hold her hand a few times."

"Did she pull away, frown at you, slap you?"

"Slap me? Good God, you've seen her slap people?"

"Just one," Owen laughed again. "Some nabob who thought he was really important in the state government. He put his hands, accidentally, you know-."

"Where did he touch her? Who was he? By all that's holy, I'll show him-"

"Relax, it was well over a year ago, and the man's gone. Seems Etta made sure the little wife back home found out about it. It's amazing what a letter can do. But," Ben felt Owen's eyes bore into him, "the important thing right now is to find out what you did."

"I swear, nothing. I don't understand it. I haven't changed, she has."

"You've tried talking to her?"

Owen polished off his beer and signaled to the passing barmaid for another round.

"Yes, if she's with someone else, she's civil, but not warm like she used to be."

"And alone?"

"She goes the other way or else rushes by."

"Does she seem angry?"

"No, sad, eaten up with sadness." Ben frowned. "This has torn me apart. I love her. I want to ask her to marry me after she finishes her time at the boarding house."

"Have you told her you love her?" Owen asked. Ben looked down at his empty beer and shook his head. "Did you mention marriage?" Same response.

"Well, it seems to me you have to gather your courage, man, if you really love her. You have to find out what is the real trouble and fix it."

"But how?"

Owen finished off his beer and paused before asking, "Do you want to use honesty or subterfuge?"

"I'm desperate. What do you have in mind?"

"How much longer does she have with the Caldwells?"

"Almost five months, until the end of the year."

"Here's what we're going to do." Owen smiled at Ben. "We'll talk to Old Lute. That's Mrs. Luttrell, the matron, and tell her what's going on. She'll help us."

Over another round of beer, Owen outlined his plan. Ben was not convinced. "You think it's going to work?"

"Absolutely, just be sure the two of you don't get carried away when she cries and you comfort her."

Owen slapped Ben on the back. "Now cheer up, I see fresh beer coming our way."

~~

"Good news, dear," Mrs. Luttrell said after Etta had taken a seat on the lumpy sofa. "A Mr. Anson, from Lexington," Etta noticed the matron glance at the envelope on her lap, "has contacted us about a position he has for an order clerk. Seems Owen sang your praises to him. He'll be at McCord's tomorrow. The interview's after hours, so of course, I'll be your chaperone."

This is not what Etta wanted to hear. "I don't want to go. I don't need another job. The Caldwells are probably going to offer me one."

"You don't know that for a fact. So you might need a new job," Mrs. Luttrell countered.

"I don't know this Mr. Anson."

"No one does. The important thing to remember is opportunity knocks only once before it moves on."

"I know," Etta answered. She did not know where the energy to try something new was going to come from. "I don't feel up to an interview."

"Nonsense, it'll be good practice. Besides, it's only twenty minutes out of your life."

Etta, exhausted by sleepless nights and her broken heart, had no strength to do battle and agreed. She would talk with Mr. Anson. But she would not be at her best. All she had energy for was crawling into the attic's hideaway and breathing and sleeping.

~~

When the two women walked into the music store the next day, Etta remembered her good manners and thanked Owen for recommending her.

"Glad to do it." His smile lit up his face. "Just head on to the back storage room. He's waiting for you." His smile grew even larger.

Etta stepped inside the backroom and froze when she saw Ben. Fury erupted from deep within. How dare they all conspire and trick her like this. She turned her back to Ben and stomped towards Mrs. Luttrell and Owen. They stood by the door, shoulder to shoulder as if to block her retreat. They would get a piece of her mind on her way out.

"Etta, please talk to me," Ben's voice reached through her anger. "I'm going mad. I don't know what I've done, but I'm so very sorry. You've got to tell me how I can make it up to you."

She turned back to look at the man she loved and whom she could not dishonor with her past. The misery on his face made her heart ache. But she knew she had to be strong.

"I can't talk about it," she whispered.

"Yes, you can." He slowly came toward her. "I'm the one person in the world you can tell anything to. I love you, Etta. You bring sunshine and song into my life. I want to marry you."

Etta stepped a few paces forward before putting her hands up to tell him not to come any closer. They stood just out of arm's length.

"Ben, it would be better if you forgot me," Etta sobbed.

Ben closed the distance between them and gathered her into his arms. "I can't forget you my love, never," his words came out in ragged breaths, and he stroked the nape of her neck. "I love you."

Her resolve, along with her backbone, weakened.

Footsteps behind her indicated Mrs. Luttrell and Owen were retreating to the other room to give them some privacy. Etta reached down, deep inside herself, for the courage to continue. She pushed herself out of his embrace and looked straight at him as she spoke.

"I have a past, Ben."

"To me, you were born the day I met you. I don't want to know about what happened to you before we met."

"You say that now, but what about the future?"

Releasing her, he raised her chin until their eyes met. "Your past belongs to you. If you want to share it, I'll listen. I promise you, no, I swear to you. I'll never pursue what happened to you before the April afternoon your song lured me into your life. Do you remember that day?"

She was so overcome with conflict that she could not answer.

But Ben must not have needed any response. He continued, "I'm always going to feel this way. Your destiny is bound to mine. We will weave them into one, and we will be strong together."

His words broke through most of her resistance. Yet, she doubted he would still love her if he ever discovered her past.

"Ben, you don't really know me."

"Yes, I do."

He took both her hands and looked deep into her eyes.

"You have a fiery temper matched with a deep ability to love and with amazing courage and strength. You'll be a wonderful wife, and our children will be fortunate to have you as their mother. I know you love me. Say you'll marry me."

She shook her head and freed her hands.

"I do love you, Ben, so much, more than I ever thought I could love anyone. But I won't agree to marry you, not yet. Let's wait six months. We'll need time to really get to know each other. At the end of six months, we'll see."

"So," Ben counted off the months on his hands, "on Valentine's Day, I'll ask you again to marry me. It'll be a proper proposal on bended knee and with a ring. I warn you though, nothing will change my mind. I want to spend the rest of my life with you."

"Hush, don't say such things. You're tempting fate," her fingertips brushed his lips.

He grasped her fingers and kissed the palm of her hand. When she heard tsking behind her, she broke from his touch.

"Okay, Mrs. Luttrell," Ben laughed at the older woman in the doorway.

"You two go on ahead now," she spoke. "Owen has to lock up. I'll follow along a little behind. You take her back to the Home and come by tomorrow evening. You two can sit on the veranda. That's how couples courted in my day."

~~~

A few hours later, Etta stopped by Mrs. Luttrell's rooms. After her knock brought a "come in," she entered and sat on the sofa by the older woman.

"Have some tea and cookies, dear."

"Thank you," Etta said.

After a sip, she also thanked Mrs. Luttrell for her help this evening.

"You're most welcome. I enjoy helping my girls," Mrs. Luttrell put her teacup down before resettling herself on the sofa. "I know Lavinia and Sophie have probably already told you about my little speech. I give every new bride advice for the bedchamber and how to have a happy marriage. I'm glad you're here. Now we can have our little talk."

Etta panicked. She did not want to hear this right now. The matron brushed away Etta's protests about how tired she was.

"I know something about your past. I also know you're not the first girl to be victimized by an older man. Unfortunately, I've seen too many girls who have suffered the same fate as you. Unlike most other people, I've never blamed them for what happened."

Tears filled Etta's eyes, and she turned away. Could what Mrs. Luttrell said be true? Was it possible she had not been at fault?

"All of you girls were children. Those nasty men took advantage of each one of you. This is the main advice I have for you tonight. You weren't responsible for what happened to you. You were an innocent. You can go to your husband as a virgin."

"I'm not. My father made sure of that."

"Look at me," Mrs. Luttrell said no more until Etta lifted her face. "You're an innocent virgin at married love. You don't know what the physical act feels like between two people who are in love and married. It is truly one of the most rapturous moments of a woman's life."

Amazed, Etta stared at the older woman, whose words offered some hope after all she had been through.

"When you go to your husband, you'll be an unblemished woman, free of guilt and sin. It's important you believe you are unsullied?" Etta nodded.

"Three years ago," the matron continued, "I advised you to start anew and forget the past. You've remade yourself. Now forgive yourself. You didn't deserve to be treated such. You're innocent."

"But how can I act like it's my first time, when it's not? I don't really remember how I acted then," she said with her eyes downcast again. This was so embarrassing to talk about.

"If it's Ben you decide to marry, trust me, he'll be nervous just like you'll be." Etta raised her eyes. "He'll be so caught up in his own reactions he won't really notice yours, as long as they're not out of the ordinary. Follow his lead, and everything will be fine. The important thing to remember is how much you love each other. You're beginning a new life together."

"Thank you Mrs. Luttrell," Etta said, and although she was still unconvinced, she hugged her advisor and left.

~~

The next day Etta joined Sophie on the front walk. Together, they started toward their jobs, Etta to the boarding house and Sophie to her bakery. They walked to work without speaking. Etta wanted to talk about what had happened with Ben yesterday but did not know how to begin.

Sophie broke through the uncomfortable silence.

"Old Lute said Ben's calling on you again. I'm so glad." Sophie's eyes splashed with joy. "Are you going to marry him?"

Etta looked at her friend and realized that though Sophie's life as an orphan was not easy, she did not have the same scars. Etta accepted she could never tell this good natured and sheltered young woman what obscenity she had endured.

"We want to be sure, so we're not rushing into marriage. He has a lot going on with getting his new store started."

"But your time at the boarding house ends in December. What happens then?"

"I'll probably stay on there for awhile. Now tell me about you and Owen. Have you set the date?"

～～

In October, the three young women readied the foyer for the double wedding of Lavinia and Sophie on November thirtieth. As they cleaned and planned the simple decorations, Etta experienced a sense of bittersweetness. She was happy for her friends, but she also envied them. Her life did not include any firm marriage plans. She still feared her stained past was too much of an obstacle.

Mr. Fielding, in his capacity as Justice of the Peace, performed the ceremony. Ben sat beside Etta and held her hand. After the two couples were pronounced married, Ben leaned over and gave her hand a gentle squeeze. He also whispered soon they would be the ones named man and wife. His pure love brought her to the brink of tears. They increased when she realized that he had mistaken her tears of pain for joy and squeezed her hand a little harder.

～～

Her time at the Home became lonelier. She retreated every night to the attic space now solely hers. There she looked at the small room and wondered what her life was going to be. Even with all of Ben's vows of love, the fear that someday her past would catch up with her never went away. When he found out, his disgust would drive him away. After he left, she would be alone, forever unloved.

～～

"They don't approve of me, do they?" Etta asked Ben two days after his parents came to stay at the boarding house in December. She cornered him in the hallway outside the dining room. Before he had time to answer, she did nothing to curb the anger within her and shot off another question.

"Why did you tell them about us? About me?"

"Whoa, why are you upset? I didn't do anything wrong. They noticed how I looked at you. At least Momma did, she sensed some sort of energy between us."

"Did she ask you last night?"

"How did you know?"

"By your father's grim expression this morning." Etta made her mouth go straight to demonstrate Mr. Darnell's look at the breakfast table. "Your mother didn't meet my eye when I asked her if she wished to have more coffee."

"They don't know you like I do. They'll come around. We have time. I promised you six months, remember?"

"What exactly did you say?"

"The truth."

"I'm a girl with no family and an unknown past. I'm an apprentice and live in the Home for Friendless Women?"

"Not in those terms, but you know I can't lie. That's why I don't play poker."

Ben gave her his usual boyish smile. But she would not allow his charm to sway her. She stared him down.

He continued, "I told them I had fallen in love with you and asked you to marry me. Momma was impressed you asked to wait six months. I told them it made no difference to me. On February 14th, I was going to ask you to marry me."

Etta felt a bit of doubt creep into her heart. "What did they say?"

"Momma told my father that proved you weren't after money."

"You're wealthy, really rich?"

"My parents are. They've got acres of land. I don't want any of it. Remember, we talked about it before."

Etta tried to remember their conversations about his family. "You did say something about land, lots of farms."

"Right, but it's not doing us much good here in Frankfort, is it?" Ben tried another smile. It made her even angrier. He did not take this whole matter seriously enough.

"It doesn't matter. Your parents will never accept me."

"Yes, they will." He kissed her nose. Her anger melted. It was difficult to stay mad at him.

"You'll see," he said. "Soon, they'll love you because I love you."
He kissed her goodbye and left to find his parents.

Over the next few days, Etta wrestled with how much the older Darnells' coldness bothered her. They stopped all conversation when she walked in upon them. They ignored her as much as possible during the dinners. Their attitude sapped her energy and robbed her of sleep until she heard Sister Justina's wise words replay in her mind.

"You can't be little Jesus and make everyone love you all the time. Be yourself."

Etta had forgotten until this moment the first time the kind nun had given her this advice. She and a girl named Sarah had gone after the same toy, a rag doll. It had turned into a particularly tearful dustup. Sarah was losing the tug of war. Etta had a firm grip and moved her hands farther along the doll's body.

Then Sarah flung her taunt. "At least, I know who my mother and father are."

Even at this moment, after so long ago, Etta remembered how painful those words were. With a start, she realized why the Darnells' actions hurt so much. They made her feel like an orphaned little girl, all over again.

Armed with Sister Justina's advice, Etta had grown stronger in the orphanage. Now she repeated the words to herself and felt stronger. She would overcome this insult and not let them win.

On New Year's Eve, the Caldwells hosted a party to celebrate the official end of Etta's apprenticeship. The guests included the residents and Lavinia and Sophie with their husbands. One by one the guests shared tales about Etta's kindness and her legendary temper.

Her laughter joined with the other guests' when Mrs. Caldwell told one of her favorite stories. Etta had threatened to let a reporter know a certain lobbyist had been found on the third floor in the act of listening through a keyhole. The intruder's cover story was he had forgotten the room where his appointment was. All the third floor residents came out of their rooms when Etta would not let go of the man's arms and screamed spy at the top of her lungs.

He managed to break away. The men chased him down the stairs and into the street while Etta yelled out the window if she ever saw him in her house again, she would report him to the opposition newspaper.

As the clock crept toward the birth of the next year, Etta along with Ben and their friends, waited for the chimes from the churches. When the bells struck the first ring, Ben kissed her, and their kiss lasted beyond the twelfth.

Chapter 23

Fayette County, January 9, 1877

Reuben Darnell found his new year had not started well. What he had seen and heard about Ben's young woman gave rise to suspicions. He did not believe, for starters, her name was Smith. It might as well have been Jones or Brown. Also Etta's appearance bothered him. She wore her clothes and walked into a room in the same manner as those born-to-wealth women he had brushed past at horse races. Even more telling were her hands. Unmarked by scars, scabs, or weather, they convinced him she had come from quality.

Next was how he had not been able to find out anything about her. There must have been a good reason. Single women did not suddenly show up someplace without a history unless there was something buried in their past. He thought he knew why, the oldest reason around.

Every path he took to discover the truth about Etta met with a brick wall. All Ambrose Fielding revealed in response to a letter of inquiry was "Etta was a sober, hard-working young woman of good habits." The closing paragraph stated no one had lodged any complaints about her behavior during the three years she had resided at the Home.

The last paragraph in particular had angered him. The words the administration used were usually reserved for letters of recommendation. There was no real information about Etta's past or true nature.

The Caldwells also gave a good report. No one, not the bankers, the priests, the newspaper owner, in Frankfort knew her true story.

So far his suspicions and investigations were a secret. He wanted to keep his efforts from his wife Araminta. He stuck each letter in the back of his desk drawer and waited until he had proof of the young woman's true nature. Then he would deal with his son, man-to-man.

But on an early January evening, the situation changed. He walked into the kitchen after taking off his barn coat and boots in the backroom and saw his wife by the table. The set of her mouth told him how angry she was. A stony silence offset the anger in her eyes. He saw his letters spread out in front of her and knew the argument was going to be about Ben.

"Now Mina, don't get your feathers ruffled. I'm trying to protect the boy."

"He's not a boy any longer."

Her words, spit out with the coldness of ice and full of contempt drove him back a few steps. He chose not to argue but to pace and listen, ready to exploit any weakness he could find in her comments.

She said, "You can't control his life. You fight him on this, and you'll drive him into her arms for sure."

He pounced on her last statement. "So you're not happy about the situation either?"

"She's not the one I would have chosen for him. But I respect his decision."

"Don't be ridiculous," Reuben said. "He doesn't have any common sense, never has."

He stopped and looked down at his letters, free of their envelopes and accusatory in his intent. Anger over his loss of privacy forced him past the restraint he had been taught to use with women.

"I'll tell you why I wrote those." He jabbed his finger toward Araminta and his correspondence. "All you've got to do is look at her and see she doesn't belong working in a boarding house. She came from wealth. Everything about her says so, her hair, teeth, hands. Someone spent a great deal of time and money on her. And," he emphasized, "no one throws time and money away unless there's been some fornication going on."

Her gasp pleased him. He gave her a withering stare before he continued. "It's the way of the world."

She reached out for the closest chair and lowered herself into the seat.

Momentum was on his side, so he pressed even harder. "Remember what happened a few years ago when the Shepherd girl skedaddled to God knows where?"

She seemed to recover and said with a little smile, "I do. Her mother said she went back east for college and then married..."

Reuben snorted at the word college and smirked when her voice trailed off. Triumph surged through his whole being when Araminta's eyes widened and a blush flamed across her cheeks. God, he was enjoying this. He leaned across the table and gathered his letters.

"The Shepherds banished their daughter. They'll never see her again. It's the same thing with the Smith girl. She's got a past, one not fit for our family."

~~

The next day Reuben took the morning train to Frankfort. A black mood settled over him the moment he stepped into the passenger car. He had sworn after their December trip he would never travel by rail again in the winter. Yet here he was, once more, on a train and confined in a space already too hot from the overheated stove.

The train bucked and gained speed, and just as he had assumed, the draft from the side window crawled down his neck. Even worse was the fact he was alone. Araminta had refused to be part of what she termed his "dirty work."

When the train pulled into Frankfort, his watch showed him they were ninety minutes behind schedule. He closed the watch case in disgust and returned it to his vest pocket. At stop after stop through the morning, he had watched the yardmen load the wood and water on board. In his opinion, men today did not know how to work outside. They had to keep moving at a brisk pace. This was a lesson Ben, unlike his other sons, had not ever learned either.

Once off the train, Reuben, with his valise, trudged the two blocks along ice-coated wooden sidewalks to Ben's store. Thank God, he thought every time he came to a patch of sawdust, some considerate storeowner had sprinkled enough to help his customers stay upright.

But in the late afternoon, the temperature had dropped, and the day's snowmelt refroze. So he picked his way carefully over the slick spots. It would not do to fall and break his hip.

He gave Ben silent approval when he stepped on the ample sawdust outside the store. It still provided good traction.

Reuben looked through the window and noticed his son was busy sorting through what looked like the day's receipts. Ben looked up as the bell on the door announced his father's arrival.

"Poppa," Ben put down his papers and started around the counter. "Is Momma ill?"

"Your mother's just fine, don't worry."

Reuben put his valise on the floor beside the inside doormat and wiped his feet. When he looked up, he saw Ben tugging at his ear. Reuben was ready to berate his son on his show of nerves but caught himself in time. Today Ben's characteristic gesture pleased him. It proved he still had the upper hand.

"Take a seat over there, sir," Ben pointed to the odd assortment of four chairs circled around the potbelly stove. "There might still be some coffee. I'll hang up your coat."

Reuben looked around the small, cramped space. The stock was again organized. So Ben had not gone to extra measures before the visit. If only the boy's life was this orderly. Ben came back to join him after he locked the door and shoved the receipts in a drawer under the counter. Reuben waited for Ben to pour two cups of coffee and sit down.

"Are you in town on business, sir?"

"No, I'm here to ask you if you've come to your senses about the Smith girl."

"Poppa, I understand how you feel, but I love her. Come Valentine's Day I'm going to ask her to marry me as soon as possible."

"There's no way you know her well enough, let alone her people. Damn it, Ben, it's important to know who she came from. You wouldn't buy a heifer without knowing her pedigree, would you? All I'm asking you to do is to postpone the wedding until I've hunted down her family."

"Etta's not a cow. She's the woman I'm going to marry. I want her to be the mother of my children."

Reuben let go of all semblance of being reasonable when he saw his son cross his arms and give him a defiant look. "I heard she's Catholic. You know what that means. Your children will be raised Catholic."

He could see his son had no answer to this charge. Probably the foolish young man had never discussed religion with the little chit. Reuben would have bet neither one attended church regular. This was further evidence she was not fit for their family. It was clear his son was so besotted he would do whatever the young woman wanted. They would end up with a Catholic in the family.

"I'm going to marry her."

"If you do, we'll not give our blessings. This marriage will be the death of your mother. The guilt will have to rest on your head alone."

"You and Momma haven't even given her a chance. You'd love her if you did."

"Write me if and when you come to your senses. Otherwise, I don't want to hear from you again. Consider yourself disowned."

Reuben put his cup down on the stove and stood. Without another word, he stomped over to the rack and put his coat on. He did not wait to button it up. He picked up his valise and jerked the door open with his free hand and stormed out into the cold. Righteous anger warmed him on the way to his favorite business hotel. He was confident the boy would soon come around.

~~

Valentine's Day, Ben's promised day to propose, fell on a Wednesday. Although it was not Etta's usual night off, the Caldwells excused her from her duties. She found Lavinia and Sophie in the foyer when she returned to the Home.

"Hurry, we don't have a lot of time before Ben gets here," Lavinia said.

"We have something for you. Open it when we're upstairs."

Sophie's words almost sang as she dangled a wrapped gift box by its ribbons. With a swish of their skirts, both of her friends raced up the stairs.

Etta joined in the game and followed. In their attic room, she chose the cushion between them and tore open the box. Inside was a small green satin hat glorious with feathers and lace. She remembered admiring one much like it in Madame Clothilde's window a few months ago. When Etta held it in front of her, she noticed the hat had those darling cloth flowers Lavinia had worked so hard to master.

"You made this for me? I love the Victorian blossoms, thank you."

Etta put on the hat and moved from her pillow. She looked for the old hand mirror the young women had used numerous times to arrange their hair and try new flirtatious looks. "Not so fast, Etta," Sophie said, "you must receive my gift." She stood and pulled a comb and brush from her dress pockets.

"Don't shake your head at me, Etta. I've been practicing the perfect hair style for your new hat."

"All right," Etta laughed and let Sophie remove the hat and take the pins from her hair.

A few minutes later, Sophie held the mirror so Etta could see the new hair arrangement.

"See how you can let these few curls escape and brush your cheeks?"

"Ah." Lavinia flourished her hand in a theatrical manner. "You look, what's the word, winsome. I believe you used the word with me before my wedding?"

"Touché, I did."

When her friends left, Sophie's parting words were, "Say yes, Etta. You deserve happiness."

Ben was due in fifteen minutes. Yet she still weighed her answer. She did not trust the happiness he had brought her. Lurking in her mind was the belief that happiness was fickle. It came and went on a whim. From what she had seen in her eighteen years, sadness and bad luck worked their way into people's lives far more readily than joy and good fortune.

Her past with her father shamed her. Even Mrs. Luttrell's words did not erase the fact she would enter marriage stained with sin. If she truly loved Ben, how could she let him marry such damaged goods? Although he claimed he did not care about her past, she wondered what he thought she was hiding. She was bothered even more by whether she should tell him the truth or not?

~~~

During their dinner at the railroad hotel, she was grateful he kept the conversation steered away from their future. He told a funny story about how a hog escaped from its pen and wandered around the state capitol building. But she could tell he was also nervous. Each time he pulled at his ear made her love him more.

On their return trip, Ben drove his carriage past the Home. She was puzzled when he continued onto St. Claire Street. Half way down the block, he stopped the horse in front of a small, one story Federal style red brick house. The moment he helped her down, she heard the bells of Good Shepherd's signaling it was eight in the evening.

Ben said, "Don't say anything yet. Trust me and wait until we get inside."

He guided her up the stone steps onto a half-moon shaped entrance stone and unlocked the front door. "Stay right here until I get the lamp lit," he further instructed.

Etta listened to him bump into a few pieces of furniture. She heard a match scrape and caught the scent of the sharp tang of sulfur. The light from his lamp lit up the hall.

"Ben, does this house belong to the man who works for you? Isn't his name Baker?"

He came back to her. "Shh, no questions, remember?"

She took his hand. "I'll try."

"Come join me in the parlor," he said after he helped her off with her coat and hung it with his on the hall tree.

Etta went through the first door on the left and sat on the small, brown paisley sofa and waited.

Ben put down his lamp on an old spindle-legged table beside the sofa and went across to the other side of the room and lit another lamp. Next he opened the side door of the cast iron stove to stir the coals and warm the room. After coming back to her, he knelt on one knee and took her hands.

"I have imagined this night so many times over the last six months. My love for you has never wavered. It's grown more than I ever thought possible. I want to spend my life with you. I see us with children and growing old together. So, I'm asking you, Etta, will you be my wife?"

She had known this moment was coming and loved him so much. Yet she struggled with the answer. Her words sputtered, "I want to very much."

"Then, say yes, please."

As she looked down at him, she remembered how he had followed her song into the boarding house parlor. At once the image reminded her of those sailors lured by the Lorelei and how the mythical women had drawn them to their deaths. She shuddered and shoved the old story from her head.

Instead, she focused on her heart. She wanted to marry this man whose eyes made her soul warm and whose love filled her breast. Maybe it was just possible that happiness was within her grasp.

"Yes, Ben. I'll marry you."

He slipped an amethyst ring on her finger before he joined her on the couch and encircled her in his arms. Resting his hands on her curls, he kissed her mouth, softly, soon more urgently.

"Thank you my love. Let's marry this month."

"So soon?"

"As soon as Old Ghostie can perform the ceremony, if it's fine with you."

Another shiver came over her. She fought back the shame of her past.

"Yes," she said and hoped he would take the tremor in her voice as joy.

"But we'd better leave this house before the Bakers come back."

"We're the owners, dearest." He kissed her nose before releasing her. "I bought it last month, fully furnished. I hope you like it."

Etta looked around at the room and heard him say, "But you can make any changes you wish."

Though the wallpaper was dingy and the lace curtains stained, one word came to her mind. Ours.

"I hope you aren't upset, Etta. Maybe I should've asked you. But, see, I couldn't."

She looked back at him. "Why?"

"Because if you'd told me no tonight, I knew I'd have to leave the boarding house right away. I couldn't bear to see you and know you'd never be my wife."

She stroked his cheek and asked, "This is really ours?"

"Legally the bank owns part."

"Show me the rest."

Ben took one of the lamps and led her on a tour of the other three rooms.

"Here across the hall is the bedroom."

Etta entered a room the same size as the parlor. This room was cooler because no fire had been lit. From the lamps Ben brought to life, she saw a simple pine bed with a dull white counterpane and windows hung with the same curtains the parlor had.

"I decided not to do anything to the inside until after tonight. If you'd turned me down, I wouldn't have cared what it looked like."

He kissed her hand. "Now you'll be able to decorate our home the way you want. Tell me you're happy with the house and marrying me."

"Yes Ben, I'm happy." She meant it. "I love our home because we'll be living here, together."

The quick tour of the remaining rooms showed the kitchen and second bedroom were smaller and their furnishings were just as worn as the other rooms. The house had been kept clean, though not in the best repair.

"Who lived here, before?" she asked when they returned to the parlor.

"A couple by the name of Riddell. They built the house in the late fifties when they married. He's from back home. I knew of the family but hadn't met him until he dropped into the store one day soon after I opened. When he told me three months ago he and his wife were having to sell out and return to her mother's house near Lexington, I offered to buy the house with all the furniture and stuff."

"They left everything?" Etta walked around the room and examined it with more care.

"I haven't really looked. It seemed like I was being nosy."

"Don't worry, it won't take long to make it feel like ours. Now, what's out the back door?"

"It leads out to a few sheds, the storm shelter, and the alley. The Riddells said we'd share the alley with some real nice neighbors on either side."

Ben moved toward the door. "Do you want me to unlock it?"

She caught his arm and said, "It's too dark and cold to look tonight."

Ben took her to the side window and pulled the curtain back.

"See the lights to the south? A widow lady named Mrs. Leander lives there. Miss Lane, the librarian, lives with her mother on the north side."

He let the curtain fall back. A bit of dust shed from the material. Etta realized she would have to give the place a good scrubbing. The notion of cleaning her own home made her smile.

"I'll bring you here on Sunday," Ben said, "after your lunch shift is over. You can see the place a lot better. Maybe we'll meet our neighbors. The people across the street are new to town, so according to the Riddells no one knows much about them."

"Yet." Etta laughed. "It won't take long. That's the way neighborhoods are. What'd the Riddells tell the neighbors about us?"

He kissed her on the nose before he answered. "I'm sure they said we're the nicest people in the world."

"Ben, can we really afford this?"

"Yes, business has been pretty good. The bank tells me the economy's finally pulled out of its slump. They predict nothing but growth for the eighties."

"We'll be so happy."

"Most certainly."

"We can entertain our friends. Your parents and brothers can come visit also."

At the mention of his parents, Ben's eyes grew wary.

"What's wrong? You've got to tell me."

"Sit in the chair near the stove."

As Etta rocked and Ben paced, he told her about his father. After a few sentences, she knew she had to try to heal the breach.

"You've got to go to your parents tomorrow. We can't possibly marry with your father so angry. It's not right."

"He's not ruling my life. I'm on my own now. I don't need him or his approval."

Etta chose not to remind him how he and his father had agreed Ben would return home if his store failed after two years. The anger in his eyes told her he was not ready to listen to the truth.

Instead, she said, "You're so lucky to have parents who love you and a home to go back to. Mine are dead. I don't even have a homeplace to go to anymore."

Ben halted his steps and looked at her. "This is the first time you've told me anything about your past." He knelt beside her. "I'm so sorry you've lost your parents, but that's all the more reason we should marry. Let my parents be damned. You're more important to me than anyone else in the world."

"You feel this way now because you're angry. If your father carries through on disowning you, you'll be an orphan like me, alone and without any family. How will you feel in a few years?"

"I refuse to borrow trouble. I know how I feel. I'm not changing my mind. My parents can't make me, and you can't either."

After a pause, he said, "Do you want to tell me about your parents?"

"No."

Etta shook her head. Her father's abuse and her mother's refusal to take her side had no right to intrude tonight.

Ben pulled her up into an embrace. "I'll make sure as long as I walk this earth, my precious one, you'll never be alone and unloved again."

To Etta, their happiness was already singed with regret and pain. On her insistence, Ben visited his parents and sought reconciliation. However, there was no good news to share the evening he returned. He told how not even his mother's tears had possessed the power to make his father change his mind.

"He called you an unknown woman. Why would you even want him at our wedding? I'm glad he's won't be there."

"You're giving up so much to marry me. Your family, your old home..."

"You're the only family I want and need until our children come. Our future together is all that counts."

~~~

The next week Lavinia and Sophie joined Etta in Mrs. Luttrell's chambers after supper to start on her wedding dress. They agreed with Mrs. Luttrell the day dress pattern Etta had selected was perfect for her.

Especially the scalloped neckline and wrists that called for lace trim. They ran their hands over the pale green silk mixed with a bit of cotton and vowed it looked and felt like fine silk.

While the four women cut and stitched, the evening bubbled with giggles. Lavinia and Sophie described scorched meat and bread baked so hard their chickens would not even eat the ruined food. Etta envied how her friends' faces glowed with joy as they talked. Their lives were full of what she had not yet experienced.

At the same time, she was also scared. Things were happening too fast. She did not doubt Ben. She doubted herself. Was she worthy of Ben and happiness? Was she truly ready to be a wife and hopefully a mother?

A bit past nine, Ben along with Owen and Daniel called at the Home. Etta walked down the steps with her friends and watched the new husbands bustle their wives out the door so quickly that she and Ben were left alone in the front foyer. She wondered if the three men had planned it.

"Soon my love," Ben said as he wrapped his arms around her. "We'll be together in our little house."

He kissed her. Etta took advantage of their stolen moments and returned his kiss. An ember of desire caught fire against the backdrop of Old Lute's approaching footsteps. Too soon Mrs. Luttrell would come in and start to cluck about him leaving. They broke apart just before the matron entered.

"Off you go, Mr. Darnell." Mrs. Luttrell held the door open. "Etta needs her rest, so she can be at work bright and early tomorrow. I'm sure you also have someplace to be in the morning."

"Good night, Mrs. Luttrell. I'm leaving." Ben gave Etta a wink and a chaste kiss on her cheek.

~~~

A little over two weeks later, Etta woke before six. Nervous yet happy because at last the day had arrived. Wednesday, March 13th, chosen because the middle day of the week was considered, according to Sophie, the best day to be married.

Etta tried to check on the wedding breakfast before her bath, but Mrs. Luttrell shooed her out the kitchen door with a pail of scented hot water and instructions to get bathed.

Lavinia and Sophie arrived soon after. As Etta brushed her hair dry, she watched them decorate the foyer. They draped the window sills and banister with garlands of paper roses. For luck, they hung a white paper dove by the side window, thus marking the spot where she and Ben would stand within the hour. Then they bustled her upstairs to dress and arrange her hair.

At the stroke of ten, Lavinia and Sophie went down the stairs. Etta waited on the landing without any regrets. Though her wedding did not resemble the ones she had grown up seeing in the cathedral in Louisville and had once believed was her due. She had long ago discarded any dream of wearing the antique lace veil from Ireland or a long train as her girl cousins had.

Nor did she miss the scent of fresh orange blossoms and stephanotis. She looked at her bouquet and felt loved. Resting inside the arrangement of ribbons and rosemary she had made were the two waxen orange blossoms her friends had carried for their weddings. They had offered the flowers as the something borrowed just before they walked down the stairs ahead of her. She had bowed, after only a little resistance, to the ageless rhyme. The something old was her pearls. The something new was her dress. The ribbons tied in lovers' knots represented the something blue. She also slid a bright new copper penny in her shoe.

Etta took a big sigh and let it out and tried to still her shaking hands. She held on to the banister and followed her friends down the stairs and toward Ben.

As a fierce snowstorm howled around the windows of the Home for Friendless Women, she took his hand and pledged her love.

~~~

The moment Etta felt she was truly married was not their first time making love. But the first time she did a batch of laundry. When she took Ben's shirts from the overhead drying racks, tears welled up inside of her. By the time she had picked up the iron from the stove to start on the collar of a shirt, tears streamed down her face.

As she sipped a cup of tea at the table, Etta tried to figure out why she had cried. It did not make any sense. She had never been happier. From eight in the morning until seven at night, she was free to decide what she wanted to do, how she wanted to do it, when she wanted to do it. There was no one to tell her otherwise. Exhilarating choices filled her days, and her nights brought newly discovered sexual joy. She never knew it was possible to be so happy.

Then she understood her tears. She cried because she was content. Her life was real and her own.

Leaving the laundry to be ironed later, she walked through rooms much smaller than any others she had lived in. Unlike her little house, the orphanage and the Home were institutions, built on a scale for housing huge numbers.

Her parents' house was also not a home. Although she and her family lived there, it had also served as a workplace for many servants and a house for entertaining the high society of Louisville.

In contrast, the low ceilings, tiny windows, narrow hallway, and dainty carpets made the cozy house on St. Claire Street a dollhouse. So she did what most little girls do with a dollhouse. She decided to host weekly tea parties with Lavinia and Sophie.

~~~

"Your home has such a nice feel," Sophie said after she propped up her feet and stretched her knitting on her pregnant belly.

Across from her, Lavinia, also due in July, turned the heels in her green knitted booties. "I agree, this is a sweet house. I can tell you're happy here. Your eyes have such a peaceful cast."

Sophie asked, "Do you miss seeing all the people at the boarding house?"

"Not at all," Etta answered. "And I can tell you what else I don't miss? Eating my meals from a tray. I will never again eat from a tray."

Her guests laughed. But Etta was serious. She treasured sharing simple and intimate meals with Ben. They reminded her of the dinners she and Willie had in their nursery so long ago. She never wanted to go back to the lavish dinners in a grand dining room and the serious business-like serving of meals in the boarding house and the Home.

Etta also rediscovered privacy, something she had not enjoyed since she came to the Home three years ago. Living only with Ben was such an abrupt change after she had shared the physical space of the Home with over sixty women every day.

At first, the sudden quietness spooked her until she enveloped herself in the mystery of silence. She had forgotten how peaceful quiet was. No background noise. No dinner bells. No bustle from so many people living close together.

If she chose, Ben might be the only person she talked to for a whole day. Freed of school and work at the boarding house, she walked from room to room and gloried in being alone, truly alone.

~~~

In October, Etta rejoiced when she realized she was going to have a baby. When she gave her news to Ben over a quiet dinner, it infuriated her that he only nodded. After she announced the due date around the second week of April, he smiled and agreed. His calmness stoked her anger

"You don't seem surprised," Etta said and narrowed her eyes at him.

"I'm not. I've suspected for about a month."

"How did you know?" Her anger continued to spark.

"I grew up on a farm, remember? I am well versed in pregnancy symptoms." Ben sat back proudly. "I've been waiting, patiently I might say, for you to tell me."

Etta hated his smugness at that moment.

"Now, don't be upset," Ben said and reached across the table for her hand. "Getting angry can't be good for the baby."

Etta gave him a nod. "I suppose I should remember you did wait."

He took her hand and brought it to his lips. "It was all I could do not to ask. I'm so happy with your news."

"Maybe your parents will accept me now since there's going to be a new Darnell."

Ben withdrew his hand. "How will they ever know? I never see them."

His sharp tone surprised her, and she tried to calm him.

"Let's extend the olive branch. Invite them to spend our first Christmas here, with us." She touched his sleeve. "Wouldn't it be special if your family visited?"

"I don't know why you're going on about this. My father made the decision to disown me, not the other way around."

This was not going the way she wanted. "I agree with you. He did, and it wasn't the right thing to do. Maybe he'll reconsider when he realizes how happy we are. If you tell your mother first, isn't it possible she'll be able to change his mind?"

Etta saw her words had not convinced him so she tried another approach, one used so well by the nuns, guilt. "Wouldn't you like for your child to know the only grandparents he has left alive?"

Ben stood so abruptly his chair rocked and almost fell. He stalked out of the room. Etta soon heard the front door slam.

For half an hour, she rocked vehemently in the parlor and fumed. She railed at him for his cut and run. How dare he leave in such fury? He should have stayed to talk it out. Tiring of both her anger and the effort of rocking at such a pace, she slowed the chair and picked up the baby blanket she was knitting. The rhythm of working the stitches from one wooden needle to another helped calm her as she waited and listened to the sleet ping the tin roof.

After the church bells struck ten o'clock, Ben had still not returned. Etta knew she had to go look for him even if she had no inkling of where he was. If he was not at the store or Murphy's, she hoped some idea would come to her. She put her knitting away and banked the coals in the stove. She had her cloak around her shoulders when Ben walked through the front door. He looked chilled and soaked all the way through his jacket.

"Ben, I'll get the fire started again. Come get warm."

"Am I forgiven?"

"Always, my love," she said and helped him take off his wool jacket. "Where were you?"

"Walking and thinking. It took me this long to realize you were right," Ben said and took the poker from her. After he stirred the coals, he stood beside her in front of the reborn fire. "Pride has no place when it comes to keeping our child from its grandparents."

She melted into his arms, and he asked, "You sure you're not mad at me any more?"

"No, after you were gone so long, I got worried," she said and looked up at him. "I just wanted you back with me. I realized I couldn't rush you. You have to sort through this by yourself. "

"I'm so glad you understand me." He kissed her cheek.

"I didn't, not at first. I rocked so furiously I'm surprised I didn't wear grooves in the floorboard. The important thing is you're back home, safe with me." She pulled away. "Ben, I never want to have another argument like this, ever again."

He held her and promised before he continued, "I'll write my mother a letter tomorrow morning and ask them to come and stay with us over Christmas."

"Maybe you could say we'll bring the baby to their house next year."

~~~

Early the next morning Ben wrote his letter. They both agreed his words should sound like a grown son willing to meet his estranged father at least half way.

"I won't apologize," he said after he disagreed with one of her suggestions.

"I'm not asking you to. I'm asking you to reconcile and accept these are the only parents you're ever going to have."

A few minutes passed before he resumed writing. When he finished, he asked, "How does this sound?"

Finally they agreed on a short note that mentioned their new address and asked Reuben and Araminta to come and visit them over the holidays. Ben closed with their good news. After he sealed the letter, he said he would drop it off at the post office in time for the morning mail.

~~~

Etta waited every day for the postman to deliver an answer. She also watched every evening as Ben pretended he did not look for his mother's handwriting on any envelope that waited for him when he came home.

~~~

As they decorated their tree on Christmas Eve, she finally put the thoughts brewing within her into words. "Be proud you were man enough to reach out to them. You're a good son."

"Didn't do any good, did it? Matter of fact, it may have made it worse."

"How can that be?"

"When you play poker and raise the bet, you reveal you think you've got the upper hand or else you're bluffing. The only person at the table who knows you're bluffing is the person with a better hand, my father. He'll think I'm weak and not playing from a strong position."

"Life isn't a poker game. You showed your parents how you're a more loving and forgiving person. They'll have to live with that knowledge. You, on the other hand, have to accept, at least for the time being, things haven't changed. Wait until the baby's here. Your mother might prevail after all."

The next morning they celebrated their own private Christmas. Ben gave her a pearl ring to go with her necklace and earrings. Etta gave him a dove gray merino wool vest with matching scarf and a pair of suspenders she had knitted. The gifts, purchased and wrapped for his parents, went unclaimed under the tree. Etta put them away when Ben went outside to chop wood.

~~~

On the gentle warm midmorning of April 12th, Edward Benjamin Darnell arrived, weighing in at about seven pounds, according to Maureen the midwife. Mrs. Luttrell was on hand to help since Etta, like all new mothers, was not allowed out of bed until the ninth day. Etta found it worse than the labor pains to lie in bed and listen to life go on without her.

Lavinia and Sophie paid her several visits. Her friends laughed and shared memories of the Home with Mrs. Luttrell while Etta realized how blessed her life had become.

Within a few weeks, Etta began to relax her guard. For over a year, good fortune had smiled on her and Ben. Now a new son had joined their charmed circle. Maybe this time fate would break its cycle of bringing bad after good.

Chapter 24

Frankfort, March 13, 1880

"Happy anniversary, my love," Ben said and kissed her when he arrived home from the store. "You're more beautiful than the day we married three years ago."

Lovely or loving was the last thing Etta felt on this anniversary. For the past two weeks, she had slept little since Edward and Charity had been ill. The croup made six-month-old Charity unable to breathe and suck well at the same time. So feedings, which usually took twenty minutes, stretched for at least an hour. Laundry and ironing piled up, and she had no energy to cook a decent meal for Ben. Also, the idea of food made her ill.

When she had woken that morning with another bout of nausea, a cup of chamomile tea put her to rights for a few hours. But the greenish feeling came back before lunch, fueled from the smells of sickness that lingered in the house. Only after she put bits of cotton soaked in vanilla extract in all the rooms, did her queasiness settle.

By afternoon the upset stomach had retreated, but it was not truly gone and threatened to return. Her back ached, her breasts sore and swollen. She was also frustrated. She was farther behind than when she had gotten out of bed this morning.

Etta looked up at her husband. His big smile and the small package wrapped in pink paper in his hand pushed her to the brink of screaming. Instead of returning his greeting and kiss, she shoved a fussy Charity into his arms and she shouted, "I need some fresh air. The walls are closing in on me."

Ben looked shocked and crestfallen. But she threw a shawl over her head and hurried out the front door. By the time she had walked twenty feet, the brisk spring breeze had chased away the remnants of her nausea. Shame replaced her anger. Ben did not deserve an irate wife who screamed like a fishmonger's woman. Sheepishly, she turned back to her house.

When she entered the kitchen, she found Ben walking and singing a song to Charity. But it was clear his efforts were futile. The baby cried and was probably hungry.

Etta rushed to apologize. "I'm so sorry I lashed out at you. I forgot it was our anniversary." With tears in her eyes, she reached toward both of them. "I'm so tired. I forgot what today was. Please forgive me."

Ben handed over their daughter and kissed her cheek. "There's nothing to forgive. I knew you've been up most nights since the babies came down with the grippe. I just assumed you napped when they did."

"They aren't going down at the same time. One of them always needs me. Even while I'm asleep, I wait for one of them to wake up and cry."

"They're getting better, aren't they?" Ben asked and ran a nervous hand through his hair.

"Yes, thank God, they're strong and recovering." Charity nuzzled her breast so Etta took a seat at the kitchen table and began to nurse. "I've gotten run down, that's all. I'll rest when they're over this croup."

"Tomorrow I'll go in early and come back at lunch so you can sleep in the afternoon."

"Thank you Ben, for understanding."

"You and our children are my life." He pulled up a chair beside her. "Nothing is more important than all of you."

Etta smiled at the thought of an afternoon nap. It was so decadent. "Maybe both children will be still asleep after my nap tomorrow. Would you like to come and nap with me?"

Ben's eyes lit up at the prospect.

~~~

Two weeks later, she joined Sophie at Lavinia's house for their monthly get together. While their babies took their afternoon naps, her old friends laughed about their foolish girlish dreams back at the Home. Their lives had diverged from owning stores and being independent women. They shared how their current lives were so much better.

Etta, however, was disappointed her life was not quite all she had hoped. Still exhausted from the last round of childhood illnesses, she was grateful her children had recovered. Others had not. But she suspected she was pregnant again. Her morning sickness had not let up. So much for the old wife's tale that promised nursing prevented pregnancy.

A switch in conversation brought Etta back from her woolgathering. Lavinia mentioned the familiar name of Mazie Raines.

"The Little Magpie," Sophie said. "How did you meet her?" She looked up from tatting an edge on a handkerchief.

"Outside Dubois' Jewelry shop."

"Better outside than inside," Etta snarled and threw down her tangled tatting.

Lavinia laughed, "You never did like her, did you?"

"She was sneaky."

Sophie broke in, "Maybe she's changed. People do, you know?"

"Maybe so," Etta answered and picked up her string to give it another try. "How'd she seem?"

"Lonely, sad. She told me she's married to a notions salesman, Richard Darby."

Lavinia tied off her yarn and examined her tatting. "She has one baby, a girl named Ruth, about two months old. We had a few minutes to visit before little Ruthie woke up."

"We can help," Sophie said. "I'm hostess next month. I'll call on her and ask her to come."

Etta nodded though she was not happy about Mazie else joining them. But Sophie and Lavinia did not seem concerned about Mazie's habit of stealing.

"Where's she live?" Sophie said.

"Yenowine's."

"They're taking families now?" Etta hoped she had kept the sneer from her voice. "They didn't when I was at Caldwell's. Most of their boarders were legislators."

"Maybe," Sophie said, "Caldwell's new boarding house took most of the legislative clientele." She paused and started on her second handkerchief of the day. "That reminds me. I knew there was something I wanted to tell you. I heard the Olympaid hired a fancy chef."

"They must be after setting a high tone," Etta said.

"What's wrong with you today, Etta?" Lavinia asked.

"Nothing," she shrugged. She was not ready to share her suspicions yet. "Maybe a little tired."

Lavinia gave her an inquisitive look before turning back to Sophie. "How'd you hear about the new chef?"

"Owen hears all kinds of things at the music store. Besides the

Caldwells want him to play the piano during the dinner hour."

"Is he going to?"

"Well, the money will come in handy. We're going to have another baby this summer."

The conversation turned from Mazie and the new boarding house to Sophie's pregnancy. When another wave of nausea crept back, Etta looked at Sophie with envy. How did her friend take everything in stride? Etta could not remember a time she had ever seen Sophie lose her temper or pout.

Maybe Etta should try to be more like her. It might be nice to have a calm peaceful life. Etta tried to think of something calm and peaceful. Nothing came to mind until she remembered the spring sunshine when she had been pregnant with Eddie. How blissful life was then. Etta felt her spirits lift as the nausea eased. There might be something to this thinking of happy memories after all.

~~

Early April brought Etta the hoped-for bright days of sunshine. With all her windows open to the fresh air, the house smelled clean again. And praise God, her morning sickness receded.

Two weeks later, the friends celebrated Eddie's second birthday and included Mazie. When Eddie unwrapped his gifts, he was just as happy with the wrapping paper as he was with his top and small wooden horse. Mazie made over all the children. She fussed over Charity's curls, how tall Eddie was. She even commented on the swirl of colors as she spun the top. Over tea and apple pie, Sophie, followed by Lavinia and Etta, told Mazie what had happened in their lives since they had left the Home and married.

Mazie, in turn, told them she had stayed on at the Home as a hired helper in the infirmary and kitchen until she met her future husband, Richard Darby. He had called on Ghostie to talk him into offering sewing classes for the residents and purchasing the needed supplies from his company.

Mr. Fielding had passed on the plan. But Mazie found she was quite taken with the salesman. Soon they were walking out together and a little over a year ago had married. Mazie said she regretted she had lost track of them after they left the Home. Her plans now included a move to Lexington as soon as her husband earned a more established route.

Mazie said, "I'll be so thrilled to get back close to home."

"Lexington's home?" Lavinia asked.

"I grew up in nothing bigger than a crossroads called Donerail, not far from Lexington. There's some shirttail cousins of mine back there."

"You'll keep in touch this time, won't you?" Sophie said.

Mazie agreed. Etta offered to host their next meeting in May and gave Mazie directions to her house. Ruthie woke up from her nap first, so Mazie left after she gathered her baby and satchel.

Danny woke up next, and Lavinia soon departed. After Etta put a few of Eddie and Charity's toys in her perambulator, she got down on her knees and started to look under the furniture.

She stopped when she saw Sophie's feet and heard her question, "What are you looking for, Etta, dust bunnies?"

"No, I can't find Eddie's new top. I thought I left it with his other toys, but it's not here."

"It's probably rolled way back under the china cabinet. I'll ask Owen to help me find it tonight when he gets home."

"You don't think... no, never mind. I'm sure it'll turn up. Thank you for the birthday party."

～～

At the dinner table, Etta revealed her suspicions to Ben. He nodded and said he had heard about such women.

"What do you mean?" she asked and fought to still the slight edge of anger in her voice.

"Some women get these urges to steal things. Things they don't need or could ever use. It happened to me after I started carrying Lavinia 's hats and your fancy work."

"How did you know it was the women doing the stealing?"

"Now calm down." He stopped cutting his ham. "Let me explain. Before I started displaying those beautiful hats and such, it was a rare woman who came into the store unless she was a farmer."

"But after Lavinia and I made things for the store?"

"It was like honey. Women came in to shop for those pretty things, not any farm items."

"Lavinia's hats looked so nice up there. You could see them from the sidewalk," Etta said and spooned some more beets onto Eddie's plate.

"After I did inventory at the end of the first month, I realized two hats were missing. I never told Lavinia since I had already paid her for them. But I knew I couldn't afford to go on losing merchandise." He shoveled some ham and potatoes into his mouth.

"And when you moved everything to the back counter behind the cash register?"

"There weren't any more stolen items, and it worked out even better."

"I don't understand."

Ben laughed, "I wished I'd thought of it right from the beginning. The women had to ask to try them on. So while the wives looked at themselves in the mirror, the men took more time to look at other things in the store. Lo and behold, sales increased."

"What's happened now since we're all too busy with our babies to make pretties for your store?"

For just a few seconds, Etta missed the satisfaction she had had when Frankfort women bought her creations. She was proud her needlework had advanced from knitting to making brooches. Her own special touch was to decorate her work with bits of velvet and fish scales left over from Lavinia's hats.

"Women have stopped coming in to shop, and the petty theft rate has decreased. I still lose some stuff, mostly small things like nails." He gave her another smile. "All of us expect to lose some of our inventory, but the women do seem to steal more than the men."

Etta decided to change the topic. "Mazie's from your part of the state. You might have heard of her people. Her last name's Raines."

"Don't think so. Where'd you say she came from?"

"Some small town outside of Lexington."

He thought as he cut another slice of bread. "Don't remember anybody by that name. Though I've heard the name of Rainey, good farm people." He stopped with his bread halfway to his mouth. "Didn't you say Mrs. Luttrell advised all the new girls to keep quiet about their pasts?"

"Yes, so I guess it's possible Raines isn't even her real name."

"And remember, in that neck of the woods, one small town is much like another. You have only her word for who she is and where she came from."

~~~

In May the four women were together again at Etta's house. This time they had a birthday party for Lavinia's second baby Eleanor, who had turned one. The baby's presents included a rattle from Sophie. Etta brought a fancy knitted summer cap woven with bright pink ribbons to set off the little girl's golden curls. Mazie's gift was Belgian lace worked into bows.

Etta had every intention of watching Mazie's movements, but her hostess duties distracted her. Once again Ruthie woke up first, and Mazie left soon after. Etta helped Lavinia gather Eleanor's gifts. The new cap was nowhere to be found.

"Now two of our babies' gifts are missing," Etta seethed. "We can't trust Mazie. She's always going to steal things. I don't want her in my house again. Do you?"

"No," both the other women said and shook their heads.

"It's so sad," Sophie said. "I guess she'll never outgrow her bad habit."

"We're probably her only friends," Lavinia said. "So what do we do? She'll expect an invitation to your house in June."

"I'd like to see her room," Etta said. "I bet we'd find Eddie's top and Eleanor's cap hidden away. I get so angry when I think she stole from our babies."

"I can see, you've got the crease between your eyes again." When Sophie touched on her forehead, Etta felt the anger melt.

Lavinia suggested, "I'll write her in a few days before we are to meet and tell her Eleanor's coming down with something."

"Let's get together in three weeks," Etta suggested. "If we stop, she wins."

"I agree. I need these meetings," Sophie said, "We can't allow Mazie to ruin our get togethers."

When the friends met in June, Sophie told them the Darby family was gone.

"Good," said Etta, "Now we don't have to pussyfoot around any more."

Chapter 25

July 13, 1880

Etta paced through the house in the middle of the night. As she opened doors and windows, she hoped to catch a stray breeze and stir the humid air. But she knew it did not really matter. The low back pain which went along with pregnancy had set in two days ago and continued to rob her of sleep.

The strangest thoughts kept her company. What was the best season to be pregnant? Her next reflection was on how the neighborhood dogs and cats never seemed to be bothered by their pregnancies. During her third round through the kitchen, she decided it had to be because they were in that condition for only a few months.

The wind chime gave off its gentle tones. She glanced out the front door and saw the clouds move in and shroud the full moon. Good, she thought, maybe the house would soon cool off and she could go back to sleep.

When the tree branches twisted and scraped against the roof and brick walls, fear began to gnaw at her. She stepped out between the front door. She could barely make out the leaves had turned, back side up. The wind howled, brewing into a storm, something she had been terrified by even as a child. Her mother had often claimed Etta had learned her fear from the only other person in the household scared to death, Aunt Helen.

And like Aunt Helen, Etta had never outgrown the fear. Early in their marriage, Ben had teased and cuddled her as the wind blew into thunderstorms. But lately his manner had sharpened, so she resisted the urge to go wake him.

Instead she shut the doors and windows. Telling herself it might blow over soon, she rocked in the parlor and tried to ride out the thunder and lightening. But soon, she resumed her pacing since the storm intensified.

When the lightening and thunder were nearly twinned, she decided enough was enough. It was time to get her babies to safety. She would just have to endure Ben's stinging remarks about how she always got het up over nothing. She rushed into their bedroom and yanked on his arm until he was awake.

"Ben, listen to that wind. You can come with me or not. You decide. But you will help me get the children to the cellar."

A shutter tore loose and hit the bedroom window. Ben nodded and joined her in gathering up lanterns and their children.

Outside Ben raised the heavy wooden cellar door and held it open against the gusts of wind. Etta climbed down the stone steps with Charity. Just as she grasped Eddie's arm, the door jerked out of Ben's hands and knocked him to the ground. Through the whirling rain, Etta saw his unmoving body lying by the back steps. He was only a few feet out of the reach of the door's rise and fall with the wind.

Etta shouted at him to get up. Over the next few moments, when he remained motionless, she tried to fight down her panic. If he did not get up soon, she would have to go get him.

The next flash of lightening showed he had not moved. So she guided the children to the dirt floor and followed with the demand that Eddie hold on tight to his sister. Next she gathered her wet skirts and held them up as she crawled back up the steps and out toward Ben.

The lantern glow from the cellar and the intermittent lightning showed the rain blew horizontally. Ben moved his legs and sat up. Etta drew upon her strength and held the heavy door with one hand. With the other, she took Ben's arm and helped him into the cellar.

A few minutes later, the storm's path crossed over their heads. She held on to the rope that secured the door. Finally, after what seemed hours, the roaring noise died. The wind dropped. The tornado must be losing its power, she thought, though the rain still lashed the wooden door.

Wet and chilled, Etta clung to her crying children and looked at Ben. He slumped a few feet across from her, against the earthen wall.

"Are you hurt?" she asked.

"No," he said. "I'll be fine. Let me rest a few minutes."

"Nothing's broken?"

"No, trust me, don't worry."

Etta turned her gaze to the water dripping around the doorframe and puddling on the dirt floor. The smell of damp earth mingled with the scent of spring apples wrapped in newspaper and stored on the shelves.

Etta leaned back. Her movement nudged something loose. Two jars of corn preserved from last year's harvest tottered from the shelf nearest her. In the weak light, the glass lay broken and glistening. The mixture of smells made her ill. She tried to ignore her rising nausea and counted the seconds between the thunderclaps.

As soon as the count grew to ten, she shook Ben awake. "I think it's safe now. I can hear the crickets again."

Ben, with Eddie held tightly, lifted the door. Etta, clutching Charity, followed them up the steps. The moonlight showed her familiar house in a strange landscape. Debris littered the yard. Someone's clawfoot bathtub sat on its side near her flattened flower garden.

Neighbors came out of their cellars and houses. Mrs. Leander, the widow from next door, rushed toward the children with dry quilts.

Etta thanked her while Ben wrapped the blankets around them and said the roof looked intact. But she knew there had to be some damage. She raised the lantern and gave the back of the house a hard look. A large tree limb had blown through the window above the sink.

Inside the kitchen, Ben left her with the children and went with one of the lanterns to inspect the attic. She stood, unable to move. The kitchen she saw was not hers. A strange leafy tree branch jutted halfway across the room. The pine pie safe had tipped forward and spilled forth cooking utensils and linens onto the table and floor. Bits and pieces of jade-colored pottery cluttered the floor and shelves.

Holding Charity on her hip, she guided Eddie around the debris and into the hallway. The rain and wind had destroyed the wallpaper and knocked the few framed pictures to the floor.

She had no words to answer Ben's overhead shouts. Instead she opened the children's bedroom door. Somehow here, nothing seemed disturbed. She changed the children into dry clothes and put them back to bed.

The kitchen appeared to have the most damage. She started to clean up. But the effort and time it would take to right the room overwhelmed her. The energy, which had kept her moving, evaporated. She collapsed to her knees by the toppled pie safe.

Ben found her a few minutes later.

"Are you hurt?" he asked.

"No," she sighed. "I'm just so upset. The fancy fruit knife you gave me for our anniversary this year is crushed." Etta held up the splintered mother-of-pearl from the folding handle.

"It meant so much to me because it was also an orphan, like me. Nothing else matched it."

"Come, you're tired. By some miracle, we're safe. The only damage's in here," he said and took her in his arms. When his head touched hers, he winced and drew back.

"What's the matter?" she asked. A tiny stream of blood had dried on his cheek. "You're the one who's's hurt. Let me see." Lifting his hair from his forehead, she saw a goose egg.

"Does your head ache?"

"Not bad. I'll rest after I get some wood for the window. It won't be fancy, but it should keep the rain out. Why don't you lie down while the babies are sleeping? We'll clean up here when I get back from checking on the store."

Etta agreed and changed out of her wet clothes. Soon she got the fire going in the cook stove and brewed a pot of tea. It was so strange. Just a few hours before she had been so hot. Now she was chilled.

She found the honey and stirred a teaspoonful into her cup of tea. They were lucky she told herself. Ben was right.

After a few sips, she realized she needed sleep. When Ben returned, they would check on their friends and neighbors. Maybe they had been as fortunate.

~~~

Later Etta woke to Eddie's cries of "Momma, Momma." A quick glance at the mantle clock told her it was almost eight. She noticed the other side of the bed was empty and the pillow undented. Ben had not come back to rest, and he was not anywhere else in the house.

By the time Charity woke up, Good Shepherd's bells had chimed nine. Etta's concern for Ben grew. He had been gone too long. After feeding both children breakfast, she left them with Mrs. Leander and set out for the center of town.

Etta walked through one heavily damaged area after another. The destruction was unbelievable. Sheared trees were everywhere. She did not have to watch for buggy traffic since the streets were too blocked for the vehicles to maneuver. She soon became disoriented because the familiar landmarks had disappeared. Gone were neighbors' houses, trees, street signs, and store fronts.

Using Good Shepherd's bent steeple as a guide, she took twenty minutes to pick her way downtown and to the store. There Ben sat amid the rubble of the collapsed storefront.

"Ben, let's go home," she said and helped him up.

"I can't see too good, Etta. My head won't stop hurting."

"You took a pretty bad bump. You need rest."

As they returned home through the litter-strewn streets, he told her about their store. Almost half their stock was no good. Mr. Trimble from the bank had stopped by and said the sheriff had deputized young men to protect the businesses from looters. But Ben was not sure he trusted the police officers and planned to return to the store before dusk.

While Ben slept, Owen stopped by to announce their new son had decided to come at the height of the storm. The midwife had told him both Sophie and the baby were doing well. The other good news was their house had only a little damage.

He also reported Daniel and Lavinia had lost the roof from their house. Fortunately the whole family was safe. They had packed up to go live with his folks until they could make the repairs to their house.

As Etta watched him leave, she wished she had family to help her and Ben. Maybe she could get Ben to write to his father or his brothers and ask them to pitch in with repairing the store.

~~~

A few hours later, Ben grumbled when she tried to wake him.

"Leave me alone. My head hurts something awful."

"Stay at home then. Your clerk can go to the store tonight instead of you."

"Don't be ridiculous, Etta," he said and put his feet on the floor. "It's my store, not his."

"But you're injured."

"I can do it." He began lacing his boots. "Get out of my way and fix me something to eat."

"Fine," Etta snapped. "If that's the way you're going to be." She slammed the door on her way to the kitchen.

A few minutes later, he sat down at the kitchen table. She put a bowl of soup down in front of him in a stony silence.

~~~

Around eight in the evening, Etta heard the Lane's dog bark.

Looking out the parlor window, she saw a group of men with lanterns draw nearer.

"Mrs. Darnell," the one in front shouted. "Mrs. Darnell, are you at home?"

Alarmed, she stepped out to the front porch. "What's the matter?"

Her heart thudded to a stop when she saw Ben, with his head down, held up by two men.

"Eldon Harris, one of your husband's customers, recognized him wandering around by the courthouse." The first man thumbed to the trio behind him.

"Harris said he wasn't acting right. We took him to Caldwell's first because that's where he said he lived. They directed us over here."

Etta started down the stepping stones, but the stranger raised his hand to stop her.

"He's out again. Best thing you can do is to show us where to put him."

Etta held the front door open. "First door on the right," she said to the two men carrying Ben. She faced the other man and said, "Thank you, Mr...?"

"Curry, ma'am."

"Mr. Curry, could one of you go by Doc Stratton's?"

"There's no need," Curry said and followed her into the bedroom. "Harris said he'd stop by on his way out of town and tell the Doc how bad off your husband is."

He lowered his voice, "Harris told me the way your husband acted reminded him of a dazed cow he once had after lightening struck it out cold."

Etta's knees buckled. Curry rushed to help her to a chair.

"Ma'am, I'm sure he'll get better real soon. The farmer said the cow was all right in a couple days. Is there anyone we can get to help you? You don't look too good either."

"Maybe my neighbor, Miss Lane?"

"The library lady? Sure, we was planning on heading her direction anyway. Heard her ma's been passing out coffee and pie to anyone that shows up on her doorstep. Let's go, fellas. Take care of yourself, ma'am."

After the front door creaked, Etta checked on Ben. He looked a little feverish. A new bruise had darkened above his eye. Guilt built within her. Here he was hurt, and she had yelled at him.

"I could use some of your coffee and pie, Miss Smith," he said.

"Ben, what are you saying? We're married. Don't you remember?"

Her heart melted when he gave her a charming boyish grin. "We're married? Isn't that just grand?" He closed his eyes and fell asleep.

A few minutes later, Etta was in the kitchen when she heard the familiar voice of Doc Stratton through the front screen door.

"Mrs. Darnell?"

"In here, sir," she said and started down the hall.

Just the sound of the doctor's words made her believe everything was going to get better.

"I heard Ben ran into a bit of trouble tonight," he said and took her hand. "You go on out to the parlor and wait for me." He guided her away from the bedroom. "This won't take long. I could sure use a cup of coffee, if you have one at hand."

Etta had his coffee ready for him when he joined her in the parlor. Between sips he told her rest was all Ben needed.

"Send for me in a few days if he doesn't improve. My advice to you is to take care of yourself and the little one you're carrying."

~~~

Two days later, Etta's concern intensified when Ben woke up and said his head felt like it was splitting in two. She ignored his protests and sent for the doctor. After Stratton examined him, he was not as comforting as before.

"It appears Ben's going to take longer than I hoped to recover from the bump on his head."

"How much longer?"

"Hard to tell. The good thing is his confusion's gone," he said. "But I'm still worried about the pain. Then there's the fact he hasn't been back to work. That's not like him."

Etta feared his answer to her next question. "Maybe I should write to his family?" The longer he took to reply, the greater her anxiety grew.

"I don't believe he is in mortal danger, Mrs. Darnell. But family's always good to have around at a time like this."

~~~

Etta sent the letter. She explained some days Ben's head pain was so intense he could not get out of bed, and the store was still a heap of rubble. She begged for help.

But the Darnells did not write back. Thinking the letter got lost,

Etta dipped into her dwindling supply of money and telegraphed Ben's parents.

"Ben hurt bad. Need help. Please come."

She did not get an answer to the telegram, either.

~~~

Two weeks after the tornado, Doc Stratton revisited the Darnell home. He spent a few moments with Ben and asked Etta to join him on the front step. Taking her by the arm, he helped her sit before he joined her.

"Mrs. Darnell, your husband's not improving like I had hoped he might. I've consulted with some colleagues from the Louisville Medical School. The prognosis isn't good. Most patients with head injuries improve quickly with rest and get on with their lives. For a few people though, life changes forever. I'm afraid Ben may be one of those."

Alarm shot through Etta. The future loomed bleak with an invalided husband, two small children, another one due in October. She panicked. How could she take care of all of them?

"Your husband reports he's having nightmares and can't sleep even when there's no pain."

"Won't he get better with rest? Maybe all he needs is a few more weeks."

"There's more to consider. He is also naturally concerned about you and the children as well as his business. None of this worry is good for him. Did you hear from his family yet?"

She could barely get the word out. "No."

"We can always hope, my dear, but I think you should prepare yourself for the worst."

"What's do you mean?" Her mouth suddenly went dry.

"He may never work again because he might not be able to concentrate or make good judgments. You could probably run the business if that happens. But," he stopped and appeared uneasy.

"Go on." Etta met his gaze. On instinct she sat up straighter.

"I want you to understand this doesn't happen all the time. But sometimes people with head injuries change so much they're no longer themselves."

He paused, and she tried to absorb what the doctor meant.

"Their spouses and children feel they no longer know who their loved ones are. Do you understand what I'm saying?"

The stained and worn stepping stones swam before her eyes. She felt faint and so alone. She shook her head.

"For example," he said, "People who never drank will suddenly consume great quantities of alcohol. Others who never showed any temper at all will become enraged over the smallest event. They easily lose control of themselves and commit the vilest of acts."

Etta's heart sank, and she asked, "How will I know if Ben is going to be like that?"

"There's no way to know until he loses control. Mark my words though, once he does, he'll no longer be himself."

"Ever?" She tried to cast the spinning dizziness from her head.

"Probably not. If it happens, for his own safety and to protect you and others, he'll have to be locked up."

Fury and despair merged within her. "No, you can't take Ben away from his family. He's a good man."

"Let's hope he never does lose control." He patted her hand and stood. "But be on the lookout for any abrupt changes in his behavior. Now let me help you up. You have to be brave for your children."

The next day she wrote another letter to Ben's parents. She said a little prayer to St. Jude as she pushed the thin envelope containing her last hope through the mail slot at the post office.

~~~

By mid-August, Etta grew even more anxious over Ben. He took to staying out late. The town guards had to bring him home from Doyle's Tavern where he routinely drank himself into verbal quarrels and fist fights.

One night the guards carried him in through the front door and dumped him onto their bed. She had his torn shirt unbuttoned and half off when he grabbed her and tried to drag her into the bed.

The smell of alcohol on his breath sickened Etta and unleashed a flashback to the times her drunken father had come to her bedroom. When she refused Ben's overtures, he erupted and forced her onto the bed beside him. His impatient hands ripped through her layers of clothing.

Etta panicked and pushed him back so hard he lost his balance and fell off the bed. Once on the floor, he lay there, unable to get up.

Gasping for air and shaken, Etta grabbed her robe, stepped over him, and rushed out of the room. Fear and disgust shot through her. She fought down the urge to vomit. Wrapping her arms around herself to quell the urge to run, she paced up and down the hallway and replayed the doctor's warning in her head.

She explored her limited options. If she knew he would sleep it off, she would be safe to stay with him through the night. But if he woke up and became angry all over again, she doubted she had the strength to fight him off a second time. She was also scared he might hurt the children.

Where could she go for help? It was well after midnight. All the decent people in the neighborhood were asleep. Even the church was closed at night. The town was not safe enough for her to walk with Eddie and Charity to Sophie's. But she could not face the Lanes or Mrs. Leander at this hour.

So Etta did the only thing she could think of. She got the clothesline rope and the heaviest iron from the back porch. Armed, she stopped outside the bedroom door to listen and heard Ben's loud snores. Slowly she opened the door and placed the lamp on the hallway floor. It gave off barely enough light to see, but at least it would not wake Ben. Removing her shoes, she tiptoed towards him. It seemed he had not moved.

He lay on his back with his arms stretched out. He did not wake up when she knelt down beside him and placed the rope and iron near her knees. Carefully she tied the rope around his right wrist and brought it to his middle. Never taking her eyes off his face, she moved cautiously to his left side.

When he did not stir, she brought his left arm close to his right and wrapped the rope snugly around both wrists. Suddenly he coughed. Etta froze and waited. After she saw he was out like a spent match, she crawled to his feet and secured them with the rest of the rope.

Not trusting her legs to remain steady, she took the iron and crawled out of their bedroom. Silent tears blurred her vision. Her heart beat so wildly she feared for her baby.

In the hallway, she hesitated before getting to her feet. His snores had not changed. She hoped she had a few hours respite before he woke. Pushing her rocker into the hallway, she dimmed the lamp and rocked to steady her nerves. Ben would be angry when he woke up, bound and trussed up like a wild hog. But for tonight she was safe, and so were her children.

~~~

It was dark when she woke. It took a few seconds to surface from her fatigue and to place where she was and what had happened. Ben's snores had changed to a deeper register. The church bells sounded. She listened as the chimes rang five times, and one by one her aches competed for her attention. Her neck was stiff. Her back ached almost as much as when she had been in labor. Using her elbows, she pushed herself up and made for their bedroom door.

Enough moonlight leaked around the window blind for her to make out Ben's shape. It looked like he was in the same position as last night. Armed once again with the iron, she softly crawled toward him. She untied his feet first and then his hands.

Backing silently out of the door still on all fours, she retreated to the safety of the hallway. After checking on the children and returning the rope and iron to the back porch, she went into the parlor and fell asleep on the sofa.

She awoke to daylight and crying, Ben's. His sobs reached through the door and grew more distinct when she opened it. He was now on his side and moaned how sorry he was. Etta wanted to go to him and comfort him but found herself afraid and frozen in the doorway.

Ben looked up at her and asked, "Etta, what happened? All I remember is drinking with the boys last night."

"The guards brought you home," she kept all expression from her voice. "They said this was your last warning. The next time, you'll be in jail."

Ben struggled to sit upright. After he was stable, he looked around the room. She watched a storm of disgust and fear march over his face as he took in the rumpled bedspread, her tired sleepless eyes and ripped bodice under her robe.

His shoulders slumped. "I'm no good, just no good to you and the children. You'd be better off if the storm had killed me."

"You should be thankful you're alive. Now stop crying and act like a man. Do something to take care of us."

"What? There's nothing I can do."

"Write your father or go see him. I can't do this alone any more, Ben. I don't have any family, you do." She turned her back on him and stomped out.

~~~

When Etta checked on him after breakfast, he was gone. At first she was puzzled. She had not even heard the front door shut. Her relief led to guilt. A good wife, she thought, would be worried. But Etta was too tired to care.

~~~

After lunch, Mr. Trimble from the bank called on her. He sat in the parlor and began by saying he did not have good news.

"I'm sorry for your trouble, Mrs. Darnell, with Ben sick and you, well, in your condition. I thought you might tell your husband the board's directed me to wire his father."

"How can you do that to Ben?"

"It's not personal, it's business. We have no choice. The elder Mr. Darnell's the co-signer. Therefore, he's also responsible for the debt."

"But we've never missed a payment. I know Ben's even paid ahead."

"The past few years, yes, he has. But since the storm, too many clients have stopped making their payments. The bank officers say we can't carry the paper on your store any longer."

"You can't take his dream away from him."

"We have a responsibility to our shareholders. They demand we pursue good business practices. Again, I'm sorry I had to bring you such bad news. Please, don't get up. I'll see myself out."

Somehow through her fog, Etta registered that the door creaked open and shut. The sounds of her children playing before her crept across the foreground of her numbed mind. A thought that she should stand and do something niggled around the edges. But she remained seated until the noise of a loud disagreement between Eddie and Charity broke through. She had no idea of how long she had sat there. Leaning over, she gathered both children and held them close until Eddie squirmed and demanded she let him go. Charity stayed on her lap and fell asleep.

Panic swept over her as she tried to think of a solution. The grim reality chilled her. Ben was damaged in some invisible way from the storm. He might get better, but Doc Stratton could not tell her when. Their store, their livelihood, would soon be gone. No one would hire Ben for any kind of job now. She was even more unhirable, pregnant and unfit to work in a decent paying job.

Any way Etta looked at her situation, she was alone and had nowhere to turn. Sophie and Owen had no room for her. They were overcrowded with their third child. Lavinia and Daniel had gone to his parents.

The money she and Ben had squirreled away, coin by coin, for emergencies was going for food and firewood and Ben's nightly trips to the tavern. A little over one hundred dollars remained in their bank account. But she could not touch the money in the bank since only Ben could withdraw any money from the account.

After Etta put Charity to bed, she pulled the coffee can from the shelf and counted what she had left in her household money. Exactly sixty-three dollars. Susan's advice from so long ago came to her. She took out a needle and some thread from the sewing basket. Within a few minutes, she had sown the money into her chemise. She did not want a repeat of last week.

Ben had again found another hiding place. He took two dollars from the broken teapot hidden in the repaired pie safe. The cache of sixty-three dollars tucked under her bodice was all she had.

Two solutions came to her. The first was to throw herself on the charity of the county even if it meant moving the three of them to the workhouse. The second was to ask the Caldwells for some work. If the Caldwells took her back, she would have to find someone to watch the children. She had only one real choice. She would die before she took her children to the county orphanage. She remembered what those places were like.

~~~

Etta returned from the boarding house after Good Shepherd's bell announced it was two o'clock more desperate than this morning. It had not gone well. The Caldwells were aware of Ben's drinking and violence and refused to hire her. The risk he might project his angry outbursts against them or their guests was too great.

Relief won over worry when she found the house empty. Life was much easier without him and his erratic ups and downs. Eddie took his sister to their room whenever he heard Ben walk up the front walk. The few times he did not retreat quickly enough, he stuttered when he had to address his father. Etta could not remember a time after the storm when Eddie had voluntarily hugged or spoken with Ben. Charity, though too young to understand, must have picked up on the tension in the home. She whimpered and cringed whenever Ben came close to her.

Though Ben was not back by nine o'clock in the evening, Etta was too tired and heartsick to even go look for him. She went to bed without knowing where her husband was. She had little control over what he did and when he did it. This she accepted and turned the keys in the doors.

Then she climbed into bed alone.

~~~

Ben was still not at home when a little before noon, a knock at the door startled her. Two unexpected visitors stood on her doorstep. Trimble, the banker, and Doc Stratton strode past her after she moved aside for them to enter. Only the doctor made eye contact and kindly took her hand as he guided her to the parlor. The banker followed. They waited for her to settle into the rocking chair before taking their seats on the sofa. So far no one had spoken. Eddie paused his toy train and looked up at the visitors.

"Eddie, would you be a big boy and take your sister to your room?" the physician asked. When the boy nodded, Doc Stratton said, "I'll come tell you when we're finished."

After the children left, Trimble began, "Mrs. Darnell, please excuse our calling, but we need to talk with you about your husband."

"Is he all right?" She feared the answer.

"He's in the jail, has been since late last night."

His information did not answer her question. She moved her gaze to the doctor. "But how is he?"

"You need to hear Mr. Trimble out first."

The banker cleared his throat and continued. "The sheriff won't let him loose without some guarantee he'll behave himself. Last night your husband attacked a woman."

"He'd never," Etta barked. But she knew the truth. Ben was capable of such an act.

"We don't know exactly what happened. The witnesses at Doyle's weren't exactly reliable. But from the looks of things, the woman gave as good as she got. She's in jail also."

"So I can get him released?"

Mr. Trimble inclined his head toward the doctor.

"What concerns us is Doc here says it's impossible for anyone to predict if and when his behavior will get better. I'm afraid he'll have to stay downtown for the foreseeable future. We don't want him hurting himself or others."

Etta's sob made the man stop and look at the doctor, who gave a slight nod to continue.

"But I have some good news. The sheriff sent a telegram to your father-in-law early this morning, and Mr. Darnell has wired he's coming in on the morning train to take control of the situation. We knew you'd be worried, in your delicate condition."

He stammered his last words, and his cheeks blazed.

"Mrs. Darnell," the doctor took over. "Let the men handle the business details. We want you to rest and concentrate on taking care of yourself and your children. They need your attention."

He tried a smile, but it slid into a frown. "I'm sorry I can't be optimistic about your husband's condition. There's still a great deal we don't know about the brain and how a person recovers from a head injury."

Etta reached deep inside for her sense of dignity. "Thank you for telling me where Ben is."

~~~

The moment the door closed on her visitors, she checked her children. They were both asleep, and Charity was under a blanket. Gently Etta uncovered her perspiring little daughter and left them to finish their naps on the floor.

Once in the hall, visions of Ben in dirty, smelly, and rumpled clothes and alone in an old dark cell saddened her. Though her jailed husband had changed so much from the man she had married, she took pity on him. Etta went into their bedroom and began to gather a few of his clean clothes.

A sudden knock on the front door was so loud her unborn baby jumped. The sound had a certain determination to it. It did not have a questioning is anyone home tone.

When Etta reached the door, she understood. Reuben Darnell glared, just as he had four years ago at Caldwell's. His shoulders were rigid, his color high.

She saw him take in her pregnancy, tiredness, and wilting spirit until his eyes moved to look behind her. She turned to see Eddie at the opened bedroom door. Reuben stared for a moment at him before he returned his attention to her.

"May I come in?"

"Yes, Mr. Darnell, come in. This is Eddie, your grandson. Eddie, this is Poppa's poppa."

Etta was amazed at how similar they were. She saw traces of Ben and Eddie in her visitor. Something about their posture, she decided when Reuben and Eddie walked ahead of her into the parlor.

"Would you like some lemonade?" she asked.

"This is not a social call. You should send the boy out of the room."

Etta hoped she did not telegraph her panic to Eddie when she took him into the kitchen and gave him some cookies and lemonade.

"You stay in here and don't wake up your sister. Your grandpa and I have to talk for a few minutes." Eddie looked at the two cookies and back at her. "Can I have Charity's cookies since she's asleep?"

"Yes," she ruffled his hair. "Along with some paper and pencils to draw with until I come get you, understand?"

He smiled and she kissed his forehead.

~~~

Back in the parlor, she decided she would be polite yet cool. After all, this was the man who had hurt Ben so much.

After he examined the room and sat down, Reuben said, "I'll get right to the point. I have a meeting with Mr. Tolliver, the bank's lawyer in a few minutes. It appears Ben needs more help than you can give him. He may never be well again. There's nothing anyone can do for him, here."

"What do you mean by here?" she asked as a coldness gripped her stomach.

"Mr. Tolliver wired me last week with his concerns about Ben's ability to work and keep the store. I then consulted a specialist in Lexington. He believes my son needs a complete rest cure, free of the stress of trying to support you. I knew he was correct when the sheriff told me this morning Ben's fixated on coming back to you, your children and this house."

"Of course he is. We're important to him."

"I'm not here to argue with you. I'm telling you the facts. He can't be released from jail without some safeguards. His drinking is out of control. He has behaved inappropriately. I gather last night he went beyond the pale. He's turned into a criminal."

He stood and towered over her.

"No," she struggled to her feet to defend Ben. "You're wrong. He's a good person."

"Remember your place, girl. Don't make a scene. You have to accept Ben will never be the same again. The specialist said his only hope of recovery is a clean break from his life with you. Otherwise he'll develop hallucinations and seizures. He could even commit suicide."

Shocked, she fell back into her chair. The rest of Reuben's words washed over her until the word divorce broke through her mental fog.

"You said divorce?"

"If you love my son," he managed to work a sneer in at the word love, "you'll want what's best for him and let him go. I'll promise you financial security. I'm prepared to give you five hundred today, and fifteen hundred when I return home." He pointed his finger, "But you must agree, right now to a divorce."

Etta gripped the arms of the chair and fought back her panic. "I can't divorce Ben. I love him. He loves me and our children."

"You have only one choice. It's simple. Are you going to take care of your children and their future and let me take care of my child?"

"You have to be out of your mind."

He leaned closer to her. "If you remain stubborn, I'll use these papers." He reached into his coat pocket and draw out a folded set of documents.

"These state I am no longer responsible for Ben or any of his debts or actions. I will also disown every last one of you and everything goes to my other sons.

Etta wondered at the depth of rancor this man had. "Why do you hate me and your own grandchildren?"

"Your stubbornness bewitched Ben from his family. His mother died exhausted by grief last year. You killed her. I'm not going to let you kill my son."

"You didn't even write to tell Ben about his mother?"

Her unborn child began to kick with renewed vigor, and she feared she might go into early labor.

He smirked. "Why should I have? Ben was lost to her. Besides, how do I even know these are Ben's children? You hid your past from our family. We know nothing about you, though I'm certain you're not who you told Ben you were."

Etta sank farther back into her chair and stared at this man in disbelief. How could Ben have come from such a person?

Charity's whine from the bedroom broke through Etta's shock. She rose and glared at him in defiance. "I agree. My children will be better off having no family at all rather than claim you."

He stalked toward the front door. Etta hoped the hate in her stare burned into his back even after he stepped over the threshold and slammed the door.

~~~

Before five o'clock, a Mr. Littleberry arrived at her house. He introduced himself as the lawyer for the senior Mr. Darnell.

"Ma'am," he said after they were seated in the parlor, "you need to sign several documents. The first one sets the divorce proceedings in order."

Etta read the three page document. It seemed to mean she was divorcing Ben on the grounds of nonsupport. She used the lawyer's ink pen and signed.

He took the paper back and rolled a blotter over her signature.

"This next one," Littleberry said, "acknowledges Mr. Darnell has deposited five hundred dollars in your savings account at the bank."

"And the remainder of the money?"

"Later."

Littleberry waved the question away and pointed to the line requiring her name.

Etta did not even bother with any more questions and accepted her defeat. All her strength now would have to go to her children. She realized the money would only be enough to get by on for several months, especially with the baby on the way. How long did it take for a divorce to become final? She had no idea and considered asking another question. But she decided against it. Etta did not want to hear another word out of his mouth.

~~~

While she peeled the potatoes for supper, she wondered if she should stay in Frankfort. She would be a disgraced woman, and the stigma would surely pass onto her children. But Frankfort had become her home. Where else could she go? Louisville was out. She realized she really had no choice until her baby was born.

The only good thing which happened, she decided as she shucked several ears of corn, was Ben's father bought her a little time. She would have the opportunity to think and plan, and more importantly to overcome her tired to the bone weariness.

Chapter 26

Frankfort, October 1880

For Etta, the unexpected bright Indian summer day brought a blessing, her daughter Della. The healthy baby started her life free of the damp and dark days common for Frankfort's fall season.

Though she had hired Mrs. Luttrell to help out, Etta missed Lavinia and Sophie. She had not seen them since their last get-together before the tornado struck the past summer. So the next week, it was Mrs. Luttrell who held her while she read the final divorce papers.

"Don't you go on like this, Etta. Your milk will dry up, and then where will you and that tiny baby be?"

Mrs. Luttrell took the papers and shoved them into her pocket. "You don't need to bother about this trash today." She stood there with her hands on her hips, and a rash of anger spilled over her cheeks. "Sounds like Mr. Darnell is nothing but an evil bastard. He's not worth even one of your tears."

But the weather soured after Mrs. Luttrell left for another lying-in job. First Eddie and then Charity came down with the measles. Etta found her world had shrunk to her house, neighbors, and correspondence with Lavinia and Sophie. So her visitor on the afternoon of December 16th caught her unaware. Mr. Trimble from the bank wore worry lines even deeper than before. He got right to the purpose of his call the moment he took a seat in the parlor.

"Mrs. Darnell, the accounts department gave me some disturbing information today. Did you know you're close to being overdrawn? We're concerned since we know you have no income. Our records show you have under twenty dollars left."

"I know to the penny how much I have at your bank. I'm waiting on Ben's father to send the rest of the money he promised after the divorce was final."

"Mrs. Darnell, evidently you haven't heard. Mr. Darnell has died, quite suddenly, it seems, some type of riding accident."

~~~

Within moments of the banker's departure, anger tore through her. Driven by her growing hatred of Ben's family and her resolve to fight for her children, she asked Mrs. Leander to watch the children. Etta was going downtown to see that no-good, low-life attorney Littleberry.

Twenty minutes later, Etta pinned her best hat into her bun and pulled on her Sunday gloves. After she thanked Mrs. Leander and kissed her children goodbye, she stomped toward the business district, now angrier at herself than anyone else. She knew better. So many times her father had gloated about closing deals with a handshake and no written contract. The cold truth was if the promise wasn't written down, chances were it was an empty promise.

Though Mr. Littleberry's office had been her destination, Etta stopped at Main and Ann Street. Maybe Mrs. Caldwell was a better choice since money was so tight. Etta realized she needed a job. It was better to keep her dwindling funds in the bank reserved for emergencies. Maybe, with Ben out of the picture, the boarding house might hire her. If not, she would talk with Old Ghostie at the Home. One of those two places from her past might provide some security for her family.

Her brother Willie came to mind. She knew he was doing well from reading the newspapers. After his marriage to their cousin Mary Margaret two years ago, he was named first vice president of the distillery. However, she gave up the idea when she realized no obituary for her Aunt Helen had been published. The old woman probably still hated her and would refuse to let Willie help. It was also possible Willie, on his own, might deny her. Louisville, as their father would have said, was a dry hole.

~~~

Etta, buoyed by her good fortune, returned to her home. Her timing had been perfect. She walked into the Caldwell's boarding house a few hours after their manager Lucinda had eloped with an itinerant well-digger. Etta promised Mrs. Caldwell she would step in and do the job.

Her children were safe for now. If Mr. Trimble's offered letter to the Darnells produced any favorable results, so much the better. For now though, she had all she needed. She did not have to count on any justice from Ben's family or the legal system. She was strong enough to work and take care of her own family. She would overcome this obstacle, just as she had the others.

~~

The week after New Year's Day, Mr. Trimble showed up during her afternoon shift at the boarding house. As Etta led the banker to the parlor, she remembered how her song had lured Ben from the street and into her life. She had been a girl then, full of spunk and fire. But although she was only twenty-three, her inner fire had over the past few years turned to cold gray ashes.

The grim lines of worry on Mr. Trimble's forehead did not promise much hope. His words, after they sat in the chairs by the window, confirmed her fears.

"Mrs. Darnell, I'm sorry," Trimble said. "I don't have good news for you. Mr. Roderick Darnell instructed his attorney to answer my letter. He claims the elder Mr. Darnell never informed him of any financial arrangement with you. Mr. Roderick refutes your story of the promised funds. I suppose you could find an attorney and try." His mouth drooped. He looked sad and resigned. "But it appears it's your word against theirs."

"And the word of any woman, especially a divorced one, has no credibility," she finished for him.

"There's also the additional expense of hiring your own attorney to counter Mr. Roderick's report about his late father's intentions."

"There's no guarantee the case will go my way," she said and realized how boxed in she was.

"Quite so." he paused. "There's another matter I need to discuss with you. It's about your mortgage and your present payments."

Etta felt her stomach churn. she struggled to keep her composure.

"My account is current, Mr. Trimble, I'm sure of it."

"Let me explain better," the banker said. After clearing his throat, he started over. "I thought you might want to reconsider the terms of your mortgage so you'd have a smaller monthly payment. Look at these figures I've run for you. You see by taking out a new loan…"

He held out some papers for her inspection.

Overwhelmed and feeling totally alone and unable to concentrate on the finer details of the new mortgage, Etta took the documents and asked for a few days to decide.

After Mr. Trimble left, Etta returned to balancing the books in the small office she had carved out for herself under the stairs. When the tears first prickled, she willed them back with the phrases that had helped rebuild her strength all her life.

"Tears are a waste of time and energy. They have no value in the survival of my family. I will not cry. I will win, *la vincero.*"

Chapter 27

The sound of Charity fussing woke Etta. Gray light edged around the drawn curtains. The wish to be a child again crept through her mind. She wanted to lie in bed and cry and have someone come and comfort her. Every hair on her head hurt. Fever played through her body. Reaching deep within, she forced herself out of sweat-sodden bedding and down the hall to the children's room. Her breath tasted gray and withered, but she was beyond caring.

Two months earlier, scarlet fever had taken her youngest child Della, an infant of ten months. Her baby's death had convinced her life would be gray with no other color offering any relief.

In the middle of many sleep-deprived, restless nights, she often reflected black was not the correct color to wear to show mourning. Its nothingness clashed with her understanding of grief. The color gray was a much better indication of her pain and the ordeal of going on, day in and day out. It was during those evenings she realized she at last fully understood the ancient Greek myth of Sisyphus. She, just as the Corinthian from so long ago, faced the unending task of moving the same boulder up the same hill for eternity.

Through the previous week, the skies stayed the color of pewter. No sunshine broke through the clouds. Fitting, she thought. The weather matched her spirit and appearance. The only color life had bequeathed was her hair, still red though streaked with a few strands of white. She had no memory of the last time sunlight or laughter or song had graced her home.

Picking up her daughter Charity, Etta folded her into her arms and soundlessly rocked the restless two-year-old back to sleep. The toddler settled, and a niggling absence haunted Etta. What was she listening for? Ah, the songbirds and their usual music to celebrate a new day. However, the overcast cold skies must have stilled the birds, and Etta, like they, did not have a comforting lullaby to offer.

Dr. Powell had told her on his last visit that the inflammation in her lungs would resolve, hopefully within six weeks or so. But he advised the pallor, which had fallen over her after Della's death, would take time to recede. She knew he spoke not from a medical viewpoint, but out of a wisdom hard earned from his own personal experience. A few years ago, one by one, beginning with his wife who had just given birth, his whole family had sickened and passed. His wife and four children lay, side by side, in the Frankfort Cemetery.

"The soul does heal, but ever so much more slowly than the body," Lewis Powell confided during his last visit. "At first it's so gradual, you'll not even be aware of it. But rest assured, with each day, you recover."

The motion of the rocking chair soon put Charity to sleep. The child's warmth spread to Etta's chest and soothed her cough. She napped in her upright position until Eddie's words jolted her awake.

"Momma, wake up. I'm hungry."

Etta forced her eyes open from the most peaceful sleep she had experienced in two months. Her son stood before her. It was evident he had tried to dress himself. His shirt was misbuttoned and half in his short pants. Below his knees were two different socks.

"Is it a work day? See I'm all ready to go to work. I even combed my hair."

Etta focused. Eddie's part switched back and forth. Only the front fringe around his face was smooth. The rest stood out in clumps and tangles.

"You look quite handsome this morning." She fingercombed his hair. "But Momma's not going to work today. Go put your old clothes on while I get your breakfast ready."

"Can I have some raisins in my oatmeal?"

Her son's hopeful expression jabbed at her conscience. Shoving her grief as far away as possible, Etta told him yes with a smile and castigated herself to get on with taking care of her children. She was lucky she still had them.

But by the time she had finished cleaning up after breakfast, her inner reserve of energy had evaporated. Fortunately Charity was back in her crib asleep, and Eddie played with his blocks at the kitchen table. She was trying to come up with a way to get him down for a nap so she could rest a bit when someone knocked at the front door.

Lavinia, wearing a bright blue shawl and a hat that cascaded with matching peacock feathers, stood on the step.

"You've been on my mind all week," her friend stated even before she was through the door. "I knew today would be a difficult day for you."

Etta did not trust herself to speak without bursting into tears. But she was grateful her friend had remembered Della's birthday.

Lavinia did not seem to notice Etta's silence. She walked in and continued. "Last night I told Daniel I was coming into town to check on you myself. So I got into the buggy right after breakfast, and here I am. And I can say you look like you're about ready to fall over. Go to bed. We'll visit when you wake up."

Etta bit back tears and hugged her visitor.

"Go rest," Lavinia said in a gentle tone and returned the embrace.

~~

Etta awoke to a sense of lightness. The sound of Eddie's giggles and Charity's delighted squeals reached her. Opening her eyes, she saw the morning gloom had burned off. One of those Kentucky golden bright warm fall days had come. The aroma of baked apples and cinnamon grabbed her attention and reminded her she was hungry. After hurriedly refreshing her face at the washstand, she gathered her bright curls into a knot and changed into a subdued lavender dress.

When Etta entered the kitchen, she took in a happy and messy scene. Charity sat on the kitchen table, her brother stood on a chair beside her, and Lavinia cut out sugar cookies with a glass. Eddie added a hunk of raw dough to a lumpy, oddly shaped animal and made it jump and gallop towards Charity, who in turn, rewarded her brother's antics with yips of joy and clapping. Etta sat down beside Eddie who immediately showed her his prize creation.

Lavinia looked at her closely from across the table. "You look better. Some of your color has come back."

"Thank you, for coming today. I was so surprised to see you on my front porch, just like a....," Etta searched for the right word, "iridescent blue bird. I'm so glad you're here."

Lavinia placed her hand on Etta's and gave a little squeeze before returning to the cookie dough. "Don't ever think you're all alone. I won't minimize what you've been through. But you're strong, deep down, where it counts."

"I'd almost given up this morning," Etta whispered. "You know that well inside you go to for strength." She put her hand on her heart. "I went there this morning and found it bone dry. It scared me because there's always been at least a little bit to draw from."

"Don't even talk that way. You've got to stay strong for yourself and your children."

"I'm better now."

"Good, how about some chicken soup and apple pie?"

Etta took in the enticing smells from the pot on the stove and the pie cooling on the windowsill.

"How did you perform this miracle? I didn't have any of these fixings in the house."

"I packed it all early this morning."

"Thank you, again."

"You're welcome."

Lavinia put a steaming bowl of soup, a hunk of brown bread, and another bowl of apple pie floating in cream before Etta.

Etta brought her face close to the pie and the other food and inhaled. "Mmmm."

"Dr. Powell said the same when he stopped around noon. He pulled up a chair and joined the children and me, right here at the table. When I offered to wake you, he said to let you sleep. He'll come by again in a few days. That man looks overworked."

Etta nodded while she savored the taste of the chicken and rice. "I guess he is. So many people are sick this fall." She evaded the real reason Lewis Powell bore a burden of melancholy. It seemed an invasion of his privacy. Instead she tore off a hunk of bread and spooned more soup.

"He's what Lute would've called an old soul. Do you ever see her?"

"Once in a while, when I'm downtown," Etta answered. "But I don't think she gets out much anymore. She's even had to give up her lying-in nursing. Her lumbago keeps her inside most days."

"Let's take the children to see her when you're better. Maybe Sophie and her brood might come too."

"Old Lute probably would like seeing all of us."

~~~

Two weeks later, Etta buttoned her coat and ended her first day back at the boarding house. She was exhausted, but she had stayed the whole day at work. Soon some money would be coming in.

After Etta bundled Eddie and Charity into their coats, she led them down the back stairs and through the alley. She did not look forward to the long, cold walk home, but if the rain held off, they would be there within twenty minutes before it got dark.

As soon as Etta stepped onto the sidewalk, she heard, "Mrs. Darnell." She recognized the voice and turned to see the tall, thin Lewis Powell beside his buggy.

"I'm on my way to your neighborhood. Let me give you and your children a ride home. You must be careful. You could suffer a relapse."

"Thank you, Dr. Powell."

Gratitude banished her fatigue. She smiled, gave him her hand, and stepped into the buggy. On the drive, Lewis let Eddie hold the horse's reins. Charity snuggled up to her and fell asleep. As the horse clopped at a slow pace, the doctor shared the big news of the day.

"Did you hear about the fight outside the capitol this morning?"

When Etta shook her head, he gave her the details about two friends who had accused each other of cheating during a horse race and decided to settle the matter without horses and on foot. They raced up toward the top of the marble steps and were tied when one tripped and rolled back down. After his friend rushed to help him get up, the fallen man yelled how he had been cheated once more.

"What happened?" Etta pictured a fist fight erupting right there on the capitol steps.

"The winner offered to buy the loser a drink, and they went off toward the nearest tavern."

Relieved, Etta joined in his laugher and thought how Dr. Powell's kind offer and conversation made the ride enjoyable.

～～

Over the next month, Dr. Powell showed up after work several evenings a week. More than once she caught herself glancing out the side window of the parlor to see if he waited for her. The happiness the sight of him brought amazed her as much as the disappointment she felt when he was not there. Gradually, almost as if she was following one of his prescriptions, her mood did lift. At last, she realized how much his company contributed to her improved spirits.

On a blustery night in late November, he asked to come in. Etta suspected his purpose. After all, she had not discouraged his attentions in any way.

In the same room where Ben had knelt and proposed, Lewis Powell spoke soft words. "It can't be any secret, I love you. I must be the most obvious man in Frankfort. Will you marry me?"

In her heart, Etta knew her feelings were different for this man. What she felt was not the giddy, girlish love for Ben, which, over time, grew encompassing. Though she did care for Lewis, much more than she ever dreamed was possible. She rationalized her doubt. Maybe life had a purpose in its huge difference between first love and the next love. She wanted him in her life. Her children needed him.

"Yes," she gave him a smile of genuine happiness. "I've been hoping you'd ask."

"Even though I am so much older than you?"

"You're not much older."

"I'm closing in on thirty-five."

Not old at all, Etta thought. In some ways she felt ancient, more than Sister Justina had ever seemed. But she would not share any of these unromantic thoughts tonight.

Instead she said, "I have something to tell you too."

"I don't care what your age is, dearest."

Etta sighed to steady herself. It was better to get it out in the open. "You do know I'm a divorced woman, not a widow, don't you?"

"Yes, but I don't care. What I do care about is you and your children."

Etta touched his arm, and he gathered her for their first kiss.

When they broke their embrace, Lewis asked, "Will you come meet my folks?"

"I didn't know you had family from around here."

"I guess we still have a lot to learn about each other. My family's from Cincinnati. Where are yours? Around here?"

Panic grabbed her. What was she going to tell him, the truth? Did it even matter any more? Both her adopted parents had been dead for so long. She also had no idea of who her real parents were.

Etta decided it was not necessary. The divorce was shameful enough even though he had to know people changed after they were wounded, especially from a head injury.

Old Lute's words given to her on the eve of her marriage to Ben came back. Through determination and pain, Etta had remade herself. For some reason, another chance to begin anew with Lewis had found her. She had no need to share any burden from her Louisville life. Though her past was always with her, Etta had kept it secret from others. Taking a deep breath, she looked at Lewis and cut him off from the person she had once been.

"No, I lost my family a long time ago."

Etta watched him wait for her to continue with more detail. It was almost as if he read her mind and had witnessed her inner struggle of sorting out what to say and what to leave unspoken.

Instead she relied on an age old stratagem of diverting his focus back to him. "Tell me about your parents." Etta said, and a bit of tension in her neck relaxed when Lewis accepted the new topic.

"They're both still in good health although my father's slowing down. A few years back he had to take on a younger doctor to help with his practice. He keeps saying he wants me to come back and take over."

"Why don't you?"

"When I was a young doctor, I wanted to prove I could be successful on my own. A few years later, I met Judith and settled here since her folks were from Lexington. After she and the children died, I decided I wanted to stay close to them."

Etta put her hand over his. The pain from his losses enveloped her and even joined with her own pain before Lewis' kind smile banished the grief. At once it went back into the part of her heart she had reserved for all her losses. There, it quieted.

"There's no real practice to go back to." Etta heard when she turned her attention back to him. "My father's partner does the lion's share. Besides I've made this my home."

He touched her cheek. "Are you happy here, in Frankfort?"

The question stunned her. No one, except Ben, had ever asked if she were happy. She answered with the first words to come to mind. "Oh, I don't know, Lewis. Like you, I feel at home here. But we can move, if you wish."

However, the idea of moving somewhere else was overwhelming. The only two true friends she had ever had were here. She did not want to lose them.

"We don't have to decide anything right now," he said.

She agreed. This was just one of many decisions stretching out before her.

"I'd like you to meet my parents, maybe over the holidays?"

Why were there always parents, Etta thought before admonishing herself. It was possible they might like her. Cincinnati was probably far enough away to keep them out of her new life.

"Will your parents mind having the children?"

"Not at all, they've despaired of ever having any more grandchildren. You see, I'm the only child. I was born when my mother was in her late thirties."

"You grew up alone?"

Etta could not imagine. She had been surrounded by McIntire cousins, aunts and uncles.

"Just the opposite," Lewis laughed, "Lots of cousins from both sides. My mother's family was German, out of North Carolina."

"They spoke German?"

"My grandparents did, especially when they didn't want us to know what they were saying."

"And on your father's side?"

"Welsh, so the family legend goes. There's no proof of any kind, but I also have lots of Powell cousins. They claim they came into Pennsylvania with William Penn. They might even have been Quakers."

His gaze held for a few heartbeats. "Is it a problem, coming from Quaker stock, I mean?"

Etta saw a flicker of doubt pass over his eyes and hurried to reassure him. "No, not at all."

"Good, but I suppose we should discuss religion. I do want to have children with you, Etta. Is it important our children be Catholic?"

Etta did not have the strength to delve into how her divorce was unrecognized in the eyes of Rome. "Lewis, I'm marrying you, not a church. We can make our own decisions."

Lewis gave her an impish grin. "Let's get married," he said, "when we're in Cincinnati. Then my parents won't have to travel down here."

"So quickly?" Etta gasped. Things were moving much too fast. "Are you sure?"

"Why not? We love each other. That's not going to change, is it?"

"No, but it's not a lot of time to plan."

"I don't want to wait. This way we can have a little honeymoon in Cincinnati at the Palace."

"With the children?"

"We'll work out something with all the cousins. A few days alone with you, just the two of us?"

He winked at her, and Etta settled into his arms. "Agreed, a wedding in Cincinnati and a small reception back here later on."

"And where would you like to live?"

"I think you'll have to move in with us. We can't all move into your room at the Olympiad." Etta laughed, and he did too.

"Do you remember the house next to my office? It's available and has more than enough room for us." His eyes lit up when he talked about its interior with its wide hallways and spacious rooms.

Instantly, Etta pictured the elegant, white three-story Queen Anne house and its wide wraparound porch and abundant windows. Though it was a lot more house to take care of and manage, she knew she was up to the task. But she would still miss her little four-room house, crowded as it was.

~~

Etta sensed her inner spark had begun to shine once more. Lewis commented on how her green eyes glowed like emeralds. She was in a festive mood for the first Christmas in a long time. Since decorating the boarding house did not depress her, she even brought the unused boughs and ribbons home.

Eddie also caught the Christmas spirit and made paper chains to put on the branches Etta arranged around the doorframes. Every evening after Charity was asleep, Eddie sat at the kitchen table and cut out paper angels to hang on the greenery and any place else he thought of.

Her holiday cards sent to Lavinia and Sophie asked for their good wishes and a promise to visit after the wedding. Their return cards sent their heartfelt blessings for her happiness.

Lavinia's also added the comment, "I thought he was more than a friend when he called the day I was there."

When Lewis read the note, Etta had to explain to him what her friend meant.

"I was acting in a truly professional manner," Lewis chuckled and kissed her forehead.

Sitting on the train and traveling north with her children and Lewis a few days later, Etta shared her astonishment at how well the last month had gone. All the wedding plans and decisions of where to live had fallen into an orderly arrangement.

"I can't believe it happened this quickly."

"What, our getting married? I knew my mother could put it all together."

"First the Caldwells were able to find a replacement for me. Then you bought the house next to your office and even found workers to make sure it'd be ready for us when we return next week. I didn't know so many good things could happen in a row and nothing go wrong."

"Why not, we both deserve a turn of good luck and happiness."

"Doesn't it make your head spin a little when you think about how your life is about to change?"

"No, but the idea of us being together does take my breath away," he whispered and put her hand in his.

"Me too," Etta answered. She really wanted to believe her life was going to be good again.

But frazzled nerves and second thoughts made Etta doubt Lewis' predictions. Not about how he loved her or her feelings about him. Her fears were about his parents. What did they really think about their son's plans to marry a divorced woman of unknown parentage with two small children? In some ways, it was even worse than Ben's parents. Now her two children were involved, and these people she was about to meet would be the only grandparents Eddie and Charity would have.

~~~

Etta's anxiety melted the moment Evan and Doris Powell opened their front door after the hired carriage rolled to a stop at their house on Madison Road. White-haired and wrapped in matching red plaid shawls, the elderly couple smiled like delighted small children. They looked enough alike, Etta thought, to pass for brother and sister.

Once they were all seated in the front parlor, Etta realized why she thought her future in-laws looked so similar. Each had the same pointed chin and high cheekbones.

Doris, so thin in her dark green satin dress, wore her braided hair wreathed about her head. Her blue eyes were clear and alert. The only jewelry she wore was her wedding band and red garnet earrings. Sitting with an erect posture, she poured tea and asked about their trip.

Evan's thinness, however, seemed new and growing, maybe because of his pallor. His eyes lacked his wife's sharpness. But he had taken care with his appearance. His face was well-shaven despite his wrinkles. He had his cane parked by his slippered feet and against the side of his brown leather chair. But his posture was so stooped he had difficulty lifting his head. He had to lean far back in the chair to see them. But even then, he rarely spoke.

The children were not frightened though. The old man won them over when he reached into the pocket of his jacket and pulled out two oranges.

"Are those balls?" Eddie asked.

"Oranges," Lewis answered, took both, and began peeling.

The orange fragrance rose and enticed first Eddie and then Charity to leave Etta's side and stand by Lewis.

"Would you like to taste a bit?" Lewis held a segment out for the boy.

When Eddie looked at her for permission, Etta smiled, nodded, and turned to thank Evan for the gift. She knew oranges were quite dear. Her children had never eaten one before. Even when she was a girl, they were the special gifts put in Christmas stockings.

Lewis gave Eddie the rest of his orange and turned his attention to the second one. Charity bit into her segment and made a sour face. Eddie took her uneaten slice and popped it into his mouth.

"May I have the rest of hers? She doesn't like it."

Charity's face clouded over, and she looked like she was going to cry.

"Here dear," Doris said, "Come by me, I have some lebkuchens. They're sweeter."

The woman held out a small china plate with three cookies. Charity rushed over and took one in each hand. After Eddie swallowed the remaining orange and joined Charity, Doris gave him his own plate.

"If you'd like the recipe, I'll give it to you," Doris said to Etta. "These were Lewis' favorites when he was a boy."

"Yes, thank you." Etta looked at Lewis before turning back to Doris. "I'd like to know all his favorite foods."

Doris tilted her head in agreement and said, "Thank you, my dear, for bringing your children to our home. Small ones always add so much joy to Christmas, don't you think?"

~~~

There were ten at table for a cheerful family dinner of roast beef and vegetables with spice cake for dessert. Lewis' cousin Andreas and his wife Sabine with their daughter Sylvia, a girl of sixteen joined them. Sylvia lived with the Powells and helped Doris run the house. When Eddie and Charity started getting restless, Sylvia led Etta and the children upstairs.

"This was Uncle Lewis' room." Sylvia opened the door onto a large room filled with children's furniture and toys.

Etta saw her children's eyes grow wide as they took in the toys. A hobbyhorse and train set took up one side of the room. In the other corner were dolls with their clothes and furniture.

Sylvia continued, "The dolls are from my house. I hope Charity will like them."

"I'm sure she will. Thank you much for your generosity." Etta took pleasure when the young woman's face glowed from the compliment.

After Etta tucked the children in, Sylvia sat down in a rocker between the beds. She pointed to the stack of books on each bed and said, "Quick like a bunny, each of you pick a story from my favorite books."

Etta kissed her children good night and returned downstairs in time to say goodbye to Andreas and Sabine. Within moments Doris led Etta to the parlor while Lewis went with Evan to the study.

"Sylvia will stay upstairs with the children," Doris said, "until we retire for the night, if you agree. I thought it was best in case one of them awakens and is frightened by being in a new place."

Doris' thoughtfulness touched Etta's soul, and she told her so.

"Both of you are so kind. Mrs. Powell, thank you for arranging all of this and the wedding," Etta moved her hand to indicate all the older woman's efforts.

"I'm the one who should thank you. I've taken such pleasure in the preparations for your visit and the wedding."

Doris took a portfolio from the table beside her. "Lewis wrote the two of you had no strong preferences one way or the other about the ceremony. Did I understand him correctly?"

After Etta agreed and thanked her again, Doris said, "I can tell you're going to be really good for him. I think the day after Christmas would be a wonderful day for a winter wedding. We'll have all the holiday decorations still in place."

~~~

Over the next two days, Etta watched the house on Madison Street transform into a festive scene of Christmas and wedding preparations. She was amazed at how tireless Doris was. The older woman oversaw everything. The food preparation, the table arrangements, the hanging of the greens, and the staging of the wedding ceremony. Doris seemed to relish every step.

Whenever Etta asked to help, Doris said she was not tired but thrilled as could be since she had never envisioned planning a wedding. The older woman seemed to have a prodigious reserve of energy for a woman of seventy-two.

Etta confided her thoughts to Lewis on the eve of their wedding. "I hope when I'm her age, I can do only half of what she finishes in one day."

"Mother has always been vigorous. She's been blessed with a strong constitution. Fortunately her mind has stayed sharp as well. Did she tell you she comes from a long line of people who have lived well into their nineties?"

~~~

The only task left to Etta was her wedding dress. Since there was not enough time to have one made, Lewis had taken her shopping their first day in Cincinnati. Etta found she really enjoyed the experience. The downtown stores reminded her so much of her earlier shopping experiences in Louisville. Upscale dress and millenary shops had not changed much in the eight years since she had moved to the small town of Frankfort.

But the dress styles differed a great deal. The latest high fashion was a two-piece ensemble with a tailored top. Gone were the flowing sleeves Etta had particularly liked, and bustles had become even larger. But the new off-the-floor skirt lengths were an improvement. They certainly allowed for more graceful movement. An impulse swept over her, and she could not stop herself. She twirled in the mirror and caught Lewis' smile in the reflection.

Even as she shook her head at some of his suggestions because she could not see herself in any of those elegant dresses in Frankfort, she gently touched the lace trims and fancy braids. Finally, they agreed on a light green silk creation with bits of delicate lace at the wrists and neckline.

In the quiet moments before the ceremony was to begin, Etta's hands trembled as she stood before the dresser mirror and clasped her pearls. It was heartbreaking to reflect on the past. What had happened to her seemed like several life-times ago. But she had survived. Often by fighting back and especially by putting her past behind her and getting on with life.

As she closed the bedroom door behind her, it struck Etta how the door was a symbol for ending one chapter of her life and beginning another. On the walk down the stairs, she whispered a promise to be the best wife she could to Lewis.

His intense gaze held and guided her past his relatives and her children gathered in the drawing room. He and Etta joined hands and stood before one of Lewis's many cousins, a justice of the peace. When he pronounced Lewis Powell and Etta Darnell man and wife at 1:38 p.m., there were some tears. A few glistened in Lewis's eyes.

After the wedding supper, she and Lewis left for the Palace Hotel, the new luxury French Empire style hotel that shocked Cincinnati. Lewis had told her no one in the city believed a sane person would pay three dollars a night to stay in one of the new hotel's luxurious rooms. At a wondrous eight stories, the hotel was the tallest building in the city.

Etta stared at the enormous building when they got off the trolley and walked around the hitching posts at the entrance. Its height made her feel like a country bumpkin.

Even more modern amazements were inside. The richly polished marble staircase was the largest she had ever seen. Etta had heard of elevators but had never ridden in one before. She gripped Lewis's arm when the wire cage began its climb. The whining noise and thuds caused her heart to beat faster. But by the time they reached the sixth floor, her fear had vanished. She took in the hotel's bright incandescent lighting and bathrooms at the end of the hall and marveled at how old and fusty Caldwell's boarding house was by comparison.

Outside their room, Lewis must have sensed her nervousness. He brought her gloved hand to his lips, and his eyes held fast to hers during the kiss.

When he spoke one of her favorite lines from Shakespeare, "A heaven on earth I have won by wooing thee," she fell in love.

Part 4

Chapter 28

Frankfort, December 4, 1889

Lewis dashed out the back door of his office toward home. His path took him over the old red brick walk lightly covered with snow and led him through the little adjoining yard.

Today, the same as every other day, he was thankful for the past eight years he and Etta had been married. Even for those years with valleys, as he liked to call their times of disagreement.

Life had changed even more two months ago when his widowed mother had moved in. It did not take long for the pricklies to come out between the two women. Some constant disagreement seemed to simmer never abate them.

Lewis stuck his head in to measure the level of tension. Most evenings the air sizzled with friction, but tonight was calm. Etta stood before the stove and stirred something which made his mouth water. A tall Ed, as he now insisted he be called, stacked wood by the stove. The young man's grumblings reached his ears and ran along the vein that it was time the family got a gas stove. Voices from the dining room told him Charity was setting the table for dinner under her grandmother's supervision. On the other side of the kitchen, Evan, barely five years old, sat at the kitchen table and glued paper chains to decorate the Christmas tree. The hired girl washed dishes.

As Lewis silently hung his coat on the rack, he hoped the peace would hold. During the day, death had confronted him three times, and he had lost each time. An elderly woman to the grippe, a father of four small children to a farming accident, and a stillborn babe to a cause only God knew.

"Poppa's home," Evan yelled. Within seconds. he was across the room and clamored for a piggyback ride.

"You're right, son. Up you go." Evan was no sooner in place before Charity stood in front of him and demanded her hug. Lewis swung Evan to the side and squeezed his daughter.

"How was school, Princess?"

"I won the spelling bee. The word was foreign. You spell it f-o-r-e-i-g-n."

"Right, what a smart girl you are."

She gave him a smile that said of course she was before she broke free and turned back to the dining room.

Ed straightened up and stopped his string of complaints. With a nod, he left the kitchen. Lewis knew Ed's destination was his bedroom where he'd escape any looming warfare between the women.

Lewis, pleased with his royal welcome from the little ones, put Evan in his chair and turned to Etta.

"If you have a few moments, you might want to read this article in the newspaper about the Palace Hotel. You do remember the Palace, don't you?"

He winked at her and kissed her on the cheek before leaning over the stove. Lifting the lids from a few pots on the stove, he found boiled potatoes, lima beans, and chicken with dumplings. His stomach rumbled.

"There wasn't another riot, was there?" Etta asked, referring to the courthouse fire of '86 when a riot led to a fire and destroyed the courthouse and jail.

"No, not at all, read here." He pulled a folded newspaper from his pocket and handed it over.

Etta glanced at the article and looked up at him with disbelief. "They shot an elephant and gave it to the Palace to cook for their guests?"

"Why not? How many times does anyone from Cincinnati get a chance to eat elephant flesh?"

"But it's not the same as being hungry and going hunting. Where's the sport in killing a chained animal?"

"Even if he's a mankiller?"

The look of disgust on her face suggested he should change to a safer topic. Chief, the elephant from the zoo, had seemed a good topic by comparison to her usual catalog of complaints. He did not want to hear as soon as he walked in the door how Ed spent all his time in his room reading instead of doing his chores. Nor did he want to hear how Charity daydreamed and never latched the back door. The worst he did not want to hear was how his mother followed behind Etta and rearranged the kitchen drawers and had added the Christmas decorations to her self-imposed daily chores.

Lewis moved toward the dining room to say hello to his mother whose deafness had probably muffled his arrival. But before he reached the doorway, Doris charged into the kitchen with two glasses. Charity hung back, half in the dining room and half in the kitchen. He thought she stood poised like a fawn ready to flee if and when the first gauntlet was flung. He smiled encouragement at his daughter and greeted his mother. Doris nodded but did not falter in her mission. She crossed in front of him and held out two glasses.

"Etta, you know I don't want to interfere. But I'm sure you don't want to have streaked glasses on the table. Charity admitted she didn't use those good linen dish towels I brought with me."

Doris then turned to Lewis. "You can't get good quality linens here." She sniffed. "Probably not enough of a demand to make it profitable. Or do you think your people here don't really know the difference?"

Lewis hated this sort of question. He knew there was no right answer so he shrugged his shoulders. Etta shook her head and faced the stove again. Without a word, he took the glasses from Doris and gave her two more.

He watched her return to the dining room and hold the glasses up to the light coming from the overhead gas fixture. They must have passed muster since she placed them on the table. He returned to Etta and held her tight until he felt the tension in her spine subside.

Dinner was thankfully uneventful. Evan did not spill his milk. Charity did not sulk over the vegetables on her plate. Even Ed gave up his usual complaints about everything being old-fashioned. Best of all, his mother and wife did not carp at each other even once.

But by the end of the meal, his dinner sat uneasily in the base of his stomach. Lewis wondered how much longer he would have to walk on eggshells around the two women before they worked out their differences.

Evan however seemed unaware of the undercurrent of tension and laid out a convincing argument that he was old enough to go sledding without a grownup this year. Lewis found his son's eyes, the same emerald shade as his mother's, fired with excitement when he boasted about his plans for the first huge snowfall. The little dark-haired boy set a jovial mood. Ed promised to take him down Guthrie's Hill when it snowed again. The next topic was his constantly changing Christmas wish list.

Lewis, though, could not shake his uneasiness and marked it up to his patients' deaths.

~~~

After New Year's, Lewis noticed subtle changes in his mother's behavior. The first sign was her sleep patterns. After she had moved in with them, she had trouble with insomnia. Her nightly ramblings had caused both him and Etta to wake up cranky and unrested.

One morning it came to him that he no longer heard her at night. When he shared his revelation with Etta over breakfast, she said the same.

On several mornings the following week, Doris still slept when he cracked open her bedroom door to check on her before he began his morning office hours.

When he noticed she was not eating and had lost weight, he asked Etta if his mother's appetite had fallen off.

"Maybe, I haven't been paying attention, Lewis." Etta put down her pencil and looked up from her market list.

"Is she forgetting to eat?" he insisted.

"She tells me she doesn't want my help or to be any bother, so she goes into the kitchen when I'm not there."

"But surely you'd notice if food is eaten or not?"

"Have you seen how hungry Ed is lately? Every day I have to go to the butcher shop and the dry goods store. I can't keep enough food in the house for him. Do you know he ate a whole pie yesterday after school?"

Etta went back to her list. "I'd better pick up some castor oil today. He could have a tapeworm."

"But my mother?"

Etta stopped writing and sighed. "You're right, she's looking frail. I promise I'll watch out for her."

~~~

By the end of January, Doris slept up to twelve hours a night. As a result, Etta was in a much better mood and reported the kitchen wars had ended. Lewis was glad life was back on a more even keel. But he had seen her anger rekindle when he urged Etta to try some new recipes to whet his mother's appetite.

While they sat in the parlor one night in early February, Lewis noticed his mother tried to scratch her arms in a ladylike manner but was failing. When he looked more carefully, he saw red spots coming through her sleeves.

"Momma, let me see your arms."

Lewis had to repeat it twice before the vacant look in her eyes disappeared. His examination revealed both arms had tiny scabs. Doris claimed she did not know how or when the sores occurred. He saw traces of alarm in her eyes for a few seconds before they regained their blank look.

"It's all right, Momma. I'll make it better with calamine lotion."

He recognized with a pang of sorrow that his mother was fading.

~~

One afternoon in mid-February, Etta, with Evan in tow, rushed through the back door of his office. He stood as soon as he saw her frantic expression and feared she had come to tell him his mother had died.

But Etta had a different story to tell. "Your mother has been dosing herself with Dr. Winter's Mint Syrup."

Etta reached into her pocket and brought out a small green bottle. "It has an awful smell, like bad whiskey."

Lewis grunted as he read the label. After he removed the lid, he sniffed, poured a little out on his finger and tasted it.

"It's laudanum with alcohol. By God," he fumed, "where'd she get this poison?"

"From the general store. The delivery boy came by a few minutes ago. He insisted on seeing her, but I told him she was asleep. When I asked him for more details, he told me she places an order every two months."

Lewis thumped down into his chair and asked, "What else did he tell you?"

"He said he made his first delivery in November when he started working there."

"I should've recognized the symptoms," Lewis moaned and rubbed his forehead.

"What are you talking about?" Etta sat in a chair and pulled Evan onto her lap.

"People take it for insomnia and pain, especially neuralgia."

"But what pain does your mother have?"

"Though it's a highly effective pain killer, some people take it to lift their spirits. But the end result is the same, addiction, and finally, if taken long enough and in large enough doses, death."

His clinical words worked against his personal anguish over his mother's prognosis. "At her age, any attempt to force withdrawal may very well kill her."

"It sounds worse than liquor."

"It's evil, pure and simple. She'll have to keep increasing her dosage until she takes too much. That's when her heart'll give out, and she'll stop breathing."

Slamming his hands down on the table, he stormed, "I hate this vile poison." Seeing her startled look, he said more softly, "During the Civil War, so many soldiers became addicted to laudanum because of their injuries that they had to continue taking it after they left the army. You remember old Henry Foster?"

"The mean crippled man who hung around the courthouse and swung his crutches at people when they walked by?"

"Yes, he was an addict, according to what Doc Stratton told me when I first opened my practice here. When he suggested I take my turn at treating the charity cases among the soldiers, old Henry was one of my first patients."

"And your mother?"

"She's declining so quickly all we can do is make her comfortable. She won't last another month."

Lewis wiped the tears from his eyes.

"Wait for me Etta, please. I'm going to close up the office and come home."

~~~

Three days later, he sat beside Doris's bed and watched his mother slip into a coma and die. Lewis found his grief was mixed with relief. At last, she had found peace.

Chapter 29

"Bye Ma," fifteen-year-old Evan shouted on his way out the door. He was gone before Etta could tell him to be careful.

She was concerned about how cold and damp winter had become. The icy temperature caused her to feel all four of her decades with every step. Along with the bite of the bitter wind, the days refused to bring any sunshine. The low slung clouds reminded her of a ceiling in a squat hovel where no one could ever stand straight.

From her bedroom window, Etta watched Evan run from the yard and tried to remember when she had last run with joy. But the memory refused to surface. She turned from her son's retreating figure to resume her explanation, once again, to the new hired girl on how to clean the woodwork with oil of cedar.

With only Evan and Lewis left at home, Etta had hoped that her workload would have lessened. Somehow though, she had more work than ever. But she and Lewis had plans for their life together after this last child was on his own. They wanted to travel around Europe. Lewis had even hired a genealogist to find out where his people had lived in Germany and Wales and was surprised when she did not want to do the same for hers. She had sidestepped the issue by claiming she would wait to see if he had any horse thieves in his family before she would start on hers. He laughed and dropped the topic.

Besides, the grandchildren's visits filled her life. She relished their time together. If asked, she thought she might even have said this was the best part of her life. She realized she would not trade youth again for what she had now, even with the discomforts from the recalcitrant winter.

~~

Evan did not understand how his mother could complain constantly about the weather. He even tried out one of his new vocabulary words on her when he told her he was impervious to the cold since his face and hands always stayed warm.

He did not feel the need to hunker down in the house and wait for the spring thaw. Freedom awaited him outside, and his small cohort of friends beckoned him. Together, they joined in great adventures they kept hidden from adult eyes.

That was good since his mother was becoming grouchier by the day. The words of wisdom spoken by his father, over and over the past six months, did not really help.

He knew he'd burst if he heard his father say once more, "Son, this is a difficult time for some women when they get to be your mother's age. There's nothing you can do but learn to live with it."

No one else spent more time with her, he said to himself, though he did not dare to backtalk to his father. It was even more unfair that Ed and Charity had escaped before their mother had come into "this difficult time." Evan knew he was the one in the family who deserved sympathy, not his mother. Most of the time, she ignored him because all her attention had turned to the life of the princess, otherwise known as Charity.

It had all started with her fancy wedding to Loren, the only son and heir to the Beauchamp fortune, four years ago. The situation grew worse when the grandchildren started coming. First his brother Ed's growing family of two whiny boys started the problem. They were always underfoot at home. Charity's son and daughter also added to his difficulties. His nephews and nieces made it impossible for anyone to notice him.

But, just when he decided being ignored was a good thing, his mother seemed to remember she was neglecting him. The questions started. What was he doing? Where was he going? Who were his friends? When would he be back? The interrogations never stopped. Sometimes she treated him like a child instead of the man of fifteen he really was. She smothered him.

His friends were much more fun to be around. They had spent last summer kitting out a small cave. It was large enough for the four of them to cram themselves into and escape curious and gossipy adults. The cave was where he was headed that afternoon, carrying his "stolen loot" and his older brother's well-used sled.

According to the plans made the day before, they would sit around their campfire, chew tobacco, and eat before they would sled down the hill near the cave. His contributions were to be a sled and canned beans stolen from Cummins' store. But he decided to take the food from his mother's pantry and lie to his pals. Evan had to admit the cover story of his theft was good. It involved how Mrs. Kerns, the fattest woman in town, blocked Old Man Cummins' view of the store shelves.

Evan found Carl and Ernest already in the cave. Carl, with a bright red plaid cap shoved over his straight brown hair, showed off the tobacco he filched from Phillip's Dry Goods last week. Ernest fed more wood scraps to the fire. He patted his pocket and said, "I've got tobacco too from Cummins'."

"We're not gonna wait on Josiah." Carl passed the tobacco around.

"He's coming, isn't he?" Evan asked and took a pinch from the pouch.

"Supposed to, he said he was bringing something special." Carl scooped a wad into his mouth.

The flames had settled into coals, so Evan pulled his cans from his pockets and put them near the fire. The three boys crouched around and kept a lookout for Josiah.

"There he is," Carl said a few minutes later and spit.

Ernest spit even farther. "He's walking funny."

"Yeah, half running, half walking," Carl mumbled with a wad of tobacco in his mouth and cast some brown juice a few inches beyond his first shot.

He added, "He's up to something."

Evan joined the spitting contest. But he could not match Carl's second try. So he said, "He keeps checking behind him."

When Josiah was closer, Evan saw a smug expression on his face.

"Boys," Josiah said from the mouth of the cave, "You'll gonna be real glad I got here today. What I've got is far better than those cans of beans."

The only thing better than beans Evan thought was rock candy.

Josiah reached into his pockets and brought out in each hand a square green bottle sealed with a stopper.

"Didn't know if you were bourbon or gin men, so I brung one of each."

Carl was the first one to try the liquor. After he stopped coughing, he passed the bottle around. Josiah handed the other one to Ernest in exchange for the tobacco pouch.

The moment Evan was afraid of arrived. Both bottles ended up in front of him. He knew his parents' beliefs on drinking, for adults only and then for a few social reasons.

"Later, I'm gonna eat first," he evaded and reached for one of the cans.

He took his time opening the beans with the can opener he had swiped from his mother's kitchen. Grabbing four spoons from his coat pocket, he stuck three, handles first, in the ground. With the fourth, he began eating.

Josiah sat down beside him, reached for a spoon, and took a can from the fire. "I went to a lot of trouble getting ahold of 'em." Josiah nodded to the bottles making another round. Evan grunted and went on eating. "You ain't too good for my liquor are you? Or are you chicken-livered?"

The last statement was accented with the universal pantomime of a chicken flapping its wings.

Evan gave another grunt, but it did not stop Josiah's goading.

"Boys." Josiah grabbed the fuller bottle. "I've got to save some for Evan here. He's almost finished with his meal. Beans and whiskey, a meal for real men, huh?"

Carl and Ernest finished off the bottle left to them and passed on Evan's offer of food.

"Put the fire out, Evan. Time to go sledding," Carl said. "Last one down the hill is a yellow egg-sucking dog."

"I'm ready," Ernest yelled and jumped up.

After Evan picked up the spoons and returned them to his pocket, he started to follow. Josiah waylaid him with an elbow and a squinty look.

"Wait," Josiah taunted, "You can't go yet. You haven't had your whiskey."

"Drink it," the other two chorused over and over.

Evan wished he had the courage to walk away, as his father had advised during one of their talks. But he needed these friends, so he did as they bid. He took up the bottle and gulped the amber liquid. The heat going down his throat took him by surprise. He broke into coughs.

Josiah sneered, "You're a sissy, Evan. You've got a sissy name. You can't even drink whiskey."

Evan flinched from their taunts when they changed their chant to "sissy Evan." He jerked the bottle up again. After draining its contents, he flung the bottle into the scattered embers of the fire where it rendered a satisfying crash of glass shattering.

"Good man." Josiah clapped him on the back. "Now go conquer

the hill."

The boys grabbed their sleds and took off laughing. They challenged each other to sled races. Evan and Josiah won the first round. They stood at the top of the hill for the final race to break the tie of the best two of three. Ernest volunteered to go the base of the hill and declare the winner. Carl agreed to call the start and passed the last bottle for one more round.

"Sledding's for sissies." Josiah pointed to the afternoon train rounding the curve over a mile away. "Let's see if you've got the nerve to hop that train."

Evan had filled many moments watching the older boys jump on the railroad cars. He understood the basics. The runner had to time the leap toward the ladder on the car and hang on long enough to prove he possessed courage. He had joined his friends in cheering the older boys' accomplishments and even imagined himself performing the same tricks when he got older.

Somewhere in his fuzzy brain, he sensed winter was the wrong time of the year for such stunts. But memories of his neighborhood heroes, his brother included, riding in triumph on top of the flat beds flashed through his mind. He also failed to reason those daredevils had held their competition in the summer when they were not wearing heavy coats and mittens. He just knew he did not want to do it.

"You know I can," Josiah crowed.

So true. A few months ago they had witnessed him leap and hang on to a coal car before he had jumped off and sprained his ankle.

"The question is can you?" Josiah nailed Evan with his eyes.

This last taunt pushed Evan past any good sense idling in his head. Visions of finally proving his courage and manhood propelled him. He tore down the hill in the direction of the train. The cheers from Carl and Ernest carried after him and spurred him to run faster.

Evan was panting by the time he reached the tracks. He sensed more than saw the train blur past. Reaching down inside to tap into his last reserve of strength, he sped forward and gained on the train. He spotted the car and ladder he needed to latch onto and ran along side and leapt. He willed his hands to grab the third rung of the ladder. His right hand brushed the cold metal but failed to curl on the rung.

~~~

"Doctor Powell, ya gotta come quick."

Lewis looked up from his exam of the town's mayor, Miles Clifford, when a boy's words reached him. They grew louder after he opened the door and saw Carl running toward him. The boy cried and yelled at the same time. He looked panicked and grabbed Lewis by the sleeve.

"Slow down, Carl, and tell me what's the matter. How can I help you?"

"It's Evan. He's been hurt awful bad."

"Where? How bad?"

"Real bad, Dr. Powell. He's been run over by the train. Come quick."

A fog fell over Lewis. It took Clifford's words and grip on his shoulder to bring him back into focus.

"Lewis," Clifford said, "Let's go get your boy."

Nodding, Lewis heard the mayor ask Carl for the exact location of the accident. He automatically grabbed his bag and followed the boy past the patients buzzing about what they had overheard. Clifford followed with his hand still pressing him forward.

At the door, the mayor turned to people seated around the room, "You all go on home now, and don't be stopping by next door at Dr. Powell's house. No sense telling Mrs. Powell about her son until we know how he is. Understand?"

The trio left the waiting room in heavy silence and walked to Clifford's buggy tied up out front.

"Tell me what happened," Lewis asked Carl when the horses started down the street.

Carl explained about Josiah's dare to hop the train and Evan's run down the hill. "I saw his hands go out. He almost made it. Then he slipped under the train."

Lewis saw the scene but could not put his son in it. Maybe the boy beside him exaggerated.

"I ran as fast as I could, to help him, you know. But there was nothing I could do." The boy stopped and shuddered. "There was so much blood in the snow."

Lewis' heart went out to Evan. There seemed to be little hope. But he willed his mind to think like a doctor. It was what his son needed most, if he was still alive.

~~~

When they reached Evan, only Ernest knelt beside Evan. Tears rushed from his eyes. Climbing down from the mayor's buggy, Lewis had prayed his son would survive.

But he knew Evan had died from the way he lay twisted by the tracks. There was nothing Lewis could do. Lewis knelt by his son and silently pleaded with God. Oh Lord, why did you have to take all of my children? Why? When he raised the boy's body to his chest, he envisioned another grave beside all the others.

Clifford wrapped Evan with an old blanket from the buggy. Together, the two men carried the boy to the rear seat. Lewis climbed in and held his son close on the hushed trip back into town. His thoughts circled. How was he going to tell Etta?

~~~

When the buggy pulled up in front of the house, Lewis glanced up and was surprised to see Reverend Humphrey get out of his carriage.

"I'm here to help anyway I can, Lewis. Do you want me to go in with you?"

Lewis shook his head. "I'll do it, alone."

"Then Clifford and I will bring in Evan. Carl, you take the doctor's bag."

Lewis assented and left the front door open after he went in. Hearing running footsteps on the stairs, he saw Etta hurry toward him. Curls had escaped her bun. Her dark green dress was covered with a dust-streaked apron.

"What's going on Lewis? I looked out the window and saw the Reverend outside."

"It's Evan, dearest."

He noticed his wife peer around him and the flushed tone of her face evaporate. In its place was now a sudden, unhealthy pallor. He took her into his arms and felt her quake.

"No, no, he can't be dead. God wouldn't take another child from me. Let me go. Evan needs me." Etta struggled to free herself.

"It's true Etta, oh God, it's true."

Lewis held tight and turned her around. His purpose was to shield her from the site of Evan when the men carried him into the front parlor where they would place the boy on the long table.

Lewis forced himself to prioritize his next steps. He beckoned Carl forward and grabbed the medical bag. With a wave, he dismissed the boy and guided Etta upstairs and into their bedroom.

"Lie down." He took in that for once she did not argue. She moved as if she were sleepwalking. She refused help untying her shoes and eventually had one shoe off and then the other.

He removed a bottle of laudanum syrup from his bag and said, "Here, take this." The dose was large enough to make her sleep. Joining her on the bed, he stretched out beside her and waited until her sobs ended, and she stilled.

~~~

Lewis, feeling decades older, shambled into the parlor and went for the whiskey decanter. He turned his back on the minister and mayor. With shaking hands, he poured himself two fingers of whiskey. Still turned, he took a sip before he put the unfinished glass back down on the side table. He faced the men.

"Reverend Humphrey, Mrs. Powell is resting upstairs. I need to return in a few minutes. Could I ask you to call Sullivan's after I call Ed and Charity?" At the mention of the undertaker's name and his children, Lewis wavered. Even more pain pierced his chest.

"Clifford," Lewis said, "Will you wait until Humphrey's finished? I have to get back to Etta after I make my calls, but I don't want my son left alone."

His friend nodded. Lewis went to Evan and unwrapped the blanket from his face. Bending down, he wiped some blood from his son's brow before giving him a final kiss.

~~~

At first, the house seemed so quiet as he sat beside Etta. Holding her hand, he watched her restless laudanum-induced sleep. There was nothing else to do but wait for Ed and Charity to arrive.

From downstairs, he heard the community fall into the familiar pattern of funeral etiquette within the next hour. He supplied the mental images to accompany the low sounds. Mrs. Burne accepted food from the church's bereavement committee. The Sullivan brothers arrived and carried Evan's body from the parlor.

A knock on the door brought him back. He looked up and saw Charity at the opened door. "I'll sit beside Momma," she offered, "Mr. Sullivan's downstairs. He said he'd wait as long as you need him to."

Lewis thought his daughter's courage won out right now over her grief. "Thank you, Princess. I won't be gone long."

~~~

After speaking with the funeral director, Lewis placed telegrams to Sophie and Lavinia. When Edward and his wife Alice arrived, Edward went up to his mother. Alice stepped in to help Mrs. Burne with the food and the tidying up for the wake.

~~~

During the evening, Lewis watched his house become a home of death. Reverend Humphrey led the family in prayer. The kitchen and dining room were filled with food for the wake and funeral dinner the next day. Edward tearfully said good-bye and departed with his wife. Charity saw her husband off and went up to her old room. From the creaking sounds of her rocking chair, Lewis knew she was vainly waiting for sleep, as he was. Only Etta, eased by her medication, slept.

~~~

Etta's memories of the wake and funeral were encased in cotton wool. Exactly who attended and who called to offer their condolences was hazy. The laudanum helped her get through the first few days.

But the day after the funeral, Lewis must have tapered her dosage. As the numbness and shock receded, the waves of pain in her soul grew. Only Charity's presence soothed her.

~~~

Two weeks later, after her daughter returned to her own home, a restlessness controlled Etta. She wandered through the house. Though she turned on every light, each room still remained dark and shadowy. The overcast skies brought no extra brightness into the house.

The only cure she knew for these troubling thoughts that robbed her of feeling alive was work. So she fired the hired girl and cleaned, waxed, or washed every thing she could. Each night she fell exhausted into bed. But her energy stayed low. Upon waking in the morning, she was no more rested than when she lay down the night before.

Winter hung on. And so did she.

~~~

In March, a month after Evan's death, Etta tackled clearing out the unused third floor. She had the idea of transforming the three storage rooms into playrooms for the grandchildren to romp around in. Inviting, toy-filled rooms might entice her children to bring the little ones over more often. What she needed was something to look forward to, some visits to brighten her life. What was better, she decided, than her small grandchildren beside her?

One large room occupied half the space, and the rest of the area was divided into two smaller rooms. The floor held the detritus of her and Lewis's lives from before and after they had married. When Doris had moved in, so had her possessions. Those joined the discards already stored on the third floor. The old woman had claimed the items included family heirlooms from Lewis' grandparents.

Throwing nothing out seemed to be a long-standing family trait, she complained to herself when she opened up a chest. She found it filled with old baby clothes and school papers which must have belonged to Lewis. Etta realized in the almost two decades of their married life, the accumulation of useless items had grown while the reasons for keeping all these belongings had lost significance.

Soon Etta discovered she gained a needed structure when she assigned herself a minimum of three hours each day to sort and clean. It took all of March and April to finish the big room.

The broken furniture was easy for Etta to let go of. Charity had stood in the doorway and declared there was nothing she wanted. Alice took home only a few pieces of Doris's china and a couple of old framed pictures. There was little the younger woman said she wanted in her house. Lavinia and Sophie also passed on the leftover items. Then, with a clear conscience, Etta ruthlessly culled the few good pieces, including a rose-patterned, bone china tea set.

The next day, Etta shoved the remaining clutter aside for the junk man. She was about to return downstairs for lunch when she noticed another one of Doris' trunks. She did not remember its contents.

"Probably just some more junk," she grumbled.

But somehow she could not walk way from it.

When Etta opened the lid, she found the trunk filled with her children's toys. She recognized Ed's miniature railroad set. She was undone. Etta recognized her level of pain was at the point where her numbness had worn off and the undeniable reality of loss would begin to oppress her.

Entrapped, she felt the present world evaporate from her brain. She accepted her mind's invitation to return to the past where all her children were safe and trains were toys, not huge machines for killing reckless boys.

~~~

It was May before Etta worked her way into the last room where she found Doris' stash of Dr. Winter's Mint Syrup in the window seat under the dormer windows. Etta's first thought echoed Lewis' words when she had shown him his mother's bottles. This liquid was vile and poisonous.

Enraged over Doris' weakness, she jerked small bottle after bottle out of the recess. Soon however tears welled up from deep inside her. Her mother-in-law had not been weak. She was a strong woman who had buckled under the grief of losing her beloved husband.

Suddenly Etta sensed Doris there with her and realized her mother-in-law was bestowing a gift upon her, the gift of how to cope with horrendous grief.

Back and forth she debated about the syrup. Doping was a sign of weak morals and personal failing. She was stronger than Doris.

What if Lewis was wrong? He had given her laudanum right after Evan's death, and it had helped. What was wrong with using a little bit to help her over the rough spots?

Then another counterargument stepped forward. Nonsense, she had not needed any such crutch after Della had died. Lewis had survived even worse, all his children, his first wife, and even his parents' deaths without relying on drugs.

But Etta remembered how far she had descended into melancholy after Della's death. She had even considered suicide though it was only a brief thought and had no substance.

She viewed the stack of bottles before her. With a flash of insight, she shrank from her future. So many little things would suddenly crop up and catch her unaware. The birthdays no longer celebrated. The holidays tinged with grief and the absence of her child. Even pulling open a drawer and finding a sock or toy.

Worse would be the sight of a child who was so similar to her own that for a few blessed moments she would forget Evan was dead.

Too much, much too much, and too unending.

Etta removed the stopper from one of the heavier bottles. The mint scent rose and reassured her. Many of Lewis' own medicines contained the same fragrance. Etta braved a small taste. She dipped her finger into the bottle and put a tiny trace of the liquid on her tongue. Pleasant, like candy. Etta took a sip and another then a bigger one.

Suddenly a small bit of sunshine began to warm within her. Etta rushed over to the dusty mirror and with her handkerchief cleared a circle to see her face. Her forehead should have been glowing. But she did not look any different than she had when, first thing in the morning, she fixed her red curls back into a knot.

How could she feel so free and light and it not show? Both times she had fallen in love Lavinia and Sophie said it was written all over her face. They teased her that the warm radiance from her green eyes announced her happiness for the whole world to see.

Even after a closer inspection, the mirror gave no indication of how the weight of grief had escaped her constricted heart. Instead her soul danced.

She turned to look at the bottles the moment the afternoon sun graced the upstairs room. Etta sat down amid Doris' treasures which had now become her temptation and reconsidered.

Grief served a purpose and was part of life. Everyone had to endure the pain. It was a test of character. If she chose instead to circumvent the pain, she was certainly a weakling and on Judgment Day she would have to reckon with her shortcomings.

But surely her past suffering counted? She had already endured so much and survived. With the exception of Lewis losing his whole family, she knew of no one who had carried the burdens she had. Also Lewis did not have to face his greatest trial until he was a grown man.

Her troubles started with being orphaned. Her father's abuse followed, and other hardships fell into a timeline. Losing her home and secure place in family and society. Both parents dead. Her brother as good as dead since he was lost to her. All these tragedies before she was even sixteen.

Her happiness with Ben was so short-lived. Lied to and cheated by her father-in-law, she was left to raise three children alone.

The thought of Della's death twisted her soul anew. Evan was the most recent tragedy in a long inventory of pain.

She opened the bottle to whiff the peppermint again. The syrup promised to ease the pain. Doris' elixir represented an escape. If she husbanded it carefully and took only a small bit no more than once, maybe twice a day, the bottles might last her some time. At least as long as it would take for her to save back enough from the housekeeping money to buy more.

Doris had showed her how to arrange delivery, how to hide her collection, and more importantly how to survive life.

So she layered another secret to her cache.

Chapter 30

Frankfort, August 24, 1899

What Etta had begun in March was at last done. She hired those nice young men, whose names she could never remember, from her church. They worked hard and, without one complaint, cleared out the clutter and cleaned the floor and walls.

After painting the playroom ceiling a sugar cookie yellow, the men hung wallpaper with fanciful animals against a sylvan background. Long flowing, sea foam green curtains graced the windows on all three sides of the room. All the furniture and toys came from mail order catalogs, the modern way to shop.

The same color scheme continued into her special room across the hall where the identical yellow ceiling and green curtains picked up intensity in the natural light.

But Etta made this room different. It was to be her haven, spare, and unseen by anyone, except her, after the workmen finished. She alone saw the delicate, pale-yellow wallpaper with bouquets of spring flowers, sat on the brocade chaise lounge with matching pillows for the window seats which hid her magical syrup, and used the lamp and the phonograph from the parlor.

Her uncluttered room evoked peace, and as summer eased into autumn, Etta took pride in the control she exercised over the syrup. While she drank from her laudanum-laced teacup every morning, she tried to ignore that the amount of syrup in the teacup increased a bit more each week as did the amount of time within those walls.

The most important feature of the room was that Evan had never seen it. As long as she did not step outside the door, she was free of pain.

~~

Charity noticed bothersome little things about her mother. Sometimes a vacant look would come into the older woman's eyes after she came down from her upstairs work. Other times, her mother would come into the room and mutter under her breath "Now what did I come in here for? I can't remember. Oh well, it must not have been important."

Both would laugh over it and talk about something else. However, after Etta became so mercurial with the grandchildren, Charity could no longer overlook her mother's mood swings. Concerned, she stopped by her father's office to discuss her mother.

"Poppa, Momma isn't herself," Charity said as soon as she sat down and propped her parasol beside the chair. "She gets so angry over the smallest things."

Lewis took his glasses off and said, "It's quite normal, Charity. Women your mother's age tend to be highly changeable. She has always been known for her temper. I can tell you, it's going to get worse before it gets better. Think of it as a storm. We just have to ride it out." His glasses, now clean, returned to his face.

"But for how long? She frightened the children so much last week. I'm wavering. Maybe I shouldn't bring them for any more visits."

"I know, she told me all about it. She knew she overreacted when little Loren chased Melissa through the parlor and knocked the tea service off the table. The teapot had been in my mother's family for so long. Though I never put much store in it, your mother thought I did."

"It wasn't because she became angry. I've seen her lose her temper, many times. This was different, Poppa. I have never seen her so enraged. The look coming out of her eyes frightened me too. She didn't seem like Momma anymore." Charity fought back feelings of disloyalty to her mother. Maybe Poppa was right. She was the one overreacting.

"She has been through so much," Lewis continued. "The change now is one more burden. Don't you think when you take all these things into consideration, it's really remarkable she's doing as well as she is?"

Charity picked up on a tone in her father's voice. It chilled her. "What do you mean?" she asked.

"Surely you've heard about women who become unhinged at this time in their lives?"

Charity nodded. She remembered Mother Beauchamp's whispers about some aunt who had been sent away for a rest cure after she had taken a knife to her husband's parts. All he swore he had done was complain about dining with cold winter air blowing in from the open window.

Charity gasped. "You think Momma might go insane?"

"No, not at all. Your mother's shown no signs of being unbalanced. One of the best indications we have is how her grandmothers handled their time."

Charity's unease heightened. Her mother had never furnished any information about her family. Every time Charity had asked about the family, Etta had always answered that the past was not important.

Even when Mrs. Beauchamp had pried into the family background, Etta gave no details. All she had said by way of explanation was the tragedies of her parents' deaths were still so painful, she could not talk about it. So Mother Beauchamp had to stop the inquisition, politely clothed as it was.

Etta did not offer any family stories after the births of Loren and Melissa either to match the Beauchamp family lore of Revolutionary War generals or Constitution signers.

"She told you about them?" Charity asked.

"Yes," Lewis said. "I asked her about a month ago." He stopped and looked over his eyeglasses at his daughter. "I have noticed, Princess, your mother isn't quite herself. The hot flashes and absent-mindedness are quite normal. Your mother's a little early with her symptoms, but she's had the shock of Evan's passing."

At these words, Charity watched her father fight to control the trembling of his chin and regain his professional demeanor before he continued.

"Probably grief has accelerated the aging process. But she told me both her grandmothers weren't bothered by their change of life. So don't you worry, you probably won't be either."

A sense of betrayal came over her. How could her mother share such family information with Lewis and not her? When the truth came to her a few seconds later, it swept away her hurt feelings. She had to leave right now to protect her mother. She knew she would give away what her mother was trying to hide.

Charity had long sensed something horrible from her mother's early life haunted her still because Etta had not shared anything about her grandmothers. Poppa must have pressed her for details, and Etta had thrown out lies as a way to divert him.

She gathered her bag and gloves. On the ride home, the sound of the horse's hooves on the cobblestones brought back a memory from before she was married.

On the way to an engagement party, Charity had mentioned how much pride the Beauchamps seemed to take in their ancestry. Her mother's temper flashed, and a derisive snort escaped from her mouth. She followed with the scalding comment that the only parent anyone could be sure of was the mother and that was only if the actual birth had been witnessed.

The bitterness behind this outburst froze Charity. After her mother filled the silence with a quick laugh, she said the world would be a much better place if more people looked to the future instead of where they had come from. She also hoped Charity would follow suit with her children.

~~~

Etta despised late autumn. It always brought a spike in illnesses, and so she became lonelier as the pace of Lewis's practice picked up. The overcast skies and cold weather drove her deeper into melancholia.

She emptied the green bottles even faster. The midmorning sip of her "medicine" was no longer sufficient. Like clockwork, she needed another dose every five hours, the first one upon rising.

One day, at eleven o'clock, Etta had her teacup in her hand and her foot on the first step of the stairs to go up for dose when she heard a knock at the front door. A woman's high-pitched voice called "Mrs. Powell." Through the lace-curtained door, she could see the outline of a short, thin woman, and conversely, the woman could also see her.

"Mrs. Powell," the minister's wife repeated after Etta opened the door. "I was just passing by after a visit with your neighbor, Mrs. Perkins, down the street."

Bessie Humphrey, a bird-like, nervous woman, turned her head to the left, and the fall flowers on her hat bobbed. The yellow zinnia lost a few petals. Etta watched them float to the threshold. The woman set one foot by her fallen petals.

"I just knew you'd want to hear about her recovery. So I just said to myself, why don't I stop in for a few minutes and tell dear Mrs. Powell all about Mrs. Perkins over a cup of tea?"

Bessie smiled and nodded at the cup in Etta's hand. "I was correct, wasn't I?" She waited for Etta to answer.

Etta knew it would not do to be impolite. Realizing the sooner the woman came in, the sooner she could get rid of her, Etta stepped aside.

"Come in, Mrs. Humphrey. I'll get you a cup of tea."

As Etta led her guest toward the parlor, she considered how long it would take to dash upstairs for her medicine and back to her visitor and the kitchen to heat the tea kettle on the stove.

Bessie ruined the plan. "I hope you don't mind," she said. "But Mrs. Burne told me all about your redecorating, and the nice young men from our church you hired. Before we have tea, could you show me your rooms?"

"Of course." Angry at herself because she had let this woman in, Etta led the way upstairs. She also vowed she would never again be without a small medicine bottle in her pocket.

~~~

Bessie gushed over the yellow ceiling. "The color lightens up the room so much. Look how you matched the same shade in the wallpaper. Your grandchildren must enjoy seeing how these delightful animals playing among the trees." The woman touched the spot where the bear danced with a deer.

"I hear you redecorated another room as well. With the same color paint but with the most charming wallpaper. Mr. Cummings showed me the pattern in his sample book, and I just said to myself, Mrs. Powell will always think it's spring with those yellow bouquets."

Etta's heart chilled. After the movers had placed the rose marble-topped table and a Tiffany lamp in her room, no one except her, not even Lewis or Charity, had ever entered it.

"I'm afraid you're going to have to leave now, Mrs. Humphrey. I've come down with a terrible headache."

"Mrs. Powell," Bessie's voice took on a serious tone. "I know how it is to lose a child."

Etta saw the hallway swim before her. This woman was not fit to talk about Evan.

Bessie grasped her hand and asked, "Would you kneel with me, right here, right this moment, so we can pray for forgiveness? God will listen."

A smoldering ember of anger lit inside her. "I have nothing to say to God. You must leave."

"Prayer is the answer, Mrs. Powell. Remember, the sins of the fathers, unto the third or fourth generation."

"Get out of my house, now, you horrible harpy."

Etta forced herself to stare Bessie down until the woman turned and fled. Etta reached for the banister and held on as she gulped air into her suffocating lungs. The door slammed. She removed the key from her pocket. Her hands trembled so much it took several tries to unlock the door. Once inside her sanctuary, she ran to the window seat.

~~~

Etta woke with her heart racing. In her dream, Evan's coffin lid had slammed shut over and over. But the sound turned out to be heavy footsteps downstairs. It was probably a patient who had found Lewis out of his office and come next door for help.

When the fog cleared, Etta rose from her chaise, smoothed her skirt, and fixed some stray curls back into her bun.

Lewis' shouts reached her. "Etta, where are you?"

He sounded angry. Suddenly the moment she had called the minister's wife a harpy crystallized. The gossip mills must have been working overtime if Lewis had already heard about it.

Etta opened the door. "Up here. I'll be right down." She glanced around the room and saw one bottle on the floor. Within a few seconds, she slid it back into the window seat and stood in the hallway to lock the door.

Etta met Lewis on the stairs. His face told the story. His lips were clamped shut. A red tinge had crept up his neck. He took her by the elbow.

"Reverend Humphrey just left my office. He told me about his wife's visit to you."

"I'm not going to stand here on the steps and argue. I just woke from a nap. I need some tea. Afterwards, I'll explain."

Etta jerked her arm free and walked past him. He stomped after her.

In the kitchen, Etta did not acknowledge Lewis's irritated sighs. Instead she brewed her tea while she sorted through different ways to defuse his anger. She could explain how vile the woman was. Or she might ask Lewis what awful sin they had committed so God was compelled to take another of their children. The final option was to listen to his rant.

One thing was certain. Her anger had exploded her melancholy to bits. For the first time since Evan's death, her thoughts seemed clear and her senses sharp. She noticed the dust motes play in the sun. She enjoyed the cleansing tang of citrus when she opened a jar of orange marmalade.

Etta turned to Lewis. Without taking her eyes off him, she crossed the room and took her seat at the table. Her mind was made up. She would wait and listen before she played the sin card. The sniveling woman and her pompous husband did not have the answers she needed.

"I'm ready now, Lewis," she said.

"Etta, you can't go flying off like a deranged harridan. I have a reputation at stake here. My good name is what pays the bills. You have to be more careful and control your moods."

"What did Humphrey say?"

"Doesn't matter, it's all the way through town. Mrs. Williams met me outside the office right after Humphrey left. The old biddy was bursting at the seams to tell me how sorry she was to hear you have fallen away from the Lord. But you're in her prayers."

Etta could not help herself, she laughed.

"It's no laughing matter, Etta, especially at your time of life."

"What are you talking about, at my time of life?"

"The change, sometimes it makes women highly strung. Do you remember Martha Manchester?"

A chill spread through Etta. Martha went to their church. "There was a short notice in the paper last week. It said she's in the county home."

"You're right, in the basement of the Home for Friendless Women."

Etta shuddered at the memory of those dark, dank rooms. The girls had spun scary stories about ghosts that haunted the little used storage rooms.

"Why isn't she at the county farm on Lawrenceburg Road?"

"The county contracted with the Home to keep the unstable women in town and made the basement more secure."

Etta pictured Martha in the familiar ill-lit place and choked back tears. "What did she do?"

"She attacked her husband with a hot iron."

"Why?"

"Don't know, but it's not important. He said she was unsound because she was going through the change. He demanded a competency hearing."

"How do you know this? Were you involved?"

"No, the judge brought in Doctor Kirkpatrick. He told me about it. He diagnosed her case as moral insanity due to menopause."

Etta's newfound clarity of mind crumbled. She needed her medicine. "I'll go write Bessie a letter of apology."

"That's my girl," Lewis said and kissed her on the forehead. "I've got to get back to the office."

Etta went upstairs to write two letters, the one she had promised, the other to Martha Manchester.

~~~

A few days later, Etta walked up the front steps of the Home and scanned the lintel for those frightening words. Home for Friendless Women. But they were gone. In their place was blank rough cement, not as gray and stained as the surrounding limestone block. Images of how scared and overwhelmed she had been when she first stood there still had the power to unnerve her. Though no longer a frightened girl of fifteen, she was even more terrified today. Only her anger over Martha's treatment provided her enough courage to walk through the door and ask to visit.

The same smell of too many bodies and too much cooking, a bit fainter than before, lingered in the foyer. The odor made her fear rise even higher. She almost left before someone might notice her. But the image of Martha locked away someplace in the basement forced her to walk into Old Ghostie's office.

Etta almost expected to see him behind the desk. Instead she found a middle-aged woman in a simple black dress with white cotton arm gaiters. Her gray-streaked hair twisted in braids around her head. The nameplate on her desk read Mrs. R. McFarland.

"May I help you?" the woman said and put her paperwork aside.

"I'm here to visit Mrs. Manchester."

"She's downstairs. Just go back outside and use the north door. Do you want someone to guide you?"

Etta shook her head and shut the door behind her. On the way to the door, she noticed the foyer walls now wore a softer green. Her anxiety notched down a bit.

Soon she stood at the foot of the basement entrance and took in the Spartan appearance. An unoccupied small desk with only a sign-in book and a hand bell, much like school teachers used, was on top. A barred gate behind the desk chair.

Etta paused and took in the changes. Beyond the desk, the walls had been removed and what looked like cells had been built in their place. Since overhead lights had been added, she could see women behind the bars of their cells. All wore the same uniforms, shapeless dark blue dresses. But she did not see Martha. Maybe her friend had been released.

When Etta reached the desk, she rang the school bell. Several women turned, and their shouts and shrieks echoed from the walls.

"I'll be right there," a voice called out over the noise. Within a moment, a plump woman dressed in a full white apron over a black dress came out of what Etta remembered was a small closet that was always locked and rumored to be haunted.

"Excuse our inmates, ma'am. Visitors always set them off."

"I'm here to visit Mrs. Manchester, if she's still here."

"She's here all right, will be for some time. The judge said at least six months."

Etta looked over the attendant's shoulder and could not imagine life in this place for so long.

"After you sign in, you can leave your coat and handbag with me. You can't take anything inside." Then the attendant picked up the desk chair and asked her to follow.

Cold rose from the floor as Etta walked behind the matron. She passed several stoves, but they put out little heat. She tried not to stare inside the cells. Out of the corner of her eye she saw some women asleep or reading. A few stared at nothing. In the last cell Martha paced the perimeter. The once pretty woman showed signs of defeat. Her face was haggard, her hair undone and tangled. Worse was the despairing look in her eyes.

"What happened?" Etta asked after the attendant placed the chair outside the cell and left.

Martha pulled her stool over, so they could talk without being overheard.

"It was all my husband's doing. He got mad at me when I told him he had to take the pledge and give up the drink." Tears fell down Martha's thin face. "He came after me. That's when I hit him."

"Did you tell the judge?"

"No, he wasn't interested in anything I had to say. Several of my husband's friends and family spoke out. They said they'd seen me fly off the handle for no good reason."

"Your family wasn't any help?"

"None live here. I've written to my brother back in Maryland. Maybe he can be of help."

～～

The visit with Martha sobered Etta and sparked an ember of her old resolve. She would wean herself from Dr. Winter's syrup. Every day for a close to a week, the warning echoed in her brain while she fought against a second dose of her medicine. Most days she worked through the urge and took only a few drops in her morning tea.

But Evan's birthday and the first Christmas without him loomed before her. Their weight overwhelmed her, and she increased the dosage. As a peaceful nothingness beckoned her, the warning she had gained from Martha's situation receded.

~~~

Etta's nerves frayed by mid-morning on Evan's birthday. First Ed and Charity called with their families, so she and Lewis would not be alone. After lunch, they left when Lavinia and Sophie arrived. The presence of visitors in her house exhausted her.

Yet she fought against a retreat upstairs to her room until she heard Reverend Humphrey's voice in the foyer. She pleaded a headache to Sophie and rushed up the backstairs. A few moments later, she escaped into her locked room. After a promise to go back to the regular dose tomorrow, she opened a full bottle and drank Dr. Winter's magic. Within a few moments, warmth radiated from her core.

~~~

Later that week, Etta discovered only empty bottles in Doris' stash under the window seat. A frantic check and recheck of each bottle hurtled her anxiety level higher. What was she going to do? It was time for her morning dose.

She added water to each container and desperately swirled the liquid. With her hands shaking, she drained the bottles into her teacup and tried to drink. More spilled on her robe than she managed to gulp. She let out an anguished sob as panic stole over her. She had to have her medicine.

Etta reached deep down to her last reserve of strength. She forced herself to return to the bedroom and dress for going out. She winced when she stood in front of the mirror and saw a gaunt and disheveled old hag. Her green eyes had even forfeited their color.

Then Etta laughed. If she covered her hair in a long scarf, no one would recognize her. She could move with impunity from store to store and buy her medicine. There would be no whispers of her purchases to make their way back to Lewis.

Her first disguised foray was successful. No one on the street acknowledged her. She purchased one bottle at a store on the other side of town. Elated, she walked home.

~~~

Two days later, she tried a different store and bought a few more bottles. Success was with her again and renewed her strength. But her third attempt at a store closer to home was different.

The clerk nodded at her when the bell jingled and announced her arrival. However, his look had no recognition in it. Etta found the patent medicine aisle and ignored the woman coming the other way. She had a bottle of Dr. Winter's in hand when she heard a voice.

"Mrs. Doctor Powell, is that you?"

Etta's teeth gritted. She hated that greeting and preferred Mrs. Powell. She pretended she had not heard, but the woman approached anyway. The aisle was too short and narrow for an escape. Etta put her hand out as if to steady herself and snuck the bottle back on the shelf.

"Yes," the woman said, "I thought it was you. Your green eyes are so distinctive. I'd know them anywhere. Would you please tell doctor how much better my little Billie is? Your husband's visit last week was just the ticket. He is such a godsend to us in this community."

Etta had no idea who this woman was and almost shared this fact. But Lewis, no doubt, would hear about it and consider her thoughtless and rude. So she smiled and said she would pass on the good news about Billie's recovery.

As she walked out of the store, she vowed never to shop this close to home again. Lewis would go berserk if he found out about her medicine especially from some busybody in town.

Chapter 31

By ten o'clock the Tuesday before Christmas, Charity at last gave in to her children. Four-year-old Loren and three-year-old Melissa had ding-donged her since breakfast. They wanted to see Nana Etta. When Charity put the telephone call through to her mother's house, Momma asked them to come over.

The three of them arrived a bit before noon for lunch. Charity thought her mother looked a little tired. Her eyes had a haunted look, but that was to be expected with Christmas so close.

Loren wolfed down his food and asked to go upstairs and play. Before Charity could answer, her mother excused him and asked Charity if she needed to run any errands.

When she answered yes, Momma said, "Why don't you go right now? You can leave the children here."

"Are you sure they won't be too much trouble?"

"No, they'll be as good as gold. Besides why shouldn't they spend the day with their nana?" Her mother hugged Melissa and touched foreheads with her. "We'll see you in a few hours. Take as long as you want."

"Thank you, there's the florist and the butcher."

"Don't worry, we'll be fine."

On her way out the door, Charity heard her mother say, "Melissa, what magic land do you want to visit today?"

~~

At four in the afternoon, Charity entered her mother's house through the unlocked back door. No one was downstairs, but that was not unusual. Loren and Melissa preferred the playroom on the third floor.

Quickly she went past the parlor. There she noticed her mother had hung garlands and arranged the familiar blown glass ornaments on the tree. On her way up the stairs, memories of childhood Christmases came over her and brought hope that the family might yet again have a festive holiday.

On the second floor, she peered into her old room now redone for Ed's children. Maybe her mother would soon resume their overnight visits.

But the quiet on the top floor unnerved her. She could not make her feet move fast enough to the playroom door. Her fingers grew thick when her hands grasped the doorknob.

After several attempts, she succeeded and opened the door. The dimming day threw shadows across the room. Her hand reached for the switch, and the lights chased the shadows into corners. That's when she saw toys scattered haphazardly around the room.

"Loren, Melissa, where are you?"

From behind a mound of pillows Loren's head appeared. His eyes were swollen from sleep, and mucus had run out of his nose and left smears hardened on his cheeks.

"Momma, Momma."

His shout awoke Melissa. Both stumbled over the pillows and headed for Charity. She scooped them into her arms. Twined together they settled onto the floor. Charity held the children tight and tried to piece together what had happened.

"Where's Nana?" He stared at her. His lower lip quivered. "Loren, do you know where Nana is?" He nodded and looked away. "Where darling? Where's Nana?" The little boy looked up and pointed toward the open door. "Nana left you here?" Again the boy nodded and looked at his sister asleep in her mother's lap.

"Nana yelled, at me and Sissy, and went bye-bye."

"Everything will be fine now. Let's go find Nana." Rising with Melissa on her hip, she reached out her hand for Loren. He shook his head.

"Loren, I need to find Nana."

Charity ran through the possibilities. Had her mother fallen? Had she had a seizure and died? Nothing made any sense.

"Momma, no." Loren grasped her skirts and tugged.

"Come help me find Nana."

He shook his head again and said, "Go home."

"After we find Nana, come on."

Loren took his mother's hand. The three crossed the hall to the other room and found the door locked. Charity called out and pounded. When she put her ear to the door, she could not hear anything. Trying to keep her panic in check, she changed her mind.

"Come darling, let's go to Gramps. He can help us find Nana."

She gathered blankets from the bedrooms and bundled the children. She hastened next door to Lewis' office and bustled through the back entrance.

"The children," Lewis said as he looked up at her. "Are they ill?" He put his pen down as Loren restarted his sobs.

"I found the children asleep and all alone, and Momma's door locked. She won't answer." Charity wiped the tears from her cheeks.

"Wait here," Lewis demanded and bolted out the door.

"I don't like Nana anymore." Loren leaned against his mother. "Nana's mean. She said no toy trains. She yelled no real loud."

"Nana loves you and Sissy. She's just sad right now. Soon she'll be better," Charity said and pulled her son closer.

～～～

Next door Lewis raced through the downstairs and up to Etta's room. He shouted and pounded but heard nothing in reply. He put his shoulder to the door and rammed three times before the door broke open. Etta lay asleep, curled on the chaise, her arms folded in a self-embrace and her unbound hair straggled across the pillow.

He checked for vital signs. Etta's chest rose and fell rhythmically. The pulse steady. But her appearance startled him. Her face was pasty and gleamed with sweat. Though when he touched her forehead, he found it cool.

The scent of peppermint reached his nose. He sniffed. The smell lingered around Etta. The green throw had begun to slip so he brought it to her chest. A small, unstoppered medicine bottle fell out of the material's folds. He picked it up and read Dr. Winter on the label.

Not again, he thought, first my mother and now Etta. His guts contracted, and he hoped the people who made and sold addiction to women had their own special place in hell. All the jigsaw puzzle pieces of their recent life fell into place. He wept tears of anger, frustration, and love.

Exhausted, he checked her once more now that he understood her true condition. She was stable and would sleep for some time. Next he searched the room and found empty bottles along with a half-dozen full ones in the window seat.

~~~

Lewis soon gathered Ed and Charity in his study. His children had to know what was going on. He pulled two empty Dr. Winter's bottles from his jacket and placed them on his desk. "Do you know what's in these?" he asked.

Neither did.

"Laudanum," Lewis said, "mixed with some alcohol and peppermint. Your mother had over thirty empty bottles hidden upstairs along with a half-dozen full ones."

Charity picked up one of the bottles and removed the lid. The scent of peppermint invaded the room.

"Didn't you give this to Momma after Evan died?" she asked.

"For a few weeks," Lewis said. "But she's now addicted."

"Like those old soldiers at the courthouse?" Ed asked.

"The same. But we're going to wean Momma off this vile stuff." He stopped and looked at them. After they nodded, he promised, "I'll find a private nurse."

"Wait," Ed asked. "Why will she need someone?"

"Primarily because of the violent physical reactions people have when they decrease their laudanum. Your mother will experience nervousness, nausea, and vomiting. She'll be angry when she realizes she can't have any Dr. Winter's whenever she wishes. Do you understand laudanum is opium?"

Charity gasped, and Ed exclaimed, "Opium?" and grabbed the other bottle. "Our mother's an opium addict?"

Lewis answered, "It's one of the dangerous side effects of laudanum if the doses are unchecked."

Charity paled, and her voice trembled when she said, "So the nurse will know she's an addict?"

Lewis nodded and waited for his children to absorb the reality of Etta's condition.

"How long before she's better?" Charity asked.

"Physically, she should be better in a few weeks to a month."

"What do you mean physically?" Ed said and rolled the bottle over in his hand.

"Your mother is also emotionally dependent. Even after she no longer physically needs this stuff, we'll have to keep her away from it."

"How long?" Charity said and put the lid back on the bottle.

"Until she's strong enough to abstain on her own."

Charity said, "What if I stayed with her for those first two weeks or so until she's well enough to have a nurse or maybe a companion?"

Lewis knew what was unspoken by his daughter. It would be embarrassing if people knew her mother was an opium addict.

"Princess, your help would be appreciated. But it's better to have a nurse or companion. They would have to know her condition."

"Why?"

"Momma has to keep away from all stimulants."

"How about a rest cure?" Charity said. "Couldn't she go to Louisville or even Cincinnati?"

"After she's out of the first dangerous phase, yes, it's possible," Lewis said. "But the good ones are expensive."

"We could both help out, couldn't we, Charity?"

Ed looked at his sister. After she agreed, he went on, "But do rest cures work? Will she get better and come back home?"

"It's worth a try," Lewis said.

"But what if it doesn't work? Does that sometimes happen?" Charity asked.

"Yes." And with that single word, sadness fell over him.

"What if she goes back to this stuff?" Charity's eyes filled with tears.

"It, it will kill her," Lewis said. "She'll have to increase the amount she takes to feel good. But once liver poisoning sets in..." He could not go on.

Charity sobbed, "Poppa, I don't want her to die. We have to help her."

"Any way we can," Ed said.

~~

Charity moved in, after explaining to her husband's family that her mother was so grief-stricken over the first Christmas without Evan that she needed some extra attention.

After a few days, Charity almost wished her story was true. Dealing with her mother was worse than she had imagined possible. Many times Charity had to stop and tell herself she could do this. After all, she had been through childbirth and nursed her two children when they were ill. But her mother's physical reactions to opium withdrawal were horrendous, far beyond what her father had described. Her mother was ill all hours of the day and night.

Caring for an adult was also more difficult. By the end of the week, Charity's resentment toward her mother boiled. After all, the addiction came from every sip out of those small bottles of evil. This was no accident, no chance disease, and it had happened from one intentional act followed by another.

Charity also was unnerved by how their relationship had changed. For the first time ever, she found her mother was not the strong rescuer, the source of all the answers to life, the one person in the whole world who would protect her, without fail. The realization scared Charity more than the night sweats and vomiting.

~~~

Etta fought through the first few days. They were a living hell. Her body craved opium. She felt her grip on sanity begin to slip, but somehow she came through the sweats and nausea. Finally sleep lasted through the night and food stayed down.

In the third week, her physical strength began its road to recovery. But at the same time her undiluted grief and resentment collided with her daughter's newfound authority and set off a firestorm.

"Charity Darnell Beauchamp," Etta said one afternoon when she was in a particularly foul mood. "I can take care of myself. I don't need your help."

Etta punctuated her anger by throwing the food tray to the floor. She enjoyed the satisfying sound of breaking pottery. Charity's moan erupted in the bedroom and brought Etta the first sense of power she had felt for almost a month. She saw no need to stop her rant.

"Besides, the food is too salty, my bed is not warm enough, and look at the filth around here."

Her daughter snapped back, "I don't want to be here either. As soon as Poppa says I can leave, I will."

"The sooner the better. This is my house and I can make my own decisions. I am your mother, not your child."

"Then you'd better start acting like one."

"Your brother would never be this mean to me."

"You are so wrong. I talk with Ed every few days. He knows what's going on and approves."

"I meant Evan." Etta glared, determined not to back down first.

~~

Charity matched her mother's look and shouted. "If it wasn't for me, you would've died. You don't appreciate how much I have sacrificed to be here with you."

She hated the moment when tears streamed down her face. It made her feel so weak.

"I've been here, taking care of you every waking moment. The only time I've seen my own children was Christmas Day."

"You can leave any time. I'm quite capable of taking care of myself."

Charity stopped her next retort because Poppa entered the bedroom. After kissing first his wife and then his daughter, he sat down. The way he seemed to ignore the tension draping the room infuriated Charity.

"Poppa, I can't stay here any more. I've tried, but I want to leave."

He put up his hand as a signal to steady her. Etta filled the lull in conversation with her own attack.

"Lewis, how could you have let this happen? I'm a prisoner in my own house. She treats me as if I've lost my mind."

"I've found a woman to stay with you, a Mrs. Kroner," Poppa intervened. "She comes highly recommended by one of my patients."

"Is she American?" Charity asked and hoped the woman was her way out of the current awful situation.

"No," he replied slowly. "She's been here for about six months." Etta sniffed her disapproval before he hurried on. "But her English is improving. I interviewed her today in the office. She can start tomorrow."

"German?" Etta said. "Does she smell of bleach? Everyone knows they clean everything with bleach."

"I think you'll like her, Etta. She's about your age, and no, she doesn't smell of bleach.

"What did you tell her, Poppa?"

"I told her your mother became ill, a stomach flare-up, and she has to have a bland diet while she recovers."

Charity wondered if her father's words would keep the new woman from becoming overcurious.

Poppa turned again to Momma and said, "I stressed to her that nothing, absolutely nothing, should be consumed by you unless I say so. I didn't go into any other details. Do you agree to have this woman come and help you?"

Etta crossed her arms over her chest and glared at her daughter. "Yes, anything as long as I don't have to look at her every day."

"Fine, I'm glad it's settled. Charity, let's get you home to your family."

His last words squashed Charity's growing guilt over abandoning her mother.

~~

The next morning, Lewis opened the back door and found Renate Kroner, an hour early, ready to work, and dressed in a bright yellow calico dress and a heavily starched white apron. Within a few minutes, the aroma of eggs and bacon drew him to the kitchen table where he ate a plateful of a delicious breakfast.

He was amazed that the woman had accomplished so much by the time he was returned for lunch. The downstairs had been put to rights. A load of laundry hung from the overhead kitchen racks. Etta was dressed. Best of all, by some miracle, she appeared cooperative.

~~

When Lewis returned home after work, he could hardly remember a time when the kitchen had been so orderly and clean. But even more surprising were Etta and Renate. They calmly sat at the kitchen table and shared a pot of tea as they tried to talk to each other. There was a great deal of pointing, nodding heads, smiling, and repeating short sentences. But the women seemed to communicate well enough. He joined them for tea and gingersnaps and thanked God for the moment of peace.

~~

As life continued to improve at his house, Lewis played with the idea of keeping Renate after Etta recovered. Etta joined him every evening for a quiet meal and an hour or two of conversation and music. She took the sleeping mixture he prepared for her fresh each night. After she was asleep, he searched the house for any vials of Dr. Winter's and found none.

~~

The anniversary of Evan's death was almost upon them when Lewis broached the subject while he and Etta ate their evening meal. "I've arranged for Dr. Phillips to make my house calls. Would you like something special at church to honor Evan?"

Etta shrugged and slid beets around her plate.

Lewis went on, "Reverend Humphrey could ask for a moment of silent prayer. Maybe the children and grandchildren might return here, if you feel up to it. I could ask Renate to come in and cook a simple meal for all of us."

"Yes, very nice."

He was disappointed by her lackadaisical answer. But, he admonished himself, Etta had been through so much. The important thing was her improvement. She was even going out on daily walks with Renate. Maybe he could soon lessen the strength of the sleeping mixture.

~~

But on January ninth, his plans changed when Hiram Cummins, owner of a dry goods store, knocked on the door a few hours after dinner.

"Come in, sir, and get warm while I get my bag. It's not your father, is it?"

Cummins took off his gloves and stuffed them into his pocket. "No, none of the family's ill." He glanced around the hall and asked, "Is Mrs. Powell available?"

"She's retired for the night."

This news did not calm Cummins, and a fear began to spread through Lewis. "Let me take your coat and then we'll talk in the study."

After Cummins sat before the fire a few minutes later, he cleared his throat and said, "Dr. Powell, we know your wife has been through so much. The last thing we want to do is to bring any more pain to your household."

Lewis got a sickening feeling in his gut and guessed what was coming next. "Go on."

"I thought you should know what happened. It must have slipped her mind to pay for the syrup."

Lewis felt the floor come up to meet him and gripped the arms of his chair to steady himself as Cummins unfolded his story of what has happened earlier in the day. While he waited on some customers and talked with Renate at the back counter, Etta moved through the aisles and nodded at several ladies. After Renate and Etta left, Mrs. Brescher told him she had seen Etta slide several bottles into the pockets of her coat."

Lewis had visions of the story making the rounds through the town. "Did she use the word shoplifting?"

"No, she said it was a shame, seeing how Mrs. Dr. Powell was not quite herself. Then I thanked her and said you and I had arranged for your wife to pick up the items."

"Thank you, Mr. Cummins, for your answer and not reporting it to the police."

"I'd never add to Mrs. Powell's grief or embarrassment."

"Thank you again for your consideration," Lewis said and removed his change purse from his pocket.

"How much do I owe you?"

"A dollar fifty."

"Here's three, for your trouble," Lewis said and rose to shake his visitor's hand.

After he saw Cummins out, Lewis returned to his study. Defeated by Etta's theft, he now realized he must not allow her out of the house. The next time, a store clerk might not be so understanding.

But her return to laudanum was even more disheartening. All the progress they had fought for and won since December had unraveled. He could no longer deny Etta was an addict and would require constant care and attention.

Lewis left the study and paced up and down the dark hallway. He had few choices left. Renate would have to know the truth. She needed to watch over his wife until the bed in Cincinnati opened up. Or he could exercise his legal power to commit his wife to the county home. He had read about such cases in the medical literature. Addicts were cured after long admissions and enforced deprivation of their drugs. Though the success rate was not high.

He could even do nothing and let the natural consequences take over. She would overdose. The thought shook Lewis so much that he abruptly stopped pacing. No, he was adamant. He would not make the same mistake he had made with his mother. He would not step aside and let Etta kill herself.

~~~

Lewis walked upstairs and checked on her. He could tell by her rhythmic breathing she was soundly asleep.

As he searched the silent house, Lewis found his mind repeating their wedding vows. For better or worse, in sickness and in health until death us do part. But his mind rebelled. By God, how bad did it have to get before they reached the worst?

He had spent his life seeing people more at their worst than at their best. Some couples truly joined together to endure their pain and suffering. However, defeated by their life trials, most pulled apart. He had always hoped he would find it within himself to stand firm and be brave. At the moment, he doubted his inner strength. He played the part of the faithful, stalwart husband, but did he really mean it? How much more could he endure?

His life had not been without pain, but he had kept going. He had not turned to mind-numbing drugs, alcohol, gambling, or another woman for comfort and his natural needs. He would leave this earth without any children to carry on his bloodline. Etta at least had two living children and four grandchildren. Besides all his children, he had lost both wives. One buried with his first family. The second, a hopeless addict and a danger to herself since she sometimes lit candles in the dead of night and wandered around the house and on a few occasions dashed without shoes or coat into the back yard.

He had not expected life to be without trouble and problems, but how much more did life have in store for him? Briefly the thought of just supplying Etta all the laudanum she wanted resurfaced before he reburied it.

"No, not yet, my love. I'm not ready to give up yet," he whispered.

~~~

His search started in her retreat and revealed no more bottles, empty or full. Then he moved to the playroom though at first glance it did not look promising. Renate kept it in good order. But something about the toys over in the corner drew him closer. The caboose and the last boxcar were off kilter from the rest of the train set.

Lewis saw they had not been aligned on the tracks properly. When he picked up the caboose, he heard something roll inside. He raised the top and found two bottles, still unopened.

He remembered Hiram had mentioned several bottles and searched for more. But he found none on the third floor.

Lewis moved to the bedrooms on the second floor. He searched

Charity's room first and came up empty-handed. Next he hunted through Ed's old room with the same results.

His hand turned the doorknob of Evan's room, and he fought down a rush of grief. Stepping over the threshold, he realized he had allowed Etta to create a shrine that would forever freeze his son as a perfect fifteen-year-old. The bedspread remained unwrinkled and hung with crisp corners. The matching curtains blocked the outside world. The books stood upright as if they were soldiers at attention. Even the odd rocks and chewing gum sticks on Evan's desk occupied their space with purpose. His baseball bat and glove did the same in the corner opposite the door.

Though Lewis was reluctant to touch his son's possessions, he forced himself to search. Tearfully he replaced the books and other items as he looked for Etta's stash and found nothing.

Soon only Etta's closet remained. He fought down his growing discomfort as he touched her personal items and invaded her privacy. However, he told himself it was imperative all of the temptation be removed. His search found five bottles in the pockets of her house coats.

Lewis was confident he had rounded up all the bottles as he took them to the trash bin. However, Etta's addiction and the solution weighed him down. It was after one in the morning before he turned off all the lights and went to bed. But, he realized as he tried to fall asleep, he still had not resolved what to do about Etta.

Chapter 32

Frankfort, January 12, 1900

After a few days of soul-searching, Lewis accepted the decision he had been avoiding. He, along with Ed and Charity, petitioned the court for an emergency competency hearing. Within the week, Judge Bigelow convened the court and called Lewis as the first witness.

"Dr. Powell, in your professional opinion, what is your wife's mental status?"

"Your Honor, I believe grief has unhinged my wife's mental capacity. She is defeated by her losses. I do feel this is a temporary situation, one which will resolve within a year of rest. I suggest she be committed to the county's care until I'm able to find a rest manor with an opening."

"Why is it necessary to involve the court?"

"I am concerned about her safety. I cannot guarantee her well-being even though I've employed a woman to attend to her and look after the house. But our woman has, on several occasions, found my wife outside in the garden without her shoes and coat. Also I have woken in the night and found her sleepwalking with lit candles."

"So if we give her over to the county, it will only be until you find a suitable place?"

"Yes, I have telegraphed several rest homes. Although none has any beds available, I'm confident my wife will soon be out of the county's care."

"Thank you, Dr. Powell. You may step down. Next we'll hear from your attorney, Mr. Shaffer."

Briefly Clarence Shaffer summarized the events in Etta's life. He focused on how the loss of her son Evan occurred at such a dangerous time in her life. He moved that she be considered unsound and recommended she be committed until she regained her sanity. He closed his argument by waving the emergency order and pointing out that even her own children had signed it. After the judge thanked him for his testimony, the lawyer returned to his seat.

Lewis saw Judge Bigelow's attention turn to Etta who sat between him and Shaffer. The judge frowned as he took in her untidy appearance and seemed to believe her dishevelment clearly indicated how unsound she was.

Lewis considered if he should stand and explain how Etta had left the house dressed to the nines with her pearls and a new hat and stumbled on her way out of the carriage and dragged her skirts through the slush at the curb. The fall, probably due to the small dose of the sleeping draught he had given her after breakfast, had knocked her hat crooked and worked her curls free. One of her warm spells must have hit while he was on the stand, and when she had yanked at her neckline, a couple buttons popped loose. But he chose to remain silent. He was here, after all, to prove she was unbalanced.

The judge asked Etta to step forward and take the stand. She refused. Bigelow stared at her, and his frown deepened. A few moments later, he signaled the bailiff to take the Bible to Etta and swear her in.

Shaffer placed her hand on the Bible and spoke in her ear until she nodded after the judge asked for her oath.

Bigelow raised his voice to get her attention. "Mrs. Powell, my questions are important. I need your full cooperation. Now please tell me how old you are."

Etta returned a shrug.

"What do you want more than anything else?"

She gave him a blank stare.

"Mrs. Powell, are you aware of our purpose here today?"

Etta shrugged again and gazed out the window.

～～

Lewis looked at the judge and could almost read what was going through the man's mind since his wife was also of a certain age. In fact, Mrs. Bigelow had been to see him only yesterday. She complained of mood swings and hot spells. More important was the fear her husband might try to put her away as he had Martha Manchester last year. Mrs. Bigelow came to tears when she retold how the judge had mentioned several times how he now considered himself an expert on mentally unsound middle-aged women. She begged for something to relieve her symptoms. Lewis had mixed a light sleeping draught for her. He hoped he had convinced her that once she slept through the night, her symptoms would diminish.

Lewis was amazed when the whole process concluded after ninety minutes. Etta was judged temporarily insane and committed to the county's care until he could find a more suitable situation for her. However, the only available opening was a cell in the Home for Friendless Women.

Lewis stood and almost asked the judge to wait until a bed came open at the regular county home on Lawrenceburg Road. He had seen this facility. It was where he wanted her to be. But his fatigue won his internal battle. He needed to sleep tonight, and hopefully Etta would be there for only a few days.

Instead the judge nodded his approval when Lewis asked if he could be the one to take her to the Home.

~~

When Renate and Lewis helped her out of the carriage and up the stairs, her mind registered the building's familiarity. Once inside, she thought she might have visited there.

The *déjà vu* moment only grew stronger when she sat in the office as a woman introduced herself as Mrs. McFarland. Etta took in the woman's kind smile and dark somber clothes. She looked around while Lewis talked to the pleasant woman.

"Etta," Lewis's voice called her back, "I'll take your pearls home, where they'll be safe."

She stroked the necklace and shook her head.

"They're mine, not yours. I won't part from them."

"Dr. Powell, leave it for now. We can always fill out the paperwork when Mrs. Powell has changed her mind." Etta looked at the woman and nodded. "Let's get you settled in, shall we?" Mrs. McFarland spoke. "Say goodbye to your husband."

Etta glared at Lewis and wondered when he had become the enemy. "I'm ready to leave now." She stood and walked to the closed door. Behind her, chairs scraped and the woman spoke again.

"Dr. Powell, we ask you wait at least a week before you come see your wife. It's important that she get accustomed to our routine here."

Lewis joined Etta. "I'll be back next Friday. Remember, I love you."

Etta refused to look at him even when she heard him sigh and after he kissed her on the cheek and left. Her only wish was to crawl into bed and forget the world.

~~~

After Mrs. McFarland took her outside and down some stairs, she whispered to a woman about her own age and made the introductions.

"Mrs. Powell, this is Mrs. Brown. She's here to help you."

Etta thought this woman also looked familiar. Though she did not quite know why, she began to fear what was ahead her.

Mrs. Brown took her arm and led her through the gate. When the latch fell into place, the sound revealed why this place looked familiar. She had visited someone here, not so long ago, and it had not been pleasant.

"Come now," the attendant said and increased the pressure on Etta's arm. "We're almost to your room."

Etta tried to free her arm but failed. Panic began to build. "Room? These aren't rooms. They're cages."

"Mrs. Powell, it's only for a few days until Dr. Powell manages to find you another place."

Etta stared inside the cages and saw gray and defeated women. They had probably been locked up a long time. Etta knew the woman on her arm lied and tried to resist, but the woman gripped tighter. Etta surrendered.

They were almost to the end of the corridor when the attendant stopped and selected a key from her large round key ring. "Here we are, your room."

Etta looked through the bars and even more dread crept through her. The cot with a small pillow, a folded gray blanket, and a white sheet resting on top offered no comfort. Bars covered the tiny window. Instead of a closet or clothes press, a few wooden pegs hung along the back wall, and one unvarnished wooden stool occupied the back corner. Nausea stirred in her stomach.

"I'm sure you'll get used to our routine in a few days, Mrs. Powell," the woman said and unlocked the door.

Etta tried to concentrate on the woman's words as she was walked forward. But the window with the bars on it captivated her attention until she heard chamber pot and corner.

When Etta saw the black-rimmed porcelain on the cement floor, bile rose into her throat. She would never use such a thing, out here in the open, before all the other women. But she heard the key turn in the lock, and she sunk onto the cot.

Through the dirt-streaked window, she saw trees naked of leaves. A weak sun struggled to come through the gun-metal gray clouds. All she could see of the few passersby were dark pant legs above boots, ankle length somber dresses, and sturdy shoes. Not many people walked by in the cold weather. Etta turned her back on the outside world. She curled into a ball, closed her eyes, and slept.

~~~

A woman's cries and her own hunger woke her. Somewhere in the back of her mind was the notion someone needed her. She had to get up to help. Her first glance told her she was not at home. She took in the barred window, the clothes pegs, the chamber pot, and the bars. Panic hit.

Suddenly another woman shouted at the first woman to be quiet. Soon others joined in. Some urged on the crying woman. The rest cursed the noise and added to the commotion. Etta inched to the head of her cot and put her back against the wall.

"Maybe I'm having a nightmare, one I can't wake up from," she whispered. But she knew no dream had ever been this real.

What she remembered was Evan had died and her family had turned against her. Coldness replaced her panic. She sank down and covered her head and body with the blanket and cried herself to sleep.

~~~

The noise of a key worked in the lock woke her. She lowered her blanket and saw a woman come closer. Something about her was also familiar.

"Etta, it's me, Mazie. Remember? We lived here? Upstairs?"

From the back of Etta's mind came the word Magpie and Ed's missing toy so long ago.

"Hungry?" Mazie moved closer.

"Yes."

"You plumb missed lunch."

Etta used her elbows to sit up and blinked. Mazie looked almost the same, maybe a little stouter but still mousy.

"Well, here's supper." Mazie took a tray from her cart and placed it on the cot.

"Thank you."

Mazie winked. "I can stay and talk later." She nodded her head to the other cells. "They're about set in to screamin'."

When she was locked in again, Etta became aware of another physical need. She had to relieve herself. She turned her back, so she did not have to see anyone watching her and used the chamber pot.

She tackled the food, weak beef and barley soup and bread with water to drink. The soup had little taste. But it and the bread took care of her hunger.

Soon Mazie was back with her cart. "I'm gonna save your tray to the last thing. We can talk that way every night," she said and sat beside Etta. "It will be just like when we lived here."

Etta did not like this woman so close and slid away, but Mazie continued her one-sided conversation.

"Pretty lonely right now, ain't ya." Mazie looked heavenward. "This too shall pass."

Etta found the pitying look coming from Mazie's eyes almost more than she could bear. She was about to demand the woman leave when Mazie mentioned she had read Etta's chart.

"What does it say?"

"I'm to dose ya with some sleeping medicine every night." Mazie stopped as if she were considering her next words. "The judge wrote down that you'd gone insane.

"Insane?" Anger exploded inside Etta over that one word. "I'm not crazy."

Etta bolted from the cell and heard Mazie ask where she was going.

The mocking voice rolled on, "Won't do you no good, you know. You're locked in."

By this time, Etta had reached the door that led upstairs. It was also made of bars. As hard as she could shake them, they would not open.

"Let me out of here, right now. I don't belong here. Let me out." Etta slumped against the locked bars and wailed.

"Shh," Mazie said when she came up behind her. "Don't go acting wild. Here, put on the clothes your nice husband brung over. "

Defeated, Etta turned from the bars and took the offered robe and gown. The scent from her lavender sachets rose to her nose. She buried her face in the soft flannel and walked into the bathroom where there were two toilets and two bathtubs and five sinks with no mirrors. After she changed into her gown and robe and returned to her cell, Mazie spooned out the sleeping medicine. Etta lay in bed and tried not to think while she waited for it to take effect.

~~~

At the end of her third day, Etta decided the best thing about her stay was the absence of any demands upon her. Nor did she have to pretend she was strong. She did not have to talk. The most she ever had to say was yes or no.

The food was bad, but it sufficed. The cold bothered her though. The steam heat and the stoves placed along the corridor did not give off enough heat to keep her legs and feet warm. So most of the time, she did not dress in her day clothes but stayed in her gown and robe and wrapped in the gray blanket. The few times she left her cot, she clasped the blanket around her.

~~~

Etta's name leapt from the crumpled newspaper Lavinia used to wipe the ammonia from her parlor window. She smoothed the wrinkles to read the write-up of Etta's trial and verdict. Her shock turned to anger when she realized from the date that her friend had been locked up for three days and Lewis had not bothered to inform her.

The next morning Lavinia strode into the Home and demanded to see Etta. When she looked through the bars a few minutes later, Lavinia was frightened. Though Etta looked younger with her hair loose and her face free from lines of care and pain, her gown and robe were unwashed, wrinkled. Lavinia could sniff Etta's body odor even from a few feet away. Worse was when Etta showed no reaction to her greeting.

Lavinia's breath caught, and her words strangled before gaining strength. "Tell me what happened."

Etta gazed at her. Lavinia noticed her friend's eyes had changed from their vivid green to a dull sea-glass hue.

When Lavinia leaned over and hugged Etta, the impression she had was that her friend was disappearing, shrinking within herself. It was almost too much for Lavinia, and she had to fight back her tears when she sat down on the cot and took Etta's hands.

Lavinia said, "You must tell me what happened so I can help you. Look at me."

"What are you doing here?" Etta's words came out unsteadily.

"I wanted to see you, to help you get out of here."

"Why trouble yourself?"

"Why?" Lavinia said in anger and inspected the cell. "How can you stay here, in this place, away from all the people who love you?"

"Go away and leave me alone."

"I can't leave you like this. This is not you. This is not how you were meant to live."

But Etta turned away and curled into a ball.

Determined to find the truth, Lavinia made her way to the door of the cell. "I'll be back Etta, after I talk with Lewis."

~~~

When a thunderous storm of fury rushed through the side door of his office, Lewis steeled himself for a bloody emergency. What he saw instead was a woman who reminded him of the valkyries he had once seen in the Cincinnati opera performances.

"Lavinia, are the children or Dan ill?"

"How dare you lock Etta up in such an awful place."

"Sit down." He rose to shut the door to his office. When he was back in his chair, he continued.

"Etta's ill. I can't protect her, so she's there until I can find a better place for her to go. She needs a rest cure."

Lavinia did not look as if she believed him and remained standing with an expression of contempt. Her words remained filled with fury.

"She needs to get out of there. When's the last time you saw her? I've never seen her so melancholy."

"It's called withdrawal. Do you know what the word means?"

"What are you talking about? Withdrawal? Etta doesn't drink."

"No, but she has been using laudanum."

Lavinia swayed, reached for the desk to steady herself, and sat down opposite Lewis.

"You gave it to her? You got her addicted?"

"Not me, my mother. You remember her living with us after my father died?" Lavinia nodded. "My mother used Dr. Winter's syrup. After Evan died, Etta found her unopened stash and started to take it. That's how she was able to numb her pain and renovate the upstairs."

Lavinia shook her head in disbelief, "We were all so proud of her, about how well she was coping."

"But she wasn't. She kept increasing her intake until she took too much to focus. Charity recently left little Loren and Melissa with her.

When Charity returned, she found the children unattended, scared and Etta locked in her room. We tried treating her at home. We thought we had succeeded until she shoplifted several bottles."

He stopped and looked through his tears at Etta's oldest friend. "It's been hell, Lavinia. We've run out of options. Either we get help for her or we let her kill herself with laudanum. What would you have chosen?"

"I had no idea this was going on Lewis, but she's not doing well there."

"She's safe. She can't get any laudanum or alcohol. She can't hurt herself. And when Lawndale Sanitarium has an opening, we'll admit her. The director thinks that after six months or so, she'll have accepted Evan's death and shaken off her dependence on Dr. Winter's. Only then can she come home from Cincinnati."

"How soon before they'll take her?"

"He wired back today. See for yourself," he said handing her a telegram. "He thinks maybe within the month, maybe less."

"I don't think she will be sane if she stays in there for a whole month." Lavinia did not even bother to read the wire.

"I love Etta, Lavinia. I'm worried about how rapidly she's declined," he said. "I'm looking into some other places as well. But there just aren't many good ones. As long as she stays in Frankfort, at least I can go and check on her."

"So you've been there?"

"Every day, I sneak in to see how she's doing. It breaks my heart, but I can't keep her here. I have to sleep sometime. I have to work so I can pay for her care."

"I'm so sorry, Lewis. I didn't understand. Let me know what I can do to help."

"Understand what we're going through, all of us, me, Ed, and Charity." Lewis wiped the tears in his eyes.

A chastened Lavinia left by the same door she had charged through thirty minutes before.

Chapter 33

Frankfort, January 29, 1900

The moment Etta felt the pressure on her neck, Aunt Helen changed her shape. Her black silks fell away and feathers, long and black, sprouted in their place. Her head twisted into the head of a buzzard. Her hands curled into long talons. But her words remained the same as when Etta was a child.

"You better be good, girl or you will be back at St. Jerome's."

However, this time, in her dream, Etta was no longer seven. She was a grown up woman. She raised her arms to fight back, but she was not strong enough to win. Aunt Helen's grip increased. Etta felt her head hit something hard.

Then darkness and nothingness, and she stopped breathing.

Chapter 34

Frankfort, same night

The abrupt staccato of fists on the front door awakened Lewis. Thinking someone was ill, he reached for the bedside light and his glasses. He hurried out from under the covers and put on his robe and slippers. At the foot of the stairs, he yelled, "I'll be there directly, just hold on."

Once he reached the front door, he unlocked and opened it to see the familiar form of the sheriff turned to the side and stamping his feet clear of snow.

"Sorry about the late hour, Lewis," announced Jim McDowell after he faced Lewis.

"It's all right, come in." From the sheriff's expression, Lewis knew he was going to be called out to an awful situation.

The sheriff gave his coat a final brushing and stepped into the hall where he removed his hat and gloves.

"I've got some bad news. It's Etta, She's dead. There was a fire."

All strength vanished from Lewis' legs. He had not expected this to be a personal call. He folded onto the hall carpet and became aware of a grasping pain in his chest as he fought for breath.

His friend waited a few beats before he continued. "Dr. Phillips examined her. He said to tell you she went quickly."

Lewis appreciated why Phillips lied. He had told similar lies to family members himself. But he knew the truth. Etta had not died quietly and without pain. "For God's sake, what happened?"

"The matron on duty, a Mrs. Darby, said after the inmates were asleep …."

The word inmates struck Lewis as cruel and harsh, not the word he wanted used for Etta.

"She heard screams and smelled smoke. By the time this Mrs. Darby got the main door unlocked, smoke had filled the hallway. Women were running in circles in their cells. When she got to your wife, Mrs. Powell was on the floor. Mrs. Darby tried to smother the flames, but it was too late. I'm sorry."

"How could a fire start?"

Jim now sat down beside him but did not quite meet his eyes. "Phillips thinks she might have caught a broom on fire from a stove in the hallway."

"It doesn't make sense, sweeping at that hour."

"That's why it's possible she might have killed herself, Lewis."

When Lewis thought of Etta committing suicide, something inside of him withered and disappeared. Guilt came in its stead and shattered his spirit.

~~

With McDowell by his side, Lewis entered the basement of the Home. The acrid smell of smoke caught in his nostrils and tightened his chest.

A woman with bandaged hands rushed toward them. "So sorry for your loss, Dr. Powell," she said. "I tried to save her."

The sheriff looked at him and said, "This is Mrs. Darby, the night matron."

"Thank you, for helping my wife."

"The fire just got the better of me."

"May I see her?"

Mrs. Darby nodded and led him down the corridor. The remnants of smoke were much stronger. He started to cough.

While Lewis had closed the distance, he saw the extensive fire damage. Scorch marks made their own map of the tragedy on the floor and walls. He noticed the charred remains of what had to be the broom and some burnt bits of cloth by a stove.

Mrs. Darby stopped outside the cell door. Lewis entered and tried to take in what had happened there. More scorch marks and a smoky residue clung to the back wall and ceiling. Etta was on the cot and covered in a clean blanket. He knelt to open the blanket.

Her body was so badly burnt Lewis's first thought was maybe they had made a mistake. This had to be another unfortunate woman lying before him. He forced himself to reach down deep and look in a more clinical manner.

"Mrs. Darby," Lewis rasped, "Are you positive this is my wife?"

"Yes sir, Mrs. Powell's the only one gone missin'."

"Will you leave us for a few minutes?"

In response, he heard her retreating steps. The pressure in his chest clenched and released. Tears followed. "Oh Etta, why? Why weren't we enough to live for?"

He put his head down and leaned against the cot. He did not know how much time had passed before he became aware of a dull discomfort under his kneecap.

Putting his hand down, his fingertips brushed over a small round pebble. He picked it up and saw a badly charred pearl. He moved his hands around under the cot and found others. Etta's prized pearl necklace. His expanded search discovered seven more pearls and several round gold segments. He pocketed them and rejoined McDowell by the entrance.

"Want me to contact the Sullivan Brothers for you?" the sheriff asked.

Lewis nodded.

~~~

Back in his kitchen, Lewis waited for the coffee to warm. He tried to picture himself telling his children about Etta's death. But his mind refused to take him there. Instead, Etta's death collided with his past. He had once thought he had experienced the worst pain death could deliver when his first family perished in their terrible illness. The loss had almost done him in. When Evan had fallen beneath the train and died, the pain seemed more unbearable. Maybe because grief had already weakened him.

But now, Etta's suicide would be even harder to live with. His guilt grabbed at him and twisted his soul. God knew he would never have put her there if he had known the county farm on Lawrenceburg Road was full. How was he going to face their children?

Chapter 35

Frankfort, January 30, 1900

Lewis paced before the elegant but cold fireplace. It was so early that Charity's maids had not yet lit the fires. On one circuit past the sideboards, he stopped and poured a small brandy. He offered it to his son, sitting by the front window. Ed shook his head. The only outward sign of grief Ed gave was his red-rimmed eyes. Lewis left the glass by the liquor cabinet when hurried footsteps on the stairs told him his daughter was near.

"It's Momma, isn't it?" Charity asked before she was even in the room.

"Princess, sit down."

"Momma?"

Lewis guided her to the sofa and sat beside her. Again he went through the morning's events. But this time, he withheld the more vivid details that he had shared with Ed. Before he finished, Charity gulped for air and shook her hands. He gently bent her head toward her lap. Her tears and deep sobs unnerved him while he tried to sooth and ease her hyperventilation.

"Take a deep breath, good, now another one. You'll be fine. Some more deep breaths. Good, is the tingling in your fingers going away?"

Charity nodded, and he offered his folded white handkerchief. After she dried her tears, he gave her the brandy snifter.

Lewis said when she was calmer, "Charity, we're going to Sullivans to plan the funeral. Do you have a favorite hymn?"

"Momma once said she liked some old song in Latin, by somebody named Gregory, I think. Would you ask the Sullivans if they know what she meant?"

Lewis promised he would.

~~~

Lewis and Ed met the elder Sullivan brother at the door and followed him to the office. For a few seconds, Lewis was taken back to the other times he had sat in the same chair and had much the same conversation. When his first wife and their children had died. When his mother had passed. Oh merciful God, just last winter when Evan died. Please, he prayed, make this the last time I have to do this. I don't think I'm strong enough to endure another death.

Lewis felt a touch on his arm and looked up. "Poppa, Mr. Sullivan was saying something about a delay."

"Delay," Lewis looked from his son to the undertaker. "What do you mean?"

"I'm sorry, Doctor Powell. It shouldn't be over a few days."

"I apologize if I seemed demanding. Of course, you have others ahead of us."

"That's not it. Dr. Phillips has asked us to wait." Sullivan cleared his throat and straightened his cravat. "It seems, huh, Dr. Phillips has decided an autopsy and an inquest are necessary."

Why would Phillips interfere? Etta did not deserve this. Lewis did not even try to contain the anger sparking through him. "Ridiculous." Lewis slammed his hand on the desk. "The man was there. He even pronounced her dead."

"He's the coroner. He has the authority to demand an autopsy."

"But why," Ed asked.

"Evidently when he and the sheriff started talking to the witnesses…"

"What, those crazy women?" Ed blurted.

"I understand how you both must feel," Sullivan raised both hands, palms out, and said, "But he and the sheriff, well, you see, they got a lot of confusing stories."

Lewis insisted it did not matter. "There's not a credible witness among those women down there."

Sullivan answered, "The problem is the newspapers have got ahold of the story. They're asking questions about how this whole thing could've happened."

Lewis grew angrier. His family, his home, his wife would all be fodder for old gossips in the whole county, let alone state. The worse part was that Etta would be remembered for how she died, not how she lived.

"I've got to stop this." Lewis got to his feet. "I'll go talk with Phillips right now, demand he stop this madness."

"Won't do you any good. Please sit back down."

Lewis felt Ed's tug on his arm. He reached over and patted he understood.

"It's out of Phillips' hands. You see, the judge got involved when a reporter bushwhacked him on the way into the courthouse. It's a real mess, Doctor Powell. The reporter's wanting details about all the women the judge has committed."

"My wife's trial, her whole story is going to be on the front page?"

"I don't have all the details. All I know is when I went to pick up Mrs. Powell, the sheriff said Phillips would contact me. So I'm waiting. But," Sullivan hesitated, "Dr. Powell, give me the information you want in your wife's obituary."

~~~

When Lewis opened his back door, he smelled fresh coffee and baking bread. Renate greeted him with a worried look.

"Mrs. Powell, she dead, ja?"

Lewis answered yes. After he took off his coat and hat, he told her the barest details.

"How did you know, Renate?" he asked when he was finished.

"Butcher delivery boy, one hour, before."

Lewis sighed and knew his telephone would ring nonstop. As if on cue, he heard the three rings that meant it was his call. He ignored it and asked for coffee and a sandwich in his study.

When he passed the telephone in the hallway, he picked up the mouthpiece and clicked the switchhook. When the operator came on the line, he told Louise to send all his medical calls to Dr. Phillips. He also asked her not to connect him to any other callers except his son and daughter.

"Mrs. Daniel Miller and Mrs. Owen Murphy asked me to tell you they called."

Lewis rubbed his forehead as the pain behind his eyes intensified. He had not even thought far enough ahead to contact Etta's oldest friends.

"Please connect me Louise."

Sophie, Owen told him, was on her way to his house. As the operator called Lavinia, Renate passed by with his coffee and sandwich. He asked her to leave them with him and to get some aspirin. Lavinia spoke through tears and asked if what she had heard was true. Was Etta dead?

Lewis gave her the same details he had told Renate. But Lavinia pressed for more. He took two aspirin and drained his cup before he mentioned how the night matron had burned her hands.

Lavinia interrupted, "Did you say her name was Darby? What's her first name?"

"Something unusual. I'm sorry, I can't think of it now."

Lewis held the hot coffee mug against his forehead. God, his head hurt even worse.

"Was it Mazie?"

"Could have been. Why?"

Lavinia ignored his question and said, "Can you ask the sheriff to find out if she is the same Mazie Darby who used to live at the Home with us?"

"Lavinia, tell me what you're getting at."

Lewis's head felt as if it was splitting in two.

When Lavinia told him about Mazie's habit of stealing, he dropped the mug and slid down against the wall.

"God," Lewis choked. "I never thought being murdered was better than suicide. Poor Etta."

"Louise," Lavinia said to the operator. "I know you're listening. Call and ask the sheriff to go to Dr. Powell's house. Lewis, I'm coming to town. I'll be there in about an hour. And Louise, don't you dare tell anyone else what we've said and that goes for anyone else listening in on the line."

~~~

A few minutes before noon, Lewis opened the door for Lavinia. She was bundled against the cold from her buggy ride with a heavy bright blue wool coat and a dark green blanket. With tears running down her wind-reddened face, she again told him how sorry she was about Etta. After he helped her with her coat and she folded the blanket, they embraced and joined Sophie and the sheriff in the parlor.

Lewis, with Jim McDowell by his side, watched Sophie and Lavinia hold each other and cry. He hoped if there was a heaven, Etta was looking down at her friends and understood how much they loved her.

After Sophie made Lavinia take the chair closest to the fireplace and have some hot tea to drink, she looked at the sheriff. "I think we're ready, Mr. McDowell."

"Mrs. Miller," McDowell began, "Before I answer any of your questions, I need to ask you some. Do you know why Mrs. Darby was admitted to the Home in the first place?"

Lavinia shook her head. "The matron, Mrs. Luttrell, always told the girls to keep their past a secret."

"But she did have this habit of stealing?" He stopped and checked his notes. "Her nickname was Magpie?"

Lavinia shuddered. "We thought it was a harmless habit. She never hurt anyone. But she never outgrew her habit, either."

"Mrs. Murphy was telling me how after all of you were married, you met, and…"

"And after she showed up, things went missing. But it was no longer little things like shiny glass buttons. She had moved on to our children's birthday gifts." Lavinia's voice shook in anger.

"You saw her take these things?"

Lavinia looked a little sheepish. "No, but we decided not to include her anymore."

"So after you met without her, no more items went missing?"

Sophie broke in. "The tornado came before our next get-together." Lewis noticed tears welled in her eyes as she looked at Lavinia. "We never had another tea party."

"I know," Lavinia said, "we have no evidence, just suspicions. But is it enough for you to go on? To see if she murdered Etta?"

"Ladies, Lewis, I don't want to get your hopes up. I'll look into it and pass along whatever I find to the coroner."

"But Sheriff," Lavinia said. "Etta was a fighter. She had been ever since I've known her. A person doesn't change and give up, even after going through so much."

Lavinia brought out her handkerchief and dabbed her tears. "What I mean is, if she was going to give up, she would've done it sooner, when her first tragedy happened. Not later, not so long after."

The sheriff closed the meeting with these words, "You all have to remember Mrs. Powell's death could also have been an accident."

~~~

Lewis procrastinated reading the early evening edition of the newspaper. The morning edition had only run a short notice about Etta and the fire. But he knew the later paper would have more details. As he at last forced himself to pick up the paper and read, he hoped Etta's friends took the time to read what Sullivan had written about her as a wife and mother in the obituary.

"Insane Wife of Prominent Physician Ends Life as Fiery Torch" blazed across the front page of his evening newspaper. The local reporter summarized her death as the most gruesome ever in Frankfort. One paragraph recounted how the gold from her earrings had melted and embedded in her ear lobes. The next paragraph gave a vivid description of how Etta's head had become detached and rolled as a fiery ball down the corridor.

Bile rose in his throat. Lewis threw the paper down and rushed to the toilet. After the nausea passed, he had the operator place a call to Loren so he could tell him to keep the newspaper away from Charity.

As soon as he finished, Lewis made his next call to the newspaper and demanded to speak with the editor. "I will own your paper by the time I'm finished with you," Lewis shouted into the mouth piece.

"Dr. Powell, please accept my apologies. We are heartsick at our mistake. Dr. Phillips has already contacted us. Be assured, we will publish a retraction tomorrow. It seems a source gave our reporter incorrect information about, er, well. Let me just say the reporter no longer works for us."

Lewis hung up and did not answer any more calls.

Chapter 36

Louisville, February 1900

Every February first the memory of his sister Etta haunted William Smith. She'll be forty-four was his first thought when he woke. The disclaimer followed, if she's still alive.

Etta had been unaccounted for so many years, but he had never given up hope that he would find her and welcome her back into the family. If Etta was ever found, he knew his wife Mary Margaret would never allow it though. Enough of Etta's story had seeped through Louisville society to ensure that. Not even his position as director of the McIntire Distillery and all his seats on charitable boards could override the long ago scandal.

But he did still hope he would one day know her fate.

At breakfast, William tried to imagine what Etta might look like. Would her hair still be so red? Would her eyes still snap in anger and dance when she sung? Mary Margaret's question broke through his revelry.

"Don't you know the Beauchamp family from Frankfort?" she asked.

"I know of them, dear. That's different than personally knowing them," he replied. "Why?"

"They've met with a terrible family tragedy. Not quite theirs, but the one their son married into."

Since the elder Beauchamp was also involved in coal mining and fuel prices were on the rise, the thought crossed his mind that it might be good to know a bit more about this tragedy. Maybe he could turn the event to his advantage. He had used other little nuggets from the newspaper before to arm his investigator Ned Palmer. So he waited for his wife to continue. There might be something here for Palmer to ferret out.

"It seems their daughter-in-law's mother committed suicide."

William agreed that was horrible and was about to finish his eggs when he heard "Her name was Etta. She was almost forty-four-years-old. Her birthday would have been today. How sad."

A chill formed in his center and raised the hair on the back of his neck.

His wife went on, "She set herself on fire. Oh, she was insane and in one of those homes where they put women," she paused, evidently in search for a delicate way to phrase it, "when they have trouble, you know, later in life."

William shook his head slightly to tell himself that he was making too much of an assumption. It was just a coincidence that this unfortunate woman had the same first name and same birthday as his sister.

He sensed Mary Margaret's attention had shifted to him. He looked at her and saw she had paled.

"Do you think this woman was your sister?" she whispered and glanced around to see if any servant was near.

"Not at all, my dear. How many Ettas do you know?"

A bit of color returned to her cheeks. "At least five."

He agreed, but his appetite had vanished, so he left the dining room for his study. After he heard Mary Margaret go upstairs and into her rooms, he slipped into the dining room to read the story. Buried on the back page where the story continued from the front-page was the closing line that the woman had been put in the same Home when she was a young woman. William told himself not to get his hopes up that he had found his sister, but the evidence indicated that this woman was his Etta. Yet, he thought, it were better if this woman was not his sister.

～～～

While his driver Max guided the horses to the distillery, William found he could not get out from under the coincidences. He realized the story would ride companion to his memories of Etta all day.

One of his first assignments to his secretary Eileen was to send out for the morning newspaper. He might need it to show to Palmer.

He had to find out more. Usually he went to his club when he wanted to trace a news story, but not today. Someone might see what he read. The library was better he decided since he knew they also kept the back issues of several newspapers.

After Eileen summoned Max, he dressed again for the cold and told his secretary he would be out for the rest of the day. He ignored the puzzled look on her face and soon climbed into his buggy.

~~~

At the library, he told Max to take the horse to the livery stable down the street and return to wait for him in the warmth of the library's main room. An idea had crystallized. If the Frankfort newspapers did not give enough details, then Palmer would have to go there to unearth details from the murky events.

William gathered the past weeks' newspapers and read the most current ones first. The grim reports and sensational headlines made his stomach turn. He prayed that this woman was not his sister. The grizzly details brought out in the inquest were repeated over and over. A local reporter summarized her death as the most gruesome ever in Frankfort. One paragraph was devoted to how the gold from her earrings melted and was embedded in her ear lobes.

But that was not the worst. The next paragraph gave a vivid description of how Mrs. Powell's head had become detached and rolled as a fiery ball down the corridor. The next day, the paper published a retraction and reported that their source had given them incorrect information.

Tears blurred William's eyes as he recalled his sister's glorious red curls. Anger took over when he realized the story of this unbalanced woman's death was displayed for all to read. There was no sensitivity for the grieving family. No one, he was certain, deserved such an invasion of privacy.

What he found strange was that there was no mention of any family members but her husband and two children, Edward Darnell and Charity Beauchamp. This Lewis Powell must have been at least a second husband since the son had a different surname. No names of parents, brothers, or sisters, no past history about where she was born, who the first husband was, nothing.

He put the newspaper down and considered. He returned his attention to the article and glanced at the other obituaries in the columns. Just as he thought, these were filled with bits of family history that gave more substance to the deceased, so the reader gained information about the person's whole life, not just their end.

Not so with Mrs. Lewis Powell.

The phrase the dog that did not bark ran through his head from one of those mystery stories he had read years ago. Anything odd must have a reason. Sometimes, what was not told turned out to be far more important than what was.

He had learned that in business negotiations. And Ned Palmer was one of the best he had used over the years to find out what others wished to keep hidden. Empowered from all that his man's strong investigations had revealed, William had been able to turn many discussions his way or know, more profitably, when to walk away from an offer that hid snares.

Palmer was the perfect choice to probe for the truth. His friendly face put his listeners at ease and opened up any blocks of reserve they desired to keep secret. He also was able to melt into a group and not draw any attention to himself.

It should not take the man long to uncover what had happened in the woman's life and find out if this Etta was his sister.

More importantly, Palmer was trustworthy. Whatever he found would never be repeated to anyone else. Of course, William paid well for this loyalty, but such was the power of money.

He went in search of his driver and found him asleep against the wall in his wooden straight back chair. Within five minutes, Max was on his way to Palmer's office a few blocks away, and William returned to his stack of newspapers and continued the search for more of the story.

"Mr. Smith?" Palmer stood before him. "Max said you wanted to speak to me?"

"That's right, sit down." William indicated the chair across from him.

"I need a quiet investigation done in Frankfort. It's different than other work you've done for me, but I trust your discretion. No one must connect you with me in any way."

"Of course, sir, I understand."

"How soon will you have that business in Ashland wrapped up?"

Palmer checked his pocket daybook. "Tomorrow if I don't go there to collect those papers for you."

"Good. Wire to have them delivered to my post office box. Make Frankfort your highest priority and stay with it until you have discovered the truth."

William showed him the stories. The two men read through the whole month of January and found the short legal notice of Mrs. Lewis Powell's commitment to the county's care.

"It'd be a whole lot easier and faster if I just sent a few telegrams to the sheriff and the newspaper editor," Palmer said.

"No, I want you there in person to listen to the town gossip and try to find some way to get into the files of the Home. Maybe you could even put a few dollars in the right hands. As usual, add it to your list of expenses. Like I said, this is your highest priority after you conclude that matter in Ashland."

~~~

On his ride home, William tried to console himself. Since he had waited this long, a week or so would not make that much difference. But another possible source of information struck him, and he directed Max to take him to the church parish hall.

Father Alios was now head priest, and maybe he would know what happened to Father John's personal papers after the old man died. What did they do with the few items a priest possessed upon his death? Did they go to his next of kin or were they kept with the church records?

He reconsidered. Did he want to get the church involved? What reason could he give for wanting to go through the old priest's papers? He would have to tell the man something. He could not go in and demand them.

William stopped Max once more and redirected the driver home again. He realized he was an amateur at this investigator business. Better to wait and plan than barge in.

Chapter 37

Frankfort, February 2, 1900

A few minutes past eleven in the morning, Ned Palmer detrained at the Frankfort depot. Dressed in a somber yet fashionable brown overcoat, he also wore his fedora in a manner that prevented anyone from looking directly into his eyes. The impression he wanted to give was that no one would recall him.

Relieved to be out of the drafts and sooty passenger car after the four-hour trip from Louisville, he stretched. When the kinks were out, he raised the collar of his coat, secured the brown muffler at his neck, and put on his warm gloves. He picked up his two satchels. One held his clothes and personal toiletries, the other his equipment.

The grey overcast sky was the same though as the one he had left in the morning. But that was Kentucky in the winter. It just made people appreciate spring so much more he reasoned.

After a shiver rolled through him, he recalled the business hotels on the riverfront. While he walked toward the water, he noticed, yet again, that Frankfort was not exactly the lively place Louisville was. People seemed to move at a slower pace.

He anticipated it would not take long to get to the end of the story here. After some lunch, he would visit the courthouse.

While he walked at a moderate pace, he mused about the amazing wealth of public knowledge anyone could uncover about the average citizen if he knew where to look. With just a little effort spent digging among the records stored by the government, Palmer knew how to find out private information.

One of his mottos was to follow the money trail, and governments were certainly about money. Collecting all those funds led to tax records, deeds, wills, court cases. It was important to know who owned what and for how long and who owned it before. He loved the challenge of finding buried nuggets of information that took him on to larger discoveries about the people in his cases.

~~~

A little past noon, when he supposed the county clerk would be at lunch, he presented himself to a young assistant in the clerk's Office as a person interested in his lineage, so he could join the Sons of the American Revolution. The young clerk gave him a quick tour of where the wills, court proceedings, marriage licenses, and tax records were. With a vague wave towards the hall, he mentioned the deeds were in the Recorder's Office directly opposite.

Palmer was a bit disappointed that he did not even have to use his prepared lie about which families he was interested in. The young man was not at all curious and closed the door that separated the office from the record room to keep the warmth from the stove with him.

He pulled some of the oldest volumes and arranged them on the worktable to hide which books he would actually use. The facts beyond the spare information given in Mrs. Lewis Powell's obituary soon came to the surface.

Palmer scanned the death record and found it held little personal information. No one had provided any leads on where Mrs. Powell had been born or who her parents were. Unknown was entered into these three lines on the official form.

He read the proceedings from the competency hearing and thought it seemed like a rush job. Everyone knew his part, and so Mrs. Powell was ruled mentally unbalanced in a short time. No other family members except the husband attended, not even her children whose signatures were below Dr. Powell's on the request for the hearing. When he closed the heavy black book, he wondered if she was discouraged that no one was present to argue in her favor.

Next he looked for her marriage license to Lewis Powell. None was listed. Following the lead of her son's last name, he moved through the earlier index and found a Benjamin Darnell married an Etta Smith. Now he had an address on St. Claire Street given for the groom. Her address was the same as the Home for Friendless Women so the reference to her ending up where she had once lived had validity. It helped his investigation that there were no other Darnell marriages for either grooms or brides.

The marriage might possibly tie up Mr. Smith's unanswered

question about where his sister had been. A few years back, after the wealthy distiller had approached him to give up all other casework and be on retainer, he had conducted his own inquiries. The research uncovered a few sketchy facts. David Smith and his wife Isabel adopted two children. The parents died at an early age, the girl disappeared from the family, and William was left alone to be raised by his maiden aunt.

Yes, it would be an end to the puzzle of what had happened to the girl if this Mrs. Etta Darnell Powell turned out to be Smith's long lost sister. Palmer allowed himself a small smile of congratulations. He did like solving puzzles.

But now another one opened before him. No death record for Benjamin Darnell. What had happened to the man? Divorce? He soon read about the court case in the proceedings of the circuit court. Looked like the poor bastard had become feeble from a head injury during the tornado of 81, he thought.

As Palmer slid the volume back, he recalled what his grandmother always said about proper ladies.

"So much for having your name in the newspaper only three times in your life, Etta. Here in Franklin County, you married, divorced, was found unstable, committed to the county's care, and died as a suicide," he said under his breath. "What else do I need to know about you?"

~~~

The increased darkness outside told him it was time to erase the trail of his work. He returned all the books except the early marriage records index so it would appear he had traced those elusive ancestors. A few minutes later, he slipped out the hallway door.

Next on his agenda was a nice dinner, but he would forgo the saloon tonight. He had a report to write and a cover story to invent for his visit at the Home tomorrow. He toyed with the idea that he would pose as an unmarried son in search of a place for his recently widowed mother. His fictionalized account involved them forced to sell their small family farm and him as a recently hired telegrapher in Louisville. The stay was only going to be for three months at the most until he had found a place for them to live. It was something to mull over during dinner.

~~~

The next morning Palmer presented himself at the Home as Ned

Walker, only living relative to Mary Walker. After he knocked on the door marked Administrator and was invited to enter, he found a woman he assumed was Mrs. McFarland because of the nameplate on her desk.. She sat behind neat stacks of loose pieces of paper. He had interrupted her bookkeeping.

"Yes?" she asked while she lifted her eyeglasses from her nose and let them fall to hang from a pewter pendent on her chest.

"I'm Ned Walker, I'm here to see if you can help us, my mother and me."

"I'll most certainly try. Please tell me about your situation."

In no time at all, Mrs. McFarland was told about Mr. Walker had died, the farm sold, the new job in Louisville, and how her caller did not know if her establishment would be a suitable place for his mother over the next few months. Mrs. McFarland suggested a tour of the main floor to see the dining hall and the rooms the older women occupied to help him decide.

"We try to keep the older women, such as your mother, here on the main floor. There's less chance of falls and broken hips when they don't have to climb so many steps."

"How many women live here?"

"Usually about thirty regular ones on the main level. Right now, we have twenty-five younger women on the second. The top floor we reserve for the youngest women who go to school or work during the day. All eat here."

They had reached the first stop on the tour, the dining room. The tall windows overlooked the side yard the Home shared with a large red brick building. Together they went over to the unshaded windows. He could now see the building next door had a circular drive and a parking lot on the other side. From his walk past it prior to his visit, he knew this was a funeral parlor.

He waited to see if she would comment on the recent tragedy, but Mrs. McFarland instead suggested they continue to the rooms.

A short walk down a dark hall brought them to a wing that jutted north. "We have these two rooms available." Mrs. McFarland opened adjacent doors. "There is only one family ahead of you, unless you sign the papers today. But I can promise that your mother will be in one of these."

He nodded he understood. The first contained two beds with their mattresses rolled up, two small dressers beside the bed, and uncurtained windows and bare linoleum floors. The other showed only one occupant would live there. The other difference was it was a corner room and so had one more window.

"You can see we have left enough space, so your mother can bring of few of her personal items with her. It would help her feel more at home."

"So your women live on just three floors?" he asked as they returned to the office. "I read about a woman who died here, not too long ago. The newspaper made it sound like she lived in the basement. You put residents there?"

"You must mean Mrs. Powell," Mrs. McFarland replied and did not stop or look at him. "The county contracts with us to take in some women who are not dangerous to others, just themselves, until there's room in another facility."

He could tell his questions made her nervous and continued, "But wasn't there a fire involved? I'm sure the newspaper mentioned a fire."

"A small one that our staff quickly extinguished." He saw her fingers go to her pendant. "We would never endanger our residents."

"I'd like to see the basement."

His firm tone brought the woman to face him. He had her full attention, so he went on, "I don't think I could rest easy unless I know for myself that my mother will be safe here."

The woman looked pained. "I understand, but I can only take you down the stairs and to the first locked gate. The main section where the special residents live is beyond that."

"I appreciate it, thank you."

～～

At the foot of the basement steps, Mrs. McFarland opened the unlocked door to step into a dimly lit hallway. A faint smell of smoke caught in his nose. She waited for him to stand beside her before she shut the door.

He saw four closed doors. The one at the end of the hall she indicated was an exit to the outside and was always locked. Only she and the matrons for the special unit had the keys. To the left was the unlocked laundry room door and coal bin and boiler heating system. Opposite that door was the entrance to the special unit. The door was also locked against intruders on this side and the escape of residents on the other side.

"So you can see, Mr. Walker, with these concrete walls and floor, there is no chance of fire spreading upstairs."

Nodding his satisfaction, he turned to the fourth door and opened it to see a totally dark room before him.

"That's our storage room, more of a closet really. It's not large, but we have many records we have to keep for our board."

"Excuse me, which door leads upstairs."

"This one here, on the left."

~~~

Once again in her office, Palmer put on his coat and thanked Mrs. McFarland for the tour.

"Is it possible to bring my mother by, maybe at the end of the week?"

Finding it was, he left, and outside he went down the sidewalk and turned toward the funeral parlor. A detour of a half a block took him past the entrance to the alley. A quick glance told him the alley probably ran past the back of the Home as well for deliveries of coal and food.

~~~

The rest of his day fell into place. He returned to the hotel for lunch and a change of clothes. Soon he exited by the hotel's back entrance dressed as a workman with a dark blue jacket and pants. On his feet were hobnail boots, and he crammed a worker's cap on his head as he crossed the street.

Within ten minutes, he turned into the alley behind the funeral parlor and the tree line of the park. From there he passed the locked basement door of the Home. He rapidly surmised the old lock was going to be an easy one to pick.

After he found out all he needed to know, he retreated to the other side of the alley and walked into the first saloon he saw for a beer before he returned to the hotel for a nap.

~~~

At dusk, Palmer woke to the sound of a light sleet hitting the hotel room window. After a low groan, he tried to convince himself that the bad weather was a good thing since it promised extra cover. He had less chance of being spotted while he hid outside and waited for the best time to enter the Home. But he did detest the thought of cold rain slipping down the back of his neck. The dampness would chill his toes even with the two pair of socks worn inside his boots. He told himself nothing for it but to get the job done. The sooner he broke in and discovered if the early records from the seventies still existed, the sooner he could leave Frankfort.

~~~

By nine o'clock, he stood by a hedge across the alley from the back entrance of the Home and watched. The windows on the main floor darkened first, followed by the other two floors. Then only the basement lights from the inmates' rooms glowed through the fog that settled over the city.

Finally after ten, the last two lights dimmed to half strength. He left the shadows and weaved in a drunken manner down the alley and into the funeral parlor parking lot before he doubled back to the basement door. Through the night silence, a train whistle indicated the approach of a night express.

He removed his winter gloves and replaced them with white formal evening ones. His profession had changed. The talk about fingerprints he had heard last fall when he was in New York had made him cautious and prompted him to have several pairs of gloves in the ready. His sources had not yet mentioned that police procedures had evolved to include this newest technique, but he was a cautious person.

The sound of a train accentuated by the chorus of chained dogs masked the sound of picking the lock. He was inside the basement entrance within one minute, well before the rumble and howls faded.

From his position, Palmer heard no human sounds. He reached into his overcoat pocket and drew out a new tool he was proud of, a flashlight for a quick look down the hall. Between him and the storeroom door was a clear path of about fifty feet. With the light now off, he took a towel from his coat pocket and wiped the floor, turned his coat inside out and wrapped it under his arms, and made his way to the storeroom door.

He tested the knob and found it unlocked. As soon as he shut the door, he stuffed his coat at the base of the door to block any light from seeping out. Next he emptied his coat pockets and brought out a small bicycle lamp and battery wrapped in another hand towel. This contraption would provide enough light to search the boxes of files stacked in the room.

Silently, he thanked the administrators who had through the years insisted that the records be kept in good order. It did not take him long to find the papers for the month of February, year, seventy-four. There was only one new admission, a Bridgette Clarissa Smith, age fifteen, admitted with Father John O'Connell of Louisville given as family member and signed by A. Fielding, Administrator.

The priest's name was unexpected, but Palmer pocketed the record in his vest and moved on to the box marked "1878", the year given on the marriage license found earlier at the courthouse. Again a neatly written document, signed by Ambrose Fielding, stated Miss Bridgette C. Smith was leaving the Home because she had married. This record joined Etta's admission paper in his pocket.

With a few minutes work, he mopped up the water he had tracked into the room, folded his towel into the satchel, and checked his watch. It was almost eleven o'clock. By eleven fifteen, he had made sure there was no water trail in the hallway and was back outside where he determined the weather was still as foul as when he had begun.

Fifteen minutes later he was back in his hotel room. It took until after midnight before he lost the night's chill and finished his report for Mr. Smith. Over his last cigar of the day, Palmer congratulated himself on a job well done. Based on the circumstantial evidence, he was almost sure he had found William Smith's sister.

But his instinct told him something had not fallen into place. He returned to the desk and put all the records into chronological order again. Admission and dismissal from the home were followed by marriage, divorce, competency hearing, commitment back into the Home, death record. Everything appeared fine.

So he worked backwards and made a list of all the facts in each document. The second time through he wondered if he had found it. It was such a small detail. Yawning, he stubbed out his cigar and climbed into bed. Tomorrow after one more call in town, he would wire his boss. Neither one of them liked loose ends.

Chapter 38

Louisville, February 4, 1900

William looked up from his desk when the housekeeper entered the study after Mary Margaret had retired for the night.

"Sorry to interrupt sir, but there's a telegram."

He took the paper, tried to ignore the slight water streaks, and said, "Thank you. Stay close by please, I may need to send a response."

William waited until the woman left the room before he read the wire. "Good hunting. Bagged limit. Suggest join me. Bigger game possible. At Essex."

William leaned back to consider what Palmer's message meant. His sister was the dead woman. He had hoped Palmer would not be able to connect Etta Powell to his banished sister. But the man had.

There was also some discovery Palmer wanted him to travel to Frankfort and see for himself. It could not be the Powell family. William had told him he did not want to get involved with them. Better to let his sister's past stay hidden. He owed her that respect.

He straightened up and checked his calendar for the rest of the week. The meetings listed there could be postponed. Mary Margaret had booked a party for the symphony on Saturday. But if he had to stay in Frankfort through the weekend, one of their many McIntire cousins would accompany her.

He wrote a reply on the back of the telegram for the gardener to take to the telegraph office and another message for his secretary which instructed her to cancel all his appointments for the next seven days. Then he asked the housekeeper to give the messages to the gardener and went upstairs to pack.

The next morning, when he told Mary Margaret he would be gone for a week of hunting, she wished him luck.

I'll need it, he thought, but not as much as Palmer if the mystery turned out to be nothing.

However, he had learned to trust Palmer when he fretted over information that did not make sense. Usually the man worked a case like a terrier and would not quit until he was satisfied there was nothing else to unearth.

Chapter 39

Frankfort, February 5, 1900

Lewis walked up the snow-covered front steps of the courthouse worn out from the funeral three days ago and all the frenzy of the reporters. Etta had not been buried the way he would have preferred, as a spirited, fiercely loving woman. Her funeral had not been a quiet, dignified one. The newspapers and their reporters had seen to that with their intrusive questions and cameras.

He hoped that before the day was over Etta would not be ruled a suicide or a murder victim. The best he could hope for, he realized, was a verdict of accidental death. Yet, if that woman had really murdered Etta, he wanted her prosecuted and hung. But the sheriff had told him no woman had ever been sentenced to death, let alone executed, in Kentucky.

On his way through the sunlit rotunda, Lewis saw Lavinia and Sophie beside the sheriff. Etta's two friends looked as if they had not slept, but they squeezed Lewis' arm when he thanked them for coming. When he entered the crowded courtroom, a stiff silence fell over the crowd as the people recognized him. He kept his gaze locked on the vacant judge's bench and took his reserved place in the front row.

Soon Jim McDowell came down the aisle. Before he sat on the opposite side, he nodded at Lewis. After Dr. Phillips entered and lowered himself into the judge's chair, the hearing began.

McDowell was the first witness. He testified that he received a call to come to the Home for Friendless Women at 12:03 p.m. He arrived twenty minutes later and found the inmates huddled and moaning in the cell closest to the entrance. Dr. Phillips was bandaging the night matron's hands.

He and the doctor walked down the corridor to look at the deceased. He briefly described the condition of the cell, how the body was positioned, the charred broom and bits of clothing scattered about the floor. After he sketched the scene in his notebook, he and the doctor lifted the body to the cot and covered it with a blanket.

His next task was to interview Mrs. Darby, the night matron, and a few of the inmates. Dr. Phillips interrupted at this point and told the sheriff to bypass the details of the interview with Mrs. Darby since she was a witness. McDowell grunted and summarized that the inmates' interviews were too confused to be credible.

After he checked the patient roll against the women in the cell and found Mrs. Powell was the only woman not marked off, he left to break the news to Dr. Powell and bring him to the Home.

Next Dr. Phillips called Mrs. Mazie Darby to the stand. A woman dressed all in black, except for the dingy white bandages on her hands, followed the bailiff into the courtroom. Her blouse and skirt were worn and plain in style. Her shawl had slid down on one side, and the large feather in her saucer-shaped hat drooped. Lewis looked at her with new eyes. How was it possible this stout, mousy woman had murdered his Etta?

After Mazie was sworn in, Dr. Phillips turned to her and asked, "How long have you been employed at the Home for Friendless Women?"

"About three years, sir."

"Did you tell the sheriff you used to live in Frankfort when you were younger?"

"Yes sir."

"Where did you live after you left there?"

"Corydon, Indiana."

"Did you come back because of family?"

"No, sir. I don't have no family left at all, nowhere."

"So why did you return?"

Mazie took a deep breath and let it out slowly. "I just wanted to find a spell of happiness. I had me some friends here, a while ago."

"I see."

The courtroom was so quiet Lewis heard Phillip's pen scratch across the paper.

"What are your duties at the Home?"

"I'm the night person. I pass out the evening meal trays and settle the women for sleeping. Sometimes…"

She stopped to look from Phillips to Lewis and back to Phillips. "I give them medicine, but only if a doctor says so. I got to enter it in the big book."

Phillips turned to a fresh page in his tablet and said, "Tell us what

322

happened on the night of January 30th."

"About midnight I finished foldin' and puttin' the laundry away. I always have some or other job to do. It's not like I sit there all night and sleep."

"I'm sure, Mrs. Darcy. Go on."

"As I was sayin', after that I took my dinner."

"Was that your usual time?"

"Yes sir. Since I get there at six, my big meal's about twelve."

"And where do you eat?"

"In the small room off the entrance. I got to prop my feet up. I have bunions something terrible, I do." Dr. Phillips motioned with his hand for her to continue. "I smelled smoke. By the time I got my shoes on, the smoke was everywhere, and I could see fire, down at the end of the cells. I unlocked the gate fast as I could and ran all out, to Mrs. Powell's cell."

Lewis felt his flesh crawl when Mazie turned her attention to him. "I'm powerful sorry, Dr. Powell. There was nothin' I could do."

"Mrs. Darby," Phillips said. "What happened when you got the cell door unlocked?"

"I kicked the broom out of the way. I just about caught fire myself. But I paid no mind and tried to squash the flames with my hands." Mazie held up her bandages.

"But the fire was too hot. I seen it twas far gone and Mrs. Powell dead."

"Why didn't you take the blanket from Mrs. Powell's cot to smother the flames?"

Lewis realized with a start he had thought the same thing when he had first entered Etta's cell.

"Oh, I know I should've, but my mind just stopped workin'. The smoke and fire was getting' the others all stirred up. The noise was somethin' fierce." Tears came down her cheeks, and Mazie fumbled with her handkerchief. At last she got most of her tears mopped up.

"Mrs. Darby, I have a few questions about what you said earlier." He turned back a few pages, and Lewis leaned forward to hear better.

"You said you had returned to the place where you had been so happy. Do you remember saying those words?"

Mazie nodded several times, and the feather on her hat fell even more.

"By place, did you mean Frankfort or the Home for Friendless

Women?"

"Frankfort, sir."

"Are you sure you didn't mean the Home?"

"Yes sir."

Phillips pointed at the bailiff who opened the door behind him. Lewis kept his eyes on Mazie as her attention remained on Lavinia and Sophie walk in and sit in chairs in the front row. A faint murmur started and grew before Phillips pounded his gavel and silenced the audience.

Mazie twisted in her seat and darted glances about the room. One glance locked briefly with Lewis before she looked back at Lavinia and Sophie. Finally Mazie stared at her hands in her lap. By now the black feather blotted out most of her face.

"Mrs. Darby," Phillips said, "Tell us again why you are working at the Home."

She looked up. Her tears started again, and Lewis willed himself to breathe.

"The truth is I used to live there with them." Her head jerk indicated Lavinia and Sophie. "And Mrs. Powell, Etta Smith she was then."

Lewis was sickened by the hissing that ignited in the courtroom.

Phillips warned the audience to remain silent, and Mazie went on, "I was real happy there. We were close as sisters. Then one by one, they married and moved out. I was left alone. Then I got married. I don't like to tell people I lived there cause they act like you're no count if youse from the Home."

"Weren't you sent there because you had developed the habit of, shall we say, taking things which weren't yours?"

"Yes sir, but I was just a wee girl. I never meant no harm."

"Were you aware you had the nickname the Little Magpie because after you came to live at the Home, you continued to take things?"

"Yes," she spoke a little above a whisper.

"Has this behavior continued?"

"No, sir," Mazie's voice was forceful. "I gave it up after I was married. You see, my Richard, he gave me many beautiful buttons and bits of lace. He was a notions salesman."

A wistful look came over her face and took away the years. Lewis saw how attractive she would have once been.

"And what about Mrs. Powell's pearls?"

"Her earrings. They was such pretty things. But they burnt and melted in the fire."

Mazie looked and sounded so convincing Lewis found he doubted

Lavinia's and Sophie's suspicions. When he looked at them, they must have read his mind. They shook their heads. Phillips continued to stare at Mazie, but she remained steady. Finally he excused her from the stand.

Phillips cleared his throat and summarized the results of his autopsy. Lewis tried to close his mind as the coroner listed his findings. But each detail struck Lewis like an arrow and renewed his guilt.

Phillips asked for a few minutes to review his notes from the witnesses. The courtroom was silent while Lewis watched Phillips go through his notebook. His pace was too fast to actually read and consider what he had written. Lewis realized the coroner had already made up his mind.

Phillips closed his notebook, looked at the people before him, and folded his hands beside the notebook. "After careful consideration of the witnesses and my autopsy, I rule that Mrs. Lewis Powell died from an accident."

The gavel pounded for the last time, and it was over. One moment deflated, the next glad Etta's death was not pronounced a suicide, Lewis watched the courtroom empty. Lavinia and Sophie kissed him on the cheek. McDowell shook his hand and mumbled something Lewis did not quite get. It sounded like the mill stones of God grind slowly, but they do grind.

Chapter 40

William was the first one to depart the 1:04 train from Louisville when it rolled into the station. It did not take him long to find Palmer outside the depot.

"I suppose you won't tell me what's got you so worked up until we're back at the Essex, right?"

"Well sir, it's better if you see what I've found."

"All right, move out." William turned to the porter and paid him a quarter to arrange his baggage delivery to the hotel.

"Palmer, can you get us to the Essex before my luggage?"

"Yes sir, I have a cab waiting."

"Good, weather's a little raw today."

"You'll be set to rights soon sir. Lunch is all set to be delivered to the room. That way we can talk, and you can decide what you want to do next."

"You certainly do have my curiosity stoked."

~~~

Back in Palmer's room, the investigator led William through all the reports he had poured over after his late night visit to the Home plus the results of his visit with the sheriff the previous evening. The disturbing details forced William to tamp down his empathy so he could concentrate on Palmer's facts and impressions.

"So," William said, "you're telling me because her second admission report to the Home listed a pearl necklace and no necklace was mentioned in the police report, you thought her death was suspicious?"

"Yes, and I'm even more convinced since it didn't even come up in the inquest."

William cleared his throat before he said, "Thank you for sparing me that ordeal."

Palmer acknowledged William's words with a nod and continued, "Remember from the newspaper story where the coroner listed the melted gold on her ears?"

"Yes, what of it?"

"See where her husband signs for her personal effects and there's no necklace given?"

"So?"

"Why isn't there a necklace? You said it was valuable and that you remembered the necklace was made of gold beads with pearls strung together."

William nodded. The memory of how his aunt had railed until her dying day that her niece should never have been allowed to leave with those family pieces of jewelry played again. His hand motioned for Palmer to continue.

"So there should have been some melted gold around her neck as well, and there wasn't."

"What'd the sheriff say?"

"I didn't ask him directly about Mrs. Powell's personal effects. I posed as a reporter and asked general questions regarding the scene." Palmer stopped to consult his notebook. "When I asked him details about the crime scene, he never mentioned anything about the necklace."

"Was the husband the only one alone with her until the undertaker came?"

"Yes, before Powell left, the matron asked him to check his wife's belongings against the list."

"No necklace," William said in a low voice. He took a few moments to sort through all the pieces of the puzzle again. He asked, "What about that crazy woman, Mildred Green? Since she was across from Etta, maybe she saw something that night?"

Palmer tapped his notebook with his pencil. "Seems her interview was inconclusive. She became rattled, and the coroner dismissed her information."

"Maybe," William suggested, "one of the other inmates wasn't locked up. She saw the necklace and tried to steal it. There might have been a struggle, and the fire set to cover up murder."

"I don't think it was one of the inmates. I got the feeling from the inquest that the sheriff and coroner tried to make the matron confess. Even brought in two women who seemed to scare Mazie. It appears she was also in the Home at the same time as your sister and had a nasty habit of taking things that weren't hers."

William shivered. "Strange, I never imagined I'd think it was better that she was murdered rather than committing suicide."

"I decided to follow up on that possibility," Palmer said after a pause. "I spent some time in the courthouse before you arrived. I looked over the death records for the unit in the basement of the Home."

William did not understand where Palmer was headed. "I would expect old women to die."

"Yes sir, but nine of them occurred at night, and I know," Palmer said and raised a hand, palm out, "what you're about to say, most deaths take place between three and four in the morning. However," Palmer now pointed to a paper before him, "I went back through the last ten years, and the Home's had a steady increase just these past three years. See, I've plotted the death rate."

William looked at the precisely drawn graph as Palmer explained, "Four years ago two women died, over the next three years, thirteen women died, including the first one this year, your sister. Guess who came to work at the Home a little over three years ago?"

"That night matron?"

"No other, and she's always been on the night shift."

"How did the other women die?"

"All were recorded as death from natural causes."

William processed these facts and said, "Nothing suspicious? No evidence of any injuries?"

"Not even one coroner inquest. Most death records listed no next of kin."

"So no one raised any doubts?" William wondered if this woman was as insane as the women she watched.

"No," Palmer reached for another stack of notes.

"Seven were buried in pauper graves."

"And the others?"

"Death records full of details about their families. Most were really up there in age in their seventies."

"The families probably thought it was a relief their loved ones had passed on."

"That's the way I looked at it."

William struggled to accept what Palmer was proposing. "Any real evidence to prove your theory?"

Palmer took sip from his coffee cup. From the grimace on his face,

William knew it had gone cold.

"Since just that before she came, the death rate was lower, I thought I would look into Mazie's background, if that's what you want."

William weighed the suggestion while Palmer used the time to refill both their cups. He thanked him for the hot coffee and said, "Why don't you chase down what you can about Mazie Darby. It might be of interest."

"And Etta's husband and children?"

"Let's leave that for now. Meet with me again for dinner and you can tell me what you have found out."

"And you?"

"I think I'll go to the cemetery and on to the Home. I want to see where she lived."

"You're going to just walk in there? What are you going to say?"

"Don't look so surprised, I'll come up with something. You're not the only one who can make up stories."

Chapter 41

Frankfort, February 5, 1900

Later that evening Palmer ran his finger over the notes and summarized his information on Mazie Darby.

"She married after your sister did, a few months later. Her husband was named in several suits within two years of their marriage. The cause was nonpayment of debt. They skipped town and moved to Corydon, in Indiana." He returned his attention to his boss.

"That last was in the courthouse records?" William asked.

"No." Palmer kept his eyes on his boss and eagerly anticipated the surprise his next words would bring. "From her."

He was not disappointed in how dumbfounded William looked.

"You interviewed her?"

"Yep, she was impressed with my press pass and eager to talk with a reporter about how brave she was. Her repeated the same story she gave at the inquest. She's a widow and has no family left. That's why she wanted to return to the only place she'd ever had any kindness."

Palmer saw the anger grow in William's eyes and heard even more anger in the harsh tones his next words held.

"So she comes back and gets a job, the night shift at the insane asylum, and begins killing old women."

Palmer shrugged and tried to keep himself from getting caught up in William's rage.

"We don't know, yet, that she is a murderess. But I have some more leads to run down. She said she stayed in Indiana until her husband died."

"When you talked with her, did she strike you as capable of murder?"

"Hard to tell, she's a little strange, but that doesn't make her a criminal. Let's see what pans out in the next few days. I don't think she's going anyplace."

Palmer watched William as he considered the situation and

unpacked his anger.

The investigator directed the conversation onto a new path. "What did you think about the Home?"

"It's such a gloomy place. I can't imagine anyone being happy there. If that was the only place this Mazie woman was ever happy, she certainly had miserable experiences since she left. Though Mrs. McFarland was gracious and helpful."

Palmer opened his notebook to a new blank page and waited for the information.

"What did she tell you?" he asked.

"She lives there, you know, and so during the first few years after she started the job, she went through the records to acquaint herself with the financial history. But soon the stories of the women and the Home grabbed her interest."

"Had to be some sad tales."

"She'd agree with you in part. However, her research turned up how devoted and capable the first director Ambrose Fielding was. She read his comments in his day calendars. Mrs. McFarland couldn't remember all the names but one group of girls named Lavinia, Sophie, and Etta had stayed in her mind. It struck her as extraordinary how all remained friends after they married and left the Home."

Palmer noticed William's voice softened when he talked about his sister's good friends.

~~~

But William's mood changed when the telegraph arrived. "This telegram from your, whatever you called that person in Coryden, isn't conclusive." William threw the paper down on the desk and stormed around the sitting room of his suite.

"I can't walk into a man's house and tell him that I think his wife, my long lost sister, has been killed, probably by a woman who has been killing other insane women and shove this telegram in his face." William's voice was close to a shout.

His boss' anger almost triggered his own. Palmer was ready to yell back before he caught himself in time.

After a pause of a few moments, he said, "It's time for the truth. I think we're on to something. There's no denying Mazie brings death with her. Those twenty-five deaths over seven years while she lived in Indiana are suspicious. But if we're right about your sister, he and her children deserve to know the truth. You will have to talk with him."

William stood up and paced back and forth with his hands stuffed in the deep pockets of his flannel robe.

Palmer knew his boss did not like family scenes. In business, William Smith was ruthless and unwavering, cold or angry as needed. But, when it came to his wife or children and grandchildren, the man avoided any emotional outbursts.

He knew he had made headway when William returned to his chair and grunted.

Palmer continued, "Tomorrow we'll put the the evidence before him."

"Not the husband. Send the information on Mazie to the sheriff. Maybe he can shake the truth out of her. I'm heading home tomorrow morning. Will you please stick around and see what he can do with your information."

He was half-way out the door before he turned back to Palmer. "Good work here in Frankfort. Regardless of the outcome, you have my deepest gratitude for returning my sister to me."

Chapter 42

Louisville, March 14, 1900

William Smith sat in his locked, pecan-paneled study and reread his investigator's reports. The first file included all the newspaper accounts of the death of Mrs. Lewis Powell. William noticed the passages he himself had underlined before he had turned the newspaper articles over to Palmer. The woman's birth date, the name of Etta, the description of her red hair and the pearl and gold jewelry. They, by themselves, did not prove that the unfortunate woman killed in the fire was his long lost sister.

The second file contained the documents Palmer had stolen from the basement storage room of the Home for Friendless Women. Every time William read the name of that institution, it never failed to chill his soul. What a horrible name to give a place. He also forced himself to go over his sister's admission record for immoral behavior. The word immoral rankled each time he had studied the document. After this ordeal was over, he would burn this record first. But the date of the record matched what he remembered of that awful day when he had peeked out his bedroom window and saw Etta leave their home for the last time. Next was her dismissal record which stated the reason she left the Home was marriage.

William removed his glasses and rubbed the bridge of his nose and considered if he had to go through the next folder that held the results of Palmer's research at the courthouse in Frankfort. He decided he had to do what Palmer called due diligence. William put his glasses back on and read. The marriage license for Etta Smith and Benjamin Darnell. The birth records of their three children. Etta's divorce from Benjamin Darnell. The deed and tax records for their house and small farm store. The competency hearing for Mrs. Lewis Powell. And it was as painful as he had suspected to read again the coroner's inquest which gave Etta's cause of death as accidental.

He knew that, without Palmer having to tell him, the only piece of missing information was how Etta Darnell got to be Etta Powell, wife of Doctor Powell. But he had promised he would discover it, and William knew he would.

The folder he opened next was marked Mazie Darby. Palmer had traced her from her marriage to her work at an old age home in Corydon, Indiana. While the administrator there could not prove Mrs. Darby was a thief and an angel of death who helped the inmates ease out of life, the death rate decreased after she moved on.

One last folder waited. William owed it to his sister to get this right. He opened it and reviewed each detail of the grand jury hearing tasked with charging Mazie Darby with murder. He understood what the county had attempted. He also understood why the case had failed. The evidence was circumstantial, and the woman had not moved from her denial of murder.

William however was not bound by the laws of reasonable doubt. He had Palmer and money. What was the word Etta used whenever she did battle with him? Vincero, that was it. Etta, vincero. I will conquer for you and avenge your death.

Book Club Questions

1. Isabel faced a difficult question about her father. Did she make the right decision? Was she guilty in her intention, even if not in deed?

2. What other forces were at work within the McIntire family? Which ones would still be in play today? Which ones were valid for the time?

3. Was Isabel right in promising Etta the princess dresses? What did Isabel's action set in place?

4. What were the reasons Etta was banished? Were they valid? Why?

5. Although the Civil War is not the central focus of the early chapters, how did it drive the characters' actions?

6. Which friend did you like better, Sophie or Lavinia? Why?

7. What part did the church have in the novel's events?

8. Were Ben's parents right in being concerned about their son marrying a woman they knew nothing about? Why/why not?

9. Describe how important gossip was in Louisville and Frankfort. Is it the same or different in your community?

10. When infant mortality rates were so tragically high, women were often told not to get too attached to their children. Do you think that was really possible?

11. How has the subject of menopause changed from Etta's time?

12. What difference did the knowledge that Etta was murdered and did not commit suicide make in the lives of Charity, Lewis, her grandchildren, her descendents?

13. The phrase la vincero empowered Isabel and Etta. What sayings has your family handed down?

Historical Notes

Coverture actually existed in the United States as it did in Europe, and gradually states passed statutes abolishing the law. By the late 1880s, most women could retain rights to their legal property.

Well-meaning people established Homes for Friendless Women through the United States beginning in the late 1860s. Friendless was code for transient women, homeless mothers and their children, unwed pregnant girls and women, the ill and destitute, as well soiled doves, the Victorian word for prostitutes. At least one Home contracted with the state and county to run a women's prison.

Although during the Renaissance women were advised to treat menopause with apples, myrrh, and a walk, by the 1890s in America and Europe, menopause was treated as either a terminal disorder or a mental illness. Some women were even committed to asylums. However, Lydia Pinkham created a vegetable compound in 1876 to ease menopausal complaints and incidentally became quite wealthy.

Acknowledgements

It has been my great fortune to have the help and support of so many. My husband deserves first place for listening to plot ideas and disasters and for what he calls "respecting the hand" on the many times he came to talk when I was in mid-thought and he was met with my raised hand. My daughters also rank high for reading the rough drafts and sending back encouragement and comments.

I have gained more than I gave to my writing groups. Their global comments and nit-picking attention to details enhanced the story. Thank you Jean, Ed, Elise, George, and Kallie for your patience and encouragement.

My editor Vicki Vanbrocklin offered corrections and suggestions with her ready pen and smile.

I leaned on my good friend Jean Airey for final layout guidance and editing. Each and every piece of advice was spot on.

Countless librarians and archivists in Florida, Kentucky, and Indiana graciously answered my emails.

I thank all of you.

Of course, any errors and mistakes are mine alone.

Kate Nixon is a transplanted Hoosier who enjoys Florida's friendliness, sunshine, and beaches. She and her husband share their home with a terrier adopted from the Humane Society. The Heirloom Pearls is her first novel.